LOST
SCROLLS
of
ARCHIMEDES

✦ TOM ROBERTS ✦

Raven Cliffs Publishing LLC

Published by Raven Cliffs Publishing LLC, Pensacola, Florida. For information, address Raven Cliffs Publishing LLC, PMB #221, 4771 Bayou Blvd, Suite C, Pensacola, FL, 32503.

www.ravencliffspublishing.com

ISBN-13: 978-1-7342462-5-4

Cover Design by Damonza

This book is dedicated to my loving wife, Charlotte Cheney; my supportive children, Melissa and Andrew; my parents, Tom and Vicki Roberts; and Dudley, faithful companion and best dog ever.

"The only thing new in the world is the history you do not know."

Harry S. Truman

THE ROMAN REPUBLIC
AT THE DEATH OF CAESAR 44 B.C

Roman Empire

States Dependent on Rome

GERMANIA

BELGICA

LUGDUNENSIS

RHAETIA

GALLIA

MARE
CANTABRICUM

AQUITANIA

Aquae

MARE ADRIA

ITALIA

Iberus

Roma

NARBONENSIS

Corsica

HISPANIA

Brund

Baleares

Sardinia

MARE
TYRRHENUM

ULTERIOR

Carthago Nova

Sicilia

MARE
IBERICUM

MAURETANIA

AFRICA

SYRTIS
MINOR

N

0   500 km

0   300 miles

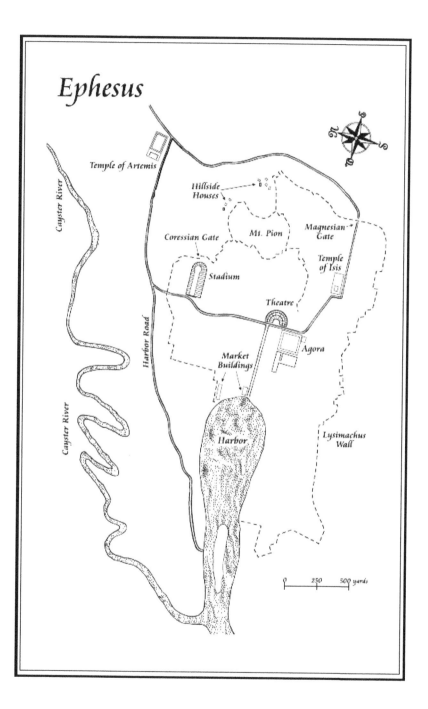

38 B.C.

CHAPTER ONE

Marcus

Ephesus, August 5

MARCUS BASSUS GRIPPED the side of the skiff and stared at the dark river. Its placid surface reflected the half-moon's light while masking the turbulent undercurrents far below.

"We must jump *now*, Marcus." Hippolytus said.

Despite the warm night air, Marcus shivered as he studied the shrouded shore fifty feet beyond the boat. The lost artifacts they sought tonight hid potent and mysterious dangers. Despite the risk to his life if he was caught, he heeded their siren call.

But I'm a scholar, not a thief.

He took a deep breath and glanced at his mentor standing in the bow. Like Marcus, Hippolytus was stripped to his loincloth, his skin blackened with ashes and pig fat.

For the third time, the small boat neared the eastern shore of the Cayster River north of the city of Ephesus in the Roman province of Asia. At the earlier locations where they sought to disembark, rocks, fallen trees, and tricky currents made the approach too dangerous. They were behind schedule.

Water splashed as Julianus, their local guide, rowed to keep the bow pointed into the swift current. Moonlight glinted off a medallion peeking above his tunic. The same Oracle medallion hung from Hippolytus's neck.

"Come on, boy," Julianus urged. His mangled nose lent a nasal tone to his voice. "This is damned hard work."

Marcus had met the man only yesterday. Julianus, whose muscled arms bulged as he heaved at the oars, said little beyond reporting the local conditions. Hippolytus said the man was obtuse, even for an Oracle.

Turning to the water, Marcus sought to calm his fears, reminding himself he often swam across the great Nile River canal in Alexandria. Still, the unknowns ahead fueled his anxiety.

"Did you hear me?" Hippolytus urged, pointing his finger at Marcus. "It's time."

Pulse racing, Marcus scooped his leather bag off the bottom boards and flung it over his back before rolling over the boat's side. He gasped as the icy water shocked him. His darkened skin blended with the inky river, and he swam against the current until Hippolytus joined him. Hippolytus waved to Julianus, who then maneuvered the skiff downstream toward the harbor at Ephesus.

With long frog strokes, Marcus swam alongside Hippolytus toward the ominous shore, where he feared soldiers waited to hack him to pieces. Soon enough his feet touched the rough river bottom, and the two invaders crawled through the shallows to a narrow strip of beach.

He scurried across the sand into the shadows of the muddy embankment. With each step, he expected an arrow from an Amazon huntress, the sworn protector of the goddess Artemis. His heart pounded in his ears, drowning out the river's soft moan. He tripped on a tree root but reached the bank and surveyed the marsh ahead. Neither sound nor motion reached his senses. His heartbeat slowed.

The serenity of the celestial glow only deepened his sense that a dark destiny was hanging over the river and land. Ahead lay the path to the Temple of Artemis, a destination for thousands of religious pilgrims. To the right, a mere mile away, the lights of Ephesus shimmered.

Marcus extracted a rope and grapnel from his bag handing it to Hippolytus, who coiled the rope over his shoulder.

Hippolytus examined the iron claws. "You sharpened these?"

"Yes," Marcus said, keeping his voice low, "before you got up this morning." In the dark, he made a sour face, recalling the effort to wake himself at such an unaccustomed hour.

In his scouting report, Julianus said one hundred priests and servants slept in the building, while scores of armed men guarded the temple's vast riches of art, gold, and sacred writings day and night.

The temple's sixty-foot height worried Marcus; that was near his tutor's limit for tossing the grappling hook.

To the southeast, lights burned at a few of the houses crowding the slopes of Mount Pion. Atop the mountain, the city walls loomed. At this distance, Marcus thanked Fortuna that he'd be invisible to the soldiers walking their rounds on the massive fortifications.

"Let's go." With his body bent low, Hippolytus darted into the reeds. Though well up in age, Marcus had observed his mentor at the Gymnasium in Alexandria. The man still retained some of the vigor from his youth as a champion athlete.

The dry reeds and cattails chafed his bare legs as Marcus followed his mentor. Beyond, he glimpsed the silhouette of the looming stadium—now empty—standing midway between the swamp and Ephesus. Julianus reported that in April, the holy month of Artemision, the stadium and city had teemed with people.

Halfway across the field, Hippolytus mouthed a fierce whisper. "Horse patrol."

They dove into the mud. Hoofbeats thudded on the soft ground, and as they grew louder and closer, the smell of horseflesh mixed with the earthy scent of decaying grass. Mud smeared his lips when he pressed his body deeper into the wet ground.

The rider gave a low order, halting his horse. A palpable silence set in, and time slowed to a crawl.

Then a horse snorted, and the clopping of hooves resumed, receding into the distance.

Several minutes passed before Hippolytus whispered new orders. "We need to move a little to the south."

Marcus wiped the bitter mud from his mouth. "That will take more time. And what about those houses near the marsh edge?" At least those houses were unlit.

"It's that or capture." Hippolytus started off into the reeds.

Marcus moved in behind his tutor, and they crept south.

As they sneaked along, the door of one house creaked open. They dropped to the ground again. Marcus heard splashing and a deep sigh of relief.

After several moments, he raised his head and stared at his face reflected in a moonlit puddle. Like his skin, his blue eyes and sandy hair were black and murky. He ducked when the door creaked again.

His mentor resumed a crouch. "He's gone. This way."

More time lost. We must meet the merchant galley before dawn breaks.

Soon, Marcus spotted the planned hiding spot—a dense thicket at the end of the swamp. Fifty feet of open ground lay between the thicket and the temple. They moved in, using the last of the tall grass as cover. This close, Marcus marveled at the temple's massive size. Walls of white marble towered over the muddy plain. Imposing columns ringed the building and supported the wooden roof he needed to climb up to. Under the pale moon, the glistening temple's beauty rivaled that of any in Alexandria. The wildness of the Ephesian landscape stood in sharp contrast to the pristine streets and manicured gardens of his city.

Large contingents of guards covered the entrances and circled the sanctuary. For half an hour, the two soon-to-be-thieves watched the perimeter patrols, and as soon as the largest gap in the defenders reappeared, Hippolytus ordered him forward.

After motioning Marcus to a safe spot several paces away, Hippolytus took a position near the building where he could spin the grapple with plenty of speed. He picked up a handful of dirt, rubbed his palms together, and then retrieved the grapnel.

Hippolytus grunted as he whirled the grappling hook in large, lazy circles before sending the iron flying toward the roof, where it landed with a dull clink. When he tugged the rope, the spikes didn't bite. He dodged the plummeting grapnel, and it struck the soft dirt with a thud that breached the quiet.

Marcus's lips were parched, and the dried mud made his skin itch. Waves of nausea rolled through his empty stomach.

I hope the Oracles' motives are pure. Temples are sacred.

While Marcus kept a sharp eye out for movement on the patrol path, Hippolytus recoiled the line. His tutor nodded at him before spinning the iron claws and releasing again.

Success.

With a tug on the rope, Hippolytus secured the grappling iron. Marcus blew a breath of relief.

It was his turn. Ignoring his conscience, he first confirmed that his short knife lay inside his leather bag before securing it across his body.

He grabbed the dangling line and started his climb, using the side of a column for support. As he ascended, he paused every few steps to take up several feet of free rope and coil it over one shoulder. The climbing practice at the Gymnasium back home was proving useful.

As he neared the roofline, Hippolytus's warbling call of a nightjar startled Marcus. Guard approaching. Several loops of rope slipped off his shoulder, leaving the end dangling thirty feet above the ground. With luck, it was too high for the guard to notice. Marcus pressed his forehead against the rope.

Back in Alexandria, I'd be sleeping or reading a scroll I had sneaked out of the Library. Tonight, I'm dangling from a temple roof. But I wanted this opportunity, right?

Marcus controlled his breathing as he watched the sentry fade into the night. Then he resumed his climb and stepped onto the roof. Soon, his heart calmed, and he gave an owl's call to Hippolytus. Marcus unsheathed his knife, dug the metal claws from the wood, and coiled the line.

Near the roof's peak, he located one of many stone-ringed vents that let out the smoke from fires and incense. A full-grown man wouldn't fit through, but a skinny, rope-climbing boy could.

Doubts crept into his mind.

Should I violate a temple? Will the Goddess be angry and seek vengeance?

Theft from a temple violated the gods, his father said, but Hippolytus promised a part in studying the significant scrolls stored there. His unquenchable thirst for the hidden knowledge of the ancient Greeks was the real reason for his willingness to be a lawbreaker. He hoped the Goddess understood.

Though the opening seemed to grow smaller with each passing moment, he knew the dark was playing tricks on him. He secured the grapnel near the vent and after seeing only darkness below, fed the line into the gloomy interior. Wishing he had more pig fat to ease his entry, he squirmed feet-first through the opening, sliding through the vent and between the roof timbers. He kept a firm grasp on the rope as he swayed high above the temple floor.

Amazed at his success in negotiating the vent, Marcus took his first look below his dangling feet. Marble columns surrounded an open space for animal sacrifices. Near the front, a single brazier cast the guards' flickering silhouettes against the walls. From his vantage point, the statue of the goddess Artemis seemed small and insignificant.

With smoke and incense filling his nostrils, he began a cautious descent toward the stone floor, slipping down alongside the many-breasted mother-goddess that now dwarfed him. His feet silently hit the marble tiles, and he crept toward the back wall of the room, using the monument and the forest of interior columns to shield against the men guarding the front entrance. In the blackness, his fingers became his eyes, searching for a mosaic panel. He found its raised edge, waist-high, and followed it to one of its ends.

That's it. Now to find the release lever.

Julianus said the mosaic contained over one hundred tiles across its width.

Gods, don't make me check each one.

He worked back toward the mosaic's middle, pressing on each small tile piece. Halfway across, none had given way.

Marcus clenched his jaws. With his finger poised to check the next tile, he heard laughter from the front. He froze and waited. A long moment passed before he resumed the search, punching each small chip one by one.

Near the mosaic's far end, one tile moved inward. Marcus flinched as the sharp click shattered the quiet, but he saw no movement from the guards.

At last.

Marcus pressed a shoulder against the wall, and the slab of stone opened a finger's width. With a harder push, it moved inward, rotating soundlessly on a central pivot.

His skin crawled as he envisioned the dangers—pits with sharpened stakes, caltrops, an endless maze—awaiting him on the other side of the black, narrow opening. He summoned his courage and slipped through the gap in the wall.

Inside the lightless abyss, he reached out into the surrounding emptiness. His fingertips struck a low ceiling and strafed along rough-hewed walls. His toes sunk into a sandy floor. Hunched over, he took small steps into the black depth of the hollowed-out void within the structure of the temple. His leg muscles tightened as his fear of entombment surged.

A slight flow of air tickled the top of his head, and he probed upward, finding emptiness. He stretched out his back in relief, inhaling the fresh air.

Far above him, a dim orb of light glowed. He traced the rough outline of a small round hole, a shaft too narrow to hold the chest containing the scrolls. He moved deeper into the stone passage.

His bare shins slammed into hard metal. He hissed in pain and fell to his knees. In front of him, he reached out and encountered metal.

Could this be it?

A rush of excitement surged through every muscle.

He caressed the cold, dusty metal, recognizing it as a chest. For a moment, his breath came in ragged gasps. When his probing fingers found the latch, he paused before unhooking it. He struggled with the stiff lid and winced as the hinges screeched.

Something slithered against his leg.

He stiffened.

His eyes shifted, hunting.

In the shaft's dim light, a faint line moved through the sand. It grew, disappearing at a snail's pace into a wall crevice. Marcus eased out the air burning his lungs and thanked the gods for sparing him a snakebite. He tried the lid again.

It opened.

Yes.

Marcus groped around inside the chest. His hands found only a single item—a small leather-bound cylinder secured with straps. Couriers favored such cases to carry documents. His heart raced as he worked to untie it. Once opened, he probed the contents. The strong smell of papyrus filled his nostrils. An excited yell formed in his throat before he stifled it with a hand over his mouth. If the guards heard him, he was a dead man.

He gripped the two scrolls and savored the moment. Hippolytus vowed the secret Oracles organization followed the path to truth. Euphoria flooded his veins, and he struggled to contain his excitement. Planned for months, the adventure yielded him the Archimedes scrolls—Hippolytus will be proud of him.

Marcus peered up the shaft. Dawn grew close, so he pushed the scrolls back into the case, refastened its straps, and secured the cylinder into his leather bag. A king's treasure might surround him, but he had what he wanted. It was time to get out before the room became his tomb.

He retraced his steps and slipped out of the entrance, clutching his plunder to his chest. He stayed low and stole back to the dangling line. Under the disapproving stare of Artemis, he ascended the rope, hand over hand.

Back on the roof, he pulled the rope up from the vent, coiling it for the descent. He rubbed his chafed palms together; what he would give for a soothing ointment.

With great caution, he stepped to the edge, listening for the patrol. Again, he gave his owl call. When Hippolytus returned the all-clear signal, Marcus pressed his heel on the grapnel, securing it into the wood. He then slid down the rope, his feet touching solid ground in seconds. He shook his hands, wincing at his rope burns before dashing over to the thicket where Hippolytus waited.

"Do you have it?" Hippolytus whispered when Marcus squatted next to him.

"I promised I wouldn't fail you." Despite the dark, he could see the grin on Hippolytus's face.

"Oh, Marcus, you're one magnificent boy." His mentor's voice trembled with emotion as he slapped Marcus on the shoulder. "I'll hug you later."

Marcus smiled, and his chest filled with pride, but he knew

the celebration would have to wait. The patrol could appear at any moment.

Hippolytus ordered an immediate retreat south toward the stone-paved harbor road. Two miles away, at the isolated western end of the harbor, they'd find Julianus.

Marcus's shoulders relaxed. Success was theirs.

His optimism dissolved when he exited the underbrush and spotted three men entering the road from around the temple's far corner. One of them carried a torch, another a bow on his shoulder; their path took them down the harbor road—the same direction he and Hippolytus planned to follow.

"Back," Hippolytus ordered in a harsh whisper.

Marcus scooted back into hiding, his leg muscles tightening once again. "Why are they here?" His voice cracked. "Did they see the rope? It will be light soon. Are we—?"

"Enough, Marcus. They're not dressed as guards. Let me think." Hippolytus peeked out toward the road. "Here's the plan. I'll let them see me, and, assuming they chase me, I'll take the main road through town. I'll lose them in some alley and meet you at the boat. You take the harbor road as planned."

Marcus's heart sank as he watched his mentor leave their cover. He took several deep breaths to calm himself.

When Hippolytus reached the road, he turned onto it and set a swift pace toward Ephesus. At first, no reaction came from the strangers.

"Stop, you. Stop." The shout from the men behind Hippolytus was in Greek, but the accent wasn't native. Roman? Dread sent a shiver down Marcus's spine. These were not city guards.

He heard Hippolytus's pace quicken, breaking into a sprint. Marcus knew they were unlikely to catch him.

Marcus waited in the thicket. He needed the men to be far down the road since he intended to go in the same direction, at least for a short stretch.

His thoughts turned to Hippolytus's escape. When the primary avenue to Ephesus branched off to the south, Hippolytus would take it and lose his pursuers in the streets and alleys.

Marcus emerged from hiding, darted to the road, and took off. Between his brisk pace and the fear of capture, his heart pounded against his chest, seeking escape.

A few minutes later, he reached a fork in the road. The main avenue to Ephesus branched left where Hippolytus would have taken his pursuers. Though the road provided a faster way to Julianus and the boat, it touched the outskirts of the town. Relief swept through him on seeing that the taverns and shops at the intersection lay quiet and devoid of people, and he whipped right toward the harbor's western end. His tense body relaxed, shifting his manic pace into a rhythm he could sustain for the next two miles.

In the gloom, Marcus searched for his path to the beach. When he found it, he cut left and dashed down the sandy trail that sliced through a mass of shoulder-height bushes.

At the river's edge, he scanned for the signal light of Julianus, who waited with the skiff. In the nerve-racking quiet, he fidgeted with the bulla around his neck, the modest gold locket of a freeborn Roman child. It served to ward off evil; he hoped it worked tonight.

Marcus expected Julianus to have the boat ready. He envisioned the men wandering around town looking for a crazy man in a loin-cloth. He suppressed the laugh the image invoked and continued to search along the harbor. A shape moved toward him.

"Julianus?" Marcus's voice was only a whisper. *Where is the lamp?*

"Over here," came the response.

He spotted a dim glow and moved in its direction.

"Did you get the scrolls?" The tall, thin figure of Julianus appeared.

"You have a boat?" Marcus posed in jest. As he approached Julianus, the man's bronze medallion shimmered in the dim lamp. "I have them."

"That's great, Marcus." Julianus pointed off to the left. "The boat's over here. Where's Hippolytus?"

Marcus filled him in on the improvised escape plan to elude the pursuers. In the lamplight, he thought he saw concern cross the other man's face.

Julianus stared skyward before focusing on Marcus. "We need to reach the mouth of the Cayster before daybreak to ensure our escape. The merchant ship won't wait."

"I know, but I am not leaving Hippolytus. You take the scrolls."

Julianus's face appeared placid, a sea of calm. "I'm sure he'll show. Let's wait by the boat. Follow me."

Silently crossing fifty paces through the sand, the two men reached the beached skiff. Julianus turned up the lamp and set it on the sand. Marcus glanced eastward along the shore. His apprehension rose when he saw a pink tinge lighting the horizon. He pulled at his hair.

Patience.

"How old are you, Marcus?" asked Julianus.

"Fourteen."

"Ah. Tell me, why are these scrolls important to you?"

Marcus thought for a moment. Hippolytus had agreed to let Marcus help decode the scrolls, but what did they mean for him? "They contain undiscovered, perhaps dangerous, knowledge from the ancient Greeks—Archimedes to be precise. As a scholar, studying them would be the chance of a lifetime." Marcus had stolen the scrolls for the Oracles and trusted Hippolytus not to lead him astray.

A distant shout interrupted Marcus, and he turned to Julianus. "Someone's coming."

He peered down the shore toward Ephesus. Before long, he

spotted torchlight, and the silhouette of a running man soon appeared against the lightening sky.

Marcus watched the runner close in on their position. "Those Romans are still chasing Hippolytus. Let's move." Marcus and Julianus shoved the boat toward the river.

As the bow hit the water, Hippolytus came running out of the night, breathless.

"Get in the boat!" yelled Julianus, the earlier calm fleeing his voice like prey before the hunter.

Marcus boarded before turning to Hippolytus. His tutor's exhaustion forced Marcus to drag him over the side. He crumpled to the floor, breathing fast, eyes closed. The stamina of the champion athlete deserted his mentor hand in hand with his youth.

With a final push, Julianus got the stern into the river.

Marcus heard the ominous whistle of an arrow before he saw it hit Julianus's leg. The man cried in pain as he grabbed the shaft buried in the back of his thigh. No longer able to hold on to the boat, Julianus lost his balance and collapsed into the water.

The current pushed the skiff rapidly downriver. Frantic, Marcus rushed to get the oars into the locks, working them to turn the vessel. He peered over his shoulder and saw Julianus regain his footing. As Julianus clutched the arrow's shaft and limped toward the boat, Marcus rowed with the full measure of his strength to close the gap between them.

Another arrow tore through the air near Julianus's head. He crouched and yelled at Marcus. "Go while you can! I'll lead these fools away." He dragged himself through the water toward shore.

"Julianus, no!" Marcus yelled, but it was too late.

Marcus ceased the vain effort to row upstream and let the boat drift. He pounded the skiff's side, tears welling in his eyes. His heart ached for his companion though he'd known him only a day.

The Agent
Ephesus, August 5

Sextus Cimber ran his fingers over his dark, cropped hair as he reviewed his letter to Octavian, the Triumvirate and Consul for Rome and its western provinces. Before tonight, his letter had contained no useful intelligence, not a scrap of evidence, rumor or gossip about Mark Antony's plans for his legions in Ephesus. Invade Italy by sea or cross to Greece and approach Rome by land?

Cimber couldn't fathom his luck, but now perhaps his prisoner might yield information for his report. As an intelligence agent for the dead Julius Caesar and now his great-nephew, Octavian, he had always provided a steady flow of information—but that had dried up recently.

He stretched his tall frame and then resumed his meal, which was losing its appeal with each gut-wrenching scream from the captive in the next room. He squeezed his eyes shut supposing that would shield his ears. The pungent odor of burning flesh filled his nose. He hated torture; it was distasteful and unreliable. Neither money nor his freedom had coaxed this prisoner into talking.

Cimber took the remaining option.

His operative inflicting the pain, Zeno, was most efficient at his job, but Cimber, in his twentieth year as an intelligence agent, had never seen anyone hold out this long. Since the capture along the river hours earlier, Cimber had learned his captive's name, Julianus, but nothing else; he remained a shadow. Gone also was the man who had appeared outside the temple, leading them on a chase through Ephesus.

Cimber, Zeno, and two other operatives were returning after another fruitless reconnaissance of Mark Antony's eastern allies gathering in Ephesus. The near-naked man's appearance out of nowhere intrigued Cimber, so they followed him. When he ran, Cimber knew he had something. A common thief? Perhaps.

"Zeno, enough. He won't talk." Cimber rubbed his eyes before returning to his meal. He looked up when Zeno appeared. The man was short and muscular with a lumpy, discolored scar running from his left eye to his jaw.

"Too late, sir." Zeno's mouth twisted in disgust. "He's dead."

"No, Zeno, you ass." He pressed his palms against his eyes. "I wanted him alive."

Such a frustrating week. The locals in Ephesus's taverns had nothing to report. The military camps remained well guarded, and the soldiers tight-lipped. "Now we have nothing." He dreaded delivering such a report to Octavian, his master in Rome.

"How's this? The apothecary in Ephesus was right." Zeno flipped a round, flat object at Cimber. It landed in his cup of wine.

"You idiot! That came from a man's bowels." The apothecary had said his potion would have the prisoner's bowels cleaned out in a few hours. "Pour me more wine. No, use the other cup." He grimaced but retrieved the object, shaking off the wine.

It was a small, thin, bronze disk. A broken link dangled from a hole punched in the metal. Cimber had spotted Julianus swallowing something a moment before they seized him.

"What's this?" Cimber frowned. One side was blank, but when he turned it over, he discovered the image of a large bird, a hawk, embossed in the metal. In its talons, the raptorial bird gripped a spear or javelin. And was that a scroll? "Strange and interesting," he muttered. He held the disk closer to the lamp, but no new details appeared.

Zeno peered at the medallion. "Never seen it, sir."

Cimber grunted and flipped the disk in the air before catching it in his open palm.

The hairs on his neck prickled as his gaze met the fierce eyes of the hawk.

CHAPTER TWO

Hippolytus
Alexandria, September 27

"Hurry up, Hippolytus," said Marcus. "The other fisherman will catch all the fish."

"Mareotis is a big lake." Hippolytus entered the kitchen. It was still dark, and the Bassus household was asleep except for the cook. "Tell him, Neema."

Neema slid a fresh loaf from the brick oven and turned to her kitchen's intruders. "He's right, Marcus."

Marcus merely grimaced and waved a dismissive hand as he rushed out the kitchen door.

Hippolytus shook his head. "Still carrying grief from his mother's death. It's not personal, Neema."

"I know. I was there." Tears misted her eyes. "Marcus is strong. He'll pull out of it, someday. He's pleasant when honey cakes come out of my oven. Take some of this." Neema cut and wrapped the warm bread. "You two will get hungry waiting for the fish to steal your bait."

Hippolytus chuckled and inhaled the bread's aroma. "Smells delightful. Might not make it to the lake."

"Save some for Marcus, teacher, or else," Neema warned, shaking a bread knife at him. He scurried from the kitchen with his wrapped prize.

*

A few hours later, Hippolytus and Marcus sat in a small boat under the bright sun. A boy from the Bassus family vineyard had joined them to work the sails and tiller.

Marcus grabbed the bait bucket. "Which bait works best, Hippolytus?" he asked. His voice cracked from the change it was undergoing.

Marcus rarely asked him for advice. This was an amusing development. When Hippolytus first met the boy, he had been unruly, stubborn, and moody. Besides endless patience and a gentle hand, he used the boy's insatiable curiosity to guide him to a more constructive path. His body was changing. Perhaps the adventure in Ephesus had matured him.

A gentle breeze rippled the lake's surface. The boat boy weaved his fingers through the water.

"Boy, stop," Marcus commanded. "You'll scare the fish."

The boy scratched his head and gave Hippolytus an imploring look.

Hippolytus frowned. "Marcus, this boy works for your father. It's not your place to instruct him." Marcus, like any teen, was still immature and sometimes insensitive. "You can bait your line, right?"

"You're asking? I'm not a ten-year-old anymore." He wiggled the cricket onto his hook. "I'm not a child after last month's adventure."

Perhaps bringing the boy to Ephesus had been a bad idea. "Toss the line over the right side. That's where the fish are." Hippolytus nodded to the water.

"No, the left side. I saw a big fish jump there." Marcus swung his line over the boat's left side.

"Good, Marcus. You can think for yourself. When faced with uncertainty, rely on reason and intuition to tell you where to cast your line. Never be afraid to make independent decisions, even when authority demands otherwise." Hippolytus knew his advice was harsh, but necessary if Marcus was to realize his potential.

"Unless it's you or Papa," added Marcus.

"That's right. Often, however, using reason and wisdom, you must choose for yourself."

Marcus stared at his line. "Papa doesn't spend much time with me... like fishing. Except in winter, he's off on voyages. He only cares about me continuing his legacy. I'm glad you're around."

Once again, Hippolytus experienced an intense protective affection for Marcus. His fondness transcended the tutor-student relationship. It had been so for years. Maybe it was the warm sun, the gentle breeze, and the lapping of the waves that made him voice his feelings.

"Marcus, you're like the son I never had." It took an effort for Hippolytus to swallow.

Marcus's face brightened briefly, but then his body slumped. He resumed staring at his line. Hippolytus was confused, unsure of what Marcus was experiencing. Abandonment? He baited his hook and cast it to the right.

After a quarter of an hour, Marcus spoke. "Made any progress on the scrolls?"

Hippolytus winced at the question. Marcus was doing some different fishing now. "None, but I'm not ready to bring them to the Oracle Prime."

"I want to help, Hippolytus. It was I who put my life in danger to snatch them."

On the journey back to Alexandria, Hippolytus had tried to turn the boy's thoughts away from Julianus and back to the potential of the scrolls. Aware that it would appeal to Marcus, he had stressed how Archimedes' work might help humanity. Hippolytus had promised to consider involving Marcus in the decoding.

"I agree you have earned some claim. However, my Oracle oath doesn't allow outsiders to view Prime Knowledge. I can, perhaps, copy a few lines of text for your study."

"Can't I do more?" grumbled Marcus.

Hippolytus saw the frustration on the boy's face. Marcus craved involvement, pressing daily, but Hippolytus couldn't keep his promise. The Oracles' goals took precedence. "Perhaps, but not right now. I don't even know if the codes are a linguistic puzzle or a mathematical one."

"Mathematics is pure and beautiful to me, truthful. It never lies, unlike Papa."

Time to distract. "Mathematics doesn't lie. People lie, but they're most often truthful, especially those who love you."

"Like you, I guess," Marcus said, smirking.

"Yes, but like your father, too. Isn't your father returning next week?"

"Yes, but he leaves the week after." Marcus tossed a stone into the water and watched the ripples spread. "I hope you're not leaving."

At a loss for words, he rubbed the boy's head and stared out over the shimmering lake. He might have to leave Marcus one day. The Oracles could call for the Archimedes scrolls without warning.

Will I be prepared—or willing—to abandon Marcus?

"Marcus…" He paused, trying for the right words. Then, he saw Marcus's fishing pole jerk. "Your pole!"

Marcus swung around and pulled back on his pole, which curved downward, touching the water.

"This is a big fish!" Marcus pulled on the line and then eased a bit before arching his body back. His gaze darted to Hippolytus. "I need your help."

CHAPTER THREE

Hippolytus
Alexandria, October 20

THE MID-AFTERNOON HEAT drove Hippolytus from the small garden and into the house he rented in the Jewish quarter. Near the door, he saw the tiny scroll with the black wax sealed with the image of the Oracle hawk. He grabbed the scroll, broke the wax seal, and spread the single sheet. A bold signature adorned the bottom: Nikanor, an Oracle Agent posted to Rome several years ago.

Hippolytus raced through the words, which were in Greek:

> *To Hippolytus: Destroy this document after reading. I write you these words with the utmost urgency. I am an Oracle Agent, a scribe, within Octavian's intelligence unit. I have discovered correspondence identifying you as wanted for a theft from the Temple of Artemis in Ephesus. The source is an unnamed teacher with the Academy of Philo in Athens. I pray to the gods this letter arrives in time. You must flee Alexandria, Hippolytus. The Oracle divines all. Nikanor*

He reread the letter twice before burning it. What was he to do? Though not an edict from the Oracle Prime, it was unambiguous. He had to flee, but could he abandon Marcus?

He stared at the flickering lamp.

And what was he to do with the scrolls?

According to legend, they were written and encrypted by Archimedes—a savant in engineering and mathematics and an inventor of many advanced mechanical devices. If Archimedes felt the knowledge in the scrolls demanded such secrecy, then they must be dangerous. For decades, the Oracles had been searching for them, knowing that in the wrong hands, the scrolls' secrets could wreak havoc on civilization.

I must run.

As much as he loved Marcus, Hippolytus recognized a higher calling. His devotion to the Oracles' goals required him to put aside personal wishes, which meant he couldn't show the scrolls to Marcus. Procuring Prime Knowledge like the Archimedes scrolls came at a price, including Julianus' death. To honor their sacrifice, he had to prevent the possibility of the Archimedes scrolls falling into the hands of power-hungry men.

His failure to decipher them weighed heavily upon him. Beyond a few lines of old Greek, his part-time decoding efforts had come to naught.

Leaving Alexandria, his home, would be painful. The city was an intellectual beacon, guiding scholars and artists as its Pharos Lighthouse guided ships at sea.

As for the scrolls, could Philotus, a friend and colleague at the Library, take them? No, the man wouldn't jeopardize his position as assistant librarian, even for an Oracle Master. He couldn't travel alone with them. Too risky. And to where would he flee? The Library of the Oracles in Ctesiphon? He didn't have time to get an Oracle escort for that dangerous journey.

Hippolytus paced the small room, reviewing every possible solution, no matter how wild. Leave the scrolls with a banker or a temple? He didn't trust either one. Bury them in the desert? He chuckled at that idea.

Don't be ridiculous, Hippolytus. Think, you fool.

He abruptly stopped his pacing, realizing what the most important question was.

Whom do I trust?

The answer rang loud and clear.

Marcus.

The boy was a phenomenon—smart and a serious student. At age ten, the boy gave his first lecture, in geometry, at the Library. Hippolytus had hoped to groom him to be the next Euclid or Pythagoras—without the latter's mysticism. Marcus loved knowledge like a brother. Yes. He could leave the scrolls with Marcus until he returned. He would stress how low risk it would be for Marcus.

But was Marcus mature enough for such a massive responsibility? Could he resist the temptation to examine the documents, even try to decode them? Though only fourteen, Marcus was much more mature than his age. Yes, for his mentor, Marcus would do it.

"Marcus. I can trust Marcus," he mumbled aloud. It must be him or no one.

*

It was *hora quarta,* the fourth hour of the night when Hippolytus approached the townhouse of the Bassus family. In typical Roman fashion, a stone wall with a stout wooden gate fronted the street. Oil lamps flanked the entry and cast a dim light. Not sure if Titus, the Bassus gatekeeper, was alert, Hippolytus pounded his fist on the door. He was about to strike again when the spy slot slid open and Titus's face appeared.

"Who's there?" Titus demanded. "The Dominus is in bed. Come back tomorrow." The slot began to close.

"Titus, wait. It's me, Hippolytus."

The sound of a bolt sliding back was followed by a creak as the gate opened slightly. "Hippolytus? Why are you here at this hour?"

"Titus, I must see young Marcus. It's urgent."

"I don't know, Teacher. Marcus is up, but the master is asleep. Tomorrow, perhaps?"

"I'll be discreet and quick. It's important I see Marcus tonight," Hippolytus said, holding out his hands in supplication.

"Very well. But be silent."

The gate swung open and Hippolytus stepped in. Titus secured the gate and lead him through a colonnaded portico that bisected a small forecourt. Hippolytus stepped into the familiar entry hall from the main door and followed the gatekeeper into the expansive atrium. Above the low, gurgling central fountain, he could see a slice of the night sky through an opening in the ceiling.

Titus lit several lamps. "Wait here," he whispered. "Master Marcus is reading in one of the day rooms." He turned and crossed the atrium toward a hall Hippolytus knew led to the public rooms and family quarters. On the opposite side of the atrium was the entry door to the servants' quarters where he stayed when his studies with Marcus ran into the late hours.

Hippolytus paced around the high-ceilinged room, wondering if he was doing the right thing in involving Marcus. As much as he tried, he found no clear-cut answer. Through his robe, he rubbed his Oracle medallion. He halted when he heard footsteps approaching.

"Teacher? What are you doing here? Is something wrong?" Marcus stepped into the light with a perplexed look on his face.

Hippolytus swallowed. He had to proceed. The preservation of Prime Knowledge depended on it. "Marcus, there's something I need to discuss. I have an urgent request, and it's a lot to ask of a young man."

"Certainly, Hippolytus," Marcus replied, with a serious expression. "Anything. Let's talk somewhere more private."

He led Hippolytus into one of the day rooms where they both sat down in richly carved chairs.

"Before you agree to anything, let me explain the situation

and what I'm asking of you. First, anything said tonight must stay between us. Understood?"

"I understand secrets." Marcus jumped up and checked the nearby corridors and the atrium. "No one's around," he said, sitting again.

"This is a vital secret, one with life-and-death consequences. Follow my directions, and the danger is minimal."

"Don't send me on another mission, Teacher. I want no part."

"No, no. I would never ask you to engage in an adventure like Ephesus again. Let me relate events that happened before I came to Alexandria and became your tutor. I must also tell you more about the Oracles."

"It's about time," said Marcus, folding his arms and posing as the injured party.

Hippolytus ignored the gesture. "The Oracles have many members all over the world, from Spain to Rome to Greece to Arabia and beyond."

"Fascinating, but how is that possible? You must have influence in many high places. It sounds intriguing, Teacher."

"Hear me out before you decide. Use your reason, your logic, not your boyish enthusiasm."

He then related the purpose of the Oracles, their ruling principle to curate knowledge for the good of humanity, and their need for secrecy. Hippolytus knew the Oracles would appeal to Marcus's own goal to use the knowledge of the ancient Greeks to build a better world.

"Let me give you a hypothetical example. If knowledge existed to make fire come from a rock, the Oracles would covet that knowledge. They would keep it safe and hidden from all men. Do you understand, Marcus?"

"The Oracles keep safe the knowledge that is dangerous and shouldn't be known?"

"Yes, until it's appropriate."

"Who decides that?"

"A council of rational, intelligent, and enlightened men. Men who have studied all their lives to evaluate how the known pieces of knowledge in the world fit together. Many have studied here in Alexandria. As you know, I possess part of that secret knowledge. The two Archimedes scrolls we recovered in Ephesus."

The boy's voice rose in volume. "Archimedes—mathematician, inventor, and engineer. I read some of his books last year." Marcus grinned, his eyes wide and staring at Hippolytus.

"I know you have. I shouldn't be, but I'm amazed at your depth of understanding."

"Tell me more about the scrolls."

"It's unfortunate," continued Hippolytus, "but I could not make sense of these scrolls. Archimedes encrypted them using some ingenious scheme." Hippolytus paused, hesitant to reveal the concept of Prime Knowledge, but then decided to put all his trust in Marcus. "The leader of our organization is called the Oracle Prime. Ultimately, I should bring the scrolls to him."

"And you haven't done so because it's a long journey?"

"In part. Winter is coming, and travel is difficult." Hippolytus paused, reluctant to admit his mistakes to Marcus but seeing no other path. "The true reason is I failed my duty. Instead of taking the scrolls to the Oracle Prime, I decided to decode the scrolls myself. However, now powerful men—Romans—who would use the knowledge for wicked purposes, are after me." He took a breath, hoping that Marcus would accept his request and his need to run. "I'm asking you to take the scrolls and keep them safe. They won't be looking for you. I, however, must..." he dreaded saying it, "flee Alexandria."

"No, no, Hippolytus! Please don't go. Don't leave me." Marcus's eyes teared up.

When Hippolytus saw Marcus's tears, doubt tore at him. "I must, Marcus." He gripped the boy's shoulders. "I don't want to, but I must. And you are the only one I can trust to protect Archimedes' scrolls."

"Take me with you."

"I can't, son, but I promise to return."

"When?"

"I don't know. It's not fair, but will you do this? I cannot tell you enough how important it is for me to leave the scrolls with someone I trust. Can you do it, Marcus?"

"You will return?"

"Don't worry. I promise to find a way back somehow. Will *you* promise to keep the scrolls hidden and to tell no one of their existence? Not a single person," his voice cracked, "not even your father."

Marcus paused and looked into Hippolytus's eyes. "But what about the Oracles? Will they come searching for the scrolls? I don't want to get Papa or myself in trouble."

"I'll be the only Oracle to know that the scrolls are with you. No one else will."

Marcus nodded. "Then, yes, I'll do it."

Hippolytus grasped Marcus's shoulder. "Thank you. One day, after I return, you can help me decode these writings." His guts twisted in self-reproach at the lie. His promise was hollow; the Romans, the Oracles, even bandits might prevent his return to see this boy he loved as a son. He paused to steady himself. "You have a place where we can hide the scrolls? Somewhere no one would find them?"

"Come with me."

Hippolytus followed Marcus to the boy's room down the hall in the family living quarters. Once inside, Marcus closed the door. "I have a floor tile I can pry up. Below, there's a little space where I can put the scrolls."

"Excellent." Hippolytus produced the Archimedes documents from under his robe.

Marcus grabbed a knife from a chest and pried up the floor tile. Hippolytus examined the space. It was dry with stone sides and bottom. He placed the precious rolls of papyrus, wrapped in lambskin, into the cavity. Marcus carefully replaced the tile, pressing it tightly into place.

"Wonderful, Marcus. Thank you. It's a clever hiding spot. Now, let me leave you with one warning. Trust no one, Marcus, not family, not friends."

"Trust no one. I understand."

Heavy pounding on the outer gate split the quiet.

"You must go, Hippolytus!" exclaimed Marcus.

"I shall return."

Hippolytus looked intently at Marcus—so much the son he never had—and then embraced the boy, holding him for several long moments, knowing it might be for the last time. He took a deep breath and released him.

Though the room's exterior door, Hippolytus ran outside into the dark peristyle garden at the back of the house. Shining in the sky above him was the Pharos lighthouse. It seemed dimmer tonight.

Time to run.

He climbed the tall garden wall, jumped to the alley below, and ran into the night.

Marcus
Alexandria, October 20

Marcus watched Hippolytus disappear over the garden wall before rushing through the house to the small, walled courtyard that separated the house from the front gate. Titus, the household gatekeeper, was sliding open the spy slot.

"Come back tomorrow," Titus ordered in a gruff voice. After hearing no response, he started to close the spy slot, but a fist burst through the opening.

"Go away, or I'll call the city guard!" the doorman yelled.

"We *are* the city guard. Open up."

Titus whispered to Marcus, "What should I do?"

"Stall them. I'll see if Papa can speak with them." Papa had staggered in from a dinner party shortly before Hippolytus left. Marcus flew back through the entry vestibule and the atrium, turning left to the family living quarters. He banged on his father's door. "Papa, wake up." Marcus waited and was about to pound the door again when it opened.

"Marcus? What time is it?" His father squeezed one eye shut and rubbed his neck.

"It's the fifth hour. City guards are at the gate," Marcus rattled off his words.

"Slow down. Speak softly," said Papa pressing his fingers against his eyes.

There had been too much drinking at his dinner party.

Marcus repeated his words as his father went back inside his room. Marcus heard water splashing, and after a few minutes, his father, dressed in a simple tunic, made his way to the gate and ordered Titus to allow the guards entry.

An officer and a trio of guards paraded in. Their officer addressed Papa. "Please pardon the intrusion at this hour, Lucius Bassus." The man's voice sounded weary. "We're looking for a Greek teacher named Hippolytus. You know him, sir?"

"Yes, he's been my son's tutor for years, but he lives in the Jewish quarter, not in this house."

"Jewish quarter?" The officer peered beyond the gate into the night.

Marcus could discern another man lurking on the edges of light from the gate lanterns. "Why are you looking for him?" Marcus asked.

Papa admonished him. "Marcus, be quiet, I'll handle this."

"When was this tutor last seen?" The officer looked toward the open house door.

"Yesterday… or the day before," answered his father, again rubbing the back of his head.

The officer turned to Marcus. "You, boy. When did you see him last?"

Marcus checked Papa, who nodded. "Yesterday at the Royal Library, but I don't know where he is now."

The officer again stared through the open gate into the dark.

Marcus heard an indistinct voice from the shadow-filled street.

"I must insist upon searching the house," said the officer stiffly. "Please step aside."

"Oh, no," said Papa, stretching his arms out. "Not unless you want Queen Cleopatra to have your head on a stake. Is Amam Kekara your commander?"

The officer nodded.

"We're drinking buddies, and I don't think he'd like you ransacking his friend's home. Do you?"

The officer glanced outside again before turning back. "I warn you, sir, that harboring a wanted man will bring trouble down upon you. Now, if you see him, contact the city guard immediately. Have a good night, sir."

As the four men made a quick exit, Marcus strained to spot the mysterious figure, but he remained cloaked in the shadows. Marcus heard the officer call out a name.

Cimber.

34 B.C.

CHAPTER FOUR

Marcus
Alexandria, May 4

MARCUS KNOCKED ON the doorframe of his father's study. "You wanted to see me, Papa?"

His father was a handsome man, with classic Roman features, including the hawk nose and black hair. Marcus took the proffered chair.

"The augur says the auspices are not right for your ceremony. I'll consult him again when I return from Massilia."

Disappointment and resentment grew in Marcus. He had to protest this unfair delay. "Papa, I'm tired of wearing this bulla and being the oldest child in Alexandria." He pulled out his amulet, talisman of a Roman male child. "I'm almost eighteen. By the gods, I'm entitled to my manhood ceremony."

"Do not invoke the gods, Marcus." His father rose and pounded his desk. "The bulla shows you're freeborn. Your lack of discipline earlier this year has delayed your ceremony—grounding a fishing boat, running a horse to near death. You've become rebellious and disobedient lately—"

"But, Father, Hippolytus understood me—"

"Don't say it; I've heard it." His father narrowed his eyes. "He spent time with you, he shared an interest in mathematics, he this, he that." His father paced across the room. "But he also neglected important social interactions. You're still a virgin, you have no friends—except Kleon." His father frowned. "*I'm* building your future and my legacy. Not Hippolytus."

"I don't want your legacy. I want you. And I want to be the one to choose my path. I don't study only for pleasure. I believe the ancient Greeks were on the verge of great breakthroughs. The Library contains undiscovered, hidden knowledge, which I must find to improve life for all men. It's what I live for."

His father shook his head. "It's a good and lofty sentiment, Marcus, but impractical. You're only one person. It's not been easy for me. I'm getting older. The business needs new blood."

"Can't you sell the business?"

"What? Sell all I have worked for in Alexandria? As an exiled Roman, it hasn't been easy conducting my trading at the whim of the Ptolemies. I can't meddle in politics without it having a direct influence on the business. I've kept my head low and my mouth shut, and my legacy won't be a pile of gold in some banker's vault."

"Please, Papa—"

"Marcus, Marcus. I love you, but you must obey my wishes. You weren't ready two years ago, but now I agree it is time for your ceremony. As a man, you will become part of Bassus Trading whether you're completely ready or not and give up this frivolous pursuit. You're becoming a lazy, indulgent schoolboy." His father slapped his desk. "Enough talk. Leave my presence. Now." He pointed his finger at the door. "I must pack for tomorrow's journey."

*

Early the next morning, Marcus escorted his father to the harbor and his ship and another trading voyage, this time to Rome and on to Massilia. The conversation was sparse until they reached the vessel.

"Marcus, trust me. It is our tradition to wait for your ceremony until the auspices are favorable."

"Yes, Father, you are wiser than I am," Marcus replied in a monotone. Though resigned to another delay, he hoped the time for his ceremony was near.

They exchanged a terse embrace. Marcus avoided eye contact and waved a brief goodbye before trudging back home. On the small altar in the family sacraria, as was the ritual, he lit incense and said a prayer to Neptune for his father's safe return. He watched the pungent gray smoke curl upward.

"Hippolytus, where are you?" he whispered.

That afternoon, he flopped onto his bed in his father's house, the grand Bassus house — his prison. His room, filled with the objects of childhood, was once more his refuge. With arms hanging over the bedside, his fingertips idly traced circles on the floor tiles. His tight muscles ached. All this built-up resentment was about to explode from his head.

Marcus' manhood ceremony had been put off, but at least Papa had agreed it was overdue. Worse was Papa's plan to make him active in the shipping business. How would he continue his studies?

The image of his last night with Hippolytus four years ago came back with vivid clarity.

The floor tile with the Archimedes scrolls. Which one was it?

A search of the floor revealed the undisturbed tile. He grabbed a knife, his hands trembling. He was about to break his promise to Hippolytus, who was more a father to him than his own was.

His anger had driven him this far, but he needed to stop and think before he executed the last step.

He concentrated, seeking clarity for his situation. His father stymied him, forcing him into a profession he had no interest in. The scrolls promised him the potential of great power. Hippolytus must have known the risks involved.

Perhaps his mentor never intended Marcus to keep his promise.

Regardless, if Marcus could quickly discover the secrets of the scrolls, then his father would have to let him continue his studies. Otherwise, Marcus would be forced to be a merchant and to forgo any chance of finding the hidden knowledge of the ancient Greeks.

He would show his father he was not a lazy, indulgent school-boy. It was up to him to set his future's course.

Carpe diem.

With the knife's point, he raised the tight-fitted floor tile. To his relief, he found the cold, dry scrolls where he had left them. Moving them to his desk, he selected one and rolled out the ancient and delicate papyrus. It was only three pages long with the end page glued to a thin wooden roller. With stones holding the scroll open, Marcus lit a candelabrum, and the black ink on the papyrus glistened in its light.

Marcus studied the script filled with strange symbols. The first page had a few lines of unfamiliar Greek script. Did the symbols represent letters in an alphabet, or a cryptic code invented by Archimedes?

A sudden knock on his door made him jump. Opening it, he found Titus standing in the hallway.

"Sorry, Dominus. He insisted on seeing you."

Behind Titus, Marcus saw a tall figure with dark hair, deep-set eyes, and an angular face. A new feature, a scraggly beard, covered his chin. It was Kleon, Marcus's good friend since childhood who worked at the Library as a scribe. Though his friend lived in the Rhacotis quarter in the western part of the city, Marcus saw him nearly every day at the Library. Kleon was like family, but as in any family, the relationship was competitive and often contentious.

"Marcus," greeted an exuberant Kleon. "I heard your father left today and figured you could use some cheering up." He lifted a wine jug and slipped by Marcus into the room.

"Honorius is calling me, Master." Titus winked. "Let me know if you wish to go out later. I'll get Mapus to walk with you."

"Thank you, Titus. I doubt I'll be going out, but I'll let you know." Marcus closed the door and scurried to his desk. He tried to roll up the open scroll before Kleon noticed it, but it slipped from his hands and rolled along the floor.

"What have we got here, Marcus?" asked Kleon, reaching the unrolled scroll first.

"*We* have nothing," Marcus said, snatching the scroll from Kleon's hands and rolling it up. During all their years of friendship, Marcus could never deceive Kleon about anything.

"I don't know what those symbols are...." Kleon scratched his chin. "They are beyond me, but I think I can read those first few Greek lines." Then, pouring out two cups of watered wine, he added, "First, we drink."

They clinked cups. "To your health, Kleon," Marcus toasted and drained his wine.

"You can read this?" Marcus waggled the scroll, his curiosity aroused again, and then unrolled it. "So, what does it say?" he demanded.

Kleon's father, a middle-level bureaucrat in Cleopatra's government, had paid for several years of language studies, providing his friend with more expertise than Marcus. In addition, Kleon had scribed part-time for several years for Eucleides, and much of the work was in translating old Greek plays and poems.

"Well, let me try..." Kleon moved the candelabrum closer. "Here goes: 'In accordance with... a pact made between P E C A and Osiris, the... Curse of Osiris, and a horrible and... torturous death, on the... unlucky one who dares read this scroll. So says P E C A.' Shit, Marcus, what is this?"

"Is there more?" Marcus crowded against Kleon and examined the scroll.

"Move your big head, and I'll see."

Marcus straightened his back.

"Yes, there's more. Ready? 'The... worthy shall find great and...

terrible powers in these documents. May the gods… grant him the… enlightenment to… wield them… with justice lest they become… destroyers of the world.'" Kleon stepped back from the desk. "Isis, protect me. Did I get cursed?"

"Don't be foolish." Marcus downplayed the idea. "You didn't read the scroll, only the curse."

"That somehow doesn't appease me." Kleon shivered.

"You know languages. Do you know the main script?" Marcus traced the first few symbols on the page.

Kleon shook his head. "Never seen it."

"I would love to know what it says."

"Where did this come from, Marcus? It's weird." Kleon cocked his head. "Did you steal this from the Library?"

"No, not the Library, never. I borrow a mathematics book, but nothing as strange as this."

"So, where is it from, Marcus?" Kleon pointed to the scroll and shrugged.

Marcus leaned back against his desk. Could he trust Kleon? Should he be attempting to read them after promising to keep them hidden? Sworn to show them to no one? He had been careless and broken half of that promise.

But it had been four years. His mentor, the man who had called him a son and had taken him beyond his grief for his mother, that man might be… dead.

His father would return in about two months. Why not see if he could meet Archimedes challenge and break the puzzle of his cursed scrolls? None had done so in two centuries. Marcus took pride in his intellectual abilities. He would best them all.

With his language skills, Kleon could help. Although, if it were a mathematical puzzle, he would obstruct progress.

"Hey, you awake?" Kleon clapped his hands. "Another dream trance?"

Marcus snapped out of his reverie. "Never mind where the

scrolls came from. Are you going to help me?" Marcus extended his hand. "In secret. No one must know."

"Marcus, for terrible powers I'm in. Yes, a secret pact. And curse you double, Marcus, if I get cursed."

Kleon grasped Marcus' hand, but the expression on Kleon's face sent an ominous chill and a feeling of foreboding through Marcus. He'd seen that look on his father's face before, right after he had concluded a successful negotiation. Kleon's narrow, all-knowing eyes and sly grin frightened Marcus.

Is my visage that of an oath breaker?

They drank the wine, and Kleon related the latest Library gossip, but Marcus's mind was on Hippolytus. After his friend left, Marcus staggered past the Archimedes scrolls, lying dark and defiant on the desk, and crawled into his bed. He thought about the nefarious shadow on Kleon's face. Did his face have that same expression? The question stayed with him during a restless night of cold sweats and chaotic dreams.

CHAPTER FIVE

The Agent
Alexandria, July 2

CIMBER CLIMBED UP to the deck of the small merchant ship right after its side scraped against the wharf in Alexandria's Great Harbor. He grabbed a rail to steady himself. Dressed in customary sailor's garb to hide his identity as a Roman agent, he surveyed the docks of Alexandria, noting changes from earlier visits. He and his head operative, Zeno, waited for the crew to lower the loading ramp before trotting off the ship.

Cimber spent the next few minutes scanning the crowds in search of the customs agent with the red armband. When he spotted the man, Cimber headed straight for him.

When they met, Cimber opened one hand to reveal a gold coin. The Egyptian palmed the coin, replacing it with a piece of parchment before moving down the dock. The parchment displayed the name of an inn where Cimber would meet his local operatives. He headed off in its direction followed by Zeno.

Octavian, his master and Triumvirate of Rome, had set a new mission for Cimber.

The primary mission was to spy on Cleopatra and her consort, Mark Antony, Co-Triumvirate—though who knew for how long, and Cimber had been given gold for infiltrating the palace and

Antony's personal guards. Perhaps a few gold coins would slip into his pocket as well.

The secondary mission was unusual—watching an old exiled Roman, Lucius Ventidius Bassus, who was 'up and coming' in Senatorial esteem but wasn't an active threat.

Lost in his planning, Cimber smashed into a large body, the collision half spinning him around.

"Your pardon, sir," said a huge man in a plain tunic.

Zeno, trailing behind, exchanged words with the stranger. Cimber couldn't make out the conversation as he walked away along the dock.

"He looks familiar," said Zeno, trotting up and appearing confused.

"Everyone looks familiar to you, Zeno."

Zeno loitered for a moment. "I know him," he muttered.

"Shut up, Zeno."

CHAPTER SIX

Talus
Alexandria, July 2

As HIS SHIP neared its Alexandrian harbor berth, Gaius Talus stared up at the magnificent Pharos Lighthouse. Next to him stood another passenger, a gem merchant.

"Ready, Trebius?" he asked the merchant. "Good luck with your trading."

"Thanks, Talus. Have a prosperous life in Alexandria."

"Aye." Talus slapped the merchant on the back. "What's life without change?" He had experienced a multitude of changes in the last few months, going from a famous gladiator in Rome to a free citizen, able to travel to new lands.

"Here we go." The loading ramp was descending. Trebius grabbed his bags. "Fortuna be with you."

"And you." Talus trotted down to the stone docks, shouldering his solid frame through the crowd to an open space amongst the slaves and stevedores working the merchant ships, the lifeblood of Egypt. The ordered chaos contrasted against the tidy stonework of the quay. Countless gleaming white marble structures, monuments, and obelisks towered over the low commercial warehouses. Soldiers in fine uniforms, posted at regular intervals, eyed the proceedings.

"Remember, Talus," called Trebius over the crowd, "head for

the Emporium. Better taverns that way." The merchant pointed toward a large, three-story building in the distance.

Talus glanced that way, but two men on the next berth drew his attention. A sailor and a customs official talked chest to chest. Gold flashed. Nearby, watching with a sharp eye, was the muscle, a rough-looking barbarian with a scar running from left eye to chin.

Out of nowhere, two other men appeared, blocking his vision of the nefarious transaction. One pointed a feathered baton at him.

"Any scrolls to declare?" asked the baton wielder.

The question puzzled Talus. "What?"

Who are these circus fools?

"You have any books or other written material in your baggage?"

"No, nothing." Talus peered at his bags, then at the officials. Talus was a tall, muscular man, big even for a gladiator, and he straightened to his full height.

"Open—" The man stopped, gazing up at Talus. "Welcome to Alexandria. Proceed."

Talus grunted and continued walking. His massive body made for rapid progress along the docks. He scanned the immediate area for the dishonest sailor and his thug, but the crowd had swallowed them. When he looked ahead, his shoulder crashed into another, causing him to look back. It was the crooked sailor. The man wasn't a commoner. His noble facial expression along with the military bent of his walk unmasked his true nature.

"Your pardon, sir." Talus spat and pressed on, glancing back. A Roman up to no good. He wanted no part of it.

The criminal's brutish companion slowed to stare at Talus. "Hey, don't I know you?" asked the brute. "From Rome? Careful who you bump into."

The man spoke in Latin with an accent he'd last heard on the narrow alleyways of Subura in Rome. For a moment, Talus stared at the brute's face, inspecting the ugly scar. He'd seen worse in the legions. Today, his first day in Alexandria, he wanted no trouble. "No, don't think we've met. Tell your friend—again—I'm sorry."

"Sure, I'll tell him. But I'm sure I've seen you." The thug turned and trotted after his companion.

Talus continued for a few paces, then halted.

"Jupiter's balls." Talus shook his head. He was going the wrong way. He searched around and, after sighting the Emporium, headed back in its direction.

Ahead, walking along the dock, he saw the broad back of the lumbering brute from earlier.

CHAPTER SEVEN

Marcus

Alexandria, July 2

THE LETTER HE had received last week announcing his father's imminent return from his latest voyage to Rome had Marcus walking each morning from his home to the docks. With the vagaries of wind and current, it was impossible to know his father's exact arrival date. As he passed the Library, he envisioned his future: a scholar, at the Mouseion, assessing and analyzing the vast knowledge generated by the Greeks in their golden age. Through that knowledge lay a better world. He would discover that knowledge and prove to everyone he had not wasted his young life in useless study.

After each morning's check of the docks, Marcus made his way back to the Library where he continued to read the works of Archimedes, hoping to find some clue for decoding the two scrolls. Yet another morning passed in which he found nothing.

Marcus left the Library at midday for another check of the docks. Today, he rode a wave of determination. He would greet Papa with respect and love—and then pin him down on a date for his manhood ceremony. Consumed by his studies, Marcus had let his sixteenth birthday—the typical day for Roman youths to celebrate their passage into manhood—and his seventeenth slip by without much concern. Then he learned—from Honorius, the

Bassus chief steward who oversaw the family house and the vineyard across the Lake—that he had no legal rights under Roman law, until after his manhood ceremony. Without those rights, he couldn't apply for work nor own property. He couldn't marry either though that was unimportant right now.

Marcus almost bumped into Kleon before he saw the man. Each of his friend's arms was around the slim waist of a young woman. Marcus recognized them from the steps of the Temple of Apollo. Prostitutes.

"Marcus, I was hoping to see you. I received my scribe wages and decided to do some drinking and other fun." Kleon gave him an impish smile. "Come join us, my friend."

"I'm s-sorry, but Papa's ship's arriving soon, and I have to meet him at the docks. Then I have a study group at the Library."

Kleon sighed. "As you wish." As he moved off, he turned and called out. "Grow up, Marcus, and see life."

Marcus had no desire to see life yet. His burning wish for discovery drove his life. He skipped parties, women, drinking, and other available social diversions. Instead, he spent his hours in the Library pursuing his dream. He stood for a moment and watched Kleon recede into the crowds.

He returned to his problem with Papa. Couldn't his father could see that commerce—and shipping, in particular—was not his fate? Though his mother had left him a small sum of money, his financial dependence on his father was a chafing yoke around his neck. He needed to throw it aside somehow.

He met Honorius at the dockside Bassus Trading Emporium, which fronted the large Bassus warehouse. With the steward was his nephew, the skinny Mapus, the family bodyguard.

After exchanging short greetings, Marcus led the men down

the docks of the Great Harbor. After dodging stevedores carrying containers of all types—sacks, crates, barrels, bales, and amphora—Marcus found Papa's colossal grain trader already docked into its double berth.

Marcus spotted his father's familiar frame on the wharf. He wore a splendid tunic with purple embroidered stripes along the hem and sleeves. His expensive leather sandals had silver buckles. His outward appearance suited a man who was once a senator in Rome.

Marcus met him with a wide grin and an enormous hug.

"Marcus, I'm glad to see you, son," said Papa, sidestepping a man carrying a sack of goods off the ship. "Let's step away from the ship before we get knocked into the sea. I've spent too much time crossing it to end up swimming in it."

A growing number of slaves and overseers were unloading the cargo of wood from Gaul. His father spotted Honorius and moved to greet the steward. An enormous crate carried by six slaves separated Marcus from the others. He saw his father and Honorius walking off and searched around for Mapus. As he turned, he saw a big, ugly thug barreling his way through the crowd of slaves carrying amphora. The thug shoved a slave aside who stumbled, sending his clay amphora crashing to the ground. Grain spilled across the dock. Slaves scattered. A dog barked.

The rough-looking man plowed onward, swinging his elbows and heading for a startled Marcus. Before he could bounce Marcus off the dock, a hand yanked him from the thug's path. Marcus hit the ground, but not before glimpsing the bully's face and the ugly eye to chin scar that marred it.

Marcus jumped up, ready to confront whoever had pulled him down. He stared into the chest of the biggest man he had ever seen.

"Are you hurt, young master?" The man spoke perfect Latin.

Marcus stepped back. No words came.

He heard workers shouting and saw many retreating from the

scene. His father and Honorius rushed up to the interloper. Honorius squeezed between Marcus and the giant.

Papa scowled at the unknown man. "You crazy barbarian! What are you doing? Son?" Papa turned to Marcus, grabbing his shoulders. "Are you all right? Honorius, call the city guard."

"Papa, I'm not a baby," Marcus said, pushing his father's arms away. "This man pulled me back from the real barbarian. You should thank him."

His father studied the big man. "What's your name?"

"Talus, sir."

"Well, Talus, I'm Lucius Bassus, owner of that ship." He extended his hand, which Talus squeezed. "Come along with us. Everyone," commanded Lucius, "head to my office in the Emporium. We'll have wine and hot food for you, Talus."

"My thanks, sir," replied Talus.

Marcus and the four men made their way through the teeming docks to the Bassus trading office. They all sat at a table with wine cups. Talus was finishing his second helping of porridge.

"The man of the day," Lucius Bassus said, raising his wine, "Talus? The name's familiar. Tell me about yourself."

"I am Gaius Talus of Rome."

Marcus examined the man. He was in his mid or late thirties, with dark hair cropped in the Roman style. He had muscles Marcus didn't know existed. But the scars on his arm and one on his cheek told of a dangerous and hard life.

"Wait, not Talus the Titan?" Lucius inquired. "The gladiator? Victor of a hundred matches? You're a legend."

Talus nodded at Lucius. "My notoriety proceeds me. Yes, I was that man." Marcus watched the gladiator's face. After a flash of pride, Talus's face wore a rueful look. "I've given up that world."

"What brings you to Egypt?" Marcus asked.

"Let's say I had a contract disagreement with my former

employer. He bet against me in a death match. Had my weapons tampered with… dead men don't collect prize money."

"Right," said Lucius, slapping his knee. "I heard some such scandalous gossip before leaving." Lucius leaned forward. "You ducked out of a match."

Marcus watched Talus's jaw set.

"That upset people you don't want to upset," said Lucius. "Bookies, gamblers—that sort."

"Those upset people forced me to leave Rome in a hurry. I'm looking for work now in a new land, so I can save to buy land of my own. Some legionnaires stationed here have served under me. We'll share a bottle or two of wine, and I'll tell my story. Perhaps they know of work."

Marcus rubbed his chin. "You know the soldiers?"

"I was in Caesar's Seventh Legion."

Marcus waited for elaboration, but Talus seemed reluctant to offer more details.

"Hear me, Talus," said Lucius. "I need a tough bodyguard. This city is never stable, with friction over Cleopatra's rule, along with discontent about the Roman troops in the country. Riots are common. Dislike—hatred is not too strong a word—of Rome is rising. The Bassus household needs protecting." Lucius pointed at Talus. "What say you? Seventy-five silver denarii a month plus room and board at my city house. And you can teach my son self-defense skills."

Marcus couldn't believe his ears. What's his father thinking? He didn't have time to play soldier.

"It's a generous offer, Master Bassus. I accept."

"Excellent. Honorius will handle the details. Search the taverns and Roman camps for a couple of men to work under you." Papa and the giant shook hands across the table. "I am hosting a dinner later this week. You will be my guest."

"Papa, you will have a slave as a dinner guest?"

Talus turned to him. "I'm no slave, Master Marcus. I'm free-born, a free man, and a citizen." Talus showed his fist, displaying the iron ring of Roman citizenship.

"I'm sorry, sir." Marcus wasn't pleased with Papa's latest plan for him. "Papa, about this training, my studies—"

"Enough, Marcus."

"No, Papa, you cannot silence me this time!" Marcus shoved away from the table, sending his chair toppling over. "I must move on with my life. Make my own plans for my work at the Library. I deserve to have my manhood ceremony. While I am a child, you hold me prisoner. If Hippolytus were here—"

"Hippolytus," Papa spoke the name with disgust in his voice. "Well, where is he? At least I'm still around." Papa stood up, his face red. "At least sometimes. Excuse my son, Talus."

"No, Papa. We must talk now. Please," Marcus pressed his palms together. "I don't have a lot of time… there's something I have to do."

"What is it you need to do?"

"I must study for a lecture at the Library—"

"Studies, discussions, lectures." His father grasped Marcus by the upper arms. Marcus winced, and the grip relaxed. "I've delayed your manhood ceremony because I knew you weren't ready. Continue like this, with no interest in practical matters, and you can expect to end up poor, living in a scholar's dormitory at the vagaries of some Ptolemaic king." Papa released him but still wagged a finger. "You know how we Romans hate kings."

"But you're not a Roman anymore," Marcus stated in a bland voice.

The flat of his father's hand swung toward Marcus. He squeezed his eyes shut, but his father stayed the blow, saving them both their dignity.

Why does Papa fight me?

Papa pointed a finger, first at Marcus, then at Talus. "Because some rabid consul pushed a decree through the Senate to exile me, it doesn't mean I'm not Roman, or you're not Roman. In our hearts, if not in the eyes of a bunch of rich, lazy Roman aristocrats, we are Roman. I act like a Roman, so shall my son."

Papa had been a victim of the hysteria around the Catilina conspiracy and exiled by Cicero thirty years ago. Back then, every senator suspected his neighbors of plotting the Republic's overthrow. Though Cicero was dead, executed a decade ago by Mark Antony, was it possible that Papa hoped the Senate would rescind the order?

"Anyway, Marcus, it's time for you to become educated in the business of merchant trading." Papa held up his hand to ward off Marcus's protests. "I've hired a man to help Honorius in his duties as the household steward, giving him time to teach you about the business… like accounting, contract legalities, ship navigation, running a farm and vineyard, proper loading of cargo, and—"

"Mucking out the stables. Yes, I understand, Papa, but is gaining a trade necessary if all I want is to be a scholar?"

"We Romans are not like the idle Greeks, who became weak, like old women, and squandered their empire. We Romans build things—roads, aqueducts, monuments, strong armies, and navies. I have helped build ships with my own hands. The Senate stripped me of my land and properties before they exiled me, so I built my company from scratch. First, I sold fish by the docks…"

Marcus had heard this speech. Papa worked his way up from nothing in a foreign land to build a prosperous business. Marcus was weary of fighting his father and no longer wanted confrontation. Maybe he could find a compromise.

"… and there were hard times when Sextus Pompey blockaded the grain trade." His father paused for breath. Looking up to the Pharos, he pointed to the lighthouse. "Study that light, Marcus. You'll see it many times as you come and go from Alexandria. It epitomizes Alexandria. Alexandria! The greatest city in the world.

Not Rome, with its rotting tenements, slave auctions, and squabbling politicians."

Marcus knew his father would take this course. It was time to throw out his counter plan. "Papa, I suggest a compromise. I want one path. You want me to take another." Over Papa's shoulder, Marcus could see an amused expression on Talus's face. "Can we work toward both? I'll pursue my studies in the mornings and business training in the afternoon. How's that sound?"

Marcus watched his father, who seemed lost in deep thought.

After several moments, he responded. "Marcus, that sounds workable but include time for training with Talus. Believe it or not, son, I don't wish to cut you off from your books; you need them. But I also need to know that when I am gone, Bassus Trading will not crumble into dust. It's time for you to move into the real world, get married, raise a family."

"Papa…"

"I'm getting old, Marcus. I've lived a full life and want to leave the business in your hands knowing it will prosper. By the gods, Marcus, I won't leave it to your Aunt Tulla." Papa shook his head. "I'll agree to your proposal, but I have one important stipulation. When the time comes, after I step down, you will engage in a *tirocinium*, a one-year apprentice in the business."

Marcus's mouth fell open.

"After you've completed the tirocinium, I'll give you a ten-percent share. I know this sounds harsh, but refuse the opportunity, and you'll face the consequences of poverty." Papa looked away.

When his father turned back, Marcus noticed his compressed lips. Anger or regret, he couldn't tell which his father felt.

"Let's go, Honorius. Mapus. I've work to do. See you at home, Marcus."

Talus rose and gave Marcus a sheepish nod.

Marcus watched them all leave, his chest heaving with a smoldering anger. He hadn't expected this. Swordplay with Talus and learning accounts from Honorius? Next, he'd be sailing the stormy seas, shoveling out the stables, and jumping whenever his father wanted something.

Marcus
Alexandria, July 5

As Marcus studied the spacious triclinium where Neema and her two kitchen helpers were making final dinner preparations, he realized this dinner was becoming more than a simple welcoming for Talus. Honorius had pulled in old Titus to arrange the couches in the shape of an upsilon, the Greek letter υ, and the guest list now included numerous interesting people, including a visiting Roman senator, Caius Plinius Tacitus, a naval architect from Rome, and Philotus, an assistant librarian. Marcus suspected his father only added the latter to placate his son's sour attitude.

Though Kleon wasn't invited to dinner, Marcus had spent the morning with his friend studying the Archimedes scrolls. It was another frustrating effort. Kleon was not proving as useful as Marcus had hoped. His knowledge of languages beyond Greek, Latin, Egyptian, and a little Phoenician was thin. His thinking was disorganized, and he was lazy, often waiting for attendants to bring him materials rather than going to the scroll shelves himself. They were both searching the Library for any clue that might lead to some insight on the strange symbols that filled the two scrolls. Week after week, nothing turned up.

As Marcus walked back to his room to prepare for dinner, he recalled his moody behavior of the past few days. He was approaching his mental prime when he should direct his energies to reading, writing, and attending and giving lectures. Instead, he was learning to run a merchant trading business and a vineyard. The latter was worthless.

His mother said he would achieve great things. "Don't settle for the mundane," she had told him at a young age. He believed doing something significant was his fate, but Papa didn't see it that way. "Your mother led a sheltered life," Papa had argued. "She never understood or appreciated how the world operates."

Once inside his room, Marcus inspected his refuge and the many vestiges of his childhood that remained: board games, a ball, a stick figure. It was a joyful time while his mother lived. She taught him the board games, tossed the ball. He remembered a time when the two of them sat in the garden and watched butterflies land on their outstretched arms. She said he should respect nature and appreciate its mysteries.

Papa had always been too busy to offer his wisdom. First, he had a fish market. Then he bought a small merchant trader. Today, he had ten ships. The business had a perpetual need for attention that was beyond Marcus's needs. Hippolytus and the Royal Library had been replacement fathers until even Hippolytus had abandoned him. Perhaps, like his mother, his old mentor would never return.

Marcus knew his father was running out of time to mold him. Within two months, he would be eighteen, and manhood ceremony or not, his father could no longer stand in his way. Though he couldn't be too bold, as he would need his father's support until he found a patron for his studies.

His mood darkened further when he remembered Papa's vow to turn the business over to him.

An hour later, Marcus stood in the entry atrium with his father, awaiting the last arrival, Senator Tacitus. His father wore his finest white toga, its folds precise and according to Roman protocol. Honorius, who excelled as both valet and steward, had seen to their perfection.

In contrast, Marcus wore a tailored, dark blue wool tunic embroidered with red and gold threads. Prior to his manhood ceremony, by Roman tradition, he could don an adolescent's toga *praetexta*, but Marcus never liked wearing it.

After a quarter hour of small chatter in the large atrium with the other guests, Marcus drifted into the front courtyard. Through the small security window in the outer gate, he observed Senator Tacitus's arrival in a litter carried by six stout Egyptian slaves. Another slave jogged up to the Bassus' gate and gave it a solid knocking. Only after Titus had opened the gate, did the huge body of the Senator leave his litter. He stepped on the back of another slave, but this one failed his task, collapsing under the weight put on him. The Senator kicked the downed slave.

That was too much.

Disgusted, Marcus left the gate to Titus and rejoined his father. A moment later, the Senator entered the atrium.

After the last introductions and polite conversations, Marcus and his father led the guests into the peristyle gardens for a quick look and from there into the open-air triclinium. His father had arranged assigned seating at the large, armless sofas, which inclined above the food tables in the center. Papa directed everyone to their places.

Marcus sat on the end of the host couch along with Papa. Talus sat between them.

Senator Tacitus took the honor of the middle couch. Opposite Marcus, the naval engineer reclined alongside Philotus, who seemed awed to be next to a Roman senator. Soon, everyone was busy with the oysters and sardines being served along with honey-sweetened wine.

Marcus, curious about Talus, now the family protector, said, "Talus, you were in the army?"

"Yes, young master, I was a centurion."

"Please, call me Marcus when we're home."

"I shall… Marcus." Talus turned toward him.

"Where did you fight?"

"I joined up when I was sixteen, living on our family farm. When Caesar's recruiters came through the countryside, I signed up with the Seventh. After training in northern Italy, I moved to a post in Gaul. The next spring, the Seventh joined Caesar on his sortie to Britain."

Marcus chuckled. "It appears none of the monsters there got you."

"Nay. After that, years of fighting in Gaul followed by the civil wars. I don't want to talk about that disaster." Talus stared off at the fresco on the far wall.

"So, after twenty years, you retired to your father's farm with the adventures over?"

Talus glanced over at Senator Tacitus before answering. "Marcus, it didn't turn out that way. During Caesar's pursuit of Pompey, an unfortunate incident occurred in Illyria during Caesar's siege of Dyrrachium."

"If my memory is accurate, that's where Caesar had Pompey trapped against the sea."

"That's right. One day I'll tell you the whole story."

Marcus nodded and took a sip of his wine. He turned his attention to the naval engineer, Quintus Fabius Buteo, who seemed in his late twenties. *What was Quintus doing in Egypt?*

"You've come to Alexandria for business, Quintus?"

"Yes, Antony hired me as a naval architect for Queen Cleopatra. She's building up quite a navy. We're here to help design and build a new trireme, larger and heavier than what the Egyptian navy has now."

"It must excite you to wrestle with new creations."

"If I had my way," said Quintus, his eyes sparkling, "I'd do something radical. A double-hull super ship with two thousand rowers and fifteen hundred marines."

"That's amazing. No one's constructed a double-hull since the fourth Ptolemy king—Philopator—built his so-called 'forty.'"

"Well, you *are* up on your naval history."

"I've read plenty of history books. My late tutor stressed it. Said it was important to gain insight from the past."

Quintus lowered his voice. "It appears Rome forgets the past. Another civil war looms."

Everyone knew of the friction between Rome's strongmen, Octavian and Antony, which was complicated by Cleopatra's involvement. If there was war, Marcus saw no way Egypt could remain independent. He thought of himself as an Egyptian. Was he destined to be a Roman?

He had to hold off further words with Quintus, as Neema and her kitchen girls now bustled about the room, serving a new wine selection and water. They returned with the first course, a simple fish soup with carrot and onion slices. As he waited for his food, he examined the exquisite frescoes Papa had commissioned last year. As though the artist had applied them only yesterday, a faint scent of fresh plaster and bright paints came to him. He loved the forest and wildlife scenes, but the centerpiece of the grouping was the Pharos Lighthouse shining out over a raging sea.

"This is an excellent wine, Bassus," pronounced Tacitus. "Is it local?"

"Yes, from my vineyard across Lake Mareotis."

"It is becoming a favorite in Alexandria," added Philotus, who knew best, being a frequent party guest because of his scholarly repute.

The servants soon reappeared to remove bowls and refill wine cups. Talus caught Neema's attention. "This is a tasty soup. Love the spices. My name is Talus, the new family bodyguard."

"I'm Neema, the cook for the Bassus household. Sometimes they let me buy the best spices though don't expect this at the servant's table. Welcome to the household, Talus. More wine?"

"Please."

Marcus glanced over at the group's quiet member, Philotus, who he valued as a friend and a great help in the Library.

Marcus had never warmed to Philotus's boss, Eucleides, who was impersonal and bureaucratic, always ready to shuffle Marcus onto someone else.

Other than Quintus and Philotus, Marcus didn't converse much with the other dinner guests. It wasn't until finishing the third course of fruit compote and nuts that he took notice of the Senator's conversation with his father. The Senator had raised his voice.

"You may have heard this when you were in Ostia, Bassus," said Tacitus, "but many senators are looking with considerable favor on you. You're an important piece in our grain trade, and Octavian knows it. The mob would have Octavian dragged through the streets were it not for his grain dole and subsidized grain prices. The Senate is reconsidering your banishment, now Cicero is no longer with us."

A pall settled over the party.

Cicero. Three decades past, the late Roman consul had exiled Lucius Bassus from Rome for his alleged part in the Catilina conspiracy. Lucius's first wife had divorced him and kept their infant son, Publius, Marcus's half-brother.

Papa had never uttered Cicero's name in the house. The Senator might have offended less had he said the foulest epithet or the blackest curse than to utter that name. Marcus could taste the rising tension in the room.

"I don't see how his death affects me," replied his father, breaking the quiescence. Marcus could hear the stress in Papa's voice.

"Come, Lucius. Don't be coy. Cicero exiled you thirty years ago. Forced your first wife to divorce you and separated you from your oldest son."

Marcus noticed the twitching of the small tic in his father's cheek—it wasn't a good sign. Marcus had never met his half-brother, who was around thirty now, and Papa never mentioned him.

"The Senate is considering a *senatus consultum* to rescind your exile," Tacitus continued. "You could have your position in Rome again, free to walk the streets of the city."

"Senator, that has minimal appeal. Why do I arouse the Senate's interest after all these years?"

"Those in Antony's camp view you as a natural ally, given your favored position in Cleopatra's court. Octavian sees your trade contacts bringing new commerce to Rome, new tax revenue for the poor treasury. He wants you in his camp."

"Everything I have, Tacitus, I made without Rome's help. See these hands? They once sold fish."

Marcus saw the Senator's nose wrinkle.

His father continued. "Am I someone the Senate respects as an equal? I think not."

"If not for yourself, Bassus, think of your son, of the opportunities for him."

Papa looked over at him. "I believe none of that would appeal to him, either."

"I was thinking of Publius. He has secured an appointment as a tribune in one of Octavian's legions."

"On the first rung of his political career. I suppose that's good, but Publius made his choice ten years ago when he allowed his stepfather to adopt him."

"Ah, the mistakes of youth," said Tacitus. "If the Senate issues a reprieve, will you accept it, Bassus?"

Marcus watched his father put down his cup. Which way would Papa go? If he accepted the pardon, would Marcus become a Roman citizen? How was it going to affect his plans to study at the Library?

"Well, Senator, if the Consuls and the Senate, and the people of Rome, wish to admit their mistake, who am I to refuse?"

The Senator's eyes became slits. "Careful, Bassus. Don't be too sure of yourself. Given the current political situation between

Octavian and Antony, being a senator could give you leverage with both. As it is, things could fall either way for you."

"Then let the people decide." His father showed a cold smile.

Marcus lost his appetite at the words. His future was murkier than ever. He had to speak now. This was his opportunity to make public his grievance with his father. It was a gamble, but his manhood ceremony was his top priority. He hoped a Roman senator would be sympathetic in a legal sense to his plight.

Jacta est alea. The die is cast.

He knew he had to frame this carefully to avoid embarrassing his father. "Senator Tacitus," he started, trying to keep his voice steady, "besides my father, the Senate's decision also affects me. Important as that decision is, my father has another decision to make. As a son nearing his eighteenth birthday, I am ready for passage into adulthood. My father, however, refuses to conduct the official ceremony for that transition. I don't…" Marcus choked off his words when he saw that his father had ceased eating and was staring at his plate.

Tacitus broke the silence. "Listen to your son, Bassus. Take decisive action for him and yourself. Linger not awaiting the people's decision. Long before that happens, Octavian will decide your fate. Act now or face destruction in the coming war. Heed my words."

Lucius Ventidius Bassus set his jaw and glared at Marcus.

CHAPTER EIGHT

Marcus
Alexandria, July 16

LOST IN THOUGHT, Marcus exited the Library through a side portal. Outside, he checked that the single Archimedes scroll under his robe was safely hidden.

His mind dwelt on two concerns as he walked the broad path taking him away from the Library complex. First, he was anxious over the veiled threat Senator Tacitus had made about the consequences of refusing the repeal of Papa's exile? If Papa accepted, would Antony seize the Bassus fleet and trade routes, ruining his father and destroying his inheritance?

If Egypt falls to Rome, will I become a Roman?

As critical as that reality was, his biggest concern was the Archimedes scroll. He had agonized over it in secret for the past two months, and because the Ptolemies coveted all written works, he had to sneak the Archimedes scroll in and out of the Library. He played on the goodwill of the guards, who knew him well, avoiding their usual searches. But beyond its curse, neither he nor Kleon had progressed in deciphering the scroll's writing. If he could discover the scroll's language, he might find a solution.

Marcus took the curving walkway leading through the Library

gardens and along the reflective pool. The far end was only two streets from home.

He soon reached the pool, and as he strolled along, he observed the quiet water, blue with the reflection of the lotus blossoms. He wished the Archimedes scrolls were as clear as the pool's crystalline water. *If only —*

A sudden collision on the path was followed by a hand striking his lower lip, and softer body parts slamming against his chest. The other person had been moving faster than he and fell backward from the force of their bodies crashing into one another. Instinctively, he reached out, grasping the thin wrists that flailed before him. A hint of jasmine was in the air.

The other person was a young woman close to his age with dark hair and honey-toned skin. Her large, pale-blue eyes captivated him and he stared, unable to break the trance. A moment passed, then words floated to his ears. They were coming from the woman he held.

"I'm sorry, I'm sorry," she said.

Marcus wasn't sorry. Her presence dazzled him, as though someone had thrown back a curtain, letting a bright light flood into his life.

Electra
Alexandria, July 16

"Hurry, Cybele." Electra was late. Her first full day of duties might be her last.

"Oh, Electra, I am envious. Being a maid to Queen Cleopatra must be so exciting. The things you must see. The men you must meet. Handsome young men, built like those Greek statues down by the theater. You know with the big—"

Electra's hand flew to her friend's mouth. "Cybele! You can't say that." She peered around the Library gardens. A few men cast casual glances in their direction.

Even bookworms appreciated young women.

She moved her hand to her friend's arm. "I can't be part of a bawdy conversation, not here in the gardens. Now come along, I don't want to be late for the queen's lunch."

"Electra, you are so proper. Embrace the modern times for your own good."

"I don't care if I'm old-fashioned. Come along," she said and picked up the pace, bringing her friend in tow. "Let's cut through the Library."

"I'd rather be outside. Can't we take the path by the pool? I love seeing the blue lotus flowers."

Electra swung around to Cybele and flung her arms up in exasperation. "Fine!" Thinking the out-of-the-way, curving walk might speed up their progress, she stormed off toward the path.

"It's only around this pomegranate—" With a yelp of surprise, Electra crashed into someone else on the path. The collision threw her off-balance. She was on the verge of falling, but strong arms caught her.

A young, attractive man held her wrists firmly. She saw deep blue eyes, wide with surprise. His olive complexion was smooth, his hair thick and wavy.

She recognized him as Marcus, son of Lucius Bassus.

"I'm sorry, I'm sorry," she managed to say.

"I wasn't watching where I was going," Marcus said. "Are you hurt?" His voice was earnest, full of concern.

Electra recovered her balance. "No, I'm fine, sir. It was my fault. My mind had wandered." She stared into Marcus's eyes and saw intelligence, concern, innocence. There was an intensity too. "What is that under your robe that poked me?"

Behind her, Cybele giggled.

"Oh, sorry. Only an old scroll I was reading."

"Don't worry, sir. Electra is clumsy, too," Cybele said, fluttering her dark eyelashes.

Electra glared at her friend. "Sir, I'm quite well now. We won't hold you up any longer." She looked from his hands, now holding hers, to his face. The warmth of his touch sent a breathtaking sensation from her hands to her arms.

Poor dear. His lip is bleeding.

He seemed frozen, staring at her.

"Are you sure you're not hurt?" he asked, his hands lingering before releasing her. "Oh, my name is Marcus Ventidius Bassus."

"Oh, Goddess," exclaimed Cybele, her eyes wide.

"I was just leaving the gardens. I guess I was hurrying…" He continued to stare at her.

Electra smoothed her dress. "I don't want to be rude, sir, but we're late. I must get to the palace."

"Yes, she must meet the queen," Cybele said, straightening her body and raising her chin, making clear her pompous self-importance.

Annoyed with Cybele's revelation, Electra tried to disengage from the unexpected meeting; she wanted no further delays.

"Yes, Marcus Bassus, I'm one of the queen's attendants. Now, we don't want her upset—so—good day. I must go now." Electra nodded at Marcus and dashed on down the path. For whatever reason, the man intrigued her. Warmth spread through her body, even in the shade of the sycamores lining the pathway.

Never mind. She didn't need this distraction and wouldn't allow it to spoil her first day as maid to the Queen of Egypt.

"What's your name?" came the call behind her.

"Electra," she replied, not daring to look back.

Cybele hurried along behind her. "Electra, isn't Marcus the son of—"

Electra whirled around. "Not another word, Cybele," she commanded. "Cleopatra made it plain that anything I heard about Lucius Bassus in yesterday's briefing is confidential. She doesn't want word to get out before her announcement next week."

"Oh, yes. Sorry."

"Don't be sorry." Electra peeked up at the sun's position. "Run."

CHAPTER NINE

Marcus
Alexandria, July 18

MARCUS TOSSED THE manuscript onto the table and watched it unroll until striking a heap of other discarded books. "Worthless. All worthless."

Kleon hadn't been much help. Although intelligent and imaginative, his friend lacked academic learning. He had read a few of the classics—the philosophy of Plato and Socrates and rhetoric of Gorgias—but not a line of astronomy, engineering, history, plays, or poems. As far as mathematics—well, Marcus had seen smarter horses.

Marcus had started out confident he could solve the scroll's puzzle, but after two months, he was running out of ideas. Archimedes' clever encryption peeved him. Marcus pulled at his hair. *Zeus and Apollo, help me.*

He grinned at his own irreverent joke. He and Kleon had named the scrolls, adopting Greek gods. His scroll was Zeus, and his colleague had Apollo. The initial two pages of each were exact matches, but Zeus was shorter overall, a mere three pages, while Apollo stretched to nine.

Except for the curse on the first page, precise, ordered rows of characters filled each page. Twenty-five rows per page and sixty characters per row. The characters were more like symbols than letters and were comprised of vertical lines and half-lines. Then, these lines were connected by one, two, or three horizontal or slanted lines. Sometimes the symbols included isosceles triangles and squares.

It was odd, but there wasn't an arc or circle in any symbol. All the known alphabets as represented by scrolls in the Library included letters with curved strokes. *What genius created such an alphabet?* A mathematical genius, one named Archimedes. He slumped down in his chair and let out a heavy breath.

At that moment, he spotted Philotus, assistant librarian and friend to Hippolytus, passing through the Reading Room. Marcus raised his arm, the universal signal in the Library for aid. The librarian noticed and hastened over.

"Marcus, how are you?"

"I'm well, sir. No word from Hippolytus, by chance?"

"No, Marcus, I'm sorry. Now, what do you need? I'm on my way to a meeting." Philotus took a half step away.

Marcus quickly said, "I need help. I'm trying to read this scroll." He gave the librarian a brief glimpse of page two of Zeus, which he had copied from the original. "Can you recommend a good linguist who might help?" Marcus gave him a sheepish expression.

"Marcus, you have been roaming around the Library for years searching for so-called secret knowledge. Is that what this is?"

Marcus shook his head. "No, sir. This is something… different."

Philotus frowned. "Very well. Let me think." He scratched his chin and then grinned. "I know the perfect person. I'll send them over."

"Great, thank you, sir." Marcus popped up from his chair and patted the librarian on the back. "I'm moving to the study room by the Isis statue."

He strolled from the Reading Room, down a hallway, and into

the Isis room, isolated and free from distractions. He sat alone and thought of Hippolytus. Even after four years, he missed his mentor.

Would Hippolytus want me to keep the Archimedes scrolls hidden, or did he actually want me to discover their knowledge? He knew my skills in mathematics and puzzles.

An hour later, he heard a knock. "Come in." The door opened and in walked Electra. His mouth fell open as he tried to form words. Nothing came out.

"Oh, it's you... Marcus." She straightened her back, gave a quick smile, and in a soft voice asked, "What can I do for you?"

"Electra, g-good afternoon," Marcus replied, standing up awkwardly. "The linguist sent you? I talked to Philotus about getting help translating—"

"He's the one who sent me here." She seemed confused. "He said there was a scholar having difficulty with a scroll's language. I expected a youngster stumbling with his Greek. This *is* the Isis room?"

"Yes, it is. I asked Philotus for help." Marcus picked up a rolled sheet of paper. "And he said he'd send a linguist. Is he coming?" Marcus tried to see around Electra.

"I'm the linguist if you haven't figured that out yet." She narrowed her eyes. "Now I see the problem..."

Marcus scratched the back of his head. "You?" He felt warm. "You're a girl."

Electra pushed back an errant strand of her shiny black hair. "Yes, me. A girl." She glared at him. "A girl Cleopatra trusts to teach languages to the future king. Well, Philotus will have a good laugh." She turned to leave.

Marcus jumped from his chair. "Wait. That's not what I meant." *Can I trust her?*

He thrust out the page two copy of Zeus. To make any progress, he needed help. "Seen anything like this?" He had to concentrate to keep his hands from shaking. He had exposed the scrolls to yet another person. Another incidence of his oath breaking.

I'm sorry, Hippolytus.

Electra turned back and raised her hands. "Marcus, I would love to help, but I have many pressing duties at the palace—"

"Please, one quick glance. I've tried every Library source I know. I'm desperate." He bit his lower lip. "Take one look, and, if you're not interested, I'll never bother you again." He stared into her eyes, with their ebony lashes, a jangle of emotions flooding through him.

"You're persistent, which is admirable." She took the outstretched papyrus and unrolled it. "Well." Her eyebrows raised. "Intriguing. Where did you get this?" She moved to the table, holding the paper in the light from a small window. "Is this part of a Library book? The writing's fresh."

"I copied it from a scroll I can't show you." He took a deep breath and released it. "I want to know what language it is."

"Language? It's not in any language I know, and I can read ten languages and recognize many more." Electra sat down and bent her head over the page to study it.

Marcus sat next to her. "So, if not a known language, what then?"

"Well, I haven't seen every possible language. How old is the original?"

"So, you will help me?" His face brightened, as hope rose in him. "And you must swear not to tell anyone," he added.

Electra straightened up. "What?" She gestured about the room. "This is a place of learning. There are no secrets here." She wagged a finger at Marcus.

Marcus glanced back at the door. "It's from an old scroll. For two centuries, a religious cult hid it from scholars."

Should its secrets stay obscure? No.

"Two hundred years? Interesting. What a strange set of

symbols," Electra said, peering again at the copied page. "It either came from an unknown land or…" Electra hesitated, then wrinkled her nose.

"Or what?" He studied the striking features of Electra's face and his skin warmed. He gripped the edge of the table and squeezed hard. *Focus.*

"It's a fake?" he asked.

"Eh? No, no. Someone from the East, beyond India, might be the author. He possesses a creative mind, that's obvious."

"Right." He released his grip, shaking his hand to get the blood flowing.

At that same instant, Electra held out the scroll to him, and his shaking hand knocked it from her grasp.

"It's fascinating," she said, watching the scroll roll along the table, "but this needs someone who can solve puzzles rather than a linguist. Do you know where it came from?"

The scroll page rolled off the table toward the floor. "Sorry, I'll get that." Marcus bent down to catch the paper.

"I'll get it." Electra said at the same time, and her arm shot out as she also leaned down to retrieve the errant papyrus.

With an audible thump, their heads knocked together.

"Ow!"

Marcus didn't hear Electra's cry of pain, nor did he feel his own. Through his watering eyes, he saw only her compelling face, whose openness drew him in. Whether from a hidden internal impetus or from the knock delivered by the crash of heads, he could not break the connection that formed. He had an intense urge to kiss her.

Electra recoiled, touching her head. "Marcus, are you all right?"

Marcus didn't answer as he searched the floor for the scroll. It had disappeared. When he straightened up, he found the page back on the table.

"Marcus, take your scroll. Did you do all this so you could kiss me?" Electra frowned at him, her lips clamped together.

"Kiss you?" Marcus blinked several times. He rubbed his head where a small knot was forming. As he examined Electra's face, he tried to remember what happened. Did he try to kiss her? Gods, he hoped not. Was she gritting her teeth or suppressing a smile or—he hoped not—a laugh?

"Did I?"

"In truth? No." Electra twirled a loose curl around her finger. "It sure appeared like you wanted to."

"I'm sorry, Electra. I respect you, and I apologize for my earlier disbelief in your abilities." She touched a part of him in a manner no other person or thing had. He didn't understand it. "But I'm desperate. I need your help with the scroll."

Without a word, she walked to the door and opened it. She poked her head into the outer hall and looked around. Her long, straight hair whipping out as she jerked her head around to look at Marcus.

A smile spread across her face.

"I like you, Marcus, so I'll help you. But first, you must tell me more about where these scrolls came from. And second... I have a request of *you*."

CHAPTER TEN

Marcus
Alexandria, July 22

MARCUS HAD NEVER been to an official palace event nor had he ever escorted a woman, but he was doing both tonight.

Beyond any doubt, he needed Electra's help with the scrolls. And her price? Be her escort to tonight's dinner party.

Marcus, wearing his best robe, and Papa, in his formal toga, arrived at the palace in separate litters provided by Cleopatra.

On this balmy summer night, they followed the other guests—haughty diplomats, stiff military men, self-important bureaucrats, talkative merchants, quiet philosophers and excited scholars—passing under the south gate into an impressive court-yard centered on a towering granite obelisk and filled with stunning marble statues. As befit Alexandria, the city of marble, their path led toward a grand flight of marble steps.

Marcus scanned the crowded courtyard for Electra.

Where are you?

Then he saw her on the edge of the courtyard. When their eyes met, Electra moved through a tall hedge into a side garden.

"Papa, will you excuse me for a minute?" He didn't wait for an answer.

"Marcus, I—" his father began.

"Go on ahead, Papa. I'll catch up," Marcus called over his shoulder.

Inside the garden, he found wide, precise walkways dividing neat rows of flowering shrubbery. Marcus inhaled the aromatic air from the blooms. He spotted Electra, attired in an exquisite silk dress, sitting on a bench by a small fountain.

"Marcus, thank you for doing this."

"And *why* am I doing this?" asked Marcus, sitting next to her.

"Because you want me to help you with…" she paused at Marcus's upheld hand. "The scrolls," she finished in a whisper.

"Yes, but what do *you* get? I'm your escort. So?"

Electra looked down. "Cleopatra's pushing me to marry."

Marcus's eyebrows shot up.

"The buffoons she's paired me with… well, they repulse me." A frown creased her forehead. "Old, fat nobles who have done nothing except occupy an exalted and undeserving position. They paw and grope. I don't intend to allow that to happen at this or future dinner parties." She stared down at her hands.

Marcus again noticed her delicate features. But she scared him. He was a moth seeking, yet fearing, the flame.

"Is there a different way I can help you?" The expression on Electra's face caused him to sag. "Tell me what you expect me to do." he said.

"Just be yourself. We will dine on a couch together, so get used to being close." She touched his hand but then drew back.

Warmth shot up his arm. Marcus swallowed. "Don't worry. I'll respect your wishes." Her presence was subtle, ethereal, yet effervescent.

Gods, being with this beautiful woman, making conversation, laughing at the correct moment—this will be hard. But I can't embarrass Papa, tonight of all nights.

"Good." She stood and grabbed his hand. "Come on. We should enter with your father."

Holding hands, they raced out of the garden and into the stream of partygoers. Before long, they caught up with Lucius.

"Marcus—" Lucius began.

"Papa, I want you to meet Electra, one of Queen Cleopatra's attendants."

"Yes, I've met Electra before. Good evening." He gave her a slight bow.

Electra returned the bow. "How are you, Bassus, sir?"

"I'm escorting Electra," Marcus blurted. "She's joining us tonight."

Lucius looked at Electra with a wrinkled brow. "How is this?"

"Oh, my escort had to attend to duties in Pelusium. I saw Marcus in the Library yesterday, and he offered to fill in." She smiled at Marcus.

"Unusual for Marcus." Papa eyed him with suspicion. "Remember your manners."

"Of course, Papa."

Past the stairs, the trio crossed a broad portico, and then on through giant bronze and oak doors, entering a long forecourt with high ceilings and illuminated by dancing blazes in enormous brass braziers. Here, the palace's fine art impressed Marcus and everyone else, based on the many gasps from the guests. His fingertips traced the curves of a green-veined marble sculpture, its surface smooth and luxurious. The sheer size of an enormous wall fresco, easily besting a galley's mainsail, stopped him in his tracks. While his father moved ahead, Marcus observed a chair of glossy ebony and creamy cedar, inlaid with lapis lazuli and carved with intricate images, and sat down in it, so as to comfortably peer up at the surrounding towering granite columns painted in multiple bright colors.

Offering silver platters of exotic finger foods, seductive servant girls swirled about, their ethereal silk gowns showing glimpses of perfect bodies. The food and women whet all Marcus's appetites, but he couldn't indulge. Instead, he rose and hurried to catch up with his father.

Burning incense, fragrant with tones of myrrh, cinnamon, cardamom and cassia, infused every breath he drew. Delightful harp music echoed from somewhere, as he entered the banquet hall with his father and Electra.

An attendant showed them to their assigned places, and Marcus was shocked to see that their seats were next to the raised platform of their host. Across from their seats and a line of low tables, Marcus saw Senator Tacitus and two diplomats. Further down, he spotted Kleon and his father, a deputy minister of trade. He gave a short wave when Kleon glanced his way.

"Marcus, decorum," his father admonished quietly, fidgeting with the folds of his toga.

He knew Papa was feeling the tension.

That morning, a courier delivered a message from Cleopatra, calling both father and son to a meeting.

Later, Papa summoned Marcus to his study. Not a man to express his emotions, Marcus found his father excited and tense. Eyes bright, he paced the room. Marcus had to sit before his father would speak. Cleopatra had handed down a momentous decision that would affect the Bassus family business—he stressed the word family—in ways Marcus feared to contemplate.

"I'm forbidden to reveal details, Marcus," Papa had said, "but you'll hear them tonight at the palace. I promise this—it will advance the date of your manhood ceremony."

Marcus jumped out of his chair. "Yes! That's wonderful news, Papa."

"Tonight," his father stressed, "remember your lessons in etiquette and diplomacy."

Tonight, I'll make Papa proud. I'll be on my best behavior and —

A percussion of drums, tambourines and bells interrupted his thoughts and ended all conversation. Marcus fidgeted with his belt. He couldn't keep his feet still as they dangled off his couch. The fanfare was immediately followed by a fast-paced dance melody that announced a troupe of young female dancers. Lithe bodies swung between the two lines of couches; their gauzy dresses forming clouds of color breezing through the room. The women's perfect shapes and brazen, sexual gyrations caused heat to rise in Marcus.

The dancers swirled away and, in their wake, six magnificent men in red loincloths juggled torches high in the air. Their oiled bodies gleamed in the fierce flames as they broke into acrobatic leaps to the piercing, intricate notes of pipes and flutes. After their precise torch catching and maneuvers, the men bowed to the crowd before flowing out of the hall.

The room fell silent for an instant before all gasped as the regal music announcing Cleopatra's presence boomed forth. A troop of young girls carrying baskets skipped into the hall, scattering fragrant lotus petals onto the floor.

As the last petal floated down, Cleopatra appeared in the entry, dressed in full royal regalia and seated on a gold and ivory throne carried by ten muscular men in traditional white loincloths. Clutched in her hands were the crook and flail of the ancient pharaohs, her ornaments of office, while an elegant wig framed her formally-painted face. She wore a white chiton sheath with colorful, flowing silk sashes that hugged her curving hips and breasts. A necklace of huge pearls adorned her neck. In raw beauty, Marcus found her less attractive than many of the dancers whose brief appearance had titillated him.

The slaves carried Cleopatra to the raised platform. An attendant took her crook and flail while another helped her onto the couch, artfully situating the folds of her dress.

"Marcus, don't stare," Electra said. She shifted her position next to him. Then, in a voice only he could hear, she added, "You're much more attractive than my recent escorts." She squeezed his bicep.

As the heat rose in his neck, Marcus tried to master his confusion. Was she teasing him or—gods—was she serious?

"What?" he croaked when he found his voice. He cleared his throat and looked into her eyes, which were pale blue, rimmed with a band of darker blue.

"Electra, forgive me," Papa said. "I expected to see you with Marcus tonight because Cleopatra mentioned you at our meeting this morning. She thought you should meet my son."

"Oh," Marcus and Electra said in unison.

"She said nothing about it—" The striking of a gong drowned out her words.

Cleopatra rose to address her guests.

"I welcome all our guests, the esteemed Senator Tacitus, our friends, family, countrymen and women." Cleopatra turned to his father. "I welcome Lucius Ventidius Bassus and his son, Marcus. I never need an excuse for a celebration…" The assembly laughed and clapped. "But Lucius has a lot to do with us gathering tonight. He has long been a supporter of my position as your queen—even before the great Caesar helped us regain our throne. Tonight, I intend to recognize that support—and Senator Tacitus, I am certain, will report this decision to Rome—not with mere words, but with royal trade concessions."

A murmur passed through the guests. Marcus watched the crowd. A scattering of men seemed animated—or agitated, perhaps. His lack of experience with the world created a black void in his perceptions. He didn't understand why these bureaucrats and merchants would be upset.

"Bassus, please stand before me," ordered Cleopatra His father joined her on the dais as one of her attendants brought her a scroll. "It is with immense gratitude that tonight, I award Lucius Ventidius Bassus one-third of our new…," Cleopatra paused for effect. "… Red Sea trade routes to India."

She handed the scroll to Lucius, and the crowd clapped and cheered. The Senator's response didn't seem enthusiastic, but Marcus wasn't sure what was proper.

"And now, let us eat and drink," Cleopatra announced, reclining back onto her couch.

When his father returned, Marcus stood and congratulated him.

"How wonderful for your father, Marcus." Electra clapped. "You'll get to travel to India, even live there. And never come back."

Again, Marcus received mixed signals. He hoped his face didn't show his rising irritation.

"Yes, that's sounds intriguing," was all he managed to say.

Electra laughed.

He liked her laugh.

"I'm joking about never returning," she said. "It would excite me to go there, but I don't know about you."

"I guess it would." Marcus shrugged. "I could study the plants and animals there."

"How boring. You could hunt for tigers or ride an elephant."

"How is that better?"

"Marcus, you can't be—" Electra cut off her words when Kleon walked up to them.

"Hello, Marcus," said Kleon.

"Hello, Kleon." Marcus looked at his friend through narrowed eyes, his jaw muscles tightening. Kleon was always trying to embarrass him, and tonight he didn't need the distraction. "What can I do for you?"

Kleon stared at Electra. "Introduce me, Marcus." He grinned, eyes bright.

Electra's smile was thin.

"Sure. Electra, this is Kleon. One of my oldest friends."

"A friend of Marcus? How unexpected. You know him from the Library, right?"

"Yes, in fact—"

At that moment, a rush of servers with food and drink crowded out Kleon. Marcus lost interest in all but the food, having not eaten since midday. Before he could take a morsel though, a slave girl handed him a silver cup of full-strength wine. He pursed his lips. Another unexpected event—he always drank watered-down wine.

His father nudged him. "Marcus, drink with care. We two must walk steady when we leave here tonight."

Electra raised her cup. "To the good fortune of the Bassus family."

"Thank you," said Papa, sipping his wine.

Cleopatra stepped from the dais. "Lucius, a word," she said, drawing his father away.

Marcus felt a fluttery sensation settle in his stomach as he observed Electra. She was even prettier than he remembered from their Library meeting.

"So, Marcus, are you in favor of Octavian or Antony?" Electra peered at him over the rim of her cup.

"Well…" The question caught him off-guard. "I didn't expect it would be necessary to make such a choice. The difficulties between the two are the subject of conversations throughout the Roman world. I understand Mark Antony has been a friend to Egypt for some time, so maybe he is the correct answer."

"You don't think he has the same designs on Egypt as Octavian?"

Marcus took a gulp from his cup, forcing the liquid down. Across the way, Senator Tacitus conversed with an Egyptian diplomat. He focused again on Electra.

"Though my father was Roman, my mother was Egyptian, and I have never been a Roman citizen. What Rome or Antony means to do is beyond me" His skin tingled from the wine.

Electra continued to press him. "Come on, Marcus. Your father has raised you Roman, not Egyptian. Your father was a senator. He travels to Rome all the time."

Marcus's face flushed. He pulled at the folds of his robe and took another swallow of wine. It warmed him more. "He does what he has to do. Because he's an exile, he can never step foot off the ship. It's forbidden." He glanced over at Tacitus. "By the Senate." His lips were dry.

He drank once more from his cup. *Why all these questions?*

Electra sat up and took a deep breath, her breasts pressing against the thin material of her dress. Her sensuality touched all his senses. "Tell me, Marcus." She stared up at the ceiling. "When Rome comes to rape and pillage our country—or should I say, my country—are you simply going to sail away?" She rolled back onto her side and gave him an intense stare.

His lips parted as he leaned in toward her. Another wave of warmth rippled through him. He wanted to reach out and touch her but instead rubbed his own forearm. Rational thought was beyond him as his body was a slave to his infatuation with Electra. He swallowed. "I—"

"Electra," Cleopatra interjected, walking over to them, "be gracious to our guests." She gave Electra a serious look and then motioned to a servant. Before Marcus could refuse, the server filled his cup. "Now drink up," added Cleopatra, smiling, "and leave politics for another time."

Marcus took only a sip, but its intoxicating effect spun his mind. He needed something in his stomach. He reached for a honey-coated peach slice that lay beyond his reach. He stretched out to grab it when Electra pulled the peach off the tray.

"Sorry, Marcus. That slice is mine."

Distracted and off balance, Marcus slipped forward. The heel of his hand landed hard on the lip of the tray, causing it to flip and fling fruit slices at him. Panicked, he tried to catch the errant pieces but knocked over his wine instead. The contents of his cup sprayed everywhere, spreading down the front of his robe and the side of the couch. Electra jumped back with a shriek, showering her own wine onto Marcus. Wine was everywhere.

"Oh, Marcus!" exclaimed Electra, her hand flying to her mouth. "I'm so sorry."

"What?" said a startled Marcus, dripping as he jumped from the couch. He slung a piece of gooey fruit off the back of his hand. "Why did you do that, Electra?" He was angry now.

Before the distressed girl could answer, the regal voice of Cleopatra rang out. "Electra! I saw what you did. How could you? And to one of our honored guests."

Marcus swallowed and glanced from the Queen to Papa. He blinked in surprise when he saw his father holding back a laugh instead of burning with rage. That worried him even more.

"I'm very sorry, Majesty. I was only playing with Marcus. This... mess I didn't know would happen." She turned to Marcus. "Please, believe me." She pressed her palms together.

"Go, you two." Cleopatra pointed to her left. "Get Marcus cleaned up. Have a slave get him a fresh robe."

"Yes, my Queen." Electra bowed, her back stiff. "Come along, Marcus. It won't take long." She beckoned him to follow.

"Excuse me, Majesty. I'm so sorry regarding the mess." As much as Marcus worried about the queen's reaction, his father's judgment mattered the most. "Papa, I—"

His father chuckled. "Just go. We'll save you some food."

Marcus scooted around his couch, came close to slipping on a peach and went after Electra, who had gone down a hallway off the dining hall. Behind him, he realized the queen and his father were talking—about him.

I hope Papa will forgive me. Gods, what a horrible first impression I have made.

He caught up to Electra in a curtained alcove down a side hallway. She was giving orders to a slave. He was prepared to tell her how embarrassing her actions were for him, but before he could, she put both hands against his chest. He gave her an angry look, and she pulled back.

"I feel so awful, Marcus. Please forgive me." Her voice was contrite, and she gazed up at him with eyes full of sincerity.

Marcus extended his arms. "All right, I understand the wine was unintentional. But grabbing the food away? That I don't understand." Marcus rubbed the back of his neck.

Electra chewed her bottom lip. "Marcus…?" She raised a finger, went to the hallway and peeked in both directions before returning. "I did all this on purpose. It got a trifle messier than I expected."

"What?" Marcus jutted his jaw forward. "Are you crazy? Do you know—"

"Lower your voice. I wanted to get you alone so we could talk. I need to warn you."

"Warn me? About what?" Marcus squeezed wine from his sleeve. "I have no enemies."

"For a time now, Cleopatra has included me in many of her policy and strategy sessions, so I can advise young Caesarion about future possibilities. I was at the meeting this morning between Queen Cleopatra and your father. Your life is about to change. Your days in the Library studying are about to end."

"I know that. Papa and I have agreed I'll spend half my time learning the business and the other half in study and research."

"That's all voided, I'm telling you. With the new India trade, your father will find himself overwhelmed. I understand he'll be taking long voyages to India and wants you to learn the business and be an active participant. You won't have time for the Library or for those scrolls Hippolytus gave you."

"No, no, no." He shook his head and paced to the hallway and back, wringing his hands.

This can't be. Papa gave me his word.

"Papa knows I don't want to be a merchant trader. It's not my path. He promised me."

"I was there, Marcus. I heard the words from his mouth. He told Cleopatra he trusts only you to run things while he's off to India."

"Gods!" He gazed at Electra. "Why are you telling me this?"

"You interest me, Marcus. You're smart. Goddess, you're smart. When I go into the Library, you're there. I hear the scribes and attendants talk. They say you're kind, respectful, and full of curiosity. A pain when they can't find what you want. Above all, a great scholar. Back there," she nodded toward the dining area, "I didn't want to see you and your father butting heads and embarrassing yourselves in front of the queen and all the important people of Alexandria. I learned about the dinner at your house. Sorry, but Philotus loves to talk. I admit I planned to spill a little wine. I never expected this… untidiness."

Marcus searched for the right words as his mind focused on Electra's warning. Was Papa betraying his word and his honor to build up Bassus Trading? He stared at the onyx floor. He had no legal or moral standing to defy Papa. Electra was right. His whole life would change, plunging him down a path he didn't want. He would never solve the scrolls, never prove to Papa that he deserved to choose his own path.

He walked over to the curtained wall and spread the curtains. Through a narrow window, he spied the harbor waters.

Is that my fate, to spend my days at sea or in a warehouse poring over account books and counting amphora? Did Archimedes, Euclid or any of the Greek philosophers start this way? No, or their books wouldn't be in the Library. I must fight Papa every step of the way. There's no turning back, no compromise possible.

Marcus slapped his hand against the curtained wall. He turned back to Electra and considered her. She intrigued him as well and not only for her undeniable beauty. Her intelligence, spunk and ability to express herself fascinated him. Conversing with women was a neglected part of his education. She had experience in the world of protocol, politics and conversation.

He could learn from her.

It was inconceivable Papa planned to do this to his own son. I will never forgive him.

His body tensed with anger at his father. Something shifted inside him, but he couldn't name it. Marcus had to act to turn aside

Papa's plans or accept his merchant trader fate, his scholarly path choked by contracts and account books.

"Next time I won't be so clumsy," he said.

"One last thing. Don't let your father find out I warned you."

Marcus nodded and rubbed his chin. "I should have seen this coming."

Before Electra could say anything, the servant returned with a fresh robe.

"You can change here," Electra directed. "Toss the wet clothes on the floor by the curtain, and I'll keep watch." She waved the slave away. "With my back turned, I assure you." She held onto the dry robe, grinning at him over her shoulder.

"Right, I'll hurry, only turn around." He took off the wet robe. "Gods! My loincloth is wet, too."

"I can't help you there. Toss it, too." She glanced back.

"Turn around." Marcus unwrapped his loincloth. "I imagine there aren't many more creative ways to get a man naked." He flung the wet underclothes to the floor.

Electra tittered. "I'll remember that."

"This isn't funny. Toss me the robe."

From beyond the room came the sound of rapid footsteps.

Electra scooted to the hallway. "Donkey crap! It's Cleopatra and a bunch of her retinue." Electra's whisper was full of alarm. She whirled around to Marcus. "She can't suspect we've been talking or see you naked. Hide behind that curtain. Now!" she commanded in a low, frantic tone.

Marcus stood with his hands before his crotch. The footsteps sounded close. He dashed for the curtain, found the opening, and plunged in. He held the heavy fabric closed and pressed his head against the wall hoping nothing was showing.

Watching through a tiny slit where the curtains met, Marcus saw Electra back deeper into the room. A moment later, slaves and several handmaidens walked pass the entrance. Marcus swallowed as he spied Cleopatra, who stopped in the hall.

"Electra, where are you?" It was Cleopatra, her voice muffled by the drapery.

"Let me get these wet—" Electra's low voice came from outside his hiding place. The curtain pressed in toward him.

"Oh, there you are, girl. What's taking you so long?" Cleopatra's voice was louder now. Footsteps approached. Marcus's heart skipped a beat. "My wig has come undone. You're the only one who can do it right and—dear cousin, why are you holding two robes? Where's Marcus?"

Marcus heard a sharp gasp followed by clothes hitting the floor. Sweet jasmine filled his nostrils, and a body pressed against his.

Jupiter! What is she doing?

Marcus tried to melt into the stone wall behind him. Warmth flooded through his body.

"Oh, Marcus? He's… he's on his way back, Your Majesty. I'm picking up. This first robe was too big." Her voice was high pitched.

"So, you have everything in hand, then?"

"Yes, my Queen."

"Come along then and fix my hair." Marcus again heard footsteps, receding now.

Her body moved away from him, banking Vulcan's hot fires. He heard a low giggle.

A few minutes later, he ventured out and flung on the discarded robe. His father's words echoed in his mind. *Decorum? Etiquette?* He failed at both.

He returned to the feast and sat by his father. His head ached from the wine, but it was clear what he had to do. He would solve the Archimedes scrolls and discover their powerful knowledge. That should convince Papa the scholarly path was his destiny. He spotted a fresh plate of peaches and groaned.

"Papa, can we go home now?"

Electra
Alexandria, July 22

Electra took another length of ebony hair from Cleopatra's ceremonial wig, running her fingers and an elegant, ivory-toothed comb through the shiny strands. Besides the dinner party, the queen had a late-night meeting with her councilors and needed to mimic freshness.

The last partygoers' voices wafted up from the courtyard. The party, the wine and the episode with Marcus Bassus all conspired to distract her attention from her task.

She reached for another hairpin, then twisted and pinned each band of hair into elegant ropes. Cleopatra's eyes followed Electra's progress in two polished-bronze mirrors.

Electra had said little, unsure of Cleopatra's mood after the incident with Marcus. She wondered how the poor man was doing. Had she been too bold? The memory of his near nude body was... stimulating. She'd seen naked men before, but this was a different experience.

"So, what do you think of Marcus?"

The queen's question startled Electra out of her reverie; she fumbled with the comb. "Marcus Bassus, Your Majesty?"

"Yes, yes, you know who I'm talking about." Cleopatra glared at her in the mirror.

"Oh, a touch different maybe, but interesting. Needs to discover some activities outside the Library."

"Interesting as in intellect? Lucius Bassus has started teaching him the shipping business and training him with a gladiator. He's pleasant to look at and seems to be rather fit."

"Yes, that's true." Electra sensed the heat rising in her face. She needed to divert the queen to other subjects. "Change your earrings, my Queen?"

"Curse the earrings." Cleopatra jerked her head around. "Tonight, I have given Lucius Bassus one-third of my India trade because my counselors say he is the best of the Alexandrian traders. That makes him and his son important to Egypt—to me. I must make ties to strengthen the connection between the Ptolemies and our Roman allies."

"Roman masters." The words slipped out before Electra could stop them.

The slap was quick and sharp, causing her to drop the comb. She rubbed her cheek. "I'm sorry, my Queen. Please, forgive me."

Cleopatra gave her an icy look before turning to the mirrors. Electra returned to her task.

"As I was saying, as head of the Ptolemy dynasty, I must ensure beneficial marriages occur in the family." The queen took her hand. "Do you understand, cousin?"

Oh, no. She never calls me cousin.

Electra's hands trembled as she picked up another hairpin. It took a moment to assimilate what the queen's words meant. Was Cleopatra going to announce a marriage match? She didn't like this. "Yes, my Queen," she said to the wavy image in the mirror.

"The Bassus family, already rich, will amass wild amounts of wealth. Marcus might be a good match. You could do worse, and you are not getting younger, you know. Time to have you married. The sooner the better, perhaps by next summer."

Electra stuck herself with a pin and recoiled. What could she say? She had turned twenty last month, ancient by Ptolemy or Roman marriage standards. "Marcus? I'm not sure. He intrigues me. He's intelligent and from a good family, but I want to marry a man I love."

"Love?" Cleopatra released a boisterous laugh. "That will come later, if the gods favor you."

Electra considered saying she could never love a Roman, but that would not sit well with Cleopatra. As queen, Cleopatra saw only a man's power, whether from armies or gold. Was Marcus a Roman? Half-Roman? She would need to watch this Marcus Bassus.

CHAPTER ELEVEN

Electra
Alexandria, July 23

THE PALACE WAS quiet as Electra walked from her rooms on the lower level. She had early morning kitchen duty as punishment for the embarrassing scene with Marcus Bassus.

She took a deep breath. One more week to go.

"Electra."

She turned to see a courier dashing up the passageway toward her. After accepting the small scroll from the man, Electra broke the unfamiliar seal. Someone named Kleon had signed it.

Ah, Marcus's friend.

The scroll was an invitation to a dinner party later this week at his house in a reputable district. Electra wanted to laugh. Was there a joke she missed? Was Kleon responding to a juvenile dare?

She heard footsteps ahead. It was Cybele. Electra hadn't seen her since the collision with Marcus.

"Electra." Cybele met her with open arms. "Are you headed to the kitchens?"

"Yes, I'm serving Cleopatra an early breakfast. I'll never understand why people get up this early. Is it because they want to?"

"What's in your hand? A love letter?" Cybele clapped her hands while bouncing on her feet. "Oh, show me."

"Sorry, Cybele. It's an absurd dinner invitation from someone I met last week."

"Oh, that's exciting. You're going, right?"

"Certainly not. Women don't go unaccompanied to dinners. As I recall, this Kleon fellow's household is of middling social status. Besides, I didn't like his ill-mannered air. Cleopatra wouldn't approve."

"How do you know? She likes boldness and adventure. She'd tell you to go. Anyway, I like that Kleon moves fast."

"Oh, Cybele, grow up." Electra turned toward the kitchens.

"Wait for me," said Cybele in a deflated voice.

*

A half-hour later, Electra entered the queen's room where she found Cleopatra at her writing desk and set the heavy silver tray on a nearby table. Under golden domes lay plates of various fruits and cheeses, poached duck eggs, freshly harvested game fish and warm bread.

"Thank you, Electra. Let me finish this last letter."

Cleopatra never ate much in the mornings; having the pick of the remains was the only reward of morning duty.

"How is your day, my Queen?"

"Oh, the usual. Scrolls upon scrolls from the bureaucrats. A pox on them!" She affixed her seal. A scribe appeared from an alcove took the letter, adding it to a stack near the door. "Now, what do we have?"

Electra removed the metal covers and served the plates out on the writing desk. While the queen picked at the food, Electra stood near a balcony. She liked watching the ships in the harbor below the palace.

"What's hanging from your belt?" Cleopatra pointed to her morning's message.

"Oh, only a letter."

"Come, come, girl. What kind of letter?"

Electra related the letter's contents.

"Kleon? Oh, yes, Marcus Bassus's friend. His father is deputy minister of farming or something."

"Should I attend, my Queen?"

"Attend? Come, Electra. Do I even need to answer that? Write an immediate reply and I'll have my scribe send it."

Electra regained her confidence and wrote a single line on the letter. "I decline your invitation." She relayed Kleon's information to the scribe, who noted it in his ledger.

Painless.

Kleon
Alexandria, July 23

Kleon increased his pace as he approached his house in the Rhacotis quarter. While adjusting the bag of meat, vegetables and fresh bread he had picked up at the market, he rubbed the ink stain on his index finger. It was a badge from today's toil scribing for Eucleides, the Head Librarian. Tomorrow, he hoped to get back to doing the research work he liked. Scribe work was beneath his abilities.

As he reached the door of his house, he met his father and hugged him. Kleon hoped his father had good news.

"Hello, Father," Kleon said.

"Kleon. Can't talk. They need me back at the ministry. There's a message inside for you." He took a few paces toward the street before turning. "Oh, don't expect Aristus today. I can only afford one session a week now. There's no money."

"What?" Aristus was his tutor. Kleon needed instruction at least twice a week to fill the gaps in his education. "Father, if you want me to contribute more of my pay—"

"I'm sorry, son, but it's not enough. Not until I get that promotion I'm waiting for."

He'd waited two years for this promotion. Kleon didn't have much hope left for it. "Please, Father."

"We'll talk later, Kleon."

He watched his frugal father walk away, then entered the house and handed his bag of food to their old servant, Min, the last remaining slave from the handful included in his mother's dowry. His father had sold the rest over the past few years.

"A message, Dominus," Min said, taking the bag.

Kleon spied a scroll sitting on the entry table and grabbed it.

"I'll be studying in my room, Min," he muttered and plunged into the gloom of the house. His father believed lamp oil was an expensive indulgence. Once in his room, Kleon disregarded household rules and lit two lamps, setting them on his desk along with the small scroll. As he sat down, he realized that it was the invitation letter he had sent Electra early this morning. With nervous anticipation, he unrolled it.

Where was the reply? Then he noticed writing near the bottom. It contrasted to the bold black ink of his hand. Someone had penned it with a delicate stroke.

At first, his eyes didn't focus. Letters appeared, incomprehensible. Then the four words on the paper struck him as if a knife to his heart.

"I decline your invitation."

No explanation. No hope. No respect.

Kleon swept the letter and one lamp from the desk. Flames sprang up and danced on the oil. He stared at the fire for a moment before snuffing it out with a blanket.

The money he spent on the dinner, borrowed from friends, was a waste.

That disrespectful bitch will pay for this humiliation. One day, she'll pay.

CHAPTER TWELVE

Kleon
Alexandria, July 25

AT THE SIXTH hour, Kleon knocked on the Bassus home's oak gate. Marcus was little more than a toddler when Kleon first started visiting this house. There was some obscure connection between the two families, though his father adamantly refused to discuss it.

Kleon looked around at the other luxury townhomes along the street. He wished he lived in this neighborhood. A statue of Serapis stared from a niche beside the door. Serapis, a blend of a Pharaonic Egypt god and a Greek god, straddled the line between present and past religions.

That will appease everyone, whether Greek, Egyptian, or Roman.

The old gatekeeper led him to a room filled with expensive furniture and art—another reminder to Kleon of his humble home. Marcus soon arrived, and they gripped forearms in greeting. Marcus's grip had grown stronger since training with the ex-gladiator. Kleon used to go to the Gymnasium but had given it up for more entertaining activities—drinking and whoring came to mind.

"We'll use Papa's day room. He's in his study planning his India trip," Marcus informed Kleon. "Follow me."

As he examined the home's interior, Kleon noticed fresh frescoes and rich furniture. No frescoes graced his house.

Marcus took a seat and pointed to one for Kleon. On a small table between them, Marcus placed the Zeus-named Archimedes scroll. Kleon did likewise with his longer document, Apollo.

"He's also planning your voyage to Massilia?" Kleon asked while scrutinizing both scrolls.

"Gods, yes, but I wish he'd forget it." Marcus picked up a small carving of a young nymph playing the lyre. "I sometimes wonder, though, if I am fighting the Fates. My gut tells me the sea is not for me."

Kleon leaned forward. "I'd love to take that voyage. My father and I went to Crete once. I love the sea." He stared into space, remembering the water, the fresh air, the talks with his father. A few days of real happiness.

"I don't dislike the sea. When my mother was alive…" Marcus studied his hands. "Anyway, back then I traveled with my father several times."

"Yes, I remember." Kleon had met Marcus's mother several times before she died some ten years ago.

Marcus fiddled with the carving. "To business. Made any progress?"

"Progress? What's that?" Kleon jumped up and walked over to a floor mosaic. "Have I seen this before?"

"Sit, Kleon. What you've tried." Marcus sounded impatient.

Kleon resumed his seat. "I've tried everything. I copied out a few symbols and showed them to several scholars, but they baffled everyone." Kleon shook his head and avoided looking at Marcus. "What about you?"

"I asked Philotus about a linguist looking at a text sample. Guess who he sent?"

"Who?"

"Electra, of all people."

Kleon wanted to slap away the smile on Marcus's face. "That dumb woman—she's worthless."

Marcus's eyes narrowed, and he dropped the carving. He glared at Kleon. "She's smart, not dumb, and she can help us. Besides, I like her."

Kleon chuckled though he didn't find his friend's sudden fondness for Electra amusing.

"Is that right?" he muttered. A burning sensation filled his stomach. Of all the women in Alexandria, why did Marcus choose this one? The gods had slapped him—again. Humiliated—again.

"Kleon? What's wrong?"

"What? Oh, nothing. Mindless thinking." With Marcus liking Electra, he would need to plan his retribution against her with care.

"I discovered an unusual pattern in the symbols that repeats every eighth letter." Marcus unrolled Zeus. "See, it's on both of my scroll's pages."

"Interesting."

Kleon stood again, as did Marcus. Behind his back, Kleon's hands balled into fists. "I don't have time for this."

"I don't understand." Marcus pushed a hand through his hair.

"Sorry, Marcus, but I remembered an important appointment." He turned to go.

"Wait, you forgot your scroll." Marcus grabbed Apollo, handing it to Kleon, who snatched it up and then stomped from the room, cursing to himself as he stormed from the house. As he stood outside in the street, his blood boiled.

I like a woman, she rejects me, then Marcus likes the same woman. And this scroll. I'll never solve it. I need a drink.

Later that afternoon, Kleon squinted through glassy eyes as Min cleared away the empty wine pitcher and the remains of a meal. His father had checked on his son, but Kleon ignored him.

In his fog-filled mind, he envisioned the life he wanted: wealth, a lovely home, and Electra as his wife. It puzzled Kleon that despite minimal family loyalty in the Ptolemies, Cleopatra cared about

Electra. His father had told him that she was part of an illegitimate line from Ptolemy Alexander II, nephew of the ninth Ptolemaic king, Soter II. That made Electra the illegitimate great-granddaughter of Soter II, while Cleopatra was Soter's granddaughter.

Kleon wished his father was more ambitious, more assertive at his ministry job instead of waiting for his promotion like a street beggar waiting for the copper coin that never comes. The promotion's extra money would get Kleon his desired education. Then opportunities would open at the Library, or he might get a decent position in the bureaucracy. Any path would be better than his current one.

There was one hope though. This Archimedes scroll—if he could figure out the impossible encryption hiding its secrets—was his best chance at gaining his dreams. Yes, he would hang his hopes on that, no matter what.

CHAPTER THIRTEEN

Marcus
Alexandria, July 27

Soon after arriving at the Library to work on decrypting the Zeus scroll, a scribe brought Marcus a note summoning him to Philotus's office.

Marcus sucked his lip and headed for the third floor. The expression on Philotus's face when he arrived seemed to foretell something unpleasant.

Philotus got to the point. "I suspect Hippolytus left certain scrolls with you before fleeing Alexandria. To safeguard, right?"

Marcus tried to swallow, but his throat was dry. "Have you heard from Hippolytus? Where is he?"

Philotus stared out the window and nodded toward it. "He's out there somewhere."

"When will—"

"Marcus, I understand your concern, but there's no new information. I risk my position even discussing him." Philotus pressed his fingers together. "You've broken your vow. Why?" His voice was sharp. "Is Kleon that important to you?"

"Why do you mention Kleon?" Marcus hated being coy.

"The fool asked me for help." Philotus threw up his arms. "He showed me an encrypted scroll right in the reading room. I assume it's one Hippolytus gave you. Am I wrong?"

Guilt flooded Marcus. He deplored forsaking the vow to Hippolytus, his only close friend.

"No, you're right, Philotus, and I'll get the scroll from Kleon." He turned to go.

"Marcus, wait," Philotus said, rising and walking over to the door. "I sense that Kleon has ambition and high expectations but lacks talent. One day, the world may corrupt him. It's dangerous to let him continue to possess the scrolls." He clapped Marcus on his shoulder. "Serve your vow and put the scrolls where they belong. Somewhere safe."

"Yes," Marcus nodded, tight-lipped, "safe."

Relief crept into his body as he walked back downstairs. Yes, he'd broken his oath, but perhaps Hippolytus planned this. He recognized that Marcus was his best—perhaps his only—chance to break the Archimedes encryption and uncover the powers of the scrolls.

Marcus understood his goal: solve the secret of the scrolls for Hippolytus and for himself. He would show Papa how scholarship was his true calling.

However, this clarity came with apprehension. Whom else had Kleon talked to or revealed the scrolls to? Might the mysterious Roman, Cimber, who once chased Hippolytus, show up again? Cimber might question him or Papa or Philotus or even Eucleides, the Head Librarian, who would not hesitate to banish Marcus from the Library. That would be unthinkable.

His decision was firm. From now on, he would keep the scrolls hidden under his floor tile and would destroy any copied pages.

Marcus didn't know where solving the Archimedes puzzle would lead, or who would oppose him, but he had to execute Hippolytus's plan.

Hippolytus will surely return then.

Kleon
Alexandria, July 27

As Kleon approached his house at midday, he noticed Marcus standing near the door. He reached to greet his friend, but Marcus moved both arms behind his back.

"The servant said you'd return soon. I need the Archimedes scroll." Marcus had a stern expression.

Kleon pulled back. "What?" His eyes got big, his jaw slack. "You solved it? Tell me."

"Calm down. I regret I ever opened the scrolls or got you involved. I should hide them again. Philotus said you talked to him." Marcus narrowed his eyes and leaned toward Kleon. "I can't allow your involvement anymore, my friend."

"What? Why? This is my big chance," Kleon retorted. Marcus remained impassive.

Marcus wants everything for himself—that cannot be allowed.

"Sorry, Marcus, you can't have the scroll." Hot blood pulsed through his temple. "And you can't make me give it back." He thrust a bony finger against Marcus's chest.

"I figured you'd respond like this." Marcus stepped back. "Return the scroll, or I'll have my father talk to your father's superiors at the ministry.

"Go ahead. You can't scare me!" Kleon yelled as Marcus walked away. His anger exploded and he kicked the door. Marcus would regret this—he would make sure of it.

CHAPTER FOURTEEN

Kleon
Alexandria, July 29

FOR THE THIRD time, Kleon's fists pounded on the Bassus front door.

"Come out, you liar, you self-righteous coward," he yelled.

His father had roused him early this morning, grilling him about the vexing Archimedes manuscript, and then sending him off to return the document to Marcus upon pain of extreme punishment. Pressure had materialized from higher in the bureaucracy. Kleon couldn't chance the scroll becoming part of a public dispute that would ruin his father.

He cursed that he hadn't made a copy.

Kleon didn't have a plan yet, but he would recover the scroll. It was his fate, his path out of an insignificant life. Where else could someone with his family circumstances go? The military? With bitter honesty, he admitted he was a coward at heart. In his childhood friendship with Marcus, brave Marcus always saved them from bullies. Business? Neither he nor his father had the funds for an enterprise.

No, he needed to take shortcuts to achieve success, wealth, power. This scroll was one of those expediencies. He didn't want to end up as a bureaucratic clerk or a low-level library scribe. The ancient manuscripts were his only chance to avoid drudgery and ordinariness. He'd no longer put up with his mediocre life.

The old doorkeeper soon opened the outer door in the stout gate. Kleon was moving to enter when Marcus came into view.

"I'll handle this, Titus," Marcus said, dismissing the slave.

Kleon stood on the threshold—Marcus blocked further entry. *How befitting to my lot.*

Marcus folded his arms. "You have something for me?"

Kleon wanted to wipe the smug expression off his friend's face, but instead, he begged.

"Yes, you know I do. Marcus, give me a second chance? It was a mistake to show the scroll to Philotus."

"Mistakes can get Papa in serious trouble," Marcus said in a low tone. "A lot is at stake, Kleon. Much more than you realize."

I know the stakes, Marcus. The winner gets power. With power comes wealth and opportunities.

"I only wanted to help you!" Kleon yelled. "I wasn't doing this for personal gain." He spoke the lie with a steady voice.

Marcus' eyebrows shot up. "No?" He smirked. "I find that hard to believe."

Yes, Marcus, you cur. I want the secrets and the power, things you have in abundance.

Power would give him status and respect. Electra would see him in a different light.

"The scroll, Kleon." Marcus stuck his hand out. It was obvious he wouldn't compromise.

Loathing his capitulation, Kleon pulled the scroll from his bag and slapped it into Marcus' open hand. "Take it, Marcus. Why don't you send them both back to Hippolytus—"

"I warned you!" Marcus shouted. "I told you not to show them to anyone!"

Kleon glowered at Marcus and countered. "Then turn them over to the Library." He could steal them from there.

Marcus saluted him with the scroll. "You've made the right decision."

"You'll regret this, Marcus." Kleon held Marcus's gaze, then stepped back. "Now, I have to be off. The Library needs me."

"Goodbye, Kleon." Marcus's tone signaled Kleon's dismissal.

"Goodbye, Marcus." He stalked off, vowing to get the Archimedes scroll back and make Marcus rue this day. *I wish I knew where he kept the scrolls.* No matter how, Kleon intended to gain the rewards he deserved.

He had taken only a dozen steps when he stumbled over a beggar laying in the shadows. "Look out, you ass." He gave the filthy man a vicious kick, eliciting a grunt. He resumed his retreat up the street.

Gods, I need a drink, wine—a whole bottle.

The Agent
Alexandria, July 29

Cimber couldn't believe his luck. A lifeless morning had produced an opportunity.

Octavian had issued strict orders—no covert actions. Observe only. After endless surveillance days in Alexandria, an unbelievable bit of intelligence had fallen his way.

He had been sitting outside the apartment building he shared with his men. It was an ideal location. Close to the Royal Quarter, but not too close, and, it was down the street from the Bassus house. Octavian wanted the man watched, so they watched.

From his inconspicuous spot, he had noticed a man headed toward the Bassus house. When the man pounded on the gate, Cimber got interested and had shuffled down closer.

Did this tie into his informant's report of yesterday's ruckus in the trade ministry? The Bassus name had come up.

In beggar's disguise and feigning a drunken stupor, Cimber

lay in the gutter near the Bassus gate as he listened in on the conversation that erupted.

Hippolytus. The name dredged up ancient memories of a man wanted for the theft of valuable temple scrolls from Ephesus. When was that? Three… four years?

To avoid suspicion, Cimber had taken Kleon's kick, then nimbly rose to his feet and shadowed him until he entered a small tavern near a temple facing Canopus Street, the primary east-west avenue.

At a nearby fountain, he cleaned the street grime from his face and removed the outer, ragged tunic he had worn over his clothes. He was now presentable enough for the tavern.

Once inside, he spotted Kleon at a table in the back. Cimber went to the bar and ordered an Egyptian beer, having developed a liking for the local beverage. Through the single room's gloom, he saw no other patrons except Kleon, whose back was to him. The man was ordering his second drink.

Let him have a couple more drinks.

When Kleon finally waved off the tavern slave, Cimber went to the bar and dropped several large silver coins on the counter. When the tavern owner reached for them, Cimber grabbed his wrist in a stout grip. "You and your slave have work to do in the back, don't you? I won't see you for a while, understand?"

When the owner nodded, the agent released his hand, and the tavern keeper scooped up the coins. Then, he grunted for the slave girl and they disappeared into the back.

He moved to Kleon's table. "Kleon, right?

When the bureaucrat's son dutifully nodded, Cimber sat down. "I'll make this short. I think we share an interest in old scrolls."

Kleon eyes widened. He scrubbed a hand across his face and shook his head. "Don't know what you're talking about," he said, his speech slurred.

Cimber ignored the remark. "Indeed, two particular ones. Does the name Archimedes seem familiar?"

Kleon gazed at him with watery eyes. "Perhaps. There are many scrolls in Alexandria, and many are old. Some written by Archimedes.

Cimber slipped a couple of gold coins out of his purse. He rolled one through his fingers. The head of Octavian flashed by. "I pay well for information. Extremely well."

Kleon howled with laughter, then abruptly broke it off.

Cimber saw a hard face that wasn't there before.

"Is that all I'm worth? A few gold coins? I can sell myself outside any temple and get a gold coin." He laughed again.

Cimber studied Kleon's face. Who was this man across from him—a drunken fool or a cold madman? He'd seen the same look on the faces of husbands who had caught him making love to their wives—right before he killed them. "More? I can arrange for more. Name your price."

Kleon stared at the moving coins for a moment and then raised his head to gaze into the Agent's eyes. "Those old scrolls are my destiny. Let me offer a different proposition for you and your gold. Listen…"

Cimber listened as Kleon talked. The small smile pulling at the corners of his mouth grew and grew as the words tumbled out of Kleon.

"Deal," Cimber announced when Kleon finished.

Kleon got to his feet, retched on the floor, wobbled a moment, and then staggered out.

Cimber sat quietly at the table—the coins laying in his palm. He nodded his head over and over.

Octavian will be pleased.

CHAPTER FIFTEEN

Marcus
Alexandria, August 1

MARCUS LAY IN bed staring at the ceiling. It had been an eventful week since Cleopatra's dinner. Two days ago, Marcus had his manhood ceremony. The solemn event began with the augur's favorable auspices at the Temple of Serapis. The ceremonial rites were a blur, though he remembered his proud father giving him the Bassus signet ring. It had ended with a processional to the Bassus house, where he walked with his father, Talus, Honorius, Philotus and Quintus. He had passed a colorful litter along the way. Inside was a veiled woman he suspected was Electra.

He had invited Kleon, but he never showed.

Papa invited many of his business clients—shippers, grain suppliers, agriculture ministers—to the celebratory feast. There Papa made the announcements that bound Marcus to his first trading voyage, in a mere two weeks' time, to Massilia on Gaul's southern coast.

During his apprenticeship, Honorius would teach him accounts and vineyard operations. He would also go with Marcus to Massilia. Talus would train Marcus on weapons, self-defense and military strategy.

As tradition required, Marcus placed his bulla amulet at its final resting place on the family altar. Afterward, he sat frozen, relieved but disappointed. Later that day, he confronted his father with his frustration.

"I cannot accomplish in commerce or any other business what I can as a scholar," Marcus lamented. "I want to continue my studies. I know Hippolytus wouldn't make me do this." This last was aimed at his father's heart, but he regretted saying it.

Papa sprang from his chair, sending it flying. "How will you earn a living writing philosophy or staring at the stars? Tell me!" His father's face was red. He swung around the desk, confronting Marcus. "Are you my son? My eldest son is a soldier, earning glory for Rome. Cleopatra expects me to travel to India, and I expect my son to run Bassus Trading while I'm gone. Not Honorius. Can you manage that from the Library?"

Marcus stared back. He couldn't match Publius in accomplishments nor suggest someone to run Bassus Trading. "I thought you... you would provide funds until I—"

"Oh, no. Not another denarius to play at the Library. Not... even... one."

His father emphasized each word, pounding his fist into his palm. "Hippolytus, left in a hurry. Who stuck his neck out when the soldiers came asking about him? Who?"

Marcus's body sagged. His father was right. Defeated again, his dreams gone. "It will be as you say, Father."

His father clasped him in his arms, holding him close, but Marcus couldn't respond.

Now as mid-morning sun streamed through his window, Marcus lay on his bed in a state of shock. There was a knock on his door.

"Come." Marcus remained on the bed, staring at the ceiling.

Titus shuffled in. "Pardon, sir, but Talus is waiting for you in the training yard."

Marcus wanted to tell Talus to soak his head in Lake Mareotis. "I'll be there."

Titus shuffled backward, closing the door behind him.

Another session with Talus.

So far, he had been doing strength and running exercises, but today would be his first weapons training session. Honorius and his accounting books had taken the whole morning.

Addition and subtraction of whole numbers; what's so hard?

At least Papa allowed him the liberty of reading at night and visiting the Library when it didn't conflict with his training. His upcoming voyage came to mind. Maybe seeing the world could prove helpful for the future.

He arrived at the training yard behind the main house wearing a short, sleeveless tunic and heavy sandals.

Talus was waiting, tapping a wooden sword against his palm. "Important rule, Master Marcus." Talus's voice boomed around the yard. "Don't be late. Irritates your trainer. He's a brute."

"My rule, Talus. Drop the 'Master.' Call me Marcus around here."

"As you wish… Marcus. Ever train with a sword, wooden or otherwise?"

"No, I've never held a sword though I have a good dagger."

"Have you ever wrestled?"

"At the Gymnasium."

"Ah, Greek-style. That's a start. You seem in good shape for a bookish fellow."

"As I told you, I exercise at the Gymnasium almost every day."

"Fine. Do some stretching and grab a wooden sword."

Marcus did as Talus instructed, and then as he walked left the weapons rack, he noticed two other household bodyguards watching from the far end of the yard.

"I must congratulation you, Marcus. You've taken the first step.

Now, ignore our spectators and concentrate on me. I found your ceremony impressive."

"Thanks, it was overdue."

"So you say."

Talus circled Marcus, his eyes focused on Marcus's. "Keep your eyes on me. Concentrate on me. So, you're a man now?" He didn't give Marcus time to answer. "Yes, a beautiful ceremony." He continued to circle, and Marcus stayed with him, his feet making scuffs in the dirt.

Talus spoke again. "My father was one of Sulla's veterans. They gave him some land up in the Po River valley. I got a manhood ceremony at sixteen, and I, too, thought I was a man. Next day, with much hubris and conceit, I joined the Legions." Talus stopped and watched Marcus's expression.

"And?" Marcus was getting bored with this exercise.

Talus resumed circling. "The Legions taught me I was not a man. Killing doesn't make you a man. Courage makes you a man. Sacrifice for your country, for the legionnaire next to you, that makes you a man." He stopped again and pointed his sword at Marcus. "You'll be commanding a ship. Men will depend on you to lead."

"But I don't know how to lead," Marcus protested, spreading his arms. "You were a centurion. Teach me to be a leader."

"In time. Now, hold your sword at the ready."

Marcus held up his sword. "Like this."

In a lightning move, Talus knocked the wooden sword out of Marcus's grip.

Marcus gasped and gave Talus an incredulous stare. "I wasn't ready."

"Lesson one. Always be ready."

As Marcus bent to retrieve the sword, a blow on his ass sent him sprawling in the dirt.

Marcus rolled over and jumped to his feet. He was breathing hard. "Hey, what was that for?"

"Lesson two. Never turn your back to your enemy." Talus raised an eyebrow. "In the arena or an alleyway, I'm your enemy."

"I'll remember that one."

"Enough lessons. See the post with the straw dummy? Go knock the straw out. Pretend it's me."

"Aye." Marcus eyed the dummy.

Not you, Talus. Papa.

Countless exercises and two hours later, an exhausted Marcus stood before Talus. The towering giant handed him a cup of water, which Marcus gulped with relish.

"You've done well, Marcus, and show potential. You may have a chance in a sword fight." He grinned. "You can do this."

"Talus, you have an impressive background. You've led men. When will you teach me to lead?"

"In time, Marcus. You're dismissed. Go read a book."

CHAPTER SIXTEEN

Marcus
Alexandria, August 15-September 7

As HE LEFT the Great Harbor aboard the *Neptune*, Marcus took in the familiar and impressive sight of Alexandria.

The city popped from the sands, draped in the light from the rising sun shining off marble and granite, its roofline of palaces, temples, obelisks, city walls, and towers standing out in stark contrast to the flat, colorless dessert of the Egyptian coast.

Approaching the harbor opening, Marcus gazed down broad north-south avenues, lined with monuments, colonnaded buildings, and gardens with fountains.

He then turned to the Pharos Lighthouse, where high in the colonnaded light chamber, an elaborate array of mirrors reflected the rising sun's brilliance to arriving ships.

Marcus loved the story of Alexander, who, after conquering Egypt, had come to this stretch of land to build his namesake city. Like Marcus, Alexander had been an avid reader of Homer, who mentioned Pharos Island in *The Odyssey*. When Alexander saw the long strip of land, the island and the protected harbor, he tasked his architects to build a great seaport, the one facility Egypt lacked. Alexandria now rivaled Rome as the world's greatest city.

As he cast his gaze around the *Neptune*, he questioned whether he could captain the ship, even with the support of its captain, Maximo, and Honorius. Though he had the vessel out twice for training and with praise for his performance, this voyage would be his first big test as a man. And while he still preferred a life of pure academic work, he vowed not to embarrass Papa through incompetence.

During the free time on the return voyage, he planned to concentrate on the Apollo scroll, the longer of the two Archimedes scrolls. He wished now that there had been time to make a copy of the scroll.

Marcus checked the loading progress amidships, but his attention soon shifted back to the main deck where his single passenger stood at the rail.

The *Neptune's* change of itinerary surprised Marcus, having learned of it only a few days ago.

"Marcus, there's been a change of plans for your voyage," Papa had said.

"Cleopatra has requested a slight deviation—a stop in Rome." Papa had spread out a map of Italy and southern Gaul. "You'll have Honorius and Maximo to help you with the navigation and ship operations."

"The *Neptune* will stop in Ostia?"

"That's correct." He pointed out the port at the Tiber's mouth, downriver from Rome. "The cargo manifest changes. You'll exchange two hundred crates of papyrus in Rome for amphorae of Falernian wine for trade in Massilia."

Marcus had chuckled. "Only the best for our Massilian friends." On the map, Marcus traced the Ostia to Massilia route. "This passage between Corsica and Sardinia with its shoals and rocks and its tricky currents worries me. Pirates were suppressed long ago, but some crew members say there have been attacks in recent years."

"Yes, the Taphros Strait. Well, Pompey and the Roman navy

took care of the pirates. Anyway, Maximo's been through the strait many times, so you should be fine. This route will, however, change our negotiating tactics."

"How so, Papa?"

"Besides gold for the Bassus wine, we'll want amber in the exchange, as much as those Timouchoi bastards will let us have."

"Why the love for Falernian?"

"The Massilians trade it to the interior's ruling elite for amber and gold. They can buy anything with those goods." His father came around the desk. "I also have a single passenger for you. At Cleopatra's request, mind you."

"Who is it?" Marcus hadn't expected any passengers.

"Electra, Cleopatra's cousin. Remember her from the royal dinner?"

Oh, yes, I remember.

"Yes." Heat had spread across his face at the memory of the dinner. Though busy with his new responsibilities, he had tried once to see Electra last week and had been told she was meeting with the queen.

As he watched her now, something about Electra's presence and the change in the *Neptune*'s route made Marcus uneasy. Though he had his own anxiety about her, his crew might consider an unaccompanied woman an unfortunate omen. Sailors were a superstitious lot.

Maybe Maximo can reassure them.

Marcus said a silent prayer to Fortuna hoping to shake off his apprehensions. He moved down the deck toward his passenger and stood by the rail until she noticed him.

"Marcus, I didn't see you there," she said at last.

"How are you?" Marcus asked.

"Well. It's a beautiful day." She looked up at the blue sky

"A good day to start a voyage." Marcus, hoping his words were prophetic, leaned on the rail, as Electra's presence filled him with unfamiliar sensations. There was an unexpected affinity and the wish to know more of her, coupled with a powerful yearning to hold her body against his. The combination unsettled him, yet he took it as a challenge to move into a new phase of being.

Electra turned to him. "Marcus, the last time I saw you—"

"Let's not bring that up." Marcus stood, his back erect, then glanced down at the deck. "Instead, consider that we have two weeks at sea. Unless you want to converse with sailors on deck or slaves below, I offer you conversation—and the great food of the captain's table—far better than sitting alone in your cabin. Join me for the midday meal?"

Electra nodded. "I accept. I'm looking forward to seeing your great mind at work."

Marcus grinned. "I feel the same about you, Electra."

Day three of their voyage found the winds shifting, but the conditions gave Maximo the opportunity to teach Marcus the necessary day-to-day sailing skills. By day's end, he had mastered much—basic navigation, knots, names of critical lines, hoisting the mainsail, and lowering the ship's boat.

The final task, though, was completely unexpected.

"Now, Marcus," said Maximo, "time to climb the main mast."

"What?" Marcus peered up at the tall pole swaying in the wind. "Is that necessary?"

"Sometimes the captain needs to see things for himself." Maximo pointed up the mast. "The best view is up there. Just go slow. There are handholds all the way. Climb in bare feet."

Marcus removed his shoes, moved to the base of the mast, took a deep breath and grabbed two handholds. He wrapped his legs around the timber and pulled himself up the mast. The climb proved effortless until he reached the halfway point and glanced toward the deck. The swaying mast and waves sliding past the hull gave him a sense of vertigo.

Climb… but never look down.

It seemed like hours, but after two or three minor slips he made it to the top. He paused for a time and enjoyed the fantastic view of the open sea. It was well worth the climb.

"Come on down, Marcus," Maximo called from the deck. "Don't rush it."

Confident now in his abilities, he proceeded down the mast to the deck. There he found Honorius waiting for him.

"He's all yours, Honorius. Good work today, sir," said Maximo.

Back in the captain's cabin, Honorius led discussions on trade and dealing with merchants, customs, and magistrates.

"Maximo tells me you're a quick learner," Honorius said. "He's pleased with your progress."

"I traveled some with Papa and observed how things worked." Marcus chuckled. "I never thought my maturing process would include nautical things."

"It strikes me that the crew respects you. I've heard no grumbling."

Marcus shook his head. "It seems unnatural for sailors to not complain."

"Aye, sir. Let's discuss trading principles. Remember," the steward advised, "always smile and be friendly before negotiations begin. Then once begun, you act serious and keep a placid expression on your face. Negotiations are give-and-take affairs. Leave concessions or extra profit on the table for the other side to feel a victory, even a small one."

Marcus nodded but then voiced his lack of confidence to negotiate with people.

"Don't worry, sir," said Honorius. "You need experience, that's all, and I'll be there for your early trading."

The instruction was necessary to fulfill his father's vision of Marcus's trading career. He took it all in and found the knowledge stimulated his mind. What he enjoyed most though were the meals with Electra, like tonight's.

"So, what is this mission for Cleopatra?" Marcus asked her at dinner that evening.

Electra sat back. "I wondered when you'd ask. It's no secret she's been writing the Senate concerning this awful acrimony between Antony and Octavian. I'm bringing more letters to explain and educate how destructive civil war would be. As a woman, I'm not allowed to address the Senate as a whole, I'll be meeting with individual senators."

"I understand it's more than ill feelings. They have a history of personal conflict. After the assassination, Antony believed Julius Caesar's mantle of power was his right."

Electra nodded. "Now Antony is gathering his eastern legions in Asia. Like spoiled children fighting over a toy that will end up broken and useless." Electra stared out one of the cabin's small portholes.

"They are following the laws of power, driven by their ambition to rule men."

Electra stopped eating. "Their struggle will destroy my country and turn it into a vassal of Rome, or worse, a province. My people will suffer enslavement or slaughter by Roman swords."

Marcus found her words troubling. Is it war that produces the most slaves with winners enslaving the losers?

"Egypt has much to fear." He wanted to comfort and hold her but dared not.

"Marcus, your family will survive regardless of the outcome. You have a foot in both camps."

Marcus considered her words. "I want Egypt to remain your Egypt, our Egypt, not a Roman one."

Electra's eyes glistened and she touched his arm. "Thank you, Marcus." Warmth spread through him. "Yet the gods and two hardheaded Romans will decide that."

Marcus put his hand over hers, his fingers soaking in the warmth of her smooth skin. Here she was, prepared to walk into a den of powerful politicians where enemies of Antony might imprison her or even have her killed. He hoped this smart, coura-geous, empathetic, and beautiful woman would not become a prize of war for a Roman conqueror.

Soon after the ship docked along the Tiber at Ostia, Marcus met Electra at the gangway.

"It won't be the same without you," he said, taking her hand.

"I'll miss you, too. It won't be long before you're back to pick me up, so enjoy your adventure into the business world. As best you can, anyway." She flashed him the smile that always warmed him.

Marcus chuckled. "It's an adventure all right. I'm not sure I want it, but I'll do my best. Good luck with the Senate. Remind them you are only the messenger."

"Don't worry. I know how to handle myself." She embraced him and stepped down the ramp.

Marcus watched her walk along the pier as Honorius escorted her to a Roman courier ship sent by the Senate.

Ostia was only a few days behind him, and Marcus already missed their mealtime talks and her smile. She occupied his thoughts during idle times on deck and appeared in vivid dreams every night in his cabin. In them, he protected her as gangs of Roman soldiers roamed a burning Alexandria.

On the positive side, Electra's absence meant he had no dis-tractions while working on deciphering the Apollo scroll hidden in his cabin.

It was late August when the *Neptune* had left for Massilia, to make the trades and deals his father entrusted to him. With the new skills taught by Honorius, he thought he had a reasonable chance for success. He hoped Electra came to the same conclusion about her task.

CHAPTER SEVENTEEN

Marcus
The Mediterranean Sea, September 17

MARCUS WOKE TO a gray dawn, the sun a dull point of light. A stiff breeze blew from the northwest, allowing full use of the sails for this homeward leg. Maximo seemed pleased with the weather.

Later, in his cabin, Marcus finished his midday meal. He sat back and thought of Electra. He hoped her trip to Rome achieved the same success as he had in Massilia.

Though the wealthy Timouchoi no longer managed an independent Massilia after Julius Caesar's forces had overrun the city fifteen years ago, they still handled the bulk of trade. They were intermediaries between inland clans traveling down the Rhone River and foreign traders. Marcus received favorable terms for all cargoes of Falernian wine.

If only his decoding of the Archimedes scroll had gone well.

On deck, the winds grew weaker but still propelled the ship toward the islands of Corsica and Sardinia. He knew that besides the ever-present shoals and treacherous currents, the coming winter would bring storms to all Mediterranean waters and curtail most trade.

"Sail!" the bow lookout yelled.

"Direction?" Maximo called.

"Off the port beam."

Marcus scanned the left side. The midday sun gave poor contrast, making it difficult to see anything low on the water, but his young eyes were the first to spot the sail.

"There, Maximo!" Marcus pointed to a white blur on the horizon.

"She's moving across our course," said Maximo.

"Helmsmen, adjust two points starboard," Marcus ordered.

The helmsmen heaved against the dual steering oars, sending spray over *Neptune's* rail.

"She's turning starboard," Maximo observed. "Recommend turning back to our original course to avoid her."

Talus had taught Marcus to be decisive. Weigh the facts, then execute.

"Do it," Marcus commanded. "Tell the rowing master to drum to cruise." He wanted the extra speed as a measure of reserve. *Neptune* had fifteen oars to each side, two men per oar. Adequate for her size, the ship deployed its rowers in headwinds or in calm conditions.

Maximo relayed the orders. The sound of chains soon rose from gangways and hatches, followed by rhythmic drum beats and the cry of the rowing Master. "One, two, three, pull."

Marcus sent Honorius to secure the chests of gold and amber in Marcus's cabin.

"Not likely to be pirates in these waters." Maximo wiped sweat from his brow. "But I'd say we not take chances."

Maximo joined Marcus at the port rail as the approaching sail came into full view, jutting well above the water. Soon the hull would be visible. Minutes passed. The winds slackened and shifted to the port side.

"Bireme!" came the lookout's yell.

"By all the hells!" cried Maximo. "She's not a merchantman. Could be a Roman warship. If we're lucky."

"What do you mean?" Marcus gnawed at a fingernail.

"A Roman warship is an inconvenience." Maximo turned to Marcus. "But pirates, pirates would be most unfortunate."

"Keep the oars at cruising speed." Marcus hoped the bireme, a bigger and faster vessel with two banks of thirty, forty, or even fifty oars per side, would ignore the *Neptune*. He hoped the unknown ship sailed with the Roman navy.

In a few moments, Marcus sensed the increase in the ship's speed. The south end of Corsica had a Roman port. If they could just make it —

"Bireme's turning!" came the masthead call.

"She's coming on fast," said Maximo. "She's chasing us, no doubt."

"Set the rowers to fast cruise, Maximo. Try to reach Corsica."

"Aye, fast cruise."

Honorius came up and whispered, "All valuables secured below the floorboards."

Marcus nodded. As he peered over the port side, another surge of speed burst beneath his feet. *Neptune* carried spare rowers, and off-shift sailors could work the oars as well; they could keep this pace for perhaps a half-hour.

He surveyed the surrounding seas. No other ships or heavy weather appeared.

"Do we have any weapons?" he asked Maximo.

"A few swords, some clubs." Maximo wiped his brow again. "That's it, sir."

Marcus peered at the closing ship as it grew larger, closer. Pirates would soon end his first voyage, his first command. He thought of his father. Would he see him again? The pirates might ransom him back. Papa would pay anything.

He wished Talus were here but realized it would still be suicide even with twenty men like Talus.

His thoughts turned to Electra. He dreamed of solving the

Archimedes scrolls with her, but it might never happen. If he survived this…

Stop it, Marcus.

Self-pity would do no good.

The trailing ship closed in, cutting across the gap. He could see tens of men at its side, but no Roman uniforms or armor or pennants. Spray flew up from the pirate ship's bow—that's all it could be now. The twin banks of oars kept a fast tempo, the blades flashing in and out of the sea.

Marcus decided his course. "Maximo, Honorius—I want no resistance. No needless deaths. Our fate is in the gods' hands. And in a greedy pirate captain. With luck, he'll ransom us back to my father."

A few sailors shouted displeasure at Marcus's decision.

"We should fight, Captain," said an older sailor. "They'll kill us, anyway."

"I'm not going down without a fight," shouted another, a hotheaded youngster. He lunged for a sword in the small pile of weapons.

"Back, you dog!" Maximo struck him with a backhanded blow and the young man crashed to the deck. "Obey the Captain, men. This is our best chance."

Two sailors manhandled the troublemaker to his feet and shoved him against the railing.

"Listen, men." Marcus jumped up on a cargo hatch. "I promise you; Bassus Trading will ransom every man. We can't do that if you're dead." Marcus scanned the deck for any defiance. "Honorius, let the rowers know they're included in any ransom deal. No one will die."

Honorius moved alongside Marcus. "Sir, this will cost your father a hundred talents," he whispered.

"You and I both know my father can afford it. Now go."

The rowers below made Marcus proud. They maintained a gap

for a while and kept up the pace for an hour before collapsing with exhaustion. The *Neptune's* speed dropped to a crawl.

Time slowed.

The pursuing ship came within archer range. Men on its deck were shaking swords while others pointed a catapult mounted before the mast, aimed straight at the *Neptune*.

Marcus wanted to prolong the chase in the unlikely chance another ship would show itself.

No ship appeared. No land popped.

As the pursuit neared its end, the pirates called for the Bassus ship to lower sails, but Marcus—defying his own logic—continued onward. After the pirates loaded their catapult and fired a grapnel onto the *Neptune*, amidships, he relented and ordered the mainsail lowered and the oars pulled in.

He could only watch as the pirates pulled in their own oars and hauled in his ship. His jaw ached from grinding his teeth in bitter vexation.

At first, he didn't recognize the object rising from the deck. Attached to a stubby mast near the bow, the pirates raised a corvus, a boarding bridge with a huge iron spike at the end.

With a lurch, the two ships ground together. Splintered wood flew as the larger bireme slid along *Neptune's* side, the collision sending a jarring shock through the entire wooden structure of the ship. The spiked bridge smashed down, penetrating the deck planking like an arrowhead into a melon. Marcus's men scattered at the impact.

Armed men ran across the intruding bridge and down onto the *Neptune's* deck. Marcus reckoned twenty pirates piled aboard the Bassus ship. He ordered *Neptune's* men back against the far rail. The menacing pirates advanced within a few feet of their victims before an order brought them to a halt. Marcus searched for the source of the command.

He was uncertain, but Marcus thought the order came in Illyrian, a language he'd heard spoken by one of the Library's linguists. The country, Illyricum, comprised wild territory along the Adriatic Sea, with an interior of craggy mountains and dense forests. Conquered by the Romans over a century ago, it stayed in near constant revolt. Last year Octavian began a campaign to put down the latest uprising. Until the Romans cleared them out, pirates used it as a haven. Based on reports his father received, many believed a pack of the pirates took refuge in Africa and Egypt.

A tall bearded man, dressed in a Roman-style tunic, threaded his way through the pirates. A gladius hung from his hip. He inspected the subdued crew of the *Neptune*.

"You are all captured prizes of me, Decimus, the Illyrian. Now… which of you sniveling cowards is Marcus Bassus?"

The mention of his name stunned Marcus, and his mind froze. *How does he know my name?*

"Speak up, dog!" shouted Decimus.

Marcus gathered his wits and took a step forward. "I'm Marcus Bassus." He struggled to stay calm. Fear crept into the edges of his mind.

"Tie him up," ordered Decimus.

Two pirates moved toward Marcus. One of his sailors jumped forward to intercept them, but a third pirate clubbed him from the back.

"Stand down, *Neptune*," Marcus shouted.

He soon found himself tied up and sitting on the deck. Two men stomped across the boarding bridge. Marcus stiffened when he recognized one as the brute who came close to knocking him off the docks two months ago.

Decimus deferred to the other, who wore a red cape and carried himself with a military bearing. This man took a position over Marcus.

"So, Marcus Bassus. I'll get right to the point. You have something my master in Rome desires. Please, tell me where it is."

A wave of nausea engulfed Marcus.

Is it the scroll he's wants?

"This is an Egyptian vessel of Queen Cleopatra—"

The man gave a quick hand signal. A lash seared his back. Stinging pain burned across his shoulders and ribs.

"You got a gentle one. It won't be gentle next time."

"What do you want?"

The red-caped man leaned in and, in perfect Latin, spoke so only Marcus could hear. "You know them as the Archimedes scrolls. And if you want to live…"

Marcus heartbeat stuttered.

No, no. How did he know?

Marcus' head spun. Pain consumed his back. His body sagged in despair. He didn't intend to give his or anyone's life for a scroll. "It's in a locked chest in the captain's cabin."

"The key?"

Marcus searched the crew. "Honorius?" Honorius stepped forward. "Give them," his voice wavered, "the key to the captain's chest."

Turning to his accomplice, the man in red gave an order. "Zeno, get the key. Get me the scrolls."

A few minutes later, the man returned with the single Archimedes scroll, the one Marcus had taken from Kleon, one of the two original scrolls given to him by Hippolytus. He cursed himself again for not making a copy.

"Only one, Marcus? I'm disappointed." He took the scroll and handed it to Decimus. "Zeno, take this to our friend in Corsica."

"Yes, Cimber."

Marcus yelled, "What about us?"

"You better get used to seeing the world from the bottom, Bassus. I'm sorry I can't talk; I'm needed in Rome to report the success of this mission." He handed another scroll to Decimus. "This paper will get you safe passage at any Roman port. After

Corsica, take this pack of mongrels to Numidia. Sell them all into slavery. Sell the ship and cargo, too. Keep twenty percent for yourself and give the rest to Zeno."

"My father will ransom us. He's wealthy and—"

"All well, Marcus, but it's just too complicated. Besides, you've seen my face. Can't have you running free, can I? And Antony might take a disliking to my piracy." He walked over to the far rail and climbed onto his ship.

With despair and pain filling him, Marcus watched the man leave. He would never again see his father; never feel Electra in his arms. Two pirates yanked him off the deck and shoved him into line with the crew. The pirates herded them all below and chained them with the rowers.

Marcus looked over the men.

We're all slaves now.

CHAPTER EIGHTEEN

Talus
Alexandria, September 17

TALUS LOVED THE game of dice. He loved the camaraderie, the exuberance of winning, the ebb and flow of Fortuna. Dice helped fill the idle time during Marcus's absence. He figured it was back to regular duties when Marcus returned in two weeks.

Tonight, as a mystical moon rose above the Pharos, he walked near the Great Harbor with Finius and Batacus, ex-legionnaire friends. Moving his friends along, he headed for his favorite bar. Without warning, Talus halted and pulled his two companions into the shadows of an alley.

"What's up, friend?" asked Finius.

"That small fellow ahead, with the sailor's cap," said Talus, "Seen him hanging around by the Bassus house. Never does much and likes the shadows."

"A local man out running around on his woman, you think?" asked Batacus, scratching his armpit.

"He's not a local or a Roman. Looks foreign by his clothes." Talus wagged a finger toward the man. "My gut says he's up to something."

Batacus's face erupted with a wry grin. "Looks kind of shifty. Want to follow him and beat the truth out of him?"

"Or we could go get drunk and save the fun for another night," Finius countered.

"Follow me," ordered Talus, striking off after the mysterious man. "We can get drunk later."

Talus followed the man through several streets and into a shadowy alley where he ducked into a cramped tavern Talus knew well.

Talus motioned toward the tavern. "I come here when I want a quiet drink. Alone," he added, seeing Batacus's questioning look.

Talus and his two companions waited in the shadows. Minutes later, with an impatient Finius ready to head out for the night's drinking, the man emerged and moved down the alley.

"Not even enough time to drink a cup," whispered Talus. He stepped out of the shadows and continued to stalk the man.

Before long the streets became familiar sights, and Talus found himself once again outside his favorite bar. The secretive man slipped inside the building.

Talus followed, beckoning to the others. He greeted the bartender, exchanging a legionnaire's salute, while Batacus and Finius slapped the bottoms of their favorite servers. The bar held a sparse but boisterous crowd. Talus's eyes swept the room until spotting his target. The light from the bar lamps showed him to be tough-looking.

He motioned his friends over to a table where he could watch the now capless man.

"Ah, he's bald," said Batacus.

"You have keen eyes, you old goat," said Finius, swiping his hand over his own bald head. He took a long pull on his Egyptian beer.

"Yeah, well, at least I won't go blind drinking that Egyptian shit," countered Batacus. He took a gulp of his cheap, unwatered wine.

Finius shrugged. "What's the plan for Baldy?"

Talus downed the last of his wine. "Finish your drinks, and then we go out back. Start a game of dice and see if Baldy follows."

"Then we beat him up?" asked Batacus.

"He must owe you money, Batacus," replied Talus. "Drink up and meet me behind the bar. I have to take a piss."

A short while later, kneeling at the spot of packed earth for the dice rolling, Talus made his first roll of the game. The rattling dice soon attracted several players from the bar.

Talus strung together an extraordinary run of luck. The coins piled up before him. His legionnaire friends grumbled and complained but also enjoyed boisterous laughter with him. One by one the bar patrons dropped out, leaving only Finius and Batacus.

Talus shook his dice for the next roll but paused when the bald stranger staggered from the bar. He lurched over to the dice game, slopping drink from his cup.

Talus greeted the man when he reached them. "Join us, friend. I'm Talus, that bald fellow is Finius, and the old one is Batacus."

"Greetings to you all." The man spoke in a Greek accent that sounded peculiar. "I'm Luka of the Daorsi."

Finius raised his cup of wine. "To a fellow hairless man."

"You're Illyrian then," ventured Talus. He'd seen a few in the Alexandrian bars. He squinted at the newcomer. "Have I seen you around before?"

"Not likely," replied Luka, "because I arrived only yesterday on the *Perseus*. Glad to be off that bitch. The captain treated us like dirt." He downed his wine and signaled a server for more. "Are we playing dice, or are we talking shit all night?"

"Sure, friend. Put up your money. *Ludus tesserarum* is the game." Talus dropped the three six-sided dice into the orca ivory cup, gave them several vigorous shakes, and then tossed them to the ground.

"Damn Jupiter's eyes!" squawked Talus. "The dog roll." Three ones. A loser.

Luka took the next turn to roll. He kept his dice in a small box.

"Here we go." He poured out his roll. Three sixes. "Yes!" he hollered. "Venus throw! I win, boys." He scooped up his winnings, then reached to recover his dice.

Talus snagged Luka's wrist in an iron grip. "Let's see those dice."

"Plain dice, Talus. Give them here." Luka gave Talus a menacing glare.

Talus picked up the dice and rolled them. They came up all sixes. "Superb dice, Luka." Again, he rolled. All sixes. Talus tossed them to Finius. "Check those out."

Finius cut a die open with his knife. "It's weighted, Talus."

Talus drew his own dagger and held it against Luka's throat. "You think we're a bunch of amateurs? Around here, cheaters get their throats cut and dumped in a canal. Say goodbye, Luka."

"Wait, wait, don't kill me," Luka pleaded.

"And why not, you cheating shit?" Talus pressed the blade against Luka's neck, drawing a drop of blood.

"Please... I... I..." Luka stammered, his voice full of desperation as his eyes darted from face to face. "Your master is Bassus?"

"So?" Talus bared his teeth.

"My shipmates plan to attack one of his ships." Luka tried to pull back from Talus's dagger. "Let me go, and I'll tell you which one."

"Oh? Tell me, and I might spare you," said Talus. Finius and Batacus came up behind Luka.

"It's... it's the one sailing to Massilia. Please—"

"Massilia?" Shit! That had to be the ship Marcus commanded. Worried now for his young master, Talus continued in his most soothing voice "I won't kill you, just tell me more, friend. Where's the attack going to be?"

"Move that blade away," Luka implored. "That's better." He

wiped at the cut and examined his hand. "It's supposed to be near the channel between Corsica and Sardinia."

"Who hired you?" Talus moved the blade back to the Illyrian's throat.

"Easy." The man stretched his neck away. His eyes shifted back and forth. "Someone named Zeno. That's all I know."

Talus released the man's wrist. "He's yours, boys."

The two legionnaires each grabbed one of the Illyrian's arms. "Let's take him to the alley," Finius said. "Don't want to bloody the playing area."

"Wait! We had a deal," protested Luka.

Finius let out a maniacal laugh. "Sorry, shit head, we never made a deal. Talus did. Don't worry. We won't kill you though you may wish we had." Luka screamed, but a quick blow from Batacus silenced him.

Talus didn't stay to watch. Lucius Bassus had to hear this dire news.

Talus
Alexandria, September 17

Talus sprinted all the way across the city to the Bassus house. He pushed by a startled Titus and hurried to Lucius Bassus's study.

"What's the hurry, Talus? Are my ships on fire?"

Talus caught his breath and reported the events at the dice game.

Lucius slammed his fist down on the table in his study. "Son of a bitch!" he yelled. "Damn the gods! I always hated Illyrians."

Talus grimaced. "If we had a fast ship, sir, we might intercept them before—"

"Grain carriers don't qualify, Talus." Lucius shook his fist. "That's all I have in port."

"Any friends who could help?" Talus asked.

"I have competitors, Talus, not friends," he replied, staring at the ceiling. "But perhaps she could loan me one of hers."

"Who's that, sir?"

"Cleopatra. I could call in a few favors she owes me. Come. Let's head over there now."

"It's the fourth hour of the night, sir. I doubt she would see us this late."

Lucius grabbed a cloak off a peg. "She's a night person. We need to get to the stables."

Talus hurried to catch up to his employer. He hated riding in a hurry at night.

Talus
Alexandria, September 18

To Talus's surprise, Cleopatra allowed them admittance past the guards and into the palace. Someone roused a few sleepy servants who led them to a small audience chamber. Talus and Lucius sat, and, after a short wait, Cleopatra appeared, clad in a thin robe over nightclothes that did little to hide her curves. Talus swallowed hard.

Bassus told her the story, leaving out the attack location. Talus figured if Cleopatra feared harm might come to Electra, she would have a more positive response.

"Is it possible the attack occurred before Electra reached Rome?" the queen asked.

She seems anxious.

"Yes, Your Majesty," said Lucius, glancing over at Talus.

Cleopatra directed the next question at Talus. "When did they plan to launch the attack?"

"It's as my master said. The man told us everything." Talus didn't like lying. His fate hung with Bassus.

The queen paced the room for several minutes, and then turned to Lucius, her face calm.

"What do you need to save them?"

"A fast ship and its crew," answered Talus. "Some marines, in case the bastards don't want to give them up."

Cleopatra paused for a moment, then signaled for a scribe waiting in the chamber's shadows. She scribbled a hasty message, pressed her seal into the hot wax, and handed the document to Bassus. "This will get you whatever you need from my admiral. Save Electra and Marcus. Soon, I leave to join Mark Antony in Ephesus. Don't give me anything else to worry about." She folded her arms across her chest.

"Thank you, Your Majesty," said Lucius.

"How long before you can reach Rome?" asked Cleopatra.

"Your Majesty," answered Talus, "it will take several weeks to reach Ostia sailing against the prevailing winds. From there I'll begin the search, though beyond Ostia I'm not sure where to look."

"I trust you will figure that out," said Cleopatra.

Talus and Bassus both prostrated themselves before standing and walking backward a few steps. They turned to leave.

"Lucius…," Cleopatra called.

Lucius turned back to face the Queen.

"Yes, Your Majesty?" asked Bassus.

"Never ask for me at this dark hour again." She turned and left the room.

CHAPTER NINETEEN

Marcus

Corsica, Numidia and Spain, September 18-29

THE *NEPTUNE* RAN before favorable winds for the passage to Corsica. Unaccustomed to the demanding physical work of rowing, Marcus struggled to keep up the pace, and his effort earned him a lash from a brute walking the rowing deck. He somehow held on until evening when the ship reached Porto Vecchio on the eastern coast.

He and his crew followed their warders to the lower level where they would sleep. After downing a cup of foul water and a crust of hard bread, Marcus trudged through the dark deck assessing each man's condition and offering words of encouragement. While a few men suffered from lashings, most held up against the brutal physical conditions. Finished with his walk-through, Marcus found a space near Honorius and collapsed into a fitful sleep filled with nightmares.

The next day, as the ship pulled out of Porto Vecchio, word spread like wildfire through the ranks of the rowers. The pirates were setting a course for the Numidian port of Hippo Regius.

Once beyond Porto Vecchio's harbor, the winds were light, so Decimus ordered the oars out. Marcus and his shift rowed for four straight hours before getting a break. The pirates passed out water buckets to the exhausted men.

One of his men complained to him. "This water is foul, sir."

Marcus took a sip. "Yes, brackish and smells of piss. My men deserve better if you expect them to keep up this pace."

The sudden lash sent searing fire across his back. It came from the row master—years of pounding the drum had built his forearms into massive blocks of muscle.

"What's that you say, pus face?" asked the row master. Another lash from the pirate's leather flail delivered burning pain. "It's brackish?" Another fiery wave of fire. "Smells of piss?" And again. "Next time, you say: 'Smells of piss, sir.'" Marcus tried to rise from his bench, but Honorius held him back, getting a lash for his effort.

After the second shift of rowers came up from below, Marcus and his men went below to rest and to eat a coarse meal on the cramped, airless lower deck. Here Honorius attended to Marcus's injuries, applying a dampened piece of his tunic to the fiery red welts.

Marcus winced with each touch but found the cool water soothed his back. "I need to learn to control my mouth," he told Honorius. "But I get so angry at Decimus and his bastards. They should have ransomed us back in Porto Vecchio. I feel helpless. Worthless."

"Ransom doesn't seem to be in their plans," said the steward. "Don't feel worthless, but at this moment, we *are* helpless against these chains and against their whips and weapons. My advice is to keep strong and stay low."

"Maybe we can escape."

"Perhaps. Now enjoy the chance you have to rest."

"What would Papa do?" Marcus asked.

"He would say the same as what I'm telling you. Now sleep," instructed Honorius.

"Yes, you too." Before laying down, he eyed the crowded deck. Various foul detritus, scum and human waste filled every crack and crevice of the space. The latrine comprised a bucket line near the forward section and was only available between four-hour shifts. During each shift, a few men didn't make it. While the pirates washed down the rowing deck with seawater, they left the sleeping quarters to wallow in filth.

Marcus lay on his stomach and plotted ways to exact his revenge on the pirates once he and his men were free. He wondered if he would ever see Papa or Electra again.

For the next several days, Marcus bit back his anger, seething in silence. Along with him, his crew suffered abusive conditions, arbitrary lashings, vile expectorant and curses from their warders. Always present was the near-constant backbreaking labor.

As they took their rowing positions on the fourth day, Marcus turned to Honorius, whispering across the aisle separating port and starboard rowers. "Do you think we can escape when we reach Numidia?"

"Perhaps. You have an escape plan?" replied Honorius.

"Quiet," yelled one of their warders.

Either Honorius believed they could escape, or he was trying to raise Marcus's spirits. Regardless, planning an escape filled his mind throughout the final day's voyage to Numidia. His attempt at self-control was earning him fewer beatings. The days slipped by, marked by a daily scratch he made on the deck.

The morning after arriving in Hippo Regius, the pirates herded Maximo and the sailing crew off to the slave auction. Despite Cimber's order to sell all the captives, Decimus followed his own plans, holding Marcus and Honorius back, along with the rowers. Through an oar port, Marcus watched Maximo and his men leave. The realization of how terrible those men's lives would become hit Marcus hard and something in him snapped, sending vile curses and vengeful threats at his captors.

"You motherless dogs, when I get free, I'll tear your black hearts out," cried Marcus. Two of the pirates pummeled him with their whips, silencing him.

Coming to investigate the ruckus, Decimus roared, "So, this is the boy captain. We need to teach this young pup some manners. Cut today's food in half for the lot."

Marcus ended up flat on the deck, his back a fiery pit of agony. Later, using strips torn from their clothes as bandages, his fellow captives tended the wounds of all who came under the lash, including Marcus.

Decimus didn't sell the *Neptune* in Numidia as Cimber commanded and seemed to have found eager buyers at the slave market because by midafternoon they sailed from Numidia. Word filtered through the lower deck that they were bound for Spain.

Marcus concentrated on the mindless rhythm hammered out on the drums, centering his thoughts on escape and seeing Papa and home again. Did Electra find success in Rome or did her mission also end in disaster?

On the night of the seventh day since his capture, rough hands pulled Marcus upright out of a deep sleep. He tried to call out, but a muscular arm gripped him in a headlock. It had taken all his strength to breathe. The thugs dragged him through the darkness to what was once his cabin. Here, only a month ago, he and Electra shared meals together. There, behind the desk where he studied the Archimedes scroll, Decimus waited—an apparition from the underworld, his face contorted into a hideous snarl.

"So, the brash pup comes for his lesson in manners." Decimus turned to his men. "Lay him over the desk. Hold his arms."

The two powerful pirates slammed Marcus face-first over the desk.

Not another beating, please.

"Decimus, you pig—" Marcus never finished.

A fist cuffed him hard on the side of his head, and for a

moment, he lost his senses. As awareness seeped back, Marcus realized the horror he faced. Decimus had thrown up Marcus' tunic and yanked down his loincloth.

"No, no," Marcus screamed. Then a rough hand grabbed and squeezed his balls, and a solid wall of pain crashed into Marcus. He cried out in agony, and another blow struck his head. Blackness roared in, but not before searing pain erupted from penetration.

Though he never regained total consciousness, it seemed like he endured hours of torture and abuse. At an unknown point in the night, he sensed the pirates were carrying him through the ship. They were laughing. After a few minutes, they dumped him on a dark, hard deck. Pain screamed from countless places in his body. With only a vague sense of his surroundings, Marcus crawled a few feet before croaking out a single word. "Papa."

Honorius appeared at his side, his face calm and his voice soothing. "Easy, Marcus. Can you walk, sir?"

"Papa, can we go home now?" Marcus asked in a weak voice.

Honorius inspected Marcus's bruised, bloody, naked body. "Never mind, I'll carry you."

Honorius and one of the crew cleaned Marcus, bandaged his many wounds, and dressed him. "Sleep now, sir."

Later that night, Marcus awoke, yelling, believing he inhabited a nightmare. The realization hit him hard that the nightmare was real. He took a deep breath, burning with shame for what happened to him, hating himself and Decimus. Through his anger, he realized that the abuse resulted from his foolish defiance.

I'm a stupid fool who's forgotten all that Talus and Honorius taught me about being a man. I must control my feelings and think of the crew first. To Hades with my pride.

He balled his hands into fists and vowed to make the survival of his men and himself his primary goal on this loathsome ship.

The next day, Marcus blocked the horror of the earlier night from his mind, masking it behind a calm exterior. He discussed the incident with no one, not even Honorius. For now, nothing could console him, neither food, nor conversation, nor Honorius's words of comfort.

When not on a rower's bench, Marcus walked the sleeping deck, trying to cheer the men, promising that his father would ransom them. Later, he sought refuge in a dark corner where he waged a battle against his doubts and his pain.

He continued protesting the mistreatment of his men, but they were at a subdued level. On the outside, he continued to express hope, voicing only positive words to his crew. Inside himself, he drew strength from his father's struggle after the exile he had endured. Marcus fought with all the tenacity he possessed to keep his horrible experience from crushing his spirit.

Marcus pulled the loose tack from his sandal and scraped another line on the deck beneath the rower's bench in front of him. Each mark brought out sharp memories of the relentless wretchedness the pirates wrought on him and the crew. Now, the twelfth day of captivity, Marcus' mood changed from fatal despair to quiet hope. Spain gave them another escape opportunity. He pushed aside his abusive treatment as something to handle later. For now, he concerned himself with his crew. He needed to encourage them to stay united.

"Keep up your spirits, men," Marcus said during the morning gruel. "Somehow, someway, we'll survive this." He lowered his voice. "We will escape, and we will enact our revenge on these dogs of Hades."

That thought became his mind's refuge. He also vowed to recover the Archimedes scroll and find the man responsible for the pirate attack. He suspected—but no, he suppressed that premise for now.

Survival first, then revenge.

Marcus

Gades, Spain, October 14

Beyond the Pillars of Hercules, the massive promontories flanking the passageway between the Mediterranean Sea and the Atlantic, Decimus spent two fruitless weeks of patrolling before deciding to put in at Gades, the Roman port in southwest Spain. The pirates herded the bedraggled captives up to the deck. Marcus eased the metal leg irons from his ankles and rubbed the abrasions that had formed. He blinked in the bright but welcomed sun and followed his crew as Decimus's men marched them onto the dock.

Decimus stood near the ramp.

Marcus stopped at the pirate leader. "Decimus, where are you taking us? We have a right to know." Though Marcus feared their fate held more abuse, he tried to maintain dignity and defiance in his voice and his stance.

Decimus unleashed a booming howl. Marcus sensed the scorn and malice.

"The young whelp can growl," Decimus said. "You're asking what shit hole is next?"

Marcus surged forward, slamming his chest against Decimus and his head into the man's lower lip. Decimus shoved Marcus back in line. A stinging lash wrapped his ribcage.

"The puppy has teeth." Decimus spat out a mouthful of blood. "I'm marching the lot of you north to work the silver mines this winter. You worthless scum will make me some coin while I relax in port. In spring, if you survive, you'll come back here, and we sail for easy pickings. I get more silver." Another booming laugh.

You bastard.

"Enjoy the mines, Marcus. Goodbye."

Marcus's legs wobbled. The mines, death pit for slaves. "We must survive. All of us," he whispered, looking at his men.

"I don't see how," came the whisper behind him.

"No talking," came a yell, followed by a lash across Marcus's back.

Marcus gritted his teeth.

We must survive.

CHAPTER TWENTY

Electra
Alexandria, November 14

ELECTRA STORMED INTO her palace room, shedding the colorful ribbons around her neck. Heavy bracelets soon followed, skipping across the floor tiles in every direction. She stopped before a cushioned sofa where she yanked out hairpin after hairpin from her styled, ceremonial hair. She plopped onto a pile of cushions but shot back up to face the woman, Cybele, trailing behind her.

"I can't believe he did this," Electra wailed, lips trembling. "He's giving their children all those lands to rule. It's political suicide. Oh, Cleopatra's smiles showed her delight with it, but she should have been smarter than that."

"Calm down, dear friend," implored Cybele, sitting beside her and putting her arms around Electra heaving shoulders. "Take a deep breath. That's better. Now, I didn't attend the announcements. Tell me what happened. What is the terrible thing Mark Antony has done that has the city celebrating and you on the verge of ripping your clothes?"

"I stood there in the courtyard of the Gymnasium, right behind those hideous golden thrones. I watched Mark Antony and Cleopatra, dressed up as Isis for the benefit of her Egyptian people, sit and made these crazy announcements. And the poor children—Caesarion, Alexander Helios, Cleopatra Selene, and Ptolemy Philadelphus—each with their own small thrones, having to sit through it all."

"But, dear Electra, as I walked over here, people shouted that Antony had restored Egypt's past glory and returned the lands lost over the years."

Electra turned blank eyes on Cybele. Antony's proclamations shocked and amazed her. With his statements, Antony had punched Octavian, and Rome, in the gut. He had given the East, with its vast wealth and territory, to Cleopatra and descendants. The letters she had carried to Rome back in August now counted as worthless paper.

"Yes, that's all true, Cybele. Cleopatra's love has addled Antony's thinking. He now thinks with his cock and not his head."

"Electra!"

Electra ignored Cybele's admonishment. "He declares Caesarion 'King of Kings' and Cleopatra 'Queen of Kings.' Then, as if that didn't get Octavian and the Senate frothing at the mouth, he anoints Caesarion as the legitimate offspring of Julius Caesar."

"How is all that so disagreeable?" Cybele cringed when Electra turned to look at her.

"Political apathy must be blissful."

"What? Did I get insulted?"

Electra squeezed her eyes shut. "You're hopeless. When Octavian hears Antony has bestowed half the East to Cleopatra and her heirs, he will rage to the Senate. Yet when he learns Antony has declared Caesarion the son of Julius Caesar, Octavian will take it as a direct threat to his power and his reaction will be more than words."

"Why would Caesarion be a threat?"

"Goddess, help me. As Caesar's named heir, Octavian inherited not only Caesar's wealth but also many senators' hatred. They now have Caesarion to hang their banners on and declare Octavian to be a false heir."

At Cybele's blank stare, Electra threw her hands in the air.

"Don't you see? Octavian will seek any excuse to declare war."

At the sudden blare of distant trumpets, Cybele rushed to the window overlooking the Great Harbor.

"They're starting Antony's triumph. I'm meeting friends in the viewing stand. Come join us.

"Another slap to Rome. Triumphs are, by tradition, held only in Rome by an act of the Senate. How could Cleopatra and Antony be so audacious?"

"All the music and horses and handsome soldiers might cheer your sour mood."

"Go, Cybele." Electra lay back on the sofa.

Cybele shook her head and left.

Electra sank into the cushions, her head pounding. It appeared another Roman civil war loomed, with Egypt going to the winner. How would it affect her? How would it affect Marcus? Did Marcus still live? Goddess, let him live. Pain slashed through her temples.

My Queen. What have you done?

33 B.C.

CHAPTER TWENTY-ONE

Kleon
Crete, January 5

KLEON HURLED THE clay cup across the workshop, shattering it into a thousand pieces.

"Remove yourselves!" Kleon yelled at the two men with him, sending them scurrying out.

His head pulsed with pain at his new failure. Initially, he had spent a month on the fruitless tactic of working alone to decode the Archimedes scroll Cimber had taken from Marcus.

Then, after overcoming Cimber's objection to exposing the scroll, Kleon had brought in a mathematician and a linguist from Athens. They left with Cimber's silver but had produced nothing.

His servant, Min, rushed into the room, agitated, bouncing from one foot to the next.

"What is it?" Kleon barked.

"Dominus, visitors," replied Min, waving a shaky arm toward the front door.

"If it's curious locals, alert the guards."

"No, no, Dominus." Min clasped his hands together. "It's the Roman, the important one."

"Gods, no," cried Kleon. "Quick, bring refreshments to the tablinum while I wait in the atrium."

The captain of the guards soon admitted his superior into the airy room. Kleon extended a hand in greeting and, trying to keep his voice neutral, said, "Cimber, a pleasant surprise. I didn't expect you for two or three months."

"I was passing by your little island," Cimber said, looking around the room, "and thought I'd check on your progress."

"Yes... I'm making headway. I had two experts here helping—"

"You mean those two fools running down the hill with my silver in their pockets?"

Panic filled Kleon—Cimber wanted results. "I had no further use for them and intend to bring in another man—" Kleon stopped, cringing at Cimber's stone-like expression.

"You've failed me, Kleon. Zeno," Cimber called over his shoulder. A hulking brute filled the doorway.

Kleon shook as a trickle of urine flowed down his thigh. "No, no, wait," he pleaded. "I have a plan."

"Oh?" asked Cimber. "Hold, Zeno, and let's permit Kleon to explain before you kill him."

Kleon's mind whirled. If Archimedes encoded the scroll using strange symbols and perhaps mathematics, then the scholar he had recently heard of might be the one to decode it. He'd use the rest of the agent's money to pay the man to solve the scroll.

If he failed, it would be the end of his dreams and his life, and Marcus, if he lived, would gloat over his defeat.

Kleon raised his hand and shook a finger in the air.

"There is a man in Babylon, a linguist and mathematician whom I've written. He's agreed to meet me at the Library of Pergamum and look at the scroll. They are proud of their scholars. And they should be. He'll solve it in no time using the resources of the world's two great libraries. And I won't even need any additional funds."

"Good, because you won't get any. If Octavian knew I allowed you to expose the scroll to Parthia, Rome's greatest enemy, he'd crucify me."

"I'll be discreet. I promise." Desperate, Kleon grabbed Cimber's cape, kneeling before the Roman. "Zeno can go with me, and if I fail—"

"You won't fail will you, Kleon? If you do, I promise a slow death. Right, Zeno?"

The brute grunted before replying, "Slow and painful."

Cimber removed Kleon's hands and headed for the door. "If this knowledge proves powerful, Octavian will be extremely pleased and might even grant you a governorship of a province, perhaps Cilicia. You have until the summer solstice. Don't make me regret this."

Then he vanished.

Kleon slumped down in a chair and rubbed his wet leg. There was no time to waste.

Provincial governor!

"Min! Min! I need to send a letter. And we need to pack."

I won't fail this time, and I'll return with the power. Cimber and Octavian will shower me with gold. And I'll be the one gloating.

But when he glanced over at Zeno, an involuntary shiver ran through him.

CHAPTER TWENTY-TWO

Talus

The Mediterranean Sea, near Tarraco, Spain, April 9

FROM THE UPPER deck where the helmsmen worked the tillers of their Egyptian ship, *Osiris*, Talus scanned the western horizon, seeing nothing except the distant coastline of Near Spain.

He considered the past seven months since leaving Alexandria. While he had spent the first month and a half at sea, the last four months had been composed of endless days at the bars, brothels, and gaming houses of Nova Carthago, Spain. After sailing from Alexandria in mid-September, his first stop was Ostia where he learned Electra was safe and leaving soon for Alexandria. He proceeded next to Corsica. In the Roman port of Porto Vecchio, he spent two days scouring the inns and taverns until he found a bartender who reported overhearing a conversation about the *Neptune* sailing for Hippo Regius in Numidia to "sell some slaves." From Corsica, he dispatched a message to Lucius Bassus, updating him.

Despite fickle winds, they made a quick passage to Numidia. In Hippo Regius, it took only a day to locate a whore who had lain with a customer claiming to be the *Neptune's* captain. She said he was selling a load of captured slaves. Then the man was going to Spain to attack Roman silver ships from the Spanish mines.

Talus spent a week locating and buying back all of Maximo's

crew from the *Neptune*. When that was finished, it was the end of October. He rolled the dice against early storms and made the passage to Nova Carthago.

Failing to find Marcus or his ship along the Spanish coast, Talus wintered in Nova Carthago rather than return to Alexandria and risk losing the *Osiris* in a storm. Even with plenty of distracting entertainment, Talus's thoughts never drifted far from concerns over the fate of Marcus Bassus. The Egyptian crew and captain of Cleopatra's warship were not pleased about wintering in Spain, but Talus had Cleopatra's writ of command. That closed their mouths. That and four months of wine and whores in the Spanish port.

In early March, Talus resumed his search along the coast of Spain, still following the information from the Numidian woman.

"We've been a month at sea now, Talus. You think we'll ever find the *Neptune*?"

Talus turned from the rail to spot Captain Socus, a middle-aged man with white hair, climbing up from the lower deck. A sea captain for Bassus Trading, his orders called for him to take over the ship upon Marcus's return from Massilia. When Talus went out last autumn seeking Marcus, Socus came along to captain the *Neptune* back to Alexandria.

"I'll tell you something, Socus." Talus knew it grated on Socus when Talus didn't address him as Captain. "In the Arena, I'd always find my man. Few places to run." He laughed and Socus looked to the sky but made no reply.

"On the battlefield," continued Talus, "the cowards always run away. The brave ones, if I didn't find them, they found me."

Socus scoffed. "Still thinking Decimus is hanging around Spain?"

"What's he to do? Become an honest merchant?" Talus chuckled. "If he wants silver, he'll be near Spain somewhere. We'll find Marcus."

"I'd like to see my wife and children again." Over the stern rail, Socus eyed the ship's wake.

"What, Spanish whores in Nova Carthago not taking care of you? Guess they get picky after laying with me." Talus laughed again but kept his gaze on the water.

"Sure, Talus, sure. Sorry, I don't share your optimism, even though we're on our third pass along this coast. When is it enough?"

Talus stared at Socus's back. His eyes narrowed, and his jaw clenched. "I'll tell you when it's enough." Talus paused as Socus turned. "Never!"

Socus held up his hands. "Look, Talus, I'm sorry for my lack of confidence in our chances. No need to get upset."

"Two ships. Behind you." Talus dashed over to the stern rail. "They're not fisherman either."

"Yes, I see them." Socus squinted at the distant sails. "They could be merchantmen. One small, one medium sized."

"I want the best lookouts on the mast," Talus called out in Greek to the Egyptian captain as he headed aft. "First, we must turn this ship around." Talus thought of directing the helmsmen himself but decided not to usurp the chain of command. He hailed the Egyptian captain who hurried up from the main deck. "Captain, see the two ships?" Talus pointed over the stern. "We need to chase them."

The captain stepped to the forward rail and bellowed orders in Egyptian. "I'm getting the marines and archers ready," he explained to Talus. "They need to stay sharp." The captain turned to his helmsmen and directed them to bring the warship about to their new course. The chase had started.

Talus watched all the activity with interest. It was reminiscent of his days in the legions. If that was the *Neptune* out there, he had one huge advantage. Talus had a warship with trained fighters, archers, and catapults, while Decimus had only a merchant galley and a band of ill-equipped pirates. Though it was a fast one for a merchant, its fifteen oars per side were no match for the *Osiris's* thirty.

After a half-hour, Socus approached Talus. "The trailing ship is chasing the lead ship, which has made several turns, none of which were for wind changes or tacking. They're trying to elude the pursuer." Socus clapped his hands together. "This will be over soon."

"And you're pleased because we're going to return your employer's son? Or is it because you'll get to see your wife soon?"

Socus studied Talus and shook his head. "Talus, you eat too much bitter fruit."

Talus chuckled. Action like this reminded him of his youth. Back then, he was indestructible, fearless, and confident. He dealt in sharp steel and death. The legions won every battle, and he bathed in the grandeur of his feats. He now knew better.

Glory is fleeting; life is short; luck runs out.

He was still confident, somewhat fearless, and no longer indestructible, as his many scars attested.

He would prefer to turn over Decimus and his men to the Roman authorities rather than kill them. How confident were the pirates? How fearless and indestructible did they hold themselves? Did they realize, if captured, they were likely to end up in a shit-hole Spanish arena as gladiator fodder? Talus had no doubt Decimus knew. Time to sharpen his gladius.

Within the hour, Socus sought Talus amidships. "It's the *Neptune* all right."

"Excellent." Talus broke into a wide grin. "We'll get Marcus before nightfall." He called over the Egyptian captain. "We'll need a small crew to take the ship into port. Then you can return to Egypt."

An hour later, *Osiris* stood off the port beam of the Bassus ship, twenty paces outside bow range but within hailing distance.

Talus called out to the *Neptune*. "Decimus, give up, man. You, more than anyone, know I never lose a match. Besides, I got catapults and archers."

A moment passed before an answer came. "Is that you, Talus? I thought it was a woman calling me. You know as well as I if you turn us over to the Romans, we're all dead men. Do you want this ship? Come get it."

Talus exhaled a deep breath. "Captain, fire a warning shot at them."

On command, the forward catapult fired, and a two-foot-long bolt streaked out in a low, flattened arc between the ships. When the missile took one of Decimus's men in the chest, driving him off the deck and into the water, Talus spun around to the captain. "What kind of warning shot was that?"

"We don't have warning shots in the Egyptian navy," the man replied, sniffing.

After sputtering for a moment, Talus shrugged. "Proceed, Captain. Close to archer range and take down the dogs."

Talus watched as the carnage started and defenseless men died. Soon, his men swept the *Neptune's* deck clear. Wounded crawled, and the dead stared into oblivion. He watched the remaining pirates retreat below to await the inevitable—death.

Talus led a boarding party over to the drifting ship, working their way below deck. Two pirates tried to conceal themselves as slaves, but the Bassus crew exposed them. One poor fellow hid in the bilge water, but they spotted him when he came up for air.

Talus ordered the release of the grateful Bassus rowers from their chains before making his way down the rower's benches searching for Marcus. The rowers were in terrible shape, a few suffered from bloody backs and most had gaunt frames. He called out. "Marcus Bassus."

"He's over here, sir."

Talus moved to find the one who spoke. "Where?"

"Right beside you, sir."

Talus examined the man on the bench beside him. Hunched over was a bearded man with unkempt hair and ragged tunic. Lashings had shredded the back of the tunic, and raw welts showed on the man's back. "What's wrong with him?" He bent down and spoke into the man's ear. "Marcus?"

"Bastard pirate punched him in the head right before you boarded."

Talus picked up Marcus, a feather's weight in his massive arms, and brought him up on deck. There were bruises, scrapes, and welts on the outside, but Talus was more worried about what the pirates broke on the inside of Marcus. He set the lethargic man onto a cargo hatch and called for water. A marine brought over a waterskin.

Talus held the water up to Marcus. "Here, drink."

Marcus gazed up at him. "Talus? Is that you?"

"Yes, now drink."

Marcus took a long pull from the skin and gawked at Talus. "What took you so long?"

Confused at first, Talus then erupted into a full, belly-shaking laugh.

An animal howl suddenly came from behind Talus, and he swiveled his head to see Decimus emerging from a storage chest two paces away. Before Talus could react, the pirate sprang up and caught the gladiator in the ribs with his shoulder. They both went down hard, where they rolled around across dead bodies before Talus got the advantage, pinning Decimus to the deck.

"So, Decimus, we meet again. Too bad I won't get to see you die a slow death in the arena."

Decimus spat. "I'll see you in the underworld, you shit."

"Talus, watch out."

Talus turned toward voice. It was Marcus, standing next to him with a pirate sword. Before Talus could say or do anything, Marcus plunged the sword into Decimus's throat. The pirate gurgled before his eyes rolled back. Marcus withdrew the sword. It clattered to the deck.

As Marcus collapsed, Talus took him by the shoulders and held him upright.

"I've never killed a man," Marcus whispered.

When Talus pulled Marcus to him, Marcus broke loose.

"Leave me be. I'm all right."

Stepping back, Talus saw Marcus's inner strength for the first time.

He's not a coddled boy anymore. For better or worse, today he's become a man.

CHAPTER TWENTY-THREE

Kleon
Alexandria, May 30

KLEON SPIED HIS villa on an inland hill long before his wagon reached its gates. Surrounded by a head-high stone wall, the building held a colonnaded courtyard with a fishpond and views of the Mediterranean.

Through the glare of the sun setting behind the hill, he noticed a handful of Roman guards on duty. One was at the outer gate, the other at the villa's front entrance. The rest played dice in the open stable. Exiting the wagon, he stretched and entered the villa's atrium. "Min, at last, we're back—to our temporary home, anyway."

"Yes, Dominus."

An old man, Min spoke few words. Kleon had bought his father's slave before leaving Alexandria but had refused to tell his father his destination. Safer for him.

Kleon reveled in the sight of familiar ground, even if it was a Roman villa in Crete, provided by Cimber. He thought of Alexandria. Cimber never told him what had happened Marcus, but whatever it was, Marcus's family and friends, even Cleopatra, would seek justice or revenge or both. Returning home while Marcus or Cleopatra lived would be a death sentence. That was fine with him for now.

They'll both be dead soon enough.

In Pergamum, he had watched the Babylonian scholar whenever he worked on the scroll. Kleon didn't understand how, but the man figured out the cipher used on the last six pages of the Apollo scroll. Kleon stopped him from decoding more than a few lines. He wanted no one to know the scroll's secrets. He had brought the scroll and the master keys back with him.

First, he planned to rest from the long sea journey from Antioch, but tonight he would start the decoding work. He didn't expect the effort to take him more than a few days.

"Min, after you've stored the baggage, put a stack of papyrus paper and extra lamp oil on the table in my study. And bring some wine to my bedroom. I'm going to rest."

If I can't sleep, I'll work on the scroll.

In the master's bedroom, everything was the same. He put on a night tunic and lay on the down-filled bed, his body sinking into its softness. His exhaustion seeped from his bones.

"Your wine, Dominus."

Kleon sat up in the bed. "Thank you, Min." Though he didn't need the extra sleep inducement, he downed the wine and lay back. He soon became drowsy. When his thoughts drifted to Marcus, he gripped the bedsheets. He had been agitated and angry that day, the day Cimber joined him in the bar. After the rejection by Electra...

Ah, Electra... I want you still... the slimy way Marcus had treated him. Cimber was... an opportunity to put... himself on top.

He had heard nothing of Marcus... likely dead... or enslaved. He felt a pang of guilt, but then sleep began to take hold.

Electra would be his... Octavian would make him wealthy... power... of Archimedes scrolls. She needed a... protector...

I'll be there, Electra. You'll be mine.

CHAPTER TWENTY-FOUR

Electra
Alexandria, May 30

ELECTRA SPED ALONG the palace corridor, streaking past a startled Cybele.

"Hey," called Cybele. "What's the hurry?"

"Marcus is back!" Months of waiting and worrying were behind her. When word came at sunset yesterday, she held off dashing straight to the Bassus house. She arranged a private litter this morning, shunning the full escort Cleopatra required.

Arriving at the Bassus house, she dashed to the gate, her face hot with excitement. Titus greeted her with a smile and guided her toward the peristyle garden.

Titus whispered, "Don't expect the same man. That was quite an experience out there."

Trepidation crept into her mind. "Thanks for the warning, Titus."

"Talus is with him, but you may go in."

Electra nodded and entered the garden. She walked along the colonnade, searching for Marcus or Talus. From behind a large fig tree, Talus appeared.

"I heard the door," Talus said. "Welcome, Princess Electra."

"I'm not a princess, more illegitimate Ptolemy. Cleopatra tolerates me."

"From what I understand she tasks you with important duties."

"Regardless, please, call me Electra. Tell me how Marcus is. I'm so overjoyed to have him back in Alexandria." She pressed her hand to her mouth. For a moment, doubt filled her that she wouldn't be able to face him and see his pain. "Will you come with me?"

"Yes, of course." Talus flashed a smile. "The rest has healed Marcus physically, I can say."

"Where is he?" Electra scanned the lush garden. "Goodness, you must drain the Nile to keep everything green."

"Well, we try. Marcus has been observing the garden's butterflies for the past half-hour. There are several bushes the creatures favor."

"He related how he and his mother liked the butterflies. They liked to land on him."

"Take this warning. Marcus isn't the same young man you left in Ostia."

Apprehension filled Electra, but she steadied herself and followed Talus to the other side of the garden. Marcus had his back to them but turned as she got close.

"Electra." His voice was soft, a whisper. "Can it be you or one of my dreams?"

Electra stopped short of Marcus and swallowed a gasp. She was unprepared for the physical changes. His shoulders were much broader and his arms more muscular, closer to Talus's than to his old self. His hair was lighter and his skin tanned. There was a small scar near his left eye and one over his nose. Honorius had told her of how they had worked in the brutal silver mines of Spain for five months after three months as a rower.

"Marcus, yes, I'm here. I am not a dream." Fighting against her distress, she laughed and ran to him, embracing him. "It's wonderful to have you back." She stroked the thick muscles spanning his upper chest and back, her fingers caressing the raised ridges along his back. *Lash marks.* She fought the impulse to pull her hands away.

Marcus put his arms around her, but the embrace seemed stilted, awkward. He pressed his face into her styled hair. She sensed the tension in his deep inhale.

"Yes, it is you." His voice was a touch stronger now. "Your hair smells the same." He broke the embrace. His unfocused eyes stared into the distance, somewhere beyond the garden. "It was a difficult time."

"Oh, Marcus, I cannot imagine what you suffered. And your men." She stepped closer and took his callused hands in her soft ones. "I'm here to support you. Everyone—Talus, your father, Honorius, Titus—we all care. Especially me. Even Cleopatra cares."

"Yes, that's true, Marcus," added Talus. "Can't speak for Cleopatra. Speaking of helping, let me get refreshments for you two. Some cool water and fruit."

"And wine, Talus."

"As you wish, Marcus." Talus looked at Electra and gave an imperceptible shake of his head before leaving.

"Talus says you're watching the butterflies."

"Oh, yes. Many butterflies. That bush," Marcus pointed to the right, "and a few others bring them to the garden." After staring at the swirling butterflies, he walked over to the bush. One of the colorful fluttering creatures landed on his arm, but he seemed oblivious to it.

"Ah, here's Talus," Electra said. "Let's sit under the cover at that table."

With a rattle of cups and dishes, Talus set down a tray of fruit and two cups of water on the table.

At the sudden sounds, Marcus came out of his reverie. "Where's the wine? Didn't I say to bring wine?" His voice was full of irritation.

"Sorry, Marcus. Slipped my mind. I'll get it now."

"Don't try to fool me, Talus." Marcus pointed a finger at the bodyguard.

Talus exchanged a look with her. The normally calm face held a pained expression. He shook his head and walked back inside the house.

She patted his hand. "Talus will bring the wine. Let's enjoy the cool water." She picked up her cup.

Marcus absently reached for his, but his inattention knocked it, spilling the contents. His arm swept out, sending the cup flying past her.

"I hate myself," he roared, jumping up and stomping down the walkway into the garden.

Electra fought tears and hurried after him. These changes—the preoccupation, the anger—were creating misgivings in her. Was his mind whole? On the surface, yes, but she worried about his psyche. And the mathematical genius? Was it still there? She prayed to the gods it was.

CHAPTER TWENTY-FIVE

Marcus
Alexandria, June 9

"How ARE YOU today, Marcus?" Electra asked.

While his father traveled to Egypt's Red Sea coast, Marcus kept company with Electra and Talus. They joined him in the garden's morning sun.

Marcus mused over his emotions before replying.

"That's difficult to answer. Earlier this week, I felt like a man climbing the final steps out of a deep pit. I went over my mistakes back on the *Neptune*. We were all helpless once they chained us below. But that didn't rally me. I stayed in the pit because I had been entrusted with the responsibility for all the men who died. That made me angry. It seemed hopeless, but now you two are with me, and I'm forgiving myself a little at a time. Perhaps I'm no longer a total incompetent."

He stood and walked over to Talus. "This man," he clapped Talus's shoulder, "has given me manly support during Papa's absence."

"You'd do the same for me," Talus replied.

"Electra, you've given me hope, just by being here."

Electra nodded and smiled.

"Papa should be here, but business, as usual, prevents that." Marcus struggled for a moment. He wanted to lash out at his father, but calmed himself and continued, "Word received from Berenike reports that Papa is building a trading post and stocking a ship. I know the India trade is critical, but I'm hoping Papa won't make the India voyage and returns home instead."

"It's understandable if you resented your father for sending you to sea," Electra said.

"I don't want to discuss my father right now. Not yet." Marcus closed his eyes, working his jaw muscles. He struggled to forgive his father, to see his view, but the feelings of anger and resentment still dominated.

Papa never understood me, but maybe he was trying to do what he thought best.

"A good father is precious," Talus interjected. "Honor him but be your own man."

Marcus spread his arms out. "Thank you both for putting up with me. For trying to help me find myself again. It's good to have such friends."

Electra said nothing but touched his arm. His heart beat faster. His feelings of attraction and want returned from that day in Ostia, but the bitter truth of his unworthiness forced the realization he must hide his affection for Electra.

"You need our help. I couldn't abandon you because I… I care." She struggled for right words. "If I can assuage your suffering just a little…"

What could or should he say? A strong attraction for Electra whirled inside him. "I'm not worthy—"

"Enough of that talk, Marcus." She moved away and stood by a nearby fig tree.

Talus remained silent and stared at his feet.

Marcus stepped over to the garden pond, focusing on the colorful fish darting below the surface, aimless in their captive world.

Electra doesn't understand me. She doesn't know of my ordeal on the Neptune, *horrors I cannot describe to her. Can I be intimate and gentle after such an abomination? I must find a healing path for myself.*

Marcus turned to Talus. "The hardest thing to overcome was my shame at not fulfilling my responsibility to my crew. I failed them."

"As I've been telling you, go easy on yourself," Talus said. "The crew told me you performed beyond the actions of the best captains. You took lashings meant for others and helped many men get through moments of despair. You kept alive their hope for freedom."

"But I didn't believe in hope. I despaired while telling them not to. I believed only in my failure. Twenty-seven men died in the silver mines and six during the rescue from Decimus. That rescue was magnificent, my friend."

Talus waved off the oft-expressed compliment. "All in a day's good work."

Electra joined Marcus by the pond. "Marcus, Honorius said many of the deaths came from accidents in the mine or the guards' brutality. Things you had no control over."

"Yes, you're right, but I should have done more." He kicked at the grass. "I have hope I will move on someday. But not today."

"That's something, Marcus." Electra's eyes were soft and her smile warm.

"But you know what I realized during my captivity? I found a new truth." He tried to keep his voice steady, finding comfort in the swirling life of the pond. "It's a complete misconception that slaves are ignorant, horrible, devious people, deserving of their status."

Talus nodded. "They're no more deserving than any man, I'd say."

Electra touched Marcus's shoulder. "I agree, but what led you to that?"

He wanted to forget his experiences below deck or in the mines, but if they understood, they might forgive his failings. He closed his eyes and let his mind move back in time. "The guards treated us alike. In truth, they may have treated me worse, but living and eating with them…" He paused as memories flooded back.

"The memories are difficult," said Electra. "But it might help the healing if you talk about them."

"Perhaps you're right. So, sharing food with the men, tending each other's wounds, sleeping against the shoulder of a man—who I would have avoided before the pirates took us—made me see them as mere men like myself with universal needs and hopes and desires. Men with compassion and vigor. I didn't perceive those things then, but now I see it with unmistakable clarity."

"Egypt," Electra added, "doesn't have a slave economy like Rome. Rather it's an agrarian one based on small farms and the annual flooding of the Nile. It's only the ruling class, the Greek elite who hold slaves. The ordinary people—farmers, tradesmen, laborers—they're all free men."

"For a time, I was a slave, a gladiator, and it was a cruel and hard life, but it didn't change the man I was—Gaius Talus, son of Servius Talus." Talus made a tight fist.

Marcus considered Talus's words. "That's what I think and feel. Being a slave is a situation, not a state of being."

Talus folded his arms. "I know this: when a free man dies, he loses all the pleasures of life; when a slave dies, he loses all the pain of his miserable life."

Electra nodded. "If you treat them well, I've found most of Cleopatra's slaves will respond in kind."

Marcus couldn't help seeing the image of the vicious beatings he and his men had suffered. Without thinking, he broke off a thick branch from the fig tree and held out the stout, arm-length stick. He clenched his teeth and envisioned the retribution he would administer.

"Marcus, are you all right?" asked Electra.

"If I had those pirate dogs right now all tied up, I'd beat the life from them."

Talus stood and grabbed Marcus's shoulder. "Easy man, you're scaring the woman."

Marcus made a deep animal sound, whirled back to the pond and hurled the stick into the water.

Talus eased down onto a garden bench, but Electra remained still, pressing her hand to her mouth.

Marcus turned back to his friends. "This morning, a thought flashed through my mind. It's not the slave who is evil and despicable, rather it is slavery itself which is the great evil of man. The only hope for an improved world is to eradicate slavery."

"That's a worthy belief," Talus agreed, rising and walking toward Marcus. "But a big task to accomplish. An impossible task if you ask me."

Marcus's shoulders slumped, and he squeezed his eyes shut. An emptiness spread through his spirit. His thoughts turned to the Archimedes scrolls. Did their promised powers offer hope or self-destruction? "Yes. Impossible. But, then again, perhaps not..."

CHAPTER TWENTY-SIX

Kleon
Fishing Village Near Alexandria, June 10

WHEN THE SIDE of the small fishing boat bumped against the wharf, Kleon jumped down and headed for the fishing village's only tavern. There he would meet Cimber's man, Zeno, if he showed. Cimber had orders from Octavian not to meddle with the Bassus family. However, money left over from Pergamum might persuade Zeno to ignore Cimber.

Kleon was confident his engineers and workmen back in Crete would soon make sense of the device described in the decoded scroll and begin construction.

Kleon hesitated outside the tavern and once more considered his decision. Marcus was his adversary now and would always oppose his plans. He still feared Marcus would break the code on the Archimedes scroll in his possession setting off a race to build the Archimedes device, a race Kleon could lose. Marcus could then oppose Kleon with the same power. It all led to one solution.

Marcus must die.

Kleon drew a deep breath and entered the tavern, his gaze searching the small, airless room. Barkeeper and one man—Zeno. Kleon pulled up a chair while Zeno motioned for the barkeeper, who soon brought a beer for Kleon before withdrawing through a door behind the short bar.

Zeno eyed him over his cup. "So, what is it you want, Kleon?"

Kleon gulped his beer. He arranged two small bags of silver on the table. "A trifling task for you. A bag now, the rest after performing the job."

Zeno hefted one bag before tossing it back onto the table. "And what would this task be?"

"Kill Marcus Bassus."

"What? Are you insane? Why don't you order me to cut my throat instead? Sons of bitches." He drained half his beer. "The Bassus whelp won't stay dead I gather. But Cimber's orders. Stay away from Bassus."

"Such loyalty. Cimber would never know. What would it take?"

Zeno eyed Kleon. "Four bags upfront. Save you some trouble finding me later."

Kleon's face was impassive as he stretched his hand across the table. "Deal."

CHAPTER TWENTY-SEVEN

Marcus

Alexandria, July 17

"I'M EXCITED TO visit the Pharos," Marcus said. He stood at the bow of the boat taking Electra and himself to Pharos Island.

"It's good you're getting out," replied Electra.

"Other than the Library, the vineyard, and a visit to thank Cleopatra, I have been nowhere."

"It's good your father returned from Berenike instead of sailing to India."

"I'm glad he's back, but he's been sending doctors to see me every day. It's annoying."

Electra laughed. "I think he feels guilt about what happened."

"You're probably right," said Marcus as the boat approached the landing near the Heptastadion, the man-made mole connecting the city to the island.

Last night he had asked Electra to join this excursion to the Pharos Lighthouse. Though palace duties had kept her late, they had boarded the boat a few hours before sunset. After disembarking, they trudged a Roman mile to the Lighthouse.

Electra scanned the top. "Are we going to the top of the octagon tier?"

"We can stop above the square tier and check the time. Both levels have fantastic views."

They climbed the wide ramp where wagons brought supplies of wood for the immense signal bonfires that guided ships. It led to the square base tier. Ahead was a group of tourists.

"Hey, let's race to the top of the ramp," Electra said with an impish grin.

"You're joking."

Electra tussled Marcus's hair. "Last one's a donkey's arse," she yelled, running for the Pharos.

Marcus groaned but raced after her, soon passing her halfway up the ramp.

At the top, they collapsed against a wall. "I'm a donkey's arse for suggesting that," Electra said between pants.

"I agree; you're a donkey's arse." Marcus snickered.

Electra swiped a playful hand at him. "Fine. No more racing. Lead on."

They followed winding stairs and ramps around the inside of the square tier which held stored fuel. At the top of this section, they found a wide terrace with a waist-high wall.

"There's the next higher viewing level." Marcus pointed upward toward the octangular section. "Let's stop here for a while."

"Let's do that." Electra headed for the wall. "Each time I come up here, it gets more magnificent."

"I know." In the warm sea breeze and purple light of the setting sun, Electra, with her long soft hair and pale blue eyes, looked particularly alluring. Her lips were calling his. He gritted his teeth. He had to stop these thoughts. She deserved the best, not someone like him. Not after what happened on the *Neptune*. Guilt swept through him. How could Electra understand, let alone forgive him?

Electra stepped back to the wall. "Cleopatra will join Antony and his forces in Ephesus. She could be away for months. I've been busy packing."

"Yes, I've had a lot to do myself," he responded, and then Electra's words sunk into his mind. "What? You're leaving Alexandria?"

Marcus touched her arm but then plucked his hand back. "I'll worry about you. I'll miss you." *Stop it. Better if she were far away.* "Perhaps you should be with your queen."

She stepped away and peered down at the city. "I told Cleopatra I wanted to stay to be with you."

"What? She granted that wish? Shouldn't you go?" Marcus swallowed. "You wanted to be with me?" Dread and joy filled him at the same time.

"Cleopatra agreed to my plans." She lowered her thick, dark lashes. "Besides, Cleopatra is making Caesarion stay in Alexandria, allowing me to continue to direct Caesarian's education. He's a delightful student." She focused her gaze on his eyes. "In truth, I wanted to help you restore yourself."

"But, Electra, that's just it. I can't go back to my previous self because that Marcus doesn't exist. He died on that ship." Shame burned his cheeks, and he turned away to stare at the sea beyond.

"You mustn't give up. You're better than this. Fight to find the man you were. You were smart, strong, and had a path you wanted to follow."

Marcus grit his teeth. "I worry about where the Apollo scroll is now and into whose hands it fell. What region should I search? Is it Rome? Or Parthia? I don't have the means—money, connections, influence—to go searching for it and can only hope that whoever has it is unable to decode it. I should have beat the information out of Decimus before I killed him. But my rage overcame me."

Electra touched Marcus's arm. "Don't blame yourself for being human. The man deserved to die. Decimus was only a hired brute. I doubt he knew anything useful."

"Perhaps you're right. But now I have a mission to accomplish and a goal to strive for. My mission is to discover the secret of the remaining Archimedes scroll." He needed Electra's help. "You'll help me?"

Electra narrowed her eyes. "Should I? Does this goal help restore the Marcus you were?"

"It will focus me. I'll be using my intellect again. I'm still drawn to the academic world of scholarly pursuits, but I realize now that knowledge is a tool, not an end in itself. If the knowledge in the Zeus scroll can help the world, shouldn't we try to discover it? It will vindicate my belief in the knowledge of the ancient Greeks. Will you help me?"

Electra contemplated her response for a long moment before answering. "Perhaps the current Marcus is a better Marcus." She smiled. "Yes, I'm here for you." She clasped his hand between hers. "What's your vision, your plan?"

"Use the scroll's power—whatever it is—to reduce the burden of labor men carry. This might involve designing and building machines. With machines replacing muscles, it's possible we could end slavery. Grandiose for certain." He studied her face. "But I need you… for your strength, your insights."

He wanted to tell her of his feelings for her, but no words came. He eased a hand onto her arm. She looked up as his head bent toward her face.

A sudden storm of footsteps filled the air. Marcus and Electra broke apart and watched a crowd of tourists descending the stairs from the octagonal tier. From the cut and design of the men's tunics and the stola worn by one woman, Marcus surmised they were Roman.

When the clamor settled, Electra turned to gaze at the sunset. "Beautiful, isn't it?"

"Yes, grand," Marcus agreed.

"But it won't last. Time to head back, Marcus." Her expression was stern, but her eyes were soft, wistful.

"Are you angry?"

"A little, but not with you. Cleopatra has forbidden me any future relationships." She reached out and touched his face. "If only it wasn't true, but I'm stuck in a netherworld between reality and dreams."

A future relationship? With me? Can't be.

"Yes, I feel the same," said Marcus, putting his hand over hers. "I'm stuck between my father's plans and my desire to decode the Archimedes scrolls." Electra removed her hand, and Marcus took in a deep, trembling breath.

An hour later, he watched Electra walk away escorted by her guard. He wasn't sure when she would return. They had spoken little on the descent from the Pharos, but he hoped they followed the same path.

His thoughts then turned to Cleopatra's decision to leave Electra in Alexandria. Understanding eluded him. Did the queen trust no one else to see to Caesarian? Or did Cleopatra have some deep strategy in mind?

What is Cleopatra planning?

CHAPTER TWENTY-EIGHT

Talus
Alexandria, July 23

TALUS TRAILED MARCUS as they entered Market Street, where Alexandrians came to shop for a variety of fruits and vegetables, meats, and bread. He marveled at the array of goods, including jewelry, pots and pans, spices from the East, perfumes and cosmetics, clothes, bolts of linen and silk, and rugs from Babylon. It was far more exotic than the Roman markets. He vowed to visit the blacksmith's stall he spotted earlier.

With Marcus becoming proficient with weapons, Talus was spending more time on tactics and strategy, but he still wanted to get the young man interested in quality weapons. At least he seemed interested in sharpening his martial arts skills. Talus now sometimes found himself at the bottom of a wrestling match.

Marcus stopped at a jeweler and poked around the ruby and sapphire necklaces. "This is a dazzling piece, don't you think?" Marcus asked.

"Aye, for a shopkeeper's wife. Not for a princess."

"I'd like to get Electra something, but I'm foolish to be buying her jewelry."

Talus started to elaborate on this opinion but found himself alone as Marcus proceeded down the line of merchants. Craning his neck, he spotted him several stalls over.

Under his breath, he grumbled curses at the bazaar crowds, which were heavier than usual today because of tomorrow's religious holiday. Egypt had more festivals than decent taverns.

After steering through a crowd at the reed basket stall, Talus joined his young patron. "Marcus," Talus called. "Couldn't you choose a more carefree day to go shopping?"

"I agree it's crowded, but it's Aunt Tulla's birthday soon. What should I get her?"

"You're asking me?" Talus laughed. "I saw a fruit stand two or three stalls over. I'll be back in a moment."

"Fine. Abandon me in my shopping crisis."

"You're smart. You'll figure it out."

He threaded his way toward the fruit stall, passing a short, burly man wearing a hooded robe. Talus glimpsed the lower part of the man's face. He had an ugly scar on his jaw. When and where had he seen that scarred face? He glanced back, shrugged, and proceeded onward.

Suddenly, he heard a woman scream behind him. Talus swung toward Marcus, pushing aside a man to get a better view.

"Knife!" someone cried.

"Look out! He's got a blade!"

Talus was unable to see the face, but it appeared to be the man he'd passed a moment ago, and the man now raced straight at Marcus. Talus started pushing and shoving people aside—men, women, and children—to reach Marcus.

"Marcus!" Talus bellowed. Marcus turned. Scar-man reached Marcus and began his thrusting motion, pushing off with his back foot.

"No!" Talus hollered. Ahead, Marcus made a swift move that astounded Talus—his young charge grabbed a large basket from the stand and swung it between the stabbing weapon and himself. The dagger penetrated the basket past the hilt, trapping it in the weave.

Talus drew his blade. The curious crowds now massing together blocked his way as he watched Marcus take off running. Talus roared his legionnaire battle cry, and a path through the market cleared. Speeding through the gap, Talus closed in on the attacker, who had wrenched his blade free of the basket and glanced at Talus before taking off after Marcus.

Talus sprinted after them but had only gone just a few paces before stumbling over a panicked dog.

After recovering his balance, Talus swept the area before spotting Marcus running from the market into a narrow passageway between buildings, with the assailant closing the gap. Talus took off running.

He was nearing the alley when, to his horror, the assassin leaped and tackled Marcus, sending both to the ground.

Closing in, Talus saw Marcus kick free and roll upright. With a fluid motion, his assailant sprang to his feet, flashing two blades now. Talus, twenty paces away, yelled the battle cry of the blue-skinned barbarians of Gaul and charged at full speed. His fearsome cry caused the attacker to flip around. He hurled a single blade at Talus, which caught the bodyguard's upper chest near the shoulder. Talus cried out and staggered back a step before continuing to plod forward.

Talus saw Marcus' leg swing up and kick the second blade from his attacker's hand. Now disarmed, the assassin apparently didn't like the odds and bolted to the side of the narrow alley where, with grace defying his large frame, he scampered over a high wall and disappeared.

At a cautious pace, Talus trudged to Marcus, who dropped his blade.

"Talus, you're wounded."

"Pull this blade out, Marcus," Talus growled through clenched teeth.

After ripping the big man's tunic open, Marcus stopped. "A leather vest. That's smart." With care, he removed the attacker's dagger from Talus's shoulder.

Talus cried out in anguish and felt a trickle of blood flow down his chest. He looked at Marcus. "Are you injured, sir?"

"No, but come along. There's a physician a few paces past the market. Let's go." Marcus torn off a large strip from his over-shirt. "Hold this on the wound."

"Bah. It's nothing. I get worse sharpening my weapons."

"He had grand knives for a thief," Marcus observed.

"Not a thief, Marcus. A hired assassin. From Rome, I'd say." Talus eyed the dissipating crowd. "You have powerful enemies, and I am only one man."

They staggered away from the market, drops of blood staining the stones behind them.

CHAPTER TWENTY-NINE

Marcus
Alexandria, August 10

MARCUS WENT UPSTAIRS to his new room, away from the household noise. His Aunt Tulla, Papa's sister visiting from Memphis, was using his old bedchamber. Upon entering, he found Electra staring out an open window through which streamed fresh air and sunshine.

"Thinking about Cleopatra?" he asked. Yesterday, as Marcus and Electra watched from a palace balcony, Cleopatra had sailed on her royal flagship, the *Antonias*, bound for Ephesus and Antony. Two hundred warships and many loaded grain carriers accompanied the Egyptian queen while the *Antonias* carried a treasure of gold talents.

His concern that Cleopatra had a devious plan involving Electra appeared unfounded. It seemed she merely wanted to spare Electra the uncertainties and discomforts of a war zone while continuing to have her tutor Caesarian.

"I'm getting used to an empty palace." She walked over to the room's worktable. "I'm worried about you, though. What if Talus hadn't accompanied you to the market?"

"I told you. The thief spotted an easy target." Marcus wanted to cut off discussion of the event. "He saw my large coin purse. If I drop the purse, he grabs it and runs. End of story."

"Oh?" She tapped the table with a finger. "What about those daggers? Talus said they were professional throwing knives."

"Who'd want to kill me? Anyway, Talus is searching for anyone with a matching dagger. Please, let's put our minds to the task at hand. Consider the second page of the two Archimedes scrolls. They're identical, as are the third pages." Marcus showed Electra a copy of the second page from his Zeus scroll.

"The subject is not closed, Marcus Bassus." Electra studied the sheet before her. "Twenty-five lines of sixty symbols each. The scroll stolen in the pirate attack had this exact layout on pages two and three?"

"That's right." Marcus pulled out another sheet of papyrus. "Check this. Page three of my Zeus scroll has twenty lines of twenty characters."

Electra scrutinized the paper. "Not much there."

"I believe these two pages will yield a location or a clue to one." Marcus rubbed his chin.

"Interesting. Even this short page has the pattern where the first symbol in each line is from the set of symbols you call…" Electra looked up at Marcus.

"Oh, stickmen, silly stick figures I drew as a boy."

"Guess I missed that part of childhood. And the remaining symbols on each line are from a different set you call River?"

"Right. They're a bunch of horizontal lines and lines at a forty-five-degree angle that remind me of a river. I've tried every number sequence and alphabet shift cipher I could come up with in both Latin and Greek."

"Plus, some additional languages that I know," added Electra. "Nothing makes sense."

"There is something we're missing back on page one with the curse. Remember the phrase 'pact made between P E C A and

Osiris'? And the final line 'So says P E C A'? What do the four letters mean? 'P E C A'? Why does he spell his name—one I've never heard of—with the extra spacing between the letters? Perhaps it's not a name."

"Or maybe," suggested Electra, "it stands for four names." She patted his shoulder. "See, we make a great team."

If you knew what I was dealing with, Electra, you would run away.

He nodded in agreement wanting to expound on his feelings, but realizing it wasn't the time. "Now I'm challenged by four minds? Jupiter, help us. It's progress, but it gets harder every time I look at it. Will we ever solve this?"

CHAPTER THIRTY

Marcus
Alexandria, August 15

IT WAS LATE at night when the scream awoke Marcus. Through its nighttime fog, his mind realized the cry must be from Aunt Tulla. He grabbed a tunic and tossed it over his head, dashing into the dark hallway. He groped his way toward the stairs.

At the stairs, there was a crashing sound of breaking wood and shattering clay. Someone had run into the wooden crockery cabinet downstairs. Marcus hurled himself down the stairs two steps at a time. At the bottom, he lost his balance and hit hard on the stone floor. There was another crash of splintering wood.

After struggling to get upright, he peered down the dim hallway. In the obscuring dark, he discerned two men twisting, pushing, and shoving each other from wall to wall along the hall. Above their heads, they grappled over a weapon.

Though clay shards littering the floor had cut his bare feet, Marcus ignored the pain and stumbled onward down the hall. He made out the figure of his father.

"Papa!" He raced ahead, but when he was two strides away, the intruder's blade plunged down into his father's chest. Marcus screamed before he crashed headlong into the attacker, dressed in black and wearing a mask. Both men hit the floor hard, and Marcus heard the man's blade clatter down the stone hallway.

Marcus tried to jump on the assailant, but the man kicked out with a hobnobbed sandal that caught Marcus in the gut, knocking the breath from him. He grabbed the man's foot as he turned to run, but a fist to his head sent Marcus reeling back in agony. He got to his hands and knees, only to watch the attacker bolt down the hall toward the back of the house, taking an abrupt turn left into Papa's room.

Marcus wobbled back up the hallway to where his father lay on his back. He knelt and touched his father's chest. "Papa?"

His father groaned and spoke in a weak voice. "I... tried... to stop him... at the stairs—"

"Don't talk Papa, let me—"

Marcus jumped at the sound of rapid footsteps pounding down the hall behind him. Afraid it might be the attacker returning, Marcus turned to see Talus with a lamp and his drawn gladius.

"Is your father..." Talus said when he reached Marcus.

"No, but he's badly injured."

"I'll run for a doctor—"

"No," Marcus said with vehemence filling his voice. "I'll get the doctor. Find the attacker and kill the bastard. He went into the garden from Papa's room."

Giving a nod, Talus wheeled and took off back down the hall.

Marcus turned back to his father. Tulla came out of her room and screamed before running up to her brother's side. "Oh, no, no, Lucius!" she wailed in grief.

"Aunt Tulla, stop. Papa needs you. Bring a lamp and water. Now!"

Tulla backed up, a horrified look on her face, before running back toward her room.

Marcus inspected his father's injury. Blood from the vicious wound soaked the front of his tunic. He was dying. "I love you, Papa."

"Marcus… be strong for our family… our name. I love you… Marcus…" His head rolled to one side; his eyes rested fully open but sightless.

"Papa? No, Papa!" Marcus screamed. Anguish surged through him like a wave of fire. Fitful sobs burst from his mouth, despite his struggle to control himself. After a moment, he regained his composure long enough to close his father's eyelids and give him a last kiss on his still warm lips. Then he collapsed against the wall.

Tulla came running from her room carrying a bronze basin of water, which she dropped on seeing Marcus and Lucius. She rushed to her brother, kneeling, and clawing at his bloody chest, but then leaned back, covered her face and cried.

A tear slid down Marcus's cheek as he stared blank-eyed into the flickering light of the lamp. He stared for a long time.

Talus
Alexandria, August 15

Leaving Marcus with his dying father, Talus sprinted down the hall and into Lucius's room. He moved past an overturned chair to the nearest window, where he found the lattice work smashed. He stepped through the wooden remnants into the night.

Outside in the moonlight, a trampled flowerbed showed the attacker heading for the wall separating the garden from the exercise yard and stables. Talus started in that direction but halted when he saw a dark shape on the ground. A sinking feeling filled him as he crouched down to investigate. It was the new bodyguard, Severus—dead—his throat cut. Talus emitted a low growl before racing for the gate in the exercise wall.

Reaching the gate, he slowly swung it open. Hearing the whinny of a horse, he took off running across the empty yard toward the stables. If the attacker meant to grab a horse, he would need to return to the yard to escape through the outer gate to the alley. There was no other exit.

Another neigh came from the dark stable.

Talus sprinted to a spot short of the double stable doors, one of which was wide open. No movement came from the darkened interior. He positioned himself, hunched down, legs wide apart, with his gladius ready. If a rider came out with a long sword or spear, he would dodge to the opposite side from the weapon and swipe at the horse's legs, sending both rider and horse down. If, as he suspected, he had a shorter weapon, a dagger or gladius, he would attack the rider. He wouldn't be at full charge in the short stretch from the barn to his position.

Even at full alert, the horse and man bursting from the stable startled him, the horseman spurring the animal for more speed. The horse was charging to Talus's right, while its rider took an attacking stance, short sword outstretched, his body leaning to strike at Talus. The dark horse closed the gap with lightning speed.

When the rider bore down to within a few feet, Talus took a half step left, planted his foot, and swung his gladius with all his strength. The collision of weapons sent a familiar shock through his arm, evoking a malicious grimace. But instead of the metallic clash he expected, there was only a dull clunking sound.

The impact sent the rider rolling off the horse's haunches to land in a crumpled heap. Talus advanced on the attacker and kicked him hard in the ribs. He heard bones crack. The assassin cried out and tried to roll away.

Talus planted his massive foot on the man's chest and bore down. His sword pressed against the attacker's throat. A wooden practice sword from the weapon rack lay nearby.

"A practice sword? Bah." The moonlight caught the pinned man's face. "Any last words? You. Scarface." He recognized the thug from the docks and the market attack. "Your executioner is Talus the Titan."

The attacker's eyes went wide. "Seen you... in the arena." The words wheezed out of the man's compressed chest.

"Right. The lanista—and the legions—paid me to kill, but for you, death is free. To the Underworld, you fucking dog."

"Wait." The words were a weak whisper.

"Be a brave man and skip your begging. Why did you kill Master Bassus?"

"I never meant... to kill the old man... just the son."

Talus sneered. "Is that so? Ready to die now?"

"Let me go, and I can tell you who hired me."

"I'll consider it." Talus's lips curled into a wicked smile. He took his foot off the man but kept the sword at his throat.

"It was... Kleon."

Marcus' friend. Kleon's committed the ultimate betrayal now.

Talus was angry. "Where can I find this Kleon?" he growled.

The assassin rubbed his chest. "Southern coast of Crete. He's got a base."

Talus looked down at the man. "I've killed a lot of wretched men in my life, so what's one more? Farewell, asshole."

"No! Wait—"

Talus drove his blade through the throat of the murderer of his employer, Lucius Ventidius Bassus, once a Roman Senator, unjustly exiled by Cicero to a foreign land.

CHAPTER THIRTY-ONE

Marcus
Alexandria, September 4

IT WAS A harrowing time. Marcus spent the day of Papa's murder in a state of shock and paralysis. He couldn't understand Papa was gone. When the embalmers and priests arrived to offer their services, he left Honorius to deal with them.

His father had died defending his home against an invader. The assassin was the man who had attacked Marcus in the market and had pushed him that day at the docks. Marcus was the target, Papa the innocent victim.

The next morning, his father lay in the atrium on a bed of carved ebony wood, the servants having anointed and dressed the body in his father's best toga. By tradition, they pointed his feet toward the door. Incense filled the residence, tended to by temple initiates hired by Honorius. The body rested in state for seven days, and by the seventh day, even the skills of the anointers and the incense could not hide the smell of decay.

Electra was a constant presence. She often arrived in the morning and remained most of the day. They spent the mornings in the garden with Marcus often relating his early remembrances of his father and mother.

His father's many clients came by, offering condolences and small gifts, bowing and pledging their loyalty to Marcus. Honorius was there to give names and the proper responses to Marcus, now the new head of Bassus Trading. Even Cleopatra and Mark Antony sent a senior advisor to extend their condolences.

In that first week, anger and guilt were his constant companions. He was angry at Papa for not hiring more bodyguards. He was mad at himself for not realizing the evil in Kleon. To Kleon, he directed his vilest anger, that passion rising from a shadowy place within himself.

On the eighth day, Marcus joined Tulla and the household, including slaves, in a funeral procession, bearing the body to the Necropolis west beyond the walls. Behind the body came the musicians playing the low notes of bronze tubas and the mournful music of the tibias. At the rear of the retinue, hired women mourners wailed their grief. The sounds almost drove Marcus into a frantic rush to escape.

Electra joined him at the Necropolis, holding his arm while he stood rigid, watching as men placed Papa's body on an elaborate pyre. After a brief prayer by a priest, Marcus lit the pyre. Its bitter smoke burned his eyes. He struggled to appear dispassionate, but he was far from calm.

When the flames had consumed the body, and the fires cooled, the bereaved collected the ashes in an urn and placed it in the Bassus marble tomb next to the one holding his mother's remains.

Marcus released his tears after the tomb's closing. Electra tried to console him but to no avail. He felt alone. In the privacy of hired litters, he cried the last of his tears. Guilt gnawed at his heart for the recent difficulties that had grown between him and Papa. Something for another day.

Two weeks after Papa's death, Marcus and Honorius met in the office of Aristoxenus, Papa's Argenti Distractores. He was the private banker handling the family's banking and legal affairs. Marcus listened as the two men summarized their actions.

Aristoxenus took out a scroll and proffered it to Marcus. "This is your father's will. Marcus, please verify the seal."

Marcus checked the wax. "It is the seal of my father, Lucius Ventidius Bassus." Marcus girded himself, worried that Papa had followed through on his threat and dropped him from the will.

"I will break the seal and read the will," announced Aristoxenus.

The banker started out by naming Marcus and Aristoxenus co-executors. He then moved on to property division.

"To the Temple of Apollo, I leave twenty-five silver talents. To Tulla Ventidius Bassus, sister, I leave one hundred silver talents. And to my eldest son, Lucius Ventidius Bassus, I give two hundred silver talents."

These bequeathals helped appeased Marcus's uneasiness. Honorius told him the cash assets exceeded fifteen hundred talents, which didn't include the ships, warehouses and other property. If nothing strange happened, Marcus was now wealthy. He hoped the money would further his goals.

Achieving wealth this way nauseated Marcus. He sought to contain his outward grief, but inside, since that terrible night, he had suffered waves of guilt and fury at himself. He knew the assassin had come for him and not his father.

"To my most beloved son, Marcus Ventidius Bassus, I leave all my remaining assets, vessels, maritime equipment and supplies, my farm on Lake Mareotis, my warehouses in Egypt, Rhodes, Rome and Massilia, my villa home in Alexandria and its contents, and all remaining cash assets deposited with my agent bankers in Alexandria. My agent, Aristoxenus of Alexandria, shall provide a complete listing within one week of this will reading. I have one requirement: Marcus must take part in Bassus Trading daily business activities for six months…"

Marcus couldn't focus on the remaining details of the will except the last clause which manumitted all household slaves. They were free while he was a slave to a business he never wanted.

CHAPTER THIRTY-TWO

Marcus
Alexandria, September 20

MARCUS SCANNED THE Bassus warehouse, discovering three men—Talus and two mercenary scouts—hunched over a map. A few hours earlier, the two spies had docked in the *Neptune* after a spying mission to Kleon's Cretan facility. Marcus joined them.

Talus nodded at Marcus. "Before we get started, I have something for you. Follow me."

In the next room, Talus pointed to a sword and shield on a table. "You'll need good equipment. These are the best."

Marcus hefted the sword. It felt like part of his arm, but as he stared into his blurry image in the shield's shiny surface, doubt crept in. "Who do I see here, Talus? A scholar or a brute with a sword?"

"A sword is only a tool like a hammer or... a pen.

"Perhaps."

Perhaps this is what Father meant by my becoming a man of the world.

"You can do this, Marcus."

"We shall see."

After Marcus and Talus rejoined the other men, Talus started the briefing. "Rufus here intercepted a delivery wagon near Kleon's villa and engaged the escort in conversation. The guards expect Kleon to pull out in late November. They expect to finish a device they're building by the end of October."

"Gods!" Marcus exclaimed, thumping the table.

"What is this device, Marcus?" asked Talus.

"I don't know," replied Marcus. "I suspect Kleon sold me out to gain possession of the Archimedes scroll and has broken Archimedes' encryption. If true, it's not good for us, not good for anyone."

Talus rubbed his chin. "If it's a weapon, we could be in trouble."

"We have a deadline—one month—if we are to stop them. We require a plan—today, men." Marcus searched the men's faces and all three began speaking at once. For two hours, they debated the raid's strategy and tactics. When Marcus raised his hand, the men stopped talking.

"Talus, explain the detailed layout again." Marcus studied the makeshift map drawn on a scrap of vellum.

"We located Kleon's base on Agios Cove, west of Hierapytna. A high headland flanks the cove entrance on the east, and a sandy spit of land sits on the west. As for the cove itself, its north shore is rocky. From there, a steep hill rises to a plateau for Kleon's villa. They work several farms to fool the locals, I presume. The cove's west side is also rocky. The east side is a sandy beach with a pier."

Marcus interrupted. "And Kleon's ship?"

"A black-sailed, light courier," Talus answered. "Kleon uses it to make short supply runs."

"Go on."

Talus pointed at the map. "Near the pier is a work complex around an open area containing several huge forges. Opposite them is an extensive wooden building for construction. Across the cove on the west side is a small engineer's office. Behind it is a low knoll with a small watchtower. Northwest, there's a steep hill with a large barrack housing fifty men and a centurion and quarters for blacksmiths, metal workers, and whoever."

"Good," said Marcus. "Anything else?"

"A road cuts between the two higher hills, running from the forges to the town of Folos. That's it."

Marcus took a deep breath. Doubts rose in his mind. Could he lead men into battle? He had to show absolute confidence regardless of his own emotions.

As they considered their options, he realized military strategy was like any problem solving. Weigh the facts, resources, and constraints, and then produce a solution. "We'll hide the *Neptune* behind this narrow island to the south and watch for the courtier ship's departure."

"What are you planning?" Talus asked.

"Here's my proposal…"

After the men withdrew, Electra joined Marcus alone in the warehouse.

"So, your plan begins?" asked Electra.

"Yes. I must stop Kleon, whatever it takes. Hippolytus was right in that we need to keep the scrolls from the wrong hands." As Marcus reached out for Electra's hand, he realized his were shaking. The impact of his plans and the consequences of defeat filled him with dread.

Electra took his shaking hands. "It will be all right. You have Talus."

Marcus smiled. "Yes, I do." But Talus and confidence would only get him so far. He had to execute as a leader.

Am I ready?

The image of his father's life bleeding out came to him. It stiffened his resolution into an iron determination to prevail.

Marcus
Southern Crete, October 12

Marcus's boat was the last one lowered from the *Neptune*. He climbed down the rope netting into the small boat, taking the tiller. Overhead, ragged clouds raced across a sliver of a moon, with occasional breaks giving brief allusions to light. He hand-signaled Talus, and the five boats, oar locks muffled, rowed for the dark shore. Four rowers, a helmsman, and a lookout manned each vessel. Sextus Rosco, the *Neptune's* captain, had maneuvered close to the beach, reducing the distance they needed to row.

After all boats made the shore, grounding onto the sand, the men separated into their assigned attack units. With one man left behind to watch the boats, the rest moved off the beach.

The dense, salty smell of the sea filled Marcus's nostrils. The soft thudding of hobnobbed boots, like a herd of camels padding across a desert dune, pervaded the night, a night that Marcus compared to falling into a vat of red wine.

Their first target was the guard post on the knoll due north of their landing.

"Talus," Marcus whispered.

His second-in-command gave the hand signal. Two archers and a runner moved out. The critical step was to kill these guards before the main force could move on the workshop complex.

Marcus planned on a quarter-hour for this phase. Kneeling in the sand, it was the longest fifteen minutes of his life. If they stayed quiet and prevented any alarms sounding, all should go well. He checked over his men, mercenaries and veterans of countless wars along the Roman frontier.

The runner from the knoll dashed in from the dark. "Sir, the knoll is secure," the man whispered. "I reminded the archers of the signals. A single flaming arrow means retreat to the boats while two flaming arrows means retreat to the pier."

Talus spat. "Marcus, two flaming arrows? Retreat to the pier?"

Marcus tried to see Talus's face in the dark. He had to show himself as the leader here. His future, whether in commerce or academia, depended on showing confidence and on getting others to follow him. They needed this backup plan.

He flicked his tongue over dry lips. "In case we're cut off from the boats. If Sextus sees two flaming arrows, he will bring the ship around to the pier, and we'll load up there."

"Good plan, sir, but fill me in next time." Talus briefed the other men.

Time for their next maneuver. Marcus raised his voice to just above a whisper. "Advanced force, move up. Take out those guards. Talus, you and your men stay at least fifty feet back."

"Will do, sir."

With five men on each side, Marcus crept up toward the workshops. If their scouting was correct, five of Kleon's men stood guard there. They crept forward through the coarse sand and across a rocky strip before Marcus signaled a halt at the foot of a gentle, grassy slope leading to the two workshops.

His signal directed two men to the front of the larger workshop to handle the guard at the pier and sent two other men behind the adjacent shop to eliminate the guard at the end of the road. The remaining men crept forward, aiming to take down the guards in the central area between the workshops.

Marcus would stay at the bottom of the slope and bring up Talus and the main force when the way was clear.

Before long, Marcus heard the barely audible sounds of a scuffle from the pier.

Jupiter, let us all get back safe.

The unexpected sound of a sword strike rang out. There was

another clang and another. In a heartbeat, the area above him erupted with the clash of steel on steel.

Marcus tried to whistle to call up Talus and his men, but his dry mouth produced only a stream of air. He wet his lips and tried again, managing a short, high-pitched whistle. Moments later, Talus and his fifteen men appeared.

"To the slope. Assist the others," Marcus ordered.

"Follow me, boys," Talus said, disappearing into the darkness with his men. A single archer remained behind with Marcus.

Marcus waited, trying not to bite his lip in half. Talus's men joined the battle, and weapon strikes split the night air with increased frequency. It reminded Marcus of a rainstorm moving across the Lake vineyard; only men didn't die from rain.

The increased intensity of the fight sped up his sense of time. Men grunted, yelled out, and screamed in death. He couldn't tell if the cries were from his men or Kleon's. Though he had confidence in Talus and his fighters, Marcus's anxiety surged, and he gripped his shield until his hands ached.

After a burst of intense action, the battle died down. One side was winning. The screams and the weapon sounds dissipated. The night became quiet again.

Marcus jumped when Talus appeared out of the night. "Report," came Marcus's nervous bark.

"We ran into more men than expected. Professionals. We lost two men, three wounded." Talus spat out a wad of blood, showing teeth outlined in red.

"Are you wounded?"

"Helmet to the face. Stings some. I'll be fine."

Marcus drew a deep breath. "Let's start on the workshops."

They entered the large building first where a quick search revealed no more guards. A few lamps were lit, and Marcus whistled on seeing the workshop. Metalworking stations covered much of the single room facility. On tables, Kleon's engineers and craftsmen had spread their drawings and notes.

Excited over the discovery, Marcus directed three men to collect everything on the tables. It took a few minutes to ascertain what he had discovered. He found large, hollow metal cylinders in different assembly stages. Kleon's men had lap-welded sheets of steel and bronze into—what? Containers? For what?

He found lead pipes, long ones, stacked in bins. They had also welded smaller tubes onto a larger central tube. It was like a giant metal spider's web.

"Jupiter's balls," exclaimed Talus. "Is Kleon building a raft to cross the river of death?"

Marcus grinned. "Too cheap to pay the ferryman. Which I hope he will see soon." They shared a quiet laugh. Marcus had considered striking the hilltop villa, cutting Kleon's throat while he slept. Revenge must wait. First, he'd smash the Archimedes devices and perhaps recover the Apollo scroll.

"Destroy all this. Save one of those shorter tubes. Hurry. We're behind schedule."

"Yes, sir," Talus acknowledged. "Those extra guards fought on even facing certain death."

"I'm worried light will catch us before we reach the boats."

The destruction of the steel drums and the spider web of tubes took longer than Marcus expected. Even with linen wrapped around the hammerheads, the clamor was ear-piercing.

A soldier hurried up to Marcus. "Sir, I've searched all the cabinets, shelves, and chests in the two workshops. We'll need two more men to carry all the scrolls and drawings we found."

"Fine. Pick a couple." He was eager to study it all back in Alexandria.

"Yes, sir. Thought you might like this ancient-looking one for yourself." He held up a scroll.

"The Archimedes scroll!" Marcus's heart leapt in his chest.

"Excellent. It's the original one taken from me. This adventure is a total success now." He clapped the man on the shoulder. "Thank you."

The soldier saluted and returned to his tasks.

Marcus spotted Talus and waved him over.

Talus ran over, holding up a piece of metal. "It's from a metal drum and is of well-crafted steel." Talus turned the metal over in his hands. "I used swords in the arena from Arabia. Could cut through a net like soft cheese."

"I wish we could haul it all off, but there's no time."

"Agreed." Talus glanced out a window. "We need to move soon. Close to dawn now. We'll be visible from the hills before long."

Marcus assessed the surrounding area. "How much longer here? We need to set the fires and move to the—"

A soldier raced into the workshop. He called out. "Marcus! Soldiers moving down from the barracks."

"Sir," said Talus, "I suggest we send most of our archers to the knoll to cover our retreat."

"Do it." Marcus turned to the men still hammering at Kleon's metalworks. "We're finished here, men. Gather down the slope."

Marcus moved out into the open yard. By the gods' bones, it was getting light. He could discern the surrounding hills now. He checked on each of the wounded that his men carried down the slope.

"Talus, grab six men and torch the buildings. We'll head to the boats when you're done."

"I love burning things," Talus replied, giving a wicked smile. "You two, you, and you three. Come on."

As Marcus watched the first fires flame up, one archer from the knoll came running. He bent down, grasping his knees, drawing gulps of air.

"What is it, man?" Marcus asked.

"Kleon's soldiers... from barracks... have formed... testudo. Our arrows... useless."

"Testudo?" Standard Roman infantry tactic against archers called for a wall of shields around and above the soldiers.

Before the archer could answer, Talus came out of the large workshop. "What's that? A testudo? Their centurion must be ex-legion." He looked at Marcus. "Fight our way to the boats, sir?"

"With our wounded? And they have twice as many men. No, we fall back to the pier. Archer, shoot off two fire arrows toward the boats. Our archers will retreat to the pier. The *Neptune* will pick us up there."

"Yes, sir." The archer prepared his arrows.

"Marcus, I'll set up a defensive position at the pier with the remaining men," said Talus. *"Neptune* needs a few minutes."

"Good. I'll be there after the signal's fired." Marcus looked around for his archer.

"Right. Listen up, boys," Talus called out. "Follow me to the pier. Won't be rowing home today." Talus and the men moved out.

Marcus grimaced as the death cart rolled by.

Jupiter, let it stop at two.

"Ready for the signal, sir." The archer stood with two flaming arrows nocked. The archer had wrapped the arrowheads in linen.

"Draw and release," Marcus commanded. The archer drew back and launched his arrows. He watched the twin flames arch across the brightening sky. The archers would soon advance to the pier. "To the pier, then."

Marcus followed the archer, glancing across at the hill where the villa sat. He spied men hurrying down a narrow path to the harbor. Was Kleon with them? Too far to tell.

At the pier, Marcus's quick glance back showed the knoll archers right behind him. Beyond, the flames glinted off the shields of Kleon's men from the barracks and the villa. They rapidly closed in on the pier. Marcus slipped through a gap in a wall of crates—

Talus's defensive position. Several more crate walls spanned the broad dock.

"Knoll archers should—ah, there they are," said Talus. "We'll need them to buy us time before the ship gets here. Kleon's troops will throw their javelins first. Better head to the farthest wall. Can't afford to lose another Bassus. Be out of a job."

"You could always try piracy," said one man.

Talus chuckled at the joke, but it invoked haunting images for Marcus.

Will I never escape the memories?

The sound of running feet on the pier took Marcus out of his thoughts. The archers had arrived. He surveyed the scene in the light of the burning buildings before taking a position behind the last crate wall. Turning to the sea, he spotted the *Neptune* not far beyond the cove's entrance. They only needed to hold out a little longer.

After his archers swept onto the pier, the first volley of javelins from Kleon's troops rained down. Some found their marks, leaving their victims prostrate on the ground. The wounded screamed.

Please, no more deaths.

A second barrage of missiles filled the air, one landing on the dock a foot away from him. The twang of his archer's bows answered the attack. A handful of Kleon's men were hit, including the standard bearer. Blood squirted from the neck of one enemy fighter struck by an arrow. Marcus steeled himself.

Out of javelins, Kleon's men retreated under fire from Marcus's archers. The ensuing lull allowed his men time to grab the *Neptune's* docking ropes. Kleon's men regrouped as Talus led the men back onto the ship. Marcus followed. Once on board, he searched for Kleon. Knowing the walk of his father's murderer, he spotted his old friend dressed in a black robe to go with his black beard. Marcus lowered his shield, cupped his hands, and yelled over the crackling of wood fires and the sounds of desperate missile fire from beyond the pier. "Kleon. I'm coming for you!"

"Is that you, Marcus?" Kleon called. "I've been expecting you. So, Zeno talked? I shouldn't have paid in advance."

"I thought I smelled something foul besides burning bodies," Marcus yelled back. He longed to run his sword through Kleon's chest.

Die like my father.

The smoke got thicker and obscured sight of his father's killer. Marcus shook his head. "Kleon, it's madness to think you can use the Archimedes powers and avoid danger and death."

There was no answer, no further bluster from Kleon.

Talus jogged up. "The job's done. We've destroyed the base."

"No, it's not over," Marcus said. "Deciphering the scrolls is no longer an academic exercise. Kleon will rebuild his device, whatever it is."

Marcus suspected it was a weapon though he hoped for a different answer. Archimedes had built several defensive machines for his beloved Syracuse in their defense against a Roman siege two hundred years ago. When the city fell, the invaders killed him, unaware of who he was.

"Kleon's alliance with Octavian means they can bring Egypt and the rest of the East to its knees. I have to stop him from spreading the knowledge of Archimedes, no matter where he goes."

It's what Hippolytus would have done.

Marcus gazed out to the open sea. The *Neptune* was rowing at top speed into the mouth of the cove. Far beyond it, he could make out another ship approaching. A black sail billowed from its mast.

CHAPTER THIRTY-THREE

Kleon
Southern Crete, October 12

Near the forges, Kleon surveyed his burning base. Embers still glowed and acrid smoke swirled in the air. The captain of his supply ship had decided against pursuing Marcus and his raiders, finding his vessel outmatched.

The workshops were a total loss, their contents burned to ashes or lumps of blackened metal. With their forges intact, the blacksmiths turned to organizing the tools the attackers had scattered around like a boneyard.

He kicked the charred remains of his main workshop. His drawings and designs—burnt, irreplaceable. The original Archimedes scroll—Marcus called it Apollo—burned or worse, confiscated by Marcus. At least he'd kept a translated copy made by the Babylonian.

He choked back a scream, not wanting to appear weak before the men.

The coming voyage to Cimber's Sicily facility would see many craftsmen abandoning him. The raid left one engineer dead and the other running into the hills. He'd need new ones.

Time to move.

With local townsmen snooping around, it wouldn't be long

before a magistrate took an interest. Kleon couldn't afford to have Antony's men sniffing into his affairs. Death by strangulation or life in prison weren't ends he desired. No, he'd load up what equipment, supplies, and men that would follow and retreat to Sicily. Though he wasn't looking forward to Cimber's unbounded fury on the loss of this complex, the Roman had promised a shipyard.

If they wanted the power he could provide, they'd pay. Ambitious, wealthy men were good allies. In time, he'd have to give them the power they obsessed over. Yet, Kleon's own desire for the power of the scrolls burned his insides, its siren call possessing his entire being.

Hiring someone to kill Marcus had been a logical, but passionate decision. His old friend was an annoyance, a rival for the scroll's power and for the woman he wanted. His hatred for Marcus arose from the childhood memories of Marcus's condescending way—not his words but the look in his eyes. Kleon saw the same thing in others—they judged him inferior because his mother wasn't Greek but Egyptian. Cleopatra and her bureaucracy had held his father down while advancing lesser deserving idiots.

Yes, he'd show those people—all those haughty sycophants surrounding Cleopatra, and those fawning, sanctimonious eunuchs. They'd be in chains soon enough.

And you Marcus? I will take great pleasure in casting you into the underworld.

CHAPTER THIRTY-FOUR

Marcus
Alexandria, November 18

Marcus enjoyed his weekly sessions with Electra. Often meeting in the afternoon, they spent much of their time upstairs trying to decode the Archimedes scrolls. Then they had dinner.

"Neema, this food tastes so much better. Sorry, I meant..." Marcus stammered. "It tasted good before but..."

"Yes, thanks to Electra and her exotic spices," Neema admitted. "Sneaks it from of the royal kitchens, I suspect."

"I grab a pinch or two," Electra said with a laugh. "I can teach you the best use of each spice."

"That sounds wonderful," the cook replied and returned to the kitchen.

"Neema stayed after your father freed her?" Electra asked.

"Both she and Titus stayed. I've also freed the remaining household servants. All work here for wages now."

"Marcus, you should be proud of that. You said slavery is wrong, and now you are acting on that belief."

"Yes, I'm proud of that, but the next step will cost me. Honorius is working on freeing all Bassus slave rowers."

Electra gasped.

Marcus nodded. "Yes, it's significant. A thousand men earning a laborer's wage is problematic for profits, but it will lift a burden from my heart. I will own no slaves."

"Placing principles above money and self-interest is a rare event in most men," Electra said bending forward and hugging Marcus.

"Walking in the shoes of a slave as I did, I experienced their pain," Marcus said, gazing into Electra's eyes. "Is it bravery to follow what is right? I think not."

"Lesser men don't think in that way." Electra took a sip of her drink. "Actually, you've inspired me, Marcus. Even though I don't live in a place like Rome where slavery is the economy, I see slavery in a different light, how destructive and demeaning it is."

"You can't imagine how much it means to hear you say that." He reached over and took her hand. "Thank you."

"Well, your passion, your emotion has touched me. You shouldn't let what happened on that ship take you down."

Marcus picked at his peppered fish fillet. "Perhaps. But your words make me have a more positive sense of myself. Maybe my resistance tactics helped the men survive on that ship and in those horrible mines."

"This is not empty praise, dear." She squeezed his hand. "This is how I see the situation and your actions, and I know Talus believes you were brave and strong for your men."

"And I thought he was trying to make me feel better."

After the meal, they walked in the garden. Electra sat on a stone bench. "I love this garden, and this fountain most of all."

Marcus sat beside her. "I've noticed you stop here every time."

As they sat, a realization crystallized in his mind.

"The Crete mission about more than recovering the scroll and destroying Kleon's base. I found a part of myself I didn't know I had," Marcus admitted.

This last statement puzzled Electra. "What? The fighting?"

"No, not that. Never have I commanded men, let alone soldiers."

"That had to be scary."

"It was. I led men in a dangerous and desperate endeavor. Somehow, I found strength from somewhere."

"See, you're not unworthy. Besides, I've heard the Library scribes describe how you help them all the time."

"That's true, but…" Marcus visualized the terrible event on the *Neptune* that made him unworthy. If Electra knew of that, she might have different thoughts. "I never thought leadership was a part of me."

"You've led me astray," Electra said. "I'm neglecting my duties."

"What? Time to count the dinner plates and spoons again?"

Electra gave him a playful slap on his head followed by a pouty look.

Marcus laughed.

"It's good to see you laugh. But tell me about leadership. Is that why you didn't want your father's business?"

"Yes, that was a big part. That and the fact I knew I belonged on the path of the scholar."

"You seem capable of much more. Are you still sure of that path?"

"No, I'm afraid I'm facing a dilemma on that."

"An unfortunate situation." She noticed the garden's sundial. "Goddess, it's late. I must go." Electra's habit was to leave for the palace before sunset, escorted by her two guards.

Marcus wanted to express his growing feelings for her. Instead, he pressed his lips together, still lacking a belief he was worthy of her after his ordeal. These past few months, whenever Marcus reached this moment, something made him withhold his affections. Guilt and self-loathing formed a stout wall which he couldn't break. His only bastion against madness was his ability to close off the terrible memories of that horrific night. He sensed Electra saw his struggle, but she seemed resigned to the future dictated by Cleopatra.

A few weeks ago, he had found his courage and had muttered an incoherent sentence to her about his fondness for her. It didn't go well.

"Marcus, give us time," she had replied. "It would only bring pain to us both. I have feelings for you, but I don't want to hurt you. The Egyptian court remains frozen in time. With Antony and Cleopatra in Greece awaiting the inevitable confrontation with Octavian, I need to stay close to the palace assisting with educating young Caesarion. In Rome, the noble women have their flirtations and affairs, but this isn't the case in Ptolemaic Egypt."

Marcus's heart had sped up at her words. "But, Electra," Marcus had pleaded, "does it hurt to talk about feelings?"

"Feelings will lead to desire, and desire will lead to the bedroom. The Stoic philosophers tell us to live in the moment and don't allow our desires or fears to control us." She spoke her mind frankly. "I do not have the sexual freedom of a Roman nobilis." Tears had misted her eyes, and she had looked away. "As long as Cleopatra rules Egypt, I must not allow myself to be… tainted."

"Yes, I understand. It's like you said on Pharos in the summer. We're stuck in a gray area until Cleopatra decides something. The death of my father…" Marcus paused, trying to control his emotions. "It's set me free on one level to pursue my goals. But now the business dominates my time."

"Control. I hate the word. I hate having anyone dominate me, even Cleopatra. It's not that I'm a slave, it's that I want my freedom to have choices, to choose my future. I don't have that. Until I do, a relationship will complicate my life. For now, let's just enjoy each other's company. I realize that's not what you wanted me to say." She had turned back to gaze out the window.

Against his desire to further their relationship, Marcus bowed to Electra's wishes. He kept his sentiments and feelings sealed away in his heart. Together, they made the best of their cheerful yet unfulfilled afternoons together.

*

One thing that cheered Marcus was the detailed drawings and partial constructions taken from Kleon's workshops. His and Quintus's study of them was now bearing fruit. Soon the secrets of the Apollo scroll, hidden for centuries, would become known.

Yet, a simple fact frustrated Marcus. Despite having both scrolls and despite spending day after day, often with Electra, in the Library researching and reading Archimedes' works, he was still no closer to decoding either scroll. He had learned much about Archimedes the man and his thinking processes, but there was no mention of the encrypted scrolls. He was losing his mental game with Archimedes despite working late, tucked away in some corner of the Library. Sometimes he fell asleep until morning when a worker from the cleaning crew would wake him.

There was one constant. He'd never give up on decoding the scrolls.

Marcus
Alexandria, December 29

Marcus examined the many drawings captured from Kleon spread out over tables in one of the Bassus warehouses. Though details on several were sketchy and handling during the raid had damaged others, he and Quintus Buteo had managed over the last two months to partially replicate the device Kleon was building.

The engineer was returning to Rome when Marcus chanced to meet him near the Mouseion. Intrigued by the opportunity to view drawings of an Archimedes device, he offered his engineering skills, and Marcus was quick to accept.

"Got this figured out?" asked Talus, walking up to Marcus. The big man rubbed his chin, peering at a drawing.

"We understand the basic design. Come along," Marcus said, leading him through the scattered parts. "Based on these drawings, we believe we know what Kleon was building."

Talus pointed at tubes of metal lying about like a giant child's toys. "And all those pipes spread on the floor? Does it make sense?"

"They confirm what we think these drawings represent." He stopped beside the tangle of pipes. "Oddly enough, this design follows that of a device described in the book by Ctesibius called *On Pneumatics*."

"What's that?"

"Pneumatics is the study of the mechanical properties of gasses. It's from the old Greek word 'pneuma,' which means wind. Air is a gas, all around us," Marcus waved his hands, "and there are others. For example, if you mix bitumen and sulfur crystals, you get a gas, one that is poisonous."

"Poisonous air?" Talus frowned. "That's amazing."

"Anyway, Ctesibius described various whimsical devices he constructed using compressed air."

"So, how do you compress air?"

"Think of bellows. Blacksmiths use them."

"I saw them used in the legions to make a fire as hot as a bolt from Jupiter. Jupiter Tonans."

Marcus brought his hands together, then spread them wide apart. "You expand a bellows and air comes into the valve, the small slit, on the side of the leather bag."

"You squeeze the bag," said Talus, "and air gushes out the nozzle. The fire roars up."

"That's right. You've taken a volume of air and squeezed it—compressed it. That trapped air is trying to get out in the time you collapsed the bag. The pieces of air—atoms, the early Greeks named them—crowd together, moving down the narrow nozzle where they have more force, more strength. The air gushes out."

Marcus stopped at the end of a large central pipe with many other pipes emanating from it.

"See this? It's like an aqueduct in Rome. Water flows down the aqueduct's main channel, and a multitude of pipes branch off to feed fountains, the public baths, and private homes."

Talus nodded his head. "So Kleon was making some odd device for water?"

"That's close."

"I know. Air. Big bellows for huge fires." Talus wriggled his hands up in the air like flames shooting into the air.

"Again, close. Air is what Ctesibius used."

"You say water is close and so is air. But it's neither. What is it?"

"When you boil water, what is that smoke rising from the pot? Is it air? No, it's steam. Boiling water produces steam. Ctesibius used his compressed air to operate miniature musical birds and open temple doors. Archimedes took a simple principle, the force potential of compressed air, and applied it to a more potent force— steam. He took Ctesibius's compressed air catapult and devised one using steam. Archimedes leap from air to steam was brilliant."

Talus held up his hands. "How come the legions are ignorant of these powerful catapults?"

"For whatever reason, no one ever constructed the air or the steam catapult."

They headed toward the front of the building, moving around the long central pipe. As the two men passed a window, Marcus spotted Electra and her escort walking toward the warehouse.

Jupiter! Have I got my days mixed up?

"We have a visitor, Talus." Marcus dashed off to the main entrance and met Electra at the door to the small front office. "Electra, don't tell me I've mixed up my days?"

"Nothing of the sort." She embraced him for a quick moment, peering beyond his shoulder. "May I come in?" She motioned her guards to stay outside the warehouse.

"Certainly." Marcus stepped aside. The smell of jasmine filled his nostrils. His chest tightened, but he took a deep breath to settle himself. "I'm sorry, but I have no refreshments to offer you. This way. I was explaining to Talus about the progress on the drawings and mechanical parts from Kleon."

"This should be interesting."

The two of them returned to where Talus waited. "It's fortunate we burned Kleon's base before he could finish a working device. It frightens me to see how close it came to completion. Kleon somehow figured out how to decrypt the Apollo scroll. I haven't."

"You will, Marcus," Electra said, patting his shoulder. "It's a matter of time."

"Time is something we don't have," said Marcus, his voice heated. "Kleon is setting up a new base somewhere and building his super ship, which would swing the balance of this upcoming confrontation with Octavian."

Electra exchanged a look with Talus. "Marcus, how can I help?"

"Continue to help me decode the two scrolls. Kleon's ahead of us with the decoding, and his threats leave us with no time. Here is Quintus's and my thinking now. Back on Crete, I saw several metal cylinders. We've determined they're designed to hold water, which is heated and turned into steam, producing a considerable force."

Talus grunted. "Can you also build these steam catapults?"

"I'm not sure. Quintus and I need to test some ideas. With Kleon's captured plans, we can build a steam catapult firing a projectile that can breach any Octavian warship's hull." Marcus studied Electra, who appeared perplexed. He continued. "Enough hits and the warship sinks. First step, we must try to build a boiler and—"

Electra gasped. "Hold on. The last six or seven pages of the Apollo scroll are plans for this catapult?"

"That's correct, based on what we found on Crete."

"Now you want to build these catapults? You intend to travel the same path Kleon has chosen? That's reckless, Marcus." Electra turned her back to him, then whirled back around, her face flushed and her eyes wide. Her voice, though, was strong. "Didn't Archimedes hide these secrets because he didn't think mankind was ready? Are you men all alike? Has anything changed in 200 years?"

"Yes," Marcus replied. "There is now the evil of Rome. Do we stick our head in the sand while the world goes insane?"

"And you plan to rescue the world by this form of insanity?"

"The alternative is to allow the barbarians to rule. Understand that this was a painful decision."

"But Marcus, why expose the powers if they might fall into the hands of Rome?"

Marcus moved closer to her. Talus had moved to the other side of the warehouse. "I remind you," he said, "Kleon, Octavian's puppet, already has this power. Thus, Rome does. Do we stand by and watch them enslave the world?"

"Do we stick to principles? This great knowledge—do we share it or keep it for ourselves? I'm just not sure." Electra held her hands to her mouth. "Marcus, I don't want you to go to war." Tears welled in her eyes.

"I don't either, but what choice is there? My moral convictions tell me to withdraw and not expose the scroll's knowledge. Is it right to suspend our principles and fight Kleon? I will not resist bending my morals if what opposes me is evil. If we defeat Kleon, we can consider burying the scrolls again."

Electra sighed. "You're right, Marcus, though all I can foresee is the world, my world, our world, burning in flames."

Marcus took her hand. "Your passion against revealing the scrolls deserves my respect. But we'll face this together. You and I. Together, we'll solve the Archimedes puzzle. We'll stop Kleon. We are, perhaps, the world's best chance at a better future, perhaps one without slavery."

"I like that plan, Marcus."

"Kleon's defeat is our priority, but I still cling to my dreams of being a scholar. I'm not good at this trading business. Without

Honorius, I'd be lost. I'll never match Papa. Though I feel like a slave to this business, Bassus Trading makes me a man of means."

Electra wiped her eyes and collected herself. "Don't be too hard on yourself. You're a quick learner." She scanned the room. "What's holding you back from building this device, this weapon?"

"I need additional stock of metal plate—iron or steel. I've sent out agents throughout our trading area to buy stocks."

Electra's face brightened. "Maybe I can help. I have friends in high places, you know."

32 B.C.

CHAPTER THIRTY-FIVE

Electra
Alexandria, March 25

IT WAS EARLY morning when Electra left her escort in the atrium and hurried to the Library's expansive Reading Room, expecting to find Marcus. His morning note requested she meet him to discuss the scrolls. She had new ideas and had been waiting for their next afternoon talk.

At the far end of the room, she spotted Marcus talking to Eucleides, Head Librarian, who moved off after seeing her enter the room. She greeted the Librarian as they passed each other and got a stern glare from the man.

Marcus gave her a brief embrace. "I'm glad you're here."

Electra eyed him. He was pale, staring off into the upper reaches of the high-ceilinged Reading Room. His embrace had been wooden, lukewarm. "Anytime, Marcus, when it's this topic." She nodded toward the retreating form of Eucleides. "What was that all about?"

"Eucleides just informed me he's revoking my Library access."

"What? Can he do that? Well, yes, he can," she said, answering her question. "But why?"

"He says since I'm not a scholar-in-residence, nor have I been giving lectures of late, he can't justify my continued acccss."

Electra cocked her head. "There's something odd here, and we can't permit him to get away with it. I'll write a letter to Vizier Horemheb and to Cleopatra."

"It's too late. The snake said today is my last day for access. Starting tomorrow, the guards will stop me at the door. There's no time to lose." The color had returned to Marcus's face.

"Follow me," said Electra.

Marcus rushed after her. They were soon in the Isis Room.

"Remember our first scroll discussion here?"

Marcus smiled. "I certainly remember, although, I didn't mention the Archimedes scrolls themselves."

"If I recall, you were circumspect." With a soft laugh, she added, "Remember the head knocking?"

"Ouch. And the collision outside the Library?"

"Seems I'm always trying to knock sense into you." She lowered her eyes.

Electra had sensed his attraction to her from that first time outside the Library. She felt a growing attraction for him, but with Cleopatra's marriage edict hanging over her, she held back. Besides, was Marcus healed? She didn't want to upset the delicate balance between friendship and something more.

"I wasn't mature enough then to understand my feelings," Marcus said. "But I experienced something on an intuitive level both times."

"Wait, we're wandering over into feelings now. But I will say, you're no longer that boy. You've changed for the better." Electra believed that. Maybe Marcus was ready for more. If she could convince Cleopatra that Marcus was the best match for her, should she? "New subject—Archimedes."

Marcus looked as if he wanted to pursue his earlier statement, but said, "Archimedes. You have an idea? I brought the Zeus scroll."

"Good." Electra rolled out the short scroll, weighing the ends with her gold bracelets. "I noticed something on Apollo last summer."

"That's a lifetime ago." Marcus rubbed his cheek. "Papa's murder, the raid, the business responsibilities, working on Kleon's drawings. Only in the last month have I been able to apply myself to the scrolls."

Electra patted his back before studying the writing. "It's like the other one. There are faint, almost invisible, dots between the letters of the signature name."

"That means they're initials, not a single name. It's four names, like you said months ago."

"Correct. Another clue for that conclusion is that the line, 'So say P.E.C.A.' Kleon read it as 'So says PECA.' That's singular, and how I've first read it. But we were both wrong. The ancient Greek on the scroll translates as plural—multiple people."

Marcus jumped out of his chair. "Gods. You've found our first clue. Now we need to determine who the four names are."

Electra straightened. "It's obvious who the letter 'A' stands for—Archimedes."

Marcus nodded. "The letter 'C.' That has to stand for Ctesibius since he came up with the air catapult, for which he had to invent the cylinder and plunger. He was also in Alexandria most of his life. Who can the other two be?"

"Wasn't Ctesibius also the first Head Librarian? As Head Librarian, he would have lived in spacious quarters in the Mouseion. He likely kept all his papers and designs here, including those for his air catapult. Who replaced him?"

"That would be Eratosthenes," said Marcus. "I have my list of consuls. And Head Librarians." He dug into his bag and pulled out a scroll, running his finger across the page. "Eratosthenes took the head position in Marcus Fabius Buteo's consulship. Two hundred and thirteen years ago."

Electra walked around the cramped room. "From what I've read about Archimedes, he came to Alexandria from Syracuse during the year Gaius Sulpicius Galus was consul." She bent over again and put her elbows on the table but stood up after noticing Marcus staring at her hips. "Concentrate, Marcus."

"Fine, taskmaster, let me check that." Marcus consulted his list. "That's amazing; it's only two years after Eratosthenes became Head Librarian. Jupiter! Three giants of engineering and mathematics in Alexandria at the same time."

"We only need to figure out who the letter 'P' stands for." Electra stared out the small window with its view of the harbor.

"We need to do some research." Marcus bagged up the scrolls. "But before we start, I need to make a request of Philotus. Follow me."

"Wait, I need my bracelets."

What is he on to now?

Marcus
Alexandria, March 25

Marcus knocked on Philotus's door. The librarian opened the door and waved Marcus and Electra in. "I heard what Eucleides did, Marcus. I'd like to help you, but there's nothing I can do."

"But there is, Philotus. My library access is good until tomorrow morning. I have this one last day to use the Library to help me solve the scroll's encoding. I—"

The librarian looked over at Electra before shaking his head. "Marcus, Marcus. I know you believe Hippolytus left the scrolls with you to entice you to solve them, and you may be right. That's between you and him. I suggest putting the scrolls away and wait for Hippolytus to return."

"It's too late for that, I'm afraid."

Marcus filled in Philotus on Kleon's success in decoding the Apollo scroll, his progress in constructing a device, the raid on Kleon's base, and Marcus's efforts to duplicate Kleon's device. He held back details on what the device was, saying only that it was a weapon.

"Gods, Marcus. What a mess you have made. Hippolytus will long regret his decision. I can't imagine the consequences if men like Octavian get this device."

"Philotus, if I can solve the scrolls, I can neutralize Kleon. Can you help? Please."

"It's our only chance, sir," added Electra.

"What can I do?" asked Philotus.

"First, give me night access to the Library. I need the extra time. Second, write an order or directive or whatever you call it giving me access and cooperation from all Library departments. I'll need their manpower in searching for and collecting documents."

"It's fortunate that Eucleides has gone to budget meetings at the palace. He won't return today. I'll do what you ask, but you're on your own after this."

With papers in hand, Marcus and Electra hurried back downstairs.

Marcus
Alexandria, March 25

Marcus led Electra to the research room and approached one of the research librarians, Sarpedos. He handed the man the directive from Philotus.

"Is everything in order?" Marcus asked.

"Yes, Bassus," answered Sarpedos. "What do you require?"

"I need copies of the personal correspondence of Eratosthenes. Not his works, his personal correspondence."

The man's eyes widened. "Sir, Eratosthenes was Head Librarian over two hundred years ago. Your request is impossible."

"Oh, no," insisted Marcus. "Since he was Head Librarian,

the Library would keep his works in a secure location here in the building."

"I'll have to pull half the scribes in the copy room. They'll fall behind schedule." Sarpedos set his jaw. "I won't do it."

"Should I bring Philotus over here?"

Sarpedos forced a smile. "That won't be necessary, sir. We'll start right away. It may take several hours."

"Make it two. We'll be back after the sixth hour," Marcus said, walking away with Electra. "This work has made me hungry. I know an eatery across the street from the Mouseion."

"I'm all for that."

On returning to their study room, Marcus found every table filled with scrolls. There was a note from Sarpedos. "Eratosthenes's personal papers as requested."

"Goddess, I hope we find the answer in all this."

Marcus threaded his fingers through his hair. "I do, too."

Two hours later, Electra discovered a significant find. A letter from Eratosthenes to the High Priest at the Temple of Artemis.

"The Temple of Artemis. Excellent." Marcus checked that he had closed the door before whispering, "Hippolytus and I stole the Archimedes scrolls from that temple."

Electra's eyes opened wide. "What? You violated a temple? Marcus—"

"I know. I was fourteen. Hippolytus said the goal justified our actions. Anyway, I remember climbing up to the roof. I was so scared… never mind. To business. Read Eratosthenes's letter."

"I haven't seen you this excited since we climbed the Pharos last summer." Electra brought the oil lamp closer and read the letter aloud.

'To the Most Faithful High Priest of Artemis: Greetings. I have

a most urgent petition, one raised for the benefit of all men's descendants. As the sanctuary of the Mother Protector Goddess Artemis, my associates and I know of no better place to harbor the great Knowledge for which we seek protection. It is a powerful and nurturing Knowledge, the work of Archimedes and others, which will free all men of the chains that hold them to their petty labors. I send this Knowledge in a locked chest marked with the seal of my Academy, the Hawk with talons holding a javelin and a scroll. Only one carrying this seal may claim the Knowledge. I send fifty talents of Gold as an offering to the Goddess for ensuring the everlasting safety of the Knowledge. In humble gratitude, I bow. Eratosthenes.'

Marcus clapped his hands and let out a cry of triumph.

"This confirms it. He sent the Archimedes scrolls to the Temple of Artemis for protection, trusting in the sanctity of the Temple."

"That didn't stop you and Hippolytus."

"Yes, I know. Tell me. What's the date?"

Electra again studied the letter. "It's dated in the seventh year of the reign of King Ptolemy Epiphanes."

"That's around the time Eratosthenes stepped down and Aristophanes of Byzantium took over as Head Librarian," said Marcus. "Poor man. Epiphanes had him imprisoned because he suspected Aristophanes planned to defect to the Library at Pergamon."

"Didn't Eratosthenes die several years after Aristophanes took over? This might be his final letter as Head Librarian."

"Could be. It connects Eratosthenes with the Archimedes scrolls and with the Oracles since the seal described is the same as that on Hippolytus's medallion. The letter says others—besides Archimedes—aided in developing the scroll's knowledge. P-E-C-A. Four initials, four men. Three of them must be Eratosthenes, Ctesibius, and Archimedes. But who is the letter 'P'?"

Electra looked over the remaining scrolls of Eratosthenes.

"Somewhere in all this, Eratosthenes must have mentioned our fourth man. It could take us hours to go through the unread scrolls."

"You're right. There must be another way." Marcus rubbed his chin.

"Meanwhile, I'll get started," Electra said, turning to the table full of scrolls.

"Wait. I thought of something. Follow me."

"Where to?"

"There is a book, a history by Agatharchides, written a hundred years ago," Marcus explained as he moved toward one of the larger book storage rooms. He and Electra passed row after row of scholars, many with heads lowered over books of ancient knowledge. Some worked on new works—poetry, astronomy, mathematics, geography, anatomy, history. Others were engaged in lively debates over interpretations of an ancient work.

"I will miss this place," Marcus said staring down a line of library stacks stretching away into infinity. "Anyway, I read Agatharchides's volume on Egypt a few years back, and I remember he made a list of famous scholars who studied at the Mouseion."

"Not every scholar, I would imagine," said Electra. "The Mouseion holds hundreds at any one time."

"It's a fortunate position to have. Free quarters and food and thousands of books from around the world."

Marcus reached his destination and engaged with one of the Library assistants. "Agenor, can you help us? I need Agatharchides's *Affairs in Europe*. The volume on Egypt."

After a short wait, Agenor brought out two scrolls. Marcus led Electra back to the Isis Room.

"What exactly are we searching for?" asked Electra.

"We're looking for scholars mentioned during Eratosthenes's time as Head Librarian, those whose names start with 'P'." Marcus went through the two scrolls, reading out names to Electra, who wrote them down.

When Marcus finished, he inspected the list of five names and began reading each. "Polyaenus of Lampsacus, Philo of Byzantium—Philo! That's it." Marcus slapped the table. "That makes perfect sense. Philo lived most of his life in Alexandria and wrote *Mechanike Syntaxis*. I've read the first chapter on mathematics where he gives a geometric construction for doubling the cube—"

"Hold it, Euclid." Electra rubbed her eyes. "How do you remember this stuff?"

"I don't know. It seems to spring into my mind like a picture. Everything I've read is there somewhere."

"That's amazing, though I'm not sure I'd want that ability. But back to our problem—the Library closes in two hours. We must find this Philo work, read it, and connect it to our Archimedes scroll. That's over two hours' work. There'll be no staff around to get material for us."

"Don't worry, I know where most works are shelved. With the night access Philotus granted us, we'll have four additional hours in here, more if we hide from the guards. Let's see what we discover in *Mechanike Syntaxis*."

"I need to check in at the palace. I'll be back in an hour, maybe less."

Marcus walked Electra out to her waiting escort and watched her leave. As he turned to go back inside, he glanced up at the Pharos Lighthouse in the distance. It was brighter than he had ever seen it.

Inside, he hurried to Sarpedos's research desk and requested a copy of Philo's work. Sarpedos consulted his master inventory, a thick slab of papyrus sheets, before silently gliding through an archway leading to the archives, an endless labyrinth of bookracks.

Over an hour later, Sarpedos reappeared, just as Electra returned. "The section holding Philo's works is being reorganized," announced Sarpedos, "It's in a delicate disposition and impossible to search until we complete the project. Come back then." He nonchalantly put away his inventory book.

Marcus squinted at the man, whose obstructiveness seemed purposeful. "You took an hour to determine that? Look, Sarpedos, I accompanied the scribe when he fetched it three years ago. I can find it again."

"Most unlikely," said Sarpedos.

"We'll try anyway," Electra said, folding her arms.

"Only Library workers can access that area. It's forbidden for others."

Marcus threw up his arms. "Philotus will have a different opinion."

"I'm sure he'll back me on this." Sarpedos gave them a smug smile.

As if he had been lurking nearby, Philotus materialized from a hallway.

"Philotus, we have an issue here," said Marcus.

Philotus seemed surprised. "Oh? What's this issue, Sarpedos?"

"Sir, as I've explained to Bassus, I'm reorganizing the Euergetes room. Its manuscripts are inaccessible right now." Sarpedos leaned back in his chair.

Philotus rubbed his chin. "Euergetes room? I don't recall a work order for that."

"It went out this morning. It probably hasn't caught up with you." Sarpedos scanned around his desk. "Here's a copy of my request."

Philotus glanced at the document. "I haven't officially approved this, so we can honor Bassus's request. Since Queen Cleopatra's cousin is also making this request," Philotus looked over at Electra, who nodded her head. "I'll take it as an official request."

"I know where the book is," added Marcus, "and I'm sure I can find it. It's Philo's *Mechanike Syntaxis*."

"Sir, I must object," said Sarpedos, rising. "This isn't protocol."

"Pleasing the queen is always protocol, Sarpedos. Keep that in mind, if you wish to further your career. Come, you two."

Marcus and Electra exchanged a triumphant look and followed Philotus.

At the Euergetes room, three scribes were emptying scroll bins.

Philotus called over the room's supervising scribe. "You will cease your activities. Ignore Sarpedos's work order for now. And help these two find whatever they need."

"Yes, sir." He nodded his head and then clapped his hands. "Take a break, everyone."

"Take this, Marcus," Philotus said. "It's an access pass that will get you into any Library area. I'll be in my office for a while longer."

"Thank you," said Electra.

Marcus addressed the scribe. "We need Philo's *Mechanike Syntaxis*. Check in bin twenty-six."

"You have an excellent memory," said the scribe.

"I have a visual picture of this whole library and much of its contents." Marcus chuckled. "But don't ask me what I had for dinner."

When they returned to the Isis room, the scribes had cleared away the Eratosthenes works and replaced them with the scrolls of *Mechanike Syntaxis*.

"So, why did you request this particular work?" asked Electra as she fingered one of the scrolls on the table.

"First, I know he was in Alexandria during the years that Archimedes was. He also studied with Ctesibius, who had similar interests in mechanics, engineering, and mathematics. *Mechanike Syntaxis* is his primary work."

"I can't argue with that logic. Let's get started."

Marcus and Electra scanned the contents page of Philo's book. "Look," said Marcus. He could hardly sit still. "The last chapter, Chapter Nine, 'Peri Epistolon' Philo titled it."

Electra gasped. "Secret Letters. Secret Letters," she repeated, hugging Marcus. They gazed into each other's eyes. Marcus swallowed. The urge to kiss Electra was strong. She was stunning, intelligent, and she put up with his quirks. He leaned in closer.

She turned back to the scroll. "This could be the key."

Marcus was close enough to smell the freshness of her hair. He forced his attention back to Philo.

"Yes, I hope it describes the encryption Archimedes used." Marcus's heart beat faster for several breaths, whether from Electra or the scroll or both, he couldn't decide. "Find the ninth chapter. You take that pile." After scanning the beginning pages of all the scrolls, they found no "Peri Epistolon."

Marcus drummed his fingers on the table. "Maybe the writing got out of sequence. We must search through everything." They began the arduous process of examining every page of Philo's writing.

An hour later, Marcus unrolled the final lines of the last scroll. They didn't find the missing chapter. "Gods, no." Marcus frowned and rubbed the back of his aching neck. "There must be more. Let's check with that scribe."

The scribe examined his records. "There was another copy of *Mechanike Syntaxis* kept in a Library warehouse by the docks. Assuming it survived Caesar's fires, it might be there."

"Is the tunnel usable?"

The tunnel, a convenient connection between the Library and the dockside warehouses, enabled quicker material transfers. During the so-called 'Alexandrian War,' Julius Caesar, attempting to drive the Egyptian navy from the Great Harbor, set fire to the docks. A casualty of that fire was the Library's book warehouses.

"I suspect it is, though it's not used much." replied the clerk.

Marcus and Electra reached the Library tunnel, where the access pass satisfied the guards. They hurried through the musty, shadowy passageway, lit only by the occasional torch. Rats and vermin scurried along the floor and across the ceiling. At the warehouse, Marcus proceeded to the records clerk.

"The records show a copy was once in a warehouse." said the ancient clerk, "It's unfortunate, but it was one that Caesar burned."

"There are no other copies?" Marcus asked.

"None I can see."

Electra slumped against the desk. "It's a dead end."

Electra's voice echoed Marcus's crushing disappointment. "Curse the gods," he said.

"Hold on," said the clerk. "Don't curse the gods yet. I recall—it's been fifteen years—some scrolls escaped the flames. The clean-up crew I was on found light damage to books in several metal chests in the lower level."

"Do you have a list of those?" Marcus said, grasping at this last hope.

"No list, but we took the material to the library annex in the Temple of Serapis for processing. Might still be there."

"Come on, Marcus. To the temple. The gods may still favor us."

At the annex, another elderly clerk led them to a small side room. Eight-foot-high wooden bins lined the walls, each crammed with scrolls. Many had blackened edges.

The clerk pulled out a dusty ledger and flipped through it. "*Mechanike Syntaxis*, you say?"

"Yes, by Philo," Marcus said. He rubbed the bulla under his tunic, dreading the clerk's answer.

"Hold on, good news. We have a copy of *Mechanike Syntaxis*."

Marcus shook both fists in the air. "Yes, that's it. This is great."

Electra and Marcus exchanged grins. "We're looking for Chapter Nine," Electra told the clerk.

"Oh. Nasty news. That scroll—Chapter Nine—was transferred to the main library." The clerk shrugged. "Have you checked there?"

"What? When?" Marcus's frowned, and a heavy stone settled into his stomach.

"Transferred over a month ago."

"By whose authority?" Electra asked.

"Let's see. The transfer had the proper authorization signed by a librarian named—the signature's hard to read. Old eyes." The clerk turned the ledger toward Marcus and Electra.

It was in a small script, but quite clear. "Sarpedos!" they both shouted.

Marcus
Alexandria, March 25

Marcus and Electra left the startled clerk and raced from the temple, narrowly avoiding a collision with two priests, and arrived at the Library at dusk. It was after hours, but Marcus showed his pass to the guards at the side entrance who waved them in.

As Marcus entered the dark and cavernous atrium, he noted the inscription over the archway to the great reading room. In Greek, it read: Sanatorium for the soul. The words gave him an odd comfort.

"Perhaps Philotus is still here," Marcus said, eyeing the dim interior. He grabbed an oil lamp before leading Electra across the atrium and up the spiral staircase to Philotus's office on the fourth level. He knocked before trying the door.

"Locked." Marcus slapped the doorframe, then paced the hall. No solution came to him. "What do we do now?" he croaked.

"Are you thinking what I'm thinking?" She barely moved as Marcus continued pacing.

Marcus halted. "Kleon. If he's following the same trail—and if he kept a copy of the Apollo scroll—he might have figured out how to decode the first three pages."

"Yes, that scares me. We need that missing chapter." Electra eyed the other offices. "Does Sarpedos have an office?"

"Third floor."

"Show me."

Marcus led Electra down a level and along its open walkway overlooking the atrium. After passing several doors, he stopped at the last one. A small wooden plaque announced the occupant's name: Sarpedos. He tried the door. Locked.

"We need to get inside."

"We can't break the door down."

He looked at Electra's hair. "Do you have any metal hairpins?"

"What? Sure, a few."

"Let me have two. I'll try to trick the lock."

"What? Another skill from my talented criminal."

Marcus chuckled. "Hardly, but Hippolytus taught me, in case I encountered locks in the Temple of Artemis."

Electra removed the hairpins holding her hair and shook her head. Cascades of long tresses flowed down her shoulders. She held out two pins.

Marcus had never seen Electra with her hair undone and the sight transfixed him. She glowed like a goddess. He fought the sensations that filled him.

"Marcus? You want these?"

Marcus broke from his reverie. "Sorry. Yes." He bent the brass pins.

Electra frowned. "What are you…"

"Trust me."

Marcus inserted the bent pins into the lock. For several minutes, he manipulated the hairpins. Something clicked. "Push the door," Marcus said, holding the pins stationary.

Electra pressed against the heavy door, and it creaked open.

"Success," Marcus whispered as they entered the dark room.

Marcus lit a small, ornate candlestick. "Search his desk. I'll check those cabinets."

Before long, Electra held up a leather bag. "I've found his journal. We're the subject of his last entry."

"The ass," replied Marcus. "Go back a month and check for any mention of the missing Philo chapter."

While Marcus searched through the cabinets, Electra skimmed the journal. "Oh, Goddess. This entry says…"

"Yes? It says what?"

"Sarpedos made a copy of the 'Peri Epistolon' chapter. A month ago. He sent that copy to…" Electra stopped and looked at Marcus.

"To who?"

Electra chewed her lip before answering. "Kleon."

"Jupiter's balls! The bastard. Electra, I fear we may be too late." Despair crept into his consciousness.

At that instant, Marcus heard a noise outside the door followed by a knock. "Anyone in there?"

"Quick, the closet." Marcus snuffed the lamp before racing to join Electra. Inside the cramped and dark space, Marcus found himself pressed against Electra's warm body. His mind spun. He concentrated—to no avail—on fighting his desires.

"I heard the door close."

Electra's whispered words brought a release of tension in Marcus. He fumbled with the door before getting it open.

Sarpedos didn't have many storage places, and Marcus had searched all but a single locked cabinet.

"Let me have those hairpins." Electra handed it over. Marcus made quick work of the simple cabinet lock and swung the doors open. Even in the dim lamplight, the Philo scroll jumped out at him like the Pyramids from the desert floor. The papyrus was dark from age or Caesar's fire, its edges blackened. Marcus rolled the papyrus out on Sarpedos's desk.

"Careful," said Electra in a low voice. "The papyrus is very dry."

"I want to make sure." His inspection of the first two pages convinced Marcus. "Looks authentic. What do you think?"

"The dialect, diction, and word choices seem appropriate for Philo's time. It's the one."

Marcus re-rolled the papyrus and slipped it under his belt. "Excellent. Maybe we'll yet beat Kleon. Let's go." Marcus took Electra's hand. "Thanks for your help."

"Like I said before, we're a good team."

Closing the door, Marcus held Electra's hand as he led her down the dark staircase. The thought of Kleon solving the encryption first made him quicken his pace.

Marcus
Alexandria, March 26

They snuck across the dimly lit Library to the Isis Room. The efficient scribes had cleared away the scrolls of *Mechanike Syntaxis*, leaving a new set.

"What are these?" asked Electra, examining one of the scrolls as Marcus lit a lamp.

"Ctesibius's collected works," said Marcus, spreading his arms. "The pure engineer in the group might offer us a clue, so before we left Philotus, I asked him to send the works of Ctesibius here. Most are original documents so we can avoid the errors in later copies."

"Tell me, Love, what we're chasing here."

"I'm hoping Philo's chapter, 'Peri Epistolon,' will yield a key of sorts—a substitution table or conversion calculation—for the stickmen symbols."

"All right, let's hurry."

They plunged into the final chapter of *Mechanike Syntaxis*. Philo's imperfect handwriting made progress slow. As the fifth hour of the night approached, Electra had translated only a few pages.

"Figured out anything yet?" she asked.

"It appears to be a treatise on cryptology. Do you agree?"

"I don't understand all the concepts, but I see cryptology's the topic. It discusses strategies for sending secret communications."

"It could be something mathematical." Marcus clasped his hands together, his anticipation verging on overwhelming.

"Ready for the next few pages?"

"More than ready."

With delicate care, Marcus rolled out the next three pages, faded and made brittle over the centuries.

For the next hour, Electra read and translated the archaic Greek, as Marcus transcribed the words onto a new roll of papyrus. Nothing relevant appeared.

Marcus's body sagged, and he put his forehead on the table.

"What's wrong?" Electra asked.

"I'm tired," he replied, rolling his neck. He considered asking for a neck rub but decided it would be a serious distraction.

Electra patted his shoulder. "So, anything useful in these pages?"

"Just general techniques like substitution ciphers. Let's hope there's something in these last ten to fifteen pages."

"Enough relaxing. Let's move on."

"All right. You vaguely remind me of someone, but he was ugly and carried a whip," he said and grinned.

Electra ignored the remark. "Time is slipping away." She fluttered her hands trying to shake her nervousness.

"I can't believe what Eucleides is doing." Marcus shook his head.

"Tomorrow, I'll petition the Vizier," said Electra. "It's doubtful, but maybe he can overrule Eucleides."

Over the next hour, they made rapid progress and only three pages remained. Marcus stood and stretched. His shoulders sagged, and he rubbed his temples to ease the pain in his head. "If I could eat, I would. Food in my stomach might prepare me for the eventual disappointment."

"You soggy rag." Electra gave him a big smile. "Dream good thoughts, because we may be on the verge of discovering the key. If not this, then something else."

They unrolled the final pages. The first was blank. When the second page was only half exposed, they both drew in a sharp breath. They gaped at each other in shocked recognition.

"It's your stickmen!" cried Electra.

"Yes! And the symbols are not letters; they're numbers." The page contained five stickmen, with a number under each. One hundred-six and four hundred-one were the first two.

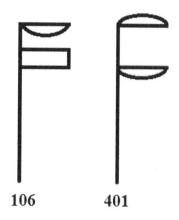

106   **401**

"Let me write these down," said Electra, excitement in her voice. "One hundred-six, four hundred-one, four hundred seven, four hundred seventy-two, one thousand eighty-eight. Does that make sense?"

"It's not clear how these five numbers provide a key," said Marcus, studying the mysterious figures, rubbing his chin in deep thought, mumbling now and then. Numbers and symbols whirled in his head as he stared at the two scrolls, head cocked to one side.

Thirty minutes passed before he spoke. "There must be a

pattern. Ah, yes. No, doesn't work. Wait. Wait." His eyes widened. "I've got it."

Electra shot him a sidelong glance. "Then, kind sir, fill in us mere mortals who aren't mathematical gods."

"As you command, cousin of the Pharaoh." Marcus took Electra's paper and drew a stick figure. He then added three arrows to it. "This upper, horizontal arrow points from right to left. It represents multiplying the previous value by ten. One becomes ten. In the stickman figure I've drawn, a vertical line, with a half circle attached to the upper right, represents the number one. If we move the half circle to the upper left, the value is now ten. To go from ten to one hundred, you move the half circle from the upper left to the lower right. Let me see you draw the number ten."

Electra took the stylus and paper. She drew while he watched. "So, if I take your figure for one and swing the half circle to the left, I get ten? Like this?" She showed the paper to Marcus.

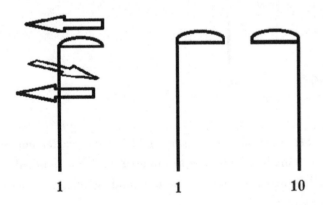

"That's it. Fantastic." Marcus squeezed Electra's shoulder. "With similar shifts, we can get the figures for one hundred and for one thousand. And so on. In the figures that Philo's given us, we have the figures for one, two, four, six, seven, and eight. We can infer the remaining three digits based on the pattern of prior ones."

"I'll take your word for it. So, how do we determine those larger numbers, like one hundred six?"

"We take the figure for one hundred and superimpose the figure for six right over it. Like this." Marcus drew out three stickmen.

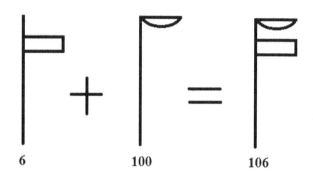

6   100   106

Electra shook her head. "And so, we end up with what?"

"We now can determine the numeric values of all stickmen from a value of 1 to 9999."

"How does that solve the Archimedes scrolls?"

"I believe the stickmen values themselves are important, but first I must check each row of symbols and convert each of the stickmen figures to its corresponding value. Then we'll see what we get."

Electra soon learned to evaluate the numeric values of the stickmen symbols and, working together, they constructed a list of the values on the twenty-five rows of page two. They analyzed the values to determine all the numbers were between 5 and 1495. Twenty-five rows of sixty characters resulted in fifteen hundred symbols, including the twenty-five stickmen at the start of each row. Marcus reckoned the stickmen values represented a position—and the symbol at that position—in the list of symbols on the Archimedes scroll.

As Marcus plotted out the positions, he found it unexpected that each row contained only one value from his list. He circled each symbol and copied them. He studied the twenty-five symbols.

They meant nothing.

One more decoding step must exist to translate the symbols to the Ionic Greek of Archimedes' time. A solution for that last step popped into Marcus's head.

"So, what's this you're proposing?" asked Electra, taking a seat next to him in the Isis Room.

"Philo left behind a key. His treatise doesn't reference the last pages of 'Peri Epistolon' anywhere. It's like it was a later addition."

Electra pressed her palms in thought. "And Ctesibius did the same thing? He left a clue?"

Marcus smiled. "You're on to me. What we're seeking is conspicuous. You won't need to read for context. We should make quick progress."

Electra handed him a scroll. "Might as well start with this one."

"It's *Belopoietica*," Marcus announced after inspecting the scroll. "It's Ctesibius work on mechanical principles and devices, especially war machines like catapults, siege towers, and battering rams. His theories on pulleys, levers, and gears, my favorite topic, fascinated me, but I lost interest in all the war machine designs and never finished. Here's my chance. I'll start at the beginning; you start at the end."

"Oh, I get to read backward," said Electra. She sounded pouty, but Marcus knew better—she wanted this as much as he did.

With all the mechanical drawings—and none had anything like the symbols they searched for—it was only an hour later that Marcus finished reading the last volume of *Belopoietica*. "Time for the next one."

Another hour later, after reading *Memorabilia and Memorandum on Mechanics*, they were down to the last major Ctesibius work, *On Pneumatics*.

"This one I haven't read," said Marcus, shuffling through the scrolls, "though others have told me it has many original and creative ideas. This time, we'll each read full volumes. You can start with the first volume, and I'll start with the last one."

Marcus glanced out a window. Dawn's first hints appeared on the horizon.

"I doubt that will make it any easier," replied Electra. "I'm finding it hard to stay awake."

"Don't give out on me now." Marcus smiled and took her hand. "There is so much at stake here. We must stop Kleon, and this decoding is the only way. His base's destruction was not the final answer."

"I know." She took a deep breath. "My motto is, and I quote from Epicurus: 'The greater the difficulty, the more the glory in surmounting it.'"

"That's the spirit." Marcus handed her the first volume. "Let's begin."

Marcus fought the urge to delve into the wondrous writings he found on every page, including the scroll on the hydraulis, or water organ.

With disappointment, Marcus finished his last scroll, "Volume Seventeen," describing an improved clepsydra, or water clock. That one deserved further study—some day. Electra was also on her last scroll. "Is that 'Volume Sixteen?'" Marcus asked when she rolled up her scroll.

"No, that was 'Volume Fifteen.' I thought you had sixteen."

"We're missing a scroll." He scanned the table but saw no errant scrolls.

"Oh, no, not another missing one." Electra's hands flew up to cover her face. "After all this work, we have another missing scroll." She dropped her hands and looked at Marcus.

He felt Electra's pain. The fog of sleep was drifting across his mind. "Don't worry. Someone just made a mistake. I'll check with the librarian," said Marcus, rising from his chair.

"Not at this hour. And tomorrow, you're banned from the Library." Electra doubled over in her chair.

"Shit." Marcus kicked the table leg.

"Wait, Marcus. Down by your feet. What's that?" She pointed at the floor.

Marcus followed Electra's finger. There, on the floor, lay a scroll. Marcus reached down and grabbed it. "This is it. The last chance." He gripped the scroll in his hand.

"Careful, Marcus. You'll crush it."

"Sorry." He unrolled the scroll. "By the gods. Or as Archimedes said, '*Eureka!* We've found it!'"

"We have? Show me."

Marcus picked up the Ctesibius scroll and showed her the page. It was full of symbols like the ones in the Archimedes scrolls. Beside each one was an Ionic Greek letter. "A substitution cipher."

Relief flooded him, but he wondered—was this the last key?

CHAPTER THIRTY-SIX

Marcus

Desert West of Alexandria, March 27

DURING THE BITTER cold of the pre-dawn ride, Marcus tried to keep up a conversation with Quintus, the engineer building the steam boiler, but the desert wind dried up his lips and mouth. Speech failed him. They had left Alexandria through the western gate and headed for the desert workshops where Quintus was constructing his boiler.

Marcus wanted to continue decoding the Archimedes scroll, but after finding the last key in yesterday's pre-dawn hours, fatigue had sent them to their beds for much of the day. Facing this early desert trip, he had decided to wait another day to solve the final puzzle piece.

Marcus glanced back once at Alexandria—the Pharos burned bright in the clear, cool air.

Three hours later, as the blacksmiths were breathing life into their infant fires with giant bellows, Marcus at last slid his sore body down from his horse and handed the reins to a stable boy.

"Marcus, join me in my office for something warm," Quintus said.

Something warm turned out to be hot wine, well-watered and spiced.

Quintus led him to a worktable with drawings of the boiler. Marcus was intrigued.

"This design is ingenious—two half-cylinders of steel plate bolted together along the long sides. We make the bolt holes during the forging?"

"They're punched out," Quintus answered. "The steel bolts are white-hot when we insert them. One bolt end has a large head. We place an anvil under the bolt head, and the other end's hammered flat. Six bolts per foot."

Marcus whistled. "It must make a very tight seal. How do you get the bolts hot enough to make them malleable?"

"The secret is the bellows that feed the fires. One man works three connected bellows at a time with six bellows per firebox. The heat is intense. A man needs relief after half an hour."

"Quintus, why the four cranes?"

"We use them to move the steel plates. Two of the wheeled cranes carry a heated plate to a stone slab where we roll the white-hot metal to the thickness we want. The blacksmiths trim the plate and punch the bolt holes."

"I'm impressed."

"Thanks, my friend, for buying all the working steel."

"Thank Cleopatra. She let me buy from the Royal stockpiles. We sourced them from the East."

"Speaking of the East, I met a Chinese engineer in Rome and convinced him to work on Cleopatra's ships. He has taught me techniques in construction and metallurgy that are unknown here or in Rome."

"We should also thank Kleon for the generous loan of his plans and drawings," Marcus said, flashing a wide grin.

"Remind me next time I see his traitorous face. Back to our work. To save weight, I will use brass piping to carry the steam from boiler to catapult. And I've received your latest changes to the catapult design."

Marcus nodded. "I know you're consumed with building and testing your boilers. Get the boiler right, and then we'll advance to the catapults."

Quintus clapped Marcus on the shoulder. "I've a surprise. We're testing our first boiler today." He beckoned Marcus to the window. "See that platform?"

Marcus peered out. "Yes." He turned back to Quintus.

"This afternoon, we run our first boiler test there."

"Quintus, don't rush things because of me."

"No," Quintus grinned. "I'm rushing things because of Kleon."

Marcus
Desert West of Alexandria, March 27

The test site was in a desert depression between low dunes. Marcus wrapped his head for protection against the merciless sun. Rivulets of sweat trickled down his brow.

Quintus pointed to a makeshift shelter with low walls of scrap wood and a canvas roof situated fifty feet from the boiler. There, Marcus gulped water brought from the nearby oasis. The cool liquid soothed his parched throat as he studied Quintus's design.

The boiler rested on its metal carriage on a low wooden platform. Wearing thick gloves, several men moved around checking fittings and connections. Below them, the firemen were throwing wood into the flames rising from the stone firebox. Atop the firebox, and slightly below the boiler, was a stout iron grate. Three bellows—ganged to a single handle—protruded from the front of the firebox.

Quintus was talking to the firemen. Laborers were bringing armfuls of split logs to feed the fire's voracious appetite.

Above and behind the boiler, Marcus noted a large wooden

tank for supplying water through a pipe and into the cap plate on the top of the sealed steam vessel.

Next to the pipe, a short brass tube protruded that would carry the powerful steam to a catapult. For testing, it ended at a metal valve fitting. A chain hung from the valve to release or shut off the flow of steam.

A similar design had been under construction when Marcus raided Kleon's base six months earlier. He wondered how much his adversary had recovered from the base's destruction.

After adding wood to the growing fire, a fireman pumped the triple bellows. Before long, Marcus sensed a low vibration and saw a thin wisp of steam drift from the brass pipe.

Quintus signaled the workmen to move back. One man climbed up to the tank and opened the valve to feed more water to the boiler. The fireman—glistening with sweat—continued working the bellows.

As Marcus watched, the mist of steam transformed into an intermittent stream of thick puffs of white before pulsating into a steady blast of hot steam. This continued for several minutes.

"All right, men," Quintus yelled over the steam's howl, "stop it down." Quintus jogged to the shelter, whooping. "Marcus, we did it!"

"You did it, Quintus." Marcus clapped his engineer's back. "It's because of your hard work."

"I couldn't have done it without your support. This advanced stuff is what we engineers live for." Quintus turned to the boiler. "I better go see we get shut down properly."

Marcus walked in the man's wake but stopped after a few paces. Something seemed odd.

A workman on a ladder near the boiler pipes shouted something at Quintus. The fire was still burning, but no steam was escaping from the brass pipe. He watched the firemen work—while one man used a long, hooked pike to scatter the fire, another was heaping dirt on the flames.

Then Marcus heard a low, rumbling growl, like an enormous wild beast on the prowl. A loud whistle followed. From the boiler's back side, Marcus spied a thin ribbon of steam hissing upward. Soon, another hot stream started on the front side.

Alarmed now, Marcus called to Quintus, who was close to the front of the platform. "Quintus, what—"

"Blessed Jupiter!" yelled Quintus. "Get away from the boiler! Run!" Quintus stumbled and fell backward. "Go! Run!" he shouted as he scrambled on all fours.

Marcus sprinted for the shelter. Violent, metallic banging sounds followed another rumbling. Marcus glanced back to see metal spinning away from the boiler. The sealed seams were failing, sending hot bolts shooting off in every direction like missiles.

Marcus dove into the shelter as a massive concussive force, like a mountainside falling to the earth, slammed him hard against the far wall. The immense blast, akin to a thunderclap, left his ears ringing. It shredded the canvas roof. A white cloud of hot, wet steam roared through and over the shelter, shattering the front wall of the rough-cut building, sending splinters flying like a storm of daggers.

Marcus stared, glassy-eyed, as the world dissolved into a swirling white whirlpool. Rivulets of hot water flowed by him before seeping into the sand. The heat seared into his skin, like the caldarium of a bathhouse. Through his deadened ears came the horrific screams of men.

CHAPTER THIRTY-SEVEN

Electra
Alexandria, April 2

IT WAS EARLY morning when Electra bounded from her litter and dashed to the gate of the Bassus house. The night of the desert accident, she had received the message from Marcus informing her he was shaken but well. Doctors had arrived for the injured, and he expected to be home in a few days. He had returned late yesterday.

Titus answered her knock and led her to the tablinum, Marcus's office. She found him seated at a window overlooking the peristyle garden. He rose when she entered. Both arms and one cheek had bandages.

"Marcus," she gasped, rushing over to him. "You said you weren't hurt." She took one of his hands.

"Nothing serious." He patted her hand. "Minor cuts. I suffered hits by a lot of giant splinters."

"How bad was it? How is Quintus?"

"It was awful. One man killed, two scalded, one lost an eye. Honorius is helping the dead man's family and those of the injured." Marcus shook his head. "I feel awful for them. It's fortunate that Quintus escaped serious injury, though a piece of stone or wood hit him in the head. He was bleeding profusely when I got to him. He's mending and is back at work already."

"I'm glad for Quintus, but it's a tragedy for the dead and injured." Electra studied Marcus. Had this incidence shaken his confidence? "Do you know what happened?"

"Quintus blames a language misunderstanding. In his excitement, he fumbled between his native Latin and his Greek. He thought he said 'Shut it down' meaning the fire, but one of his boiler tenders heard, 'Close it' thinking he meant to close the steam output valve. With the valve closed, pressure built up, and the boiler exploded before the men could extinguish the fire or reposition the valve setting."

"Are your plans affected? I'm worried you could get hurt the next time." Electra embraced Marcus, who returned it before breaking away.

Marcus lowered his eyes. "I'm sorry, I can't—"

"Don't be sorry. You need time." Electra smiled and took a few steps toward the atrium but then turned around. "So, how are you and Quintus going to fix this?"

"We have a new design with a second steam output pipe. It will have a clay-like seal that will shatter under high pressure and let the steam safely escape. No more accidents."

"Are you sure it will be safe?"

"We'll make it safe. And test it many, many times." Marcus pressed his palms together.

"Good. Now, I must hurry off to the Serapeum to offer prayers to Serapis that Cleopatra's injured men receive the god's healing. Then, I'm meeting Tulla at the market. Can I come by later?"

"Most definitely. I'm tired, though, from working all last night on the scrolls. I may have figured out the message on the first scroll."

"Thank the goddess, at last!" Electra squealed and clapped her hands. She hadn't worked on the scrolls since they broke the encoding and couldn't wait for Marcus's report. "Tell me everything when I return. You get some sleep."

A half-hour later, Electra joined the throng surrounding the Temple of Serapis in the southwest of the city by the lake.

"How long will Princess Electra pray today?" asked her senior guard.

She had asked the guards not to use that title, but they persisted. It made them feel important, she figured. "An hour, maybe two," she replied, heading off through the crowd for the main entrance.

Inside, she purchased a votive bird mummy. A silver coin bought her a private viewing alcove facing the giant bearded statue of Serapis, whose animal companion, the three-headed dog, Cerberus, sat at his feet.

On a marble bench, she cast up her prayers to Serapis. She was almost complete with her litany when a priest, dressed in a traditional robe, entered.

He bowed to her. "May the Blessed Serapis grant your petitions."

"Thank you. Can I help you?"

"Princess Electra." She frowned at the word, but the man ignored the action. "The High Priestess would like to speak with you."

Her skin tingled. "Very well." Did the Serapis temple have a high priestess?

The man bowed again. "This way, please."

Electra followed the priest from the alcove and down a corridor.

She found it odd that this priest had a full head of hair. Serapis priests shaved their heads or cut their hair short. Shaking off her uneasiness, she followed the priest as he turned down a semi-dark corridor. She passed a few closed doors along the hall, guessing they were priest quarters. It seemed an odd place to meet the High Priestess.

She was coming up to a corner. As she neared the last door, someone wrenched it open, and a man stepped out. She tried to avoid him, but he reached out and flung an arm around her waist.

"What are—" Before she could finish, the priest wheeled and clamped his hand over her mouth from behind.

The sudden attack sent her heart racing. The other man pulled her toward the open door despite her kicks and punches at the priest who responded by yanking her off her feet and hauling her into the small room. All the while, she tried but failed, to scream for help. Desperate, she bit into the priest's finger, tasting salty blood. He yelled and pulled his hand away.

Electra managed the beginnings of a scream, but the second man pressed his big hand over her mouth. Despite the choking smell of sweat and grime, she continued kicking and flailing, but her efforts did not deter her captors.

"Enough." The priest drew a dagger from his robe and waved it in her face. She stopped struggling, finding her feet back on the ground. "No more screaming," he commanded, easing his hand from her mouth.

Electra sucked in a ragged breath. "Release me." She struggled to keep her voice steady. "And explain yourselves." She scrutinized their appearances. "You fools are not priests. Do you know who I am?"

A third man stepped into the room. Dressed in black, he was tall and wore a thick, black beard. "Oh, yes, Princess, we know who you are."

Electra's heart skipped a beat. "Kleon! You bastard. I thought you were off licking your wounds? Release me, or Cleopatra will have you... you... executed."

"Come, Princess. Cleopatra is somewhat busy fighting Octavian. Or perhaps she's fending off attacks from Antony's own inner circle."

"What am I to you? I'm a handmaiden. Couldn't you find any cheap Roman women you could impress into your bed?"

Kleon grimaced, his white teeth a sharp contrast to his beard. "True, Princess, but with you, I hang a sword over Marcus's head. He'll give me his Archimedes scroll and cease his efforts to construct a weapon. Or you die."

"Marcus will never give in to your bestial action. He will—"

She never finished her threat. Kleon struck her on the side of her head. Her world went black.

*

A flash of light. A snatch of sound. A gentle swaying. Dense, salty air. Pain. It brought Electra back from the whirlpool of vertigo and nothingness. Her head rolled from side to side. She was moving, laying on her back. She opened her eyes but saw nothing at first but spinning black spots. When her vision cleared, she saw slivers of light. She was in a constrained space, her arms tied to her sides. The rough linen gag in her mouth tasted like dirt, causing saliva to trickle from the corner of her mouth.

She squirmed around in the dark and rough wood scratched her skin. She was in a heavy woven basket. The swaying, undulating motion of the basket cast a trance on her, so she concentrated on the pain in her head. That centered her, and she forced her mind to work and forget the close, dark prison she was in.

Where are they taking me?

She heard bits and pieces of conversation, of shouts, of seabirds calling. She inhaled deeply and smelled the sea.

Through a small gap in the basket weave, she glimpsed the Pharos Lighthouse. They were taking her through the docks of the Great Harbor. *Kleon was taking her away from Alexandria!* She had to get out before they reached a ship. She kicked at the basket with her feet and tried to scream, but a muffled wail was all she managed. Her cry died in her throat when a sharp blade pierced through the top of the basket, stopping inches from her chest. It was immediately pulled out, but then thrust in from the basket's side near her head. The blade slid under her nose and came close to slicing her upper lip. As fast as it entered, the knife retreated. She shivered in fear.

"Don't make me kill you, Electra. We'll both lose."

Kleon.

Her chest tightened and breathing became difficult which, along with the gag, prevented her from responding to Kleon. All she could manage was a whimper. She fought back the tears, wanting to scream. The dizziness was trying to return, but she shook her head to clear it. She focused on one thought, one goal.

I must live until Marcus rescues me. I must live for Marcus. For myself, I must live.

CHAPTER THIRTY-EIGHT

Marcus
Alexandria, April 2

THE SUDDEN SHOUTING of a child caught Marcus in mid-sentence of a letter he was writing. The child's voice sounded familiar, and it was getting closer.

"Marcus. Marcus," came the shouts. Into the study burst Perimedes. "It was Kleon!" The boy was gasping.

"What? Slow down, Perimedes. Take a breath. What is this all about? Shouldn't you be at the market?"

"I saw Kleon. Down by the docks near the Emporium. He was walking toward the Western Harbor."

"Wait. How do you know Kleon?" Marcus asked.

"I was visiting once when you and Kleon were arguing at the front door. He gave you a scroll, but I don't think he wanted to."

"How do you know it was Kleon? He's grown a beard."

"He has a funny walk."

"I never noticed. Thank you, Perimedes," Marcus said in a calm voice. The boy was alarmed; he knew Kleon had killed his Uncle Lucius. "Talus and I will see that Kleon does no mischief. Neema will take you back to the market and find your mother."

"There's more, cousin. He had men with him, and they were carrying a big basket."

"A big basket?" Marcus was puzzled. What trouble was Kleon causing? He thought of Electra. Her guards should keep her safe. "I'll head over there now." Marcus called for Neema. "Neema will take you to find Aunt Tulla and—"

A loud banging interrupted him. Someone was at the front gate. Marcus hurried out into the hall. There were loud voices. Then Talus came running up the passageway, followed by a palace guard.

"What's the problem?" Marcus demanded.

"Sir, this is Peleus, one of Electra's guards." The man nodded to Marcus. "He has a report for you."

"What is it, Peleus?" Marcus swallowed. A cold chill descended his neck. *Blessed Jupiter, let it not be about Electra.*

"Sir, Electra has been missing going on four hours. We took her this morning to the Serapeum, but she is no longer there." Marcus reeled from the hammer blow of the guard's words. "They found no sign of her at the palace. The Minister of Security is dispatching a patrol to search the city for her. A detachment from Mark Antony's guards is also being—"

"Peleus, I have a report that a..." Marcus paused, not wanting to involve Perimedes, "customs official may have seen her at the docks. I suggest you go over now. Talus and I will not be far behind you."

"I'm on my way, sir. We'll find her." The guard bowed his head and headed out.

In the meantime, Neema had appeared. Marcus sent her off with Perimedes.

"Now, Talus, I have a report someone saw Kleon in the city. We may end up chasing him to find Electra. But first, find Honorius and bring him to me. He should be back in his quarters."

"Yes, sir. Back in a minute."

Marcus raced to his room and threw on a more presentable tunic. He added a belted dagger and a linen overshirt to hide the blade.

Returning to his study to await Honorius, his thoughts wanted to dwell on Electra, but he distracted himself with business paperwork Honorius would need while he was away.

Could Kleon grab her off the streets? Would he? Kleon, if you hurt Electra, I'll kill you... slowly.

Talus and Honorius dashed into the study. Marcus apprised the steward of the situation. "Honorius, I want you to get the *Neptune* ready to sail. You have two hours."

"But, sir, the *Neptune* is being loaded with wine for—"

Marcus cut off the steward. "She's the fastest ship we have. Unload as much cargo as you can. I don't know how long we'll be out. Assume ten days and load the proper supplies."

"Yes, Bassus," Honorius replied. "I'll get right on it."

"First, I have documents for you." Back in the study, Marcus handed two sealed scrolls to Honorius. "The first gives you complete authority to operate Bassus Trading in my absence. The second gives you authority to withdraw bullion from my banker, if the need arises, subject to the banker's review. I've sealed both with the Bassus ring. Finally, here's my ring. You'll be able to open new shipping contracts, pay debts, whatever may come up."

"Sir, how long will you be gone?" asked Honorius in his usual calm, serious manner.

"If Kleon's involved, that's unknowable, but let's say a month, two maybe."

"Yes, sir. I'll head to the *Neptune* at once." Honorius turned to leave.

"And Honorius, see if you can find a physician or surgeon to accompany us. Pay what he asks. Now hurry, man." Honorius dashed from the room.

Marcus called in Talus. "I need you to pack gear and hire as many mercenaries as you can—in two hours. Offer a month's worth of work."

"A month, sir?" said Talus cocking his head.

"Kleon could head anywhere, assuming he's involved." Marcus punched a fist into his palm. "If he is, I want enough manpower to convince him to release Electra."

"Should get us thirty men. More if I had the time."

"Offer a two-week bonus, if you need to. Get those men, Talus, and bring them to the *Neptune.*"

"Will do, sir." Talus's face was somber. "I'd like to get my hands around Kleon's scrawny neck. Bah. Let me get my kit and some extra clothes. I'll meet you with the mercenaries on the ship."

"Good man. I'll head over with a couple of the house guards."

Marcus and two strapping bodyguards set a rapid pace for the western-most of Alexandria's two harbors. They dodged through workers, litters, and loaded wagons, before reaching the Heptastadion, the artificial causeway linking Alexandria to Pharos Island. It divided the two Alexandrian harbors.

Marcus raced along the docks, headed for the harbormaster's office. Once there, he hurried in and stood among mounds of scrolls and clay tablets piled up in the cramped office.

The harbormaster was contentious at first, refusing to waste his time reviewing the day's sailings, but a small bribe bought his cooperation. In a moment, he produced a tablet listing a recently departed Roman ship.

Marcus grabbed the tablet. The Roman vessel, *Fortuna*, a five-oar merchant Sicily-bound, left Berth Eight. Fortuna, the god of luck.

We'll see about that, Kleon.

Marcus dashed out of the harbormaster's office and headed to Berth Eight. He arrived to find the space empty. Marcus hailed a sailor on the ship in the next berth. A copper coin loosened the man's tongue. The Berth Eight ship's destination was Apollonia, Cyrene's port city. The sailor added that the *Fortuna's* captain was tall and sported a thick black beard.

Anger raged inside Marcus at the thought of Electra in Kleon's power. He checked his emotions before sending one bodyguard to inform the palace security captain of the possibility that someone had kidnapped Electra and taken her away on the Roman ship, *Fortuna*.

He hurried over to the *Neptune's* berth farther down the Western Harbor. Honorius was overseeing the loading of supplies. The workers had stacked amphorae of wine in carts nearby.

"The crew is aboard, and all wine unloaded, Bassus. Except for ten amphorae in the third mate's quarters."

"Good thinking," said Marcus. "I'm headed for Cyrene. Send any news to our office there. Take care of things here."

"Yes, sir, we'll load supplies for crew and mercenaries in half an hour."

Marcus sent his remaining bodyguard back to the Bassus house with instructions to return if any news arrived. Electra's guard reported no sightings.

Marcus could do nothing further but wait. His bodyguard returned from the Palace with no new information. The security captain reported that the Navy had no ships to spare to search for Electra.

Bastards.

Marcus knew Agrippa, Octavian's admiral, had made it near impossible for the Egyptian navy to keep communications and supply lines open between Alexandria and Antony's field army. He and his men would be Electra's search party.

At that moment, Talus arrived leading a contingent of men. "Got us thirty-two of Alexandria's finest. Or most vile. Depends."

Marcus grinned and nodded. "I'll take them. You keep them in line, my friend."

Together, they led the mercenaries onto the ship. Marcus watched as they made themselves at home in the empty hold.

On deck, the crew prepared for departure, pulling back the heavy loading ramp and moving the rowers to their positions.

Several men on the wharf used long poles to push the ship away from its berth.

They were underway.

Marcus waved to Honorius. "We'll be back, soon."

With Electra, I hope.

Marcus

The Mediterranean Sea and Deserts of Syrtica and Cyrenaica, April 6-May 1

Four days out of Alexandria, Marcus awoke mid-morning to gentle seas and ordered Captain Socus to turn north. The *Neptune* followed the African shore for most of the day before resuming a westerly track. Since Alexandria, the seasonal northwest shift of the winds had slowed their westward progress. They made headway only through their rowers and by use of tacking. The busy helmsmen, both port and starboard, exhausted their strength by the end of each shift at the tillers.

Soon, the ship entered the Egyptian territory called Pentapolis, land of five cities. Marcus gazed over the bow as Cyrene, the principal city, came into view.

Marcus considered the *Neptune* fast for her size. With fifteen oars on each side versus five on Kleon's ship, Marcus had an edge and expected to arrive in Cyrene first.

Talus joined Marcus on the helmsman's deck. "Any sign of Kleon?"

"Not yet," Marcus replied. He swung to the first mate. "Davos, let's get a lookout on the mast."

"Yes, sir."

"Talus, get your best-eyed mercenaries at the rails. And have them prepared for action."

"They're ready. They'll be fighting each other if we don't catch

Kleon soon." Talus chuckled. "Bit of a nasty bunch, but I'll show them who's got the biggest balls."

"Talus the Titan." Marcus chuckled. Talus let loose a big laugh.

Two hours later, the low sun in their eyes, the masthead watch called. "Sail! Starboard bow. Heading southwest."

"Davos, get the oars going," Marcus commanded. "Set course to cut them off from the shore."

"Yes, sir."

The captain came up to Marcus. "Is it Kleon's ship?"

"Can't tell, Captain. I'm waiting on word from aloft." Marcus had yet to spot the unknown ship.

"The wind has backed, so we'll get more headway."

In a few minutes, Marcus and men at the rails spotted the dark red sail. He called down to the main deck. "Talus, roust the mercenaries and await my orders."

"Aye, Marcus," came Talus's retort. "You're liking this."

"I had a good teacher." The afternoons he spent with Talus going over classic sea battles of the Greeks, Persians, Egyptians and Romans—strategies, tactics, logistics—invigorating knowledge for his ever-hungry mind, flashed in his mind.

The rowing master's drum started its rhythmic beat at its slowest cadence—harbor speed. It would prepare the rowers for faster speeds.

Another call came from the masthead. "Five oars!"

Marcus peered over the starboard bow. The two ships had closed and stood less than two miles apart. Marcus couldn't count the oars, but it wasn't many. The other ship wasn't altering course.

"New sail! Off the port bow."

Marcus swiveled to port. The new sail belonged to a big ship, perhaps a returning grain carrier caught in Rome for winter. Its course was crossing the *Neptune's*.

"It's a grain carrier," announced Socus. "Doubled masted. She's riding high, carrying ballast stones only. We may have to veer off to avoid that beast."

"Keep me advised. How's our small ship?" Marcus peered starboard again. "She's swinging away."

"Masthead," Socus yelled up to the lookout. "Position of first sail."

"Moving away and picking up speed."

Socus turned to face the mass of Africa. "Damn. We're getting a land breeze off the desert. This will make the chase interesting."

"Yes, I feel it," Marcus said. He hailed Talus. "Do your mercenaries enjoy a rabbit chase?"

"They do, sir," Talus grinned.

"Captain, seems the wind is also benefiting our grain ship. Better ramp up our oars to cruising speed." Marcus worried that the grain ship would get in their way. The *Neptune* was fast, but he couldn't risk the grain ship cutting her in half. If they avoided a time-wasting maneuver, it would allow the *Neptune* to catch the smaller vessel. His gut said it was Kleon. Marcus wanted him—alive or dead.

A half-hour passed. The grain ship had moved to the north, prolonging the interval when the two ships would be crossing. Marcus paced the deck. The mercenaries' rowdy conversations hardly penetrated his consciousness. Marcus was working out the crossing angles, wind direction and speed, the condition of his rowers, and closing rates of the three ships.

It's just a geometry problem.

"Marcus, with the wind picking up, we need more speed."

Marcus observed that Captain Socus was sweating. He wasn't accustomed to this level of action.

"Recommend we advance rowers to attack speed," Socus added.

Marcus grimaced. "Can't do that, Captain. The rowers will have nothing left for the chase. The sun's setting, meaning we'll lose Kleon in the darkness. We need to close before the light goes."

"It's your ship, sir." Socus walked back and stood near the port helmsman.

Marcus peered at the grain ship. Each heartbeat brought it closer. He eyed the main deck. The mercenaries were getting restless. Some glared up at his position.

Marcus considered his options. He could stay on his current course, slowing to let the bigger ship pass. Kleon would gain enough space to slip into the darkness. He could go to attack speed, but that pace would consume the rowers' strength. His last choice was to stay his course and speed and see what happens. He could veer off at the last minute though that meant losing track of Kleon.

Over a hundred men's lives depended on his decision. Marcus chose the third option. He leaned against the starboard rail and eyed the oncoming behemoth. Below, the mercenaries were all tracking the same object, some pointing. The conversation was more subdued. Many were impassive—the veterans, who had withstood many charges in battle. They knew it was all the choice of the gods.

Don't fail me, Neptune.

Talus climbed up to Marcus. Sweat beaded his brow. "Marcus, you got this?"

Marcus nodded but continued to watch the other ship where he could now see individual men on its deck. Some were waving both arms, others signaled with strips of sailcloth over their heads. He looked up at the masthead.

"Masthead. Status on first sail."

"Course northwest. We're gaining on her."

That was good news. But the decision point was approaching. He perceived grain ships for what they were. Titans of the sea. Two hundred feet long. Twelve hundred tons bearing down on them. The *Neptune* was half that.

The drum of the row master pounded out its steady beat.

Marcus assessed the situation. It was not good. He snapped a command to Socus. "Captain! Attack speed!"

In a booming voice, Socus gave the order that sealed their fate. "Attack speed!"

At once, the drums started their frantic pace. The *Neptune* heaved forward. Time itself was running faster for Marcus. The gap between the ships closed. Sailors and soldiers were streaming away from the port side. Shouts of warning and panic rose.

For an instant, Marcus froze. The chaotic action moved in distinct steps. The faces of men nearby showed marked horror. To hesitate now meant death. He yearned for it to be done.

"Socus! Ramming speed!"

He never heard the relayed command. It was inconceivable, but the drums beat faster. In the wind of the ship's new surge, Marcus's hair flew back.

The monstrous prow of the titan, a hundred feet away, headed straight for the midsection of the *Neptune*. Marcus spied the ship's deity figurehead with its angry snarl. Socus and the two helmsmen scattered off the rear deck. Marcus gripped the rail. It was in the gods' hands now.

Fly Neptune! *Fly*!

In a single beat of his terrified heart, the grain ship, its crew yelling curses, slid by the stern of the *Neptune*. They were safe.

"Captain Socus. Oars, all stop," Marcus croaked, unable to muster the energy to yell. He heard the groans and tortured gasps of exhausted men. On deck, there was a buzz amongst the men, which quieted when Talus bellowed an order, sending them below deck.

Kleon was getting away, sliding into the gloom of twilight. Marcus could only watch.

*

After stopping in Hesperides for supplies, Marcus sent the ship south into the Gulf of Syrtis. He gambled that Kleon would sail west. There were no real ports in the eastern Gulf except for a few fishing villages. Still, Marcus wanted to check that shoreline in case Kleon was foolish enough to land and enter the desert without horses or fresh supplies. It would be suicide. Marcus judged Kleon would try for one of the southwestern ports, maybe Charax.

Midmorning, Talus joined Marcus at the rail. "Marcus, you know where Kleon is headed?"

"When I returned from the desert camp, after the boiler explosion, I stayed up all night trying to figure out the last puzzle piece for the scrolls Hippolytus had left me. We had translated twenty-five Ionic Greek letters into modern Greek. The jumbled letters formed an anagram, and that night I figured it out. I put the letters together and came up with: 'Rock Well 7 Cyrene Alexandria.'"

Talus scratched his head "What does that mean?"

"I believe it's a location. If someone travels south from Cyrene and someone else comes west from Alexandria, they'll eventually cross at a point in the desert south of the Green Mountains in Cyrenaica."

"And that's where Kleon is heading?"

"Yes. I don't know yet what the word 'rock' means. Perhaps 'well' means water well. The question is from what direction will he be traveling? East? Unlikely. He would have done so soon after leaving Alexandria. South from Cyrene? That's possible. I'm hoping our near-intercept of him yesterday persuades him to avoid that route."

"He'll come from the west?"

Marcus stared at the blue-green water as it slid by the ship. "Yes. I hope we can cut him off somehow."

*

The second day in the Gulf, late afternoon, Marcus was at the bow with a lookout. Charax, with its excellent anchorage, rose on the horizon, and Marcus ordered an approach from the east.

After an hour of sailing, the masthead lookout cried, "Sail! Well off to starboard."

Marcus searched the sea before spotting the dark sail. Soon, he determined the ship was southbound, on a strong wind from that quarter. It was on a perpendicular path to his.

Is it Kleon?

Marcus passed Talus on the way aft. "Alert your mercenaries," Marcus advised him. "That ship could be Kleon."

At the helmsman's deck, Socus greeted him. "Bassus, we'll know soon whether that incoming ship is Kleon's. I've alerted the row master."

A quarter of an hour later, the Captain made his assessment. "By Jupiter, it's the same ship we chased near Cyrene. That dark red sail on that size ship is quite distinct."

As Marcus watched, the two ships paths began to converge. At a mile apart, Marcus was amazed to see someone on the other ship waving a white cloth or banner. It was only there for a few heartbeats before it stopped. "Someone on that ship just signaled to us," Marcus exclaimed.

"Where?" Socus searched the far ship. "I see nothing."

"It's stopped. It has to be Electra."

"They're turning away." Socus pointed to the red-sailed ship.

"Set a course for that ship and put the rowers at cruising speed. We've got you now, Kleon, you bastard."

"Helmsmen, come to starboard," Socus ordered. For a long minute, they heeled about before Socus called the mark. "Center your helms."

On the lower deck, Marcus saw Talus bringing up his men. Marcus called to him, "Talus—"

A cry from the masthead drowned Marcus's words. "Sandbank! Dead ahead!"

"Hard starboard!" Socus yelled.

Marcus grabbed the rail as the ship heeled hard to the right. A heartbeat later, there was the grinding noise before the ship slammed to a halt, sending Marcus tumbling along the rail and down the steps to land face-first on the deck. He heard loud metallic sounds of armored men crashing to the deck and against the rails. Cries of shock and pain filled the air.

Marcus crawled back to his feet. A trickle of blood ran down from a split lower lip. Still dazed, he wobbled to the rail and peered over the side. The bow of the ship had cut into a sandbank. They were notorious in this quadrant of the Gulf.

They were dead in the water.

Marcus scrambled back up to Captain Socus's position. The man's head must have struck the ship's rail as blood flowed from a gash on his head. A sailor brought him a scrap of linen which Socus applied to his wound.

"Are you all right, Captain?"

"I'll see the ship's surgeon soon. I must have misjudged the tides. Excuse me, but I need to access the damage." He headed forward.

Marcus gazed out over the port side where he saw the red sail fading into the horizon.

*

Half a day was lost in making repairs. The *Neptune* came off the sandbank during the evening tide, backing away under oar power.

They sailed from Charax at noon the next day. For the following three days, they stopped at every port and small fishing village along the southwestern and western shores of the Gulf of Syrtis. Nobody reported seeing the *Fortuna*.

In Thubactis, it was a different story. The ancient Phoenician city, now Roman, existed because of its proximity to an inland oasis. Kleon had stopped there. A few merchants had sold him supplies of bread and water. They said Kleon sailed to the west.

Studying the Bassus Periplus of the coastline around Cyrene, Marcus spotted the likeliest port for Kleon—Leptis. It was another Phoenician and Carthaginian settlement, and Bassus ships often traded there for ivory and gold. Kleon needed food, and the city had many coastal farms. He also required horses and pack animals.

The map blurred before Marcus as his mind wandered. He searched his memories for a time when Kleon had meant friendship and camaraderie. They were there somewhere in his memories, but his hate overwhelmed them. He turned back to the map and tapped the city of Leptis before ordering Captain Socus to sail for it. The *Neptune* was also running low on supplies.

From the upper deck, Marcus watched several of the mercenaries loitering on the main deck. Talus soon showed up, and Marcus filled him in on his plans.

Talus rubbed his short-cropped hair. "Glad Kleon's going to ground. Gives these men something to do. I'm tired of seeing all those sour faces."

"I understand." Marcus again scanned the mercenaries, who were now checking their gear.

"If he's not gone to ground at Leptis, you'll have my sour face to look at as well." Talus released a terse laugh.

*

Leptis had a harbor protected by two breakwaters. As the *Neptune* slid by the harbor's lighthouse in the late morning of the twelfth day, Marcus was taut with nervous energy when he spotted Kleon's small merchant ship.

After docking, Marcus, Talus, and ten mercenaries made their way along the wharf to Kleon's ship. They found the ship deserted except for a couple of sailors lounging on crates stacked on the main deck. Reluctant to talk initially, their lips loosened when Marcus offered them a handful of silver coins.

"We docked here yesterday," a bald sailor, coughing, informed Marcus. "Kleon bought supplies and horses." More coughing. "Kleon and ten or twelve men took off this morning heading east. He ordered the rest of us back to Sicily."

"Where's the young woman he had on board?" Marcus knew better, but he hoped somehow that Electra was in Leptis.

"Went riding, too. Now, that was a sweet morsel. And feisty as—"

Marcus wanted to pull his sword and run the man through but checked his anger. "Careful of your mouth, you worthless dog," Marcus growled. Two of Marcus' men moved up, but he waved them back.

"Sorry, sir," the sailor said in a subdued voice. "I meant no offense."

Marcus calmed himself and sent Talus to buy horses.

As he hurried back to the *Neptune*, he considered the sailor's words. It gave Marcus all the confirmation he needed that Kleon was headed for the desert south of Cyrene to recover something, perhaps more scrolls. Back in his cabin, he again consulted the Periplus for the Gulf of Syrtis's desert coast.

Kleon had a half day's head start, but Marcus was confident they would catch him and rescue Electra.

Every night at sea, he would lie awake thinking of the woman he loved. Their frozen feelings for each other awaited the outcome of the all but declared civil war. Only last month, after Octavian made an ominous threat on the floor of the Senate, several hundred senators had fled Rome to join Antony in Greece. When he would finally fall asleep, he would be plagued by fitful dreams of Kleon and Electra. Somewhere mixed in, he felt the presence of his father.

A few hours later, Talus entered the cabin. "Sir, I could get only twenty horses and five mules. Even offered twice the market price. Fools."

"We'll make do with whatever supplies you found." Marcus still believed he would outnumber Kleon's forces.

"I found a local guide who knows the desert road between Leptis and Cyrene. Worked the caravans for twenty years. Knows the oasis' locations."

Marcus clapped. "Great. We'll need that water along the way, that's for sure. Now, one more task for you. I need a stake to serve as my gnomon."

"What? Are you making a sundial?" Talus asked, confusion in his voice.

Marcus chuckled. "In a sense, yes. Here, let me write down the exact length I need. Find a woodworker or a furniture maker."

"Whatever you say, Marcus." Talus headed out.

As the big man was leaving, Captain Socus entered. "Bassus, sir, we bought all the supplies you wanted and they're ready for packing on the horses."

"Excellent," Marcus replied. "Captain, here are your orders. Sail back to Apollonia. If all goes as planned, I'll meet up with you there in three weeks or so. If I don't show in four…," Marcus considered his next words, "… I'm probably dead, so return to Alexandria and report to Honorius. He'll know what to do."

Marcus took eighteen men plus Talus and hired Talus's guide. Each man had provisions of food and water while the pack animals carried another week's worth.

After everyone had a midday meal in their bellies, Marcus rode out of Leptis. The coastal road was in passable condition, with the

Romans improving it over the years, and allowed a pace of thirty to forty miles on a good day.

Marcus and his force rode for ten days through the blistering heat, traversing most of the entire windswept Gulf coastline. Their only stop was in Charax for fresh food and fodder.

For the last two of those ten days, heading north along the Gulf's eastern shore, Marcus had stopped his force at midday to take a sun reading. He had Eratosthenes's *Geography*, describing his method for calculating the Earth's circumference and also a copy of Hipparchus's *Table of Climata*. Marcus consulted the tables that recorded the lengths of shadows of a standard gnomon—his stake—as seen at Alexandria on specific days of the year. Marcus would have to interpolate in the table because there were no entries for the current date—April twenty-fifth. He had to locate the parallel for Alexandria.

On the third day, while the men sheltered out of the sun in hastily pitched tents, Marcus sat on a rock and scribbled his calculations on a clay tablet.

Talus came up and peeked over his shoulder. "So, Learned One, discovered anything?"

Marcus held up a hand, then scribbled for several moments. "Based on my crude calculations, we're not far south of the parallel for Alexandria."

"The 'para'—what was that word?

"Parallel. How can I explain it? The Earth is a sphere, not a flat plane. Draw a circle around the sphere running east-west at the point mid-way between the top and bottom of the world, and you'll have the parallel that geographers call the equator. It's an imaginary line where the sun is directly overhead on the summer solstice. Every point on that line lies an equal distance from the poles. Every point on earth has a parallel running through it. I want to find the parallel for Alexandria. From anywhere on Earth if you follow that parallel—however long that might take—you will arrive at Alexandria. Clear? The gnomon, this stick, casts a shadow like a sundial. By knowing the date and the length of the shadow, I can calculate which parallel we're at."

"Bah. You scientists. Sorry for asking. Just point me to where I can find Kleon so I can run him through."

Marcus shook his head. "That'll happen soon enough. If we head east along the Alexandria parallel, we should cross the north-south line running down from Cyrene."

"How will we know when we get there?"

"I'm not sure, Talus," Marcus replied. "Not sure at all."

The guide, Erginus, joined them. "Sir, will we be continuing further north? I ask because there is an oasis a few hours ride north."

Marcus considered the guides information. "What do you think, Talus? Continue to the oasis, camp, then head east?"

Talus grunted. "Sounds good to me."

"East?" asked the guide. "Sir, are we going to turn east? At the oasis ahead, an old smuggler's track travels east across the desert to the coast on the far side of Cyrene at the border with Marmarica. It's a rugged road but still easier than going cross country."

"I'm all for roads," said Talus.

"I can't argue with that, Erginus. We ride north."

*

At sunrise, Marcus led his men east under an azure sky. To conserve water, they continued their daily plan, riding out at dawn for four or five hours, then sheltering either in tents or in the shade of low dunes. Before dark, they resumed the trek along the ancient route.

In mid-afternoon on the first of May, the fifth day on the old road, Marcus approached Talus. "We're getting close to the line south from Cyrene, but the caravan track is bearing to the north."

"I noticed," said Talus. "Should we strike out east?"

"I'm not sure. The two of us should scout what's ahead."

When Talus agreed, Marcus informed the men. "We'll be back in two hours."

He and Talus galloped east from camp. The deepening sands soon slowed the horses to a walk. The winds blew stronger with each step away from the road. Marcus tied a wet cloth over his face to ease the discomfort of the unbearable heat and the choking dust. Only his eyes showed.

After riding an hour, Marcus approached a low ridge. At the top, he halted and scanned ahead but saw only endless miles of sand. To the north toward Cyrene, he thought he could detect the tips of mountains through the flickering mirages hovering on the horizon.

"Not much to see, Talus. I guess we should head back." Marcus turned his horse. That's when he saw it. He pulled back on the reins.

Talus expressed both their feelings. "Shit."

CHAPTER THIRTY-NINE

Marcus
Cyrenaica Desert, May 1-3

A WALL OF sand was moving from the south across the path back to camp.

Marcus tried to catch his breath. Around him the sand stirred, mimicking his rising panic. Talus moved his skittish horse alongside, grimacing and shaking his head. Marcus saw something rare on his friend's face: fear.

Marcus had seen powerful sandstorms in Alexandria and knew they often ravaged the deserts of Cyrenaica. Two such eruptions had struck them last week along the Gulf's southern coast. Each time the storm had quickly blown out to sea. This inland storm was different.

He stared at it, black and angry, swirling sand and chaos high into the air. Lightning flashes pierced the turbulent mass as it marched across the landscape. The disturbance had risen without warning along the southern horizon moving north, placing them in the path of the storm's broad front.

They had to reach the camp's shelter.

Marcus shouted, "We need to return to camp. Let's go." He kicked his horse's ribs and bolted forward. He heard Talus whip the reins across the shoulders of his horse and follow. Behind them, he saw their dust cloud billowing into the torrid desert air.

They rode hard, but after a quarter of an hour, Marcus reined in his horse. It was hopeless. The storm was moving too fast. It was still miles away, but the unsettled air was already stirring up the surrounding desert, and thunder rolled overhead. Marcus felt his heartbeat pulsing in his ears.

Talus halted beside him. "What's the plan?"

Marcus stared ahead. "It's clear we can't make it to the men. I hope they've found shelter, which is what we need to do."

"Not much around here." Talus scanned the area toward the approaching wall of flying sand.

"Over there," Marcus pointed north. "See that dark smudge a mile out?"

Talus squinted. "Could be a rock outcrop or gully?"

"We've got to go for it. Come on."

After five minutes of hard riding, their destination came into focus—a limestone uplift. Maybe they'd find a cave. Marcus would settle for a ledge he could dig under for shelter. On reaching the leeward side of the rocks, he halted his horse and dismounted. Sand stung his face.

"The weathered-out space under that rock ledge," Talus shouted over the swirling wind. "It's the best we got."

"What about the horses? We can't leave them loose." Marcus yelled back. The dull roar of the maelstrom grew louder.

"There's a sturdy bush over in the lee of the storm." The big man jumped down, handing over his reins.

Marcus struggled to hold the prancing horses as Talus retrieved the tethers. Gusts of wind-whipped sand beat against his body.

"I'll take the horses and tie them down." Talus tossed Marcus a trowel. "Here, dig out more space." He led the two horses behind the rocks.

Marcus dug under the large rock shelf. Blowing sand stung

every inch of exposed skin. His eyes burned. The angry demon, only minutes away, was obliterating the daylight with frightening speed. He worked like a madman, racing to gorge out enough space for both of them.

Talus returned, carrying a waterskin, two blankets, and tent stakes. "I found a narrow cut in the rocks. The horses should be fine." Talus studied the storm. "Hold up, Marcus. No more time. The beast is here." He tore a couple of strips from a blanket. "Wet this and put it over your mouth and nose. Keeps sand out. Now in you go. Face the rocks."

Marcus wedged in as far as he could and pressed the wet blanket to his face. He heard Talus pounding the stakes, covering the exposed side with the blankets. Before the big man slid in behind him, Marcus thought he picked up the shrill whinny of the horses.

The storm struck with god-like violence. Marcus squeezed his eyes down to narrow slits. The scream of the wind, the roar of the sand, and the rumble of thunder assaulted his ears. An image of the dark abyss in the Temple of Artemis's treasure room filled his mind, bringing a taste of bile. He fought his panic.

"Hang on."

He couldn't tell if that was Talus or his own mind speaking to him.

The tempest raged into the night. It was hours before it abated, and an eerie silence settled on the desert. Marcus fell into a fitful sleep.

*

Dawn lighted the horizon as Marcus helped Talus tend the bedraggled horses, watering and feeding them. They had water for one more day.

They mounted and rode west into the still unsettled desert, searching for the road and any sign of the men. The night's sandstorm had blown the landscape into a smooth, featureless plain. After resting out of the searing afternoon sun, they continued a weaving search line, dipping south, then north.

As the fiery sun dipped below the horizon, Marcus heard a shout ahead from Talus.

"Marcus! The road." Talus dismounted as Marcus rode up. Using his trowel and his huge hands, Talus scraped away at the hot sand, exposing the packed surface of the road.

"Thank the gods," Marcus exclaimed.

"Follow it west or east?" asked Talus, remounting.

"We'll go west until dark." Marcus slumped forward, weary from the two-week ride. He thought of Electra, and a new determination rose in him, restoring his energy. "I expect we'll find the men somewhere toward the oasis."

The next day, after losing the road a few times, Marcus spied a party of men in the distance. "Talus, it's them!" He wanted to cheer.

As they galloped closer, he saw the men camped behind a small dune. Erginus was first to greet them.

"Sir. Talus. We thought the storm took you."

Marcus dismounted and clapped the guide on the shoulder. "We thought the same of you. How are the men? And you?"

The guide pointed to the men. "They are well enough. That storm was straight from Hades. We lost most of the tents. We found water in an old well near the road. It's often dry, but this winter was wetter than usual." Erginus wiped his brow. "We got lucky. But eight men deserted, taking water and supplies."

"Those bastards," growled Talus. "After I paid them double."

Marcus scanned the roused men. "That leaves us nine?"

"Yes, including me," said Erginus. "We have horses and enough donkeys. Some nomads came through yesterday. We traded some abandoned gear from our deserters for feed for the animals and a little food for us, too. We've got water from the oasis. Is nine men enough?"

Marcus didn't need to think. "It has to be. We'll move out at first light. Talus, can you see to the horses?" Marcus went over to the quiet group of mercenaries, trying without success to gauge their mood. He offered another month of employment, and despite their mutterings about more storms, the men all begrudgingly agreed to continue.

He grabbed a blanket and found shade for a nap, his body aching. He fell into a deep, dreamless sleep.

Talus shook him awake hours later. "Hungry, sir? One of our archers shot a gazelle this morning."

"Fresh meat? I won't turn that down."

After the best meal he'd had in weeks, Marcus led his reduced party back east along the road. When it turned northeast, Marcus continued to follow the road.

"Do you think he's out here?" Talus asked, his voice subdued.

"He has to be. He just has to be."

"Aye, Commander."

As night descended, Marcus heard a shout and rode ahead, with Talus close behind. Erginus had dismounted and was inspecting a dark shape on the sand.

"Dead horse," said Talus. He jumped down and walked over to the dead animal.

"Broken leg," said Erginus. "I'd say the carcass is three days old."

"Throat's cut," added Talus. "Didn't suffer."

Marcus dismounted and joined the two men. "Nomad's horse, do you think?

"No, tribesmen wouldn't leave good horse meat."

Talus walked ahead several paces before calling out, "Over here. Got the body of a man."

Marcus and Erginus ran to the spot. Erginus knelt to examine the partially-buried body. "I know this man," he said. "He's from my town and works as a guide and caravan guard. He must have been guiding Kleon."

"Appears Kleon has no guide now," said Marcus.

"Well, there's a bunch of tracks leading north," observed Talus.

"It has to be Kleon," said Marcus. "We'll camp here tonight. In the morning, we ride north. All day if we must, by the gods."

After remounting, he noticed the dusty and exhausted men now gathered about and staring at him. Even in the fading light, he could tell they weren't pleased.

CHAPTER FORTY

Marcus

Cyrenaica Desert, May 4

FOR HALF THE morning, Marcus and his men followed the tracks they had found yesterday. The hoof prints were prominent in the softer ground but barely visible where exposed to the winds. At the base of a line of high dunes, Marcus ordered a halt to rest the animals.

Leaving their mounts below, Marcus, Talus and Erginus climbed one of the higher dunes, which promised a view to the north. The climb was steep, forcing Marcus to scramble with his hands as much as with his feet.

Surmounting the dune's shifting sands, he sat on its thin cap, flushed from exertion. The morning sun glinted off the wavy sand that stretched endless to north and south. Tall, swirling dust devils reminded him of the sandstorm.

Between the glare and the imposing lines of dunes, Marcus didn't get the view he wanted.

"Gods, not much to see," said Erginus, panting.

"An army could hide in those dunes," added Talus. "Good view there." He pointed to the west.

Marcus scanned left. A massive slanting slab of rock interrupted the dune line. The rock jutted into the sky, dominating the landscape.

"Let's head there."

Marcus slid halfway down the dune before regaining his feet. On reaching his horse, he examined the rough faces of the mercenaries and thought about his idyllic days in the Library. Life always seemed to push him toward unsavory choices.

An hour later, the party had trekked over to the uplifted rocky slab.

"Quite the rock pile," observed Erginus.

The slab's base was a jumble of rocks. After a short search, the men found a manageable passage. Marcus and Talus walked their horses through the narrow rift and onto the hard-packed slope of the hill.

"Is it safe for the horses?" Marcus kicked the ground. "It seems firm enough."

"Agreed. Be careful of holes. Breaks legs."

Marcus mounted his horse and ordered the others to find shade and rest. The footing was tricky. Marcus, sensing his horse slipping, found his heart in his throat several times. The rock slab was steep, hard-packed, and devoid of vegetation.

After a quarter of an hour, Marcus dismounted, marveling at the incredible vista. Several hundred feet below was the desert floor where line after wavy line of dunes rolled northward toward Cyrene. There, the tops of hills approaching the Green Mountains peeked over the horizon. Each dune line flowed east and west across the plain. Far to the east, he saw a thin smudge of color, likely the road preferred by tax-evading caravans running between Cyrene and Siwa in Egypt's western desert. The purity and starkness of the land held a unique beauty.

Marcus broke away from the panorama. He saw Talus staring at an area below them. "What is it?"

"There." Talus pointed north. "Little dust cloud."

Marcus gauged the cloud was two miles away. "It's a rider, moving north."

"Kleon's man?"

Marcus moved close to the edge of the rock slab. That's when he saw the line of riders emerging from the dunes to the northeast. "Talus, look there. They're headed west to intercept the single rider. It can only be Kleon with Electra." Sweat burst from every pore. He leaned forward trying to catch more detail. So close now, he felt a mixture of dread and hope. A realization dawned, and he took a step toward the cliff's edge.

Talus yanked Marcus back. "Are you sun sick? You can't go that way."

"I'll take my horse." Marcus tried to step forward, but Talus held him tight.

"It's a sheer drop, Marcus. You'll kill yourself. Worse, you'll kill a good horse."

"Very funny. But I understand the anagram now. 'Rock' is where we're standing. It's the end of the north-south line from Cyrene. Where the lone horseman heading north meets the riders from the east is where the old well is with the additional Archimedes scrolls. The ones with the real power. We have to stop them and get Electra."

From his elevated position, Marcus examined the panorama below. It was unambiguous in his mind now. The Apollo scroll, with its catapult design, was a mere demonstration of steam's power. The true power of steam—or something even more powerful—lay buried in the desert sand near the well.

Marcus slapped his hands together. Kleon was not going to escape with Electra and the Archimedes scrolls. Somehow, he would stop the bastard.

Marcus went back to the edge, his fists clenched. "Kleon! Kleon!" He yelled as loud as he could, but the vastness of the desert swallowed his voice.

When he realized the ride to intercept Kleon would take hours, Marcus rushed over to his mount and leaped onto it. "Come on. Let's get that ass." Without waiting, Marcus slapped his horse and tore off down the slope.

"Marcus, slow down," cried Talus.

Marcus didn't react to the warning in time. His horse, propelled ever faster down the steep slope, could not keep its footing. Marcus pulled back on the reins, but the horse's front legs collapsed, launching him forward over the head of the animal. He landed hard on his chest and knees and slid down the slope, trailing dust and a hail of small stones. A large rock rose out of the ground ahead of him.

It was the last thing he remembered.

Kleon
Cyrenaica Desert, May 4

Excitement rose in Kleon's chest. For days, he had measured the shadow cast by his crude gnomon. This last measurement was dead on for the Alexandrian parallel.

Yesterday's reading showed him too far north, so he had ridden south. The discovery of the huge rock slab, with its sheer side facing north to Cyrene, had convinced him it was the reference in Archimedes' cryptic anagram: RockWell6CyreneAlexandria. He couldn't thank Sarpedos enough for providing the last piece for solving the scroll's puzzle.

Now he was riding with Electra and his men to the spot of the final clue—a desert well. The flatness of the landscape gave him hope that, in the two centuries since Archimedes buried his scrolls, the shifting sands had not inundated the well.

Kleon glanced back at Electra, her horse tethered to his by a rope. The captivity, the riding, and the heat were taking their toll. Despite her exhausted appearance and hollowed eyes, she maintained a stubborn expression. Kleon had never seen such determination.

What a wife she would make.

For now, his hope was that Marcus was far away. They needed rest before continuing to Cyrene.

Kleon resumed his search of the desert while his mind mulled over the wisdom of going behind Cimber's—and Octavian's—back. Not trusting either, he didn't tell them he had solved the writings on page two and three. Whatever he found out here must give him leverage to bargain for power after his super-ship defeated Antony. Electra was his leverage against interference from Marcus.

Kleon had tried to tempt Electra again this morning, promising to wed her when he became a provincial governor. Again, she rejected him. No matter, that would be her fate.

One of his men galloped up beside him.

"Pardon, sir. The men were wondering. Do we still need the woman? She slows us down."

Kleon laughed. "She's my security against Marcus Bassus. Now, keep to your tasks. I'll worry about the woman."

"Yes, sir." The man fell back.

Kleon broke out of his thoughts at a strange sound. Was someone yelling? A trick of the wind? Was it his man riding from the rock slab? Wait. He heard it again. A low, drawn-out note of… anger. It almost sounded like his name. He pulled up and searched in all directions.

Is that you, Marcus? You're too late, fool. The scrolls are mine. I win. You lose.

CHAPTER FORTY-ONE

Marcus
Cyrenaica Desert, May 6

MARCUS WOKE UP with a terrible pounding in his head. Though he had never lost consciousness completely, he had been too dizzy to ride. How long had he slept? He looked around and saw the horses, including his, tied in a line nearby, munching at the thin grass. He then spotted Talus trotting toward him.

"You all right, Marcus?" the big man asked. "That was a nasty knock. You were loopy there for a few minutes."

Marcus rubbed his head where a knot had formed. "I'll be fine. Please get me some water and food."

A half-hour later, he ordered the men to mount up for the ride after Kleon. After inspecting his horse, he found no broken bones. Still a little dizzy, he carefully mounted his horse and fell in with his men.

After two hours of hard riding, he and his men reached the area of the well where Marcus found several small digs and one large one from which the top of a well was visible. Tracks led away to the north.

For two days, they tracked toward the mountains. Marcus knew where Kleon was going—Cyrene, due north from the uncovered dry well. Kleon must have found the additional manuscripts that Archimedes described in the scrolls stolen from the Temple of Artemis. These new scrolls, he surmised, held the knowledge of terrible powers leading the four men—Archimedes, Ctesibius, Eratosthenes and Philo—to hide the scrolls in the first place.

"We have an advantage, Talus," Marcus remarked. "We know Kleon's destination."

"Aye. We can drive the men somewhat harder." Talus glanced at the men following behind. "They won't mind."

Marcus knew that the unrelenting heat, poor food, rationed water, and the endless riding were taking their toll on his men. Every day, he pushed the mercenaries that extra hour. On the second day, significant grumbling began. Even Talus was not his even-tempered self, often lashing out at every provocation.

Erginus and Talus tracked Kleon through the desert plain and into the foothills, still soft from recent rainfall. As they moved further north, the rocky ground of the hills and mountains was proving difficult, and they lost Kleon's trail several times.

Out of the scorching desert at last, Marcus noticed the sky darkening. As he and his men neared the first slopes of the Green Mountains, they stopped for the afternoon rest and watched sheets of cold rain, the first since Leptis, crash onto the parched desert. Lightning cracked across the sky, and thunder echoed off the mountainsides.

During the evening ride, the storm broke but not before drenching every man and animal. Beginning their climb into the mountains, Erginus told Marcus the slopes often ended at cliffs or promontories, but many valleys and passes allowed the passage to the north.

As the sun settled, they lost Kleon's trail again, eliciting curses from Marcus. If they didn't regain the track, and soon, hope was slim that they would rescue Electra. The scrolls—with all their knowledge—would fall into the hands of Octavian, a power-crazed tyrant.

To add to his misery, more lightning sliced the darkening sky ahead. He was just drying out from the earlier deluge.

Marcus called a short rest and then turned to his trackers. "If another storm hits before we pick up his trail, Kleon might slip away, and we'll lose Electra." Unpleasant thoughts crept into his mind.

"It's getting dark," Erginus added. "I can't track in the dark."

Talus rubbed his chin. "Could use torches."

"That would work," Erginus acknowledged.

"If the rain doesn't return," Marcus said. As his eyes swept north, a bright bolt of lightning struck the top of the mountain to the east. Rather than a brief shattering of the gloom, this strike went on for many seconds. Silhouetted against the flashes were a line of riders less than a quarter mile away.

Marcus couldn't believe his eyes, and for a moment, couldn't find his voice, but then he shouted, "There! Did you see that? Riders. On that ridge a little to the east." He pointed northeast.

Erginus stared up the slope. "If he's on that ridge, we have him. It ends in a huge outcropping; a promontory called the King's Throne. It's sheer cliff on three sides with only a narrow neck connecting it to the approach ridge."

"It's already raining up ahead," added Talus. "Coming this way."

A streak of lightning flashed across the sky, followed by a blast of thunder causing several horses to jerk their heads and whinny. Marcus patted his horse, feeling a kindred unease. Going up the naked slope in a thunderstorm wasn't his first choice, but Electra was going through the same danger. He wouldn't fail her now.

Marcus lifted his chin, saying. "We must reach that ridge before Kleon realizes his mistake. Let's get moving."

Talus called to the men. "Mount up, boys. We've trapped us a wild pig."

In the failing sunlight and growing lightning, Marcus and his men raced up the ridge. Erginus, the best horseman, led the way followed by Talus. Soon, he pointed to a piece of cloth dangling from a thorny bush.

Marcus hastened upward, taking in the dank, earthy smell of the mud churned up by the horses. He took a quick glance at the thin, soggy linen that flapped in the wind gusts. Was it a sign from Electra?

A chill passed through him. He avoided thinking of her suffering, concentrating instead on what he would do to Kleon. His thoughts were dark and shamed him. In the Greek plays he had read in the Library, men were often the playthings of the gods, without a will of their own. If so, he would defy the gods. They would not bend his will away from his goals. He would save Electra, and Kleon would receive the swift justice he deserved for his father and for the men who died in the Spanish mines.

Consider your situation, Kleon. A fronte praecipitium a tergo lupi. A precipice before, wolves behind.

*

An hour later, the ridge leveled off, and Marcus was closing in on the narrow bridge of land that led to the King's Throne. With the soft ground and the echoing thunder covering the sound of their approach, they pressed the horses. They now rode the high escarpment that overlooked Cyrene and the fertile coastal plain. A few lights glowed in the far distance.

"It's a beautiful view in daylight," said Erginus. "Can't see much now."

As they neared the promontory, the storm abated, passing through the mountains, where it would dry up over the desert. The lightning, however, was undiminished, and in a bright flash of light, Marcus spotted riders ahead.

"There," yelled Talus. "Three hundred feet ahead."

"Kleon must have realized his mistake by now. Fan out," Marcus ordered. "Archers, prepare your bows. Remember; do not fire on the woman."

Another flash exposed Kleon's party galloping back toward the land bridge leading to the ridge and Marcus's position. Kleon must soon realize the futility of his situation and surrender without a bloody fight.

Seconds later, flickering lightning showed two riders, swords drawn, entering the connecting neck, twenty feet wide and fifty feet long. Marcus could not spot Electra.

The distance between his party and the two charging men closed. Marcus drew his gladius.

"Archers, prepare to fire at will." The noise from the galloping horses echoed off the cliffs.

Would they spring out of the dark, hacking and slashing their way through his line?

His answer came in the next flash as Kleon's men charged across the connecting neck.

"Fire," Marcus yelled, an instant before thunder shook his chest.

Three arrows shot out. From the darkness, came the screams of men and horses. A moment passed before a flurry of flashes showed the results. A body with two arrows protruding lay on the ground. Beside it lay a horse in its death throes, an arrow in its neck. Now running free, the second horse dashed past Marcus's line, down the ridge, and into the night.

Another flash of light across the sky revealed the unhorsed rider racing back to the King's Throne. An arrow found the leg of the warrior who screamed in pain before darkness closed in. A moment later, a scream melted into the night. Then, Marcus heard nothing. The man must have fallen off the precipice.

"Close up, boys." It was Talus. He dismounted and walked

forward, gladius in hand. "Take up defensive positions across the narrows."

Marcus was relieved to delegate, if only for a while, the military maneuvers to Talus. The man had years of experience in the legions. Marcus dismounted and moved beside Talus. "What's the plan? Do we attack now?"

"Not tonight, Marcus." Talus's face was unreadable in the dark, but his tone was confident. "Too risky. We can hold this small front against Kleon's forces. If Erginus is right about no way down, we can starve Kleon out."

"But he still has Electra. If he threatens to…" Marcus couldn't say the unthinkable. "I can't risk her life."

"Kleon's a dead man if he harms Electra. It's a stalemate."

"Yes, you're right." Marcus gripped the pommel of his sword to stay his trembling hand.

"The men and horses are both exhausted." Talus scanned up and down the shadowy rank of men. "I'll set up the watch. You should get some rest."

Sleep eluded Marcus. In the first hour, he bolted upright when he heard men screaming from across the neck of land. There was a scream of terror that ended abruptly. Kleon must have sent a man down the cliff face.

"One less man to fight," Talus said. "Foolish to descend that cliff in daylight; madness in the dark."

"That may be true," replied Marcus, "but we need to avoid a fight and make Kleon consider one option—surrender." Marcus paced. "We need a plan."

Talus held out his hand, stopping Marcus. "I have an idea."

Marcus peered up at the big man, his face vague in the darkness. "I need a good idea right now."

"I didn't say it was a *good* idea."

CHAPTER FORTY-TWO

Electra
King's Throne, Cyrenaica, May 7

ELECTRA'S MIND SPUN in dizzying patterns as events of the last few weeks flashed across her consciousness. Ocean waves and seasickness. Endless days along the coastal road with its meager farms and herds of emaciated livestock, all the while bouncing against a horse's hard back. Hunger and thirst gnawed at her. Food and water had been scarce during the past couple of days. Lying on the rough, wet ground, her eyes furtively scanned her immediate surroundings, but she saw no one, perceived nothing but the miserable rain.

Where are they?

A guard watched her day and night. When they traveled, they roped her horse behind that of one of Kleon's smelly men. A faint smile formed on her parched and cracked lips—no doubt her body smelled as rotten. Voices came from the back of the promontory, the section away from the narrow neck of land they had traversed earlier. After crossing, they dragged her from her horse, then rode off. Maybe this was her chance to escape.

Electra sat up and allowed her dizziness to subside. Little by little, she rose to her feet, hoping no one saw her. The pitch-black night hid the spot where the narrow path crossed back to the ridge and her rescue. Earlier in a flash of lightning, she had spotted a group of pursuing horsemen on the ridge, so close now. A cautious step brought the snap of a stick under her foot. She stopped and listened, again hearing voices.

Now. Go now, her mind screamed.

"Where ya going, woman?" came a gruff voice.

She whirled around and got a brief glimpse of a cruel face before a rough hand squeezed her throat. She closed her eyes in terror, fighting futilely against a muscular arm. Her broken fingernails clawed the arm, causing the brute to yelp, but his grip never wavered.

Electra gasped for air, and her world faded, replaced by blackness. Her legs quivered. She was cold.

Sometime later she awoke, flat on her back. It was still dark with no visible stars overhead. A rough piece of cloth gagged her mouth, and ropes bound her hands and feet. She shifted onto her side, and the blackness still filled her vision. Sliding her feet forward, she scrapped across some loose rocks. The stones rolled away, gathering more rocks as they slid.

They had put her next to a cliff!

With the gag, her scream turned into a muted croak. She rolled back and wriggled and pushed away from the precipice. Sharp stones raked across her back and hips, causing her to wince in pain and choke back a cry.

"Going somewhere, princess? Not a good move."

It was Kleon's voice. Her attempt to cry out only resulted in muffled sobs escaping her gag. Rough arms grabbed her by the back of her tunic and jerked to her feet. With her tunic pulled to the top of her thighs, she stared at her vile captor, a lascivious grin on his face. Though defenseless, weak and frightened, her narrowed eyes poured hatred at Kleon.

Kleon gave a signal, and the brute holding her up dragged her across the rocky ground.

Through her restraint, she shouted crude epithets at Kleon, vile words picked up from Mark Antony. The gag soaked up her words.

When the dragging stopped, Electra was next to a near-dead tree that clung to the cliff, near to the neck. Kleon stepped forward and tossed a rope over a long, stout branch that extended over the cliff face.

Electra's heart slammed against her chest.

No, he can't do this. Why would he do this?

Kleon walked over, and she stared at him, shaking her head in a slow, deliberate motion. Through her gag, she voiced a single, extended word, "No."

"Come, come, Electra. I would never do that." Kleon lowered his voice, the words barely audible. "This is only a negotiating tactic. I would never hurt that lovely neck. You were once my true love."

A mixture of shock and relief swept through her.

Kleon, you do not understand what love is.

He tossed the rope to his man. "Tie it under her arms. You know what to do. Get two men to gather firewood."

Kleon stepped close and pulled down her gag. She screamed, but his rough hand clamped over her mouth. "If you cooperate, I'll remove the gag. No screaming. Understand?"

She nodded, and the hand moved away. "Kleon, release me. Marcus will let you go. We'll ride away."

"Sorry, Princess, but Marcus won't let me go while I have those scrolls. I have my own plan." He leaned in close to her. "If he loves you, you might live." His breath was hot against her face.

She turned her head and squeezed her eyes shut, jumping when she heard wood dropping on the ground near her. Kleon's face remained inches from hers. "Don't," she pleaded.

He gave her a crazed look.

"You're mad," she said, her voice cold.

He stepped back and slapped her. "Stupid, bitch. Pull her up."

Spots of light spun before her vision, and her body fought against unconsciousness. Then the rope tied around her began pulling her upward. A mixture of horror and hopelessness filled her mind as her feet lost contact with the ground.

Marcus...

CHAPTER FORTY-THREE

Marcus

King's Throne, Cyrenaica, May 7

TALUS'S IDEA WAS a risky one, but Marcus went along with it. Alone now, he doubted his decision. He missed the big man's steady presence. Would the men follow his orders without Talus? He had paid them to do a job, but that didn't console him.

After watching Talus leave, Marcus didn't even try to sleep. He paced back and forth behind the line of men. While a few slept, others sat around a small fire sharpening their swords.

His thoughts focused on Electra. She had proved herself tenacious in running the daily operations of the palace in Cleopatra's absence. How was she handling her captivity and the month-long chase? The mercenaries were grumbling at the conditions. What must Electra be experiencing? Was she even alive?

She has to be.

Marcus shifted his mind to Kleon, and hatred settled in his gut. What would the trapped dog do? Surrender? That was Marcus's hope, but was it realistic? Would Kleon try to use Electra to bargain for his freedom? Marcus thought of the scrolls. Hippolytus said their importance, their preservation, towered over any consideration, over any man—or woman. But Hippolytus wasn't here facing this dilemma. On this barren ridge top, could he allow someone as unscrupulous as Kleon to claim the Archimedes scrolls? He couldn't lose Electra. He loved her and was ready to die to save her.

With sudden fury, several bright balls of light burst from the dark on the outcropping across the neck of land his men guarded. Marcus held his hand before his face and peered into the light. Twenty paces from him, flames from two places roared and danced against the night.

Kleon had lit two large bonfires. Their light illuminated a large flat area. Shadowy images of men, rocks, and bushes flickered on the landscape. One fire was near a dead tree. Marcus continued to squint. What was in the tree?

Oh, gods, no! A woman with long dark hair dangled from a long tree branch that extended over the precipice. Her bare legs kicked in the air.

It was Electra.

"Electra!" Marcus's cry was a mix of horror, anguish, and rage as he raced to the edge of the ridge opposite her.

"Marcus," her voice drifted in return.

The sound tore at his heart. Instinct made him draw his gladius and rush toward the short strip connecting ridge and precipice. His men grabbed him as he tried to push past them.

"Hold, Bassus, hold," shouted a mercenary.

"He wants you to attack," added another fighter. "You'll be killed. And the woman."

Marcus panted, feeling his blood surge through his veins.

"That you, Marcus?" came Kleon's taunting call from across the narrow chasm.

Marcus's face twisted in rage.

The desert had been rough on Kleon. He was thin, caked in dust, and wore a ragged tunic. He was so close Marcus could hit the man with a rock

"Let's be reasonable, Marcus. Aren't you the level-headed boy who said reason and logic are what separates us from the beasts?"

As the words sank in, Marcus tried to calm himself with deep breaths. Even then, his voice was rough when he yelled back. "What do you want, Kleon?" His gaze swung over to Electra, and a knife twisted in his heart.

A low menacing laugh came back from Kleon. "Well, everything, naturally." There was another laugh. "But for you, Marcus, I'm willing to be reasonable, to negotiate."

"I don't negotiate with scum," Marcus shot back but then cursed his antagonizing tone. He sheathed his sword. There'd be time for that later.

"Come, Marcus. Consider the situation."

Confusion filled Marcus. What did he mean?

He peered at Electra and the rope looped under her arms. It seemed strong enough. He followed its line to the trunk of the tree. Where was it tied? It wound behind the tree into the light and then back toward the shadows. When he peered beyond the bonfire, he saw the rope ended at a stake. Gods.

Kleon knelt by the stake, holding a dagger to the rope.

I must put you down, Kleon.

"Kleon," Marcus yelled. "Don't even think about it. I'll cut you into pieces."

Kleon laughed. "Spoken like a man in love. But you haven't seen all of my little stage."

Marcus scanned across the promontory. Then he saw it. One of Kleon's men stood on a rock by the second fire, swinging a heavy sack a hand's width above the licking flames. It had to be the Archimedes scrolls. These new scrolls, he was sure, held the primary knowledge that Archimedes and his colleagues had discovered. The Archimedes scrolls contained the potential to change the world for the better. Or for worse, if Kleon and Octavian have their way. Kleon wouldn't dare set them aflame.

Anger pushed aside Marcus's raw emotions and allowed him to

think. His gaze swept across the scene before him, sorting through every solution running through his mind.

"Well, Marcus?" Kleon called. "My arm's getting weary. It might slip. Perhaps, I might burn those Archimedes scrolls."

"Marcus, be careful," Electra implored.

Her concern for his safety ripped his insides. He averted his eyes. All his men stood around, watching, awaiting his command. He shuddered, his mind on the edge of despair.

Composing himself, he yelled back, "So, what's your deal, Kleon?"

"Just a contract between two honorable men," Kleon answered, emulating the tone of a merchant. "Like the promise your father made to you before I had him killed."

Marcus's breath caught, and rage filled him again. He bent down to clear his head.

You go too far now, Kleon.

Marcus straightened his back. His burst of fury seemed to clear his mind. "Tell me what you want."

"Well, at last, negotiations begin." Kleon's laugh was short this time. "I know what you want, Marcus. You want this prickly woman dangling so precariously from this rotten tree."

"You're a bastard, Kleon." The voice was Electra's. Although she hung limply, her spirited voice was defiant. "If you live, it'll be as a eunuch in the deepest hole in Egypt."

Kleon turned toward her. "Princess," he mocked her. "And I used to think of you as refined."

"Enough, Kleon. Give me your terms," Marcus pressed. He pushed back his anger and motioned to his men to gather closer.

"To business then," called Kleon. "You want Electra, right?"

A brief wind blew up from the cliff face, causing Electra to twist around slowly. Marcus concentrated on Kleon. "That's right," Marcus replied.

"You can have her. I'm thrilled to rid my hands of her."

Marcus spoke in a low voice to his men. "Archers, stand by. The rest of you defend the neck. Let no one get by you."

"Where's Talus?" asked an archer.

"He's around," Marcus snapped, examining each man's face. "Just do your jobs." The men moved to their positions.

Marcus raised his voice again. "I ask again, Kleon. What do you want?"

A long moment passed. Marcus glanced at Electra before walking toward the land bridge.

"Stay where you are, Marcus," Kleon commanded. "What do I want? I want the Archimedes scrolls I so cleverly found. Octavian's very interested in seeing what I make with them."

Marcus watched Kleon's dagger. The blade pressed against Electra's rope.

"And I want safe passage down this mountain," Kleon continued. "If dawn comes and I see you or any of your men, Electra dies. Worse—and I believe it would be a horrible blow for all men—my man will burn the scrolls, their secrets rendered to ashes."

"Kleon," Marcus called out. "Besides robbing me of the pleasure of cutting your throat, you are asking me to give up tremendous power and to give that power to a Roman madman. I need time to consider your offer."

There was a loud groan from Electra.

"Patience, darling," said Marcus. We'll both get our revenge before long.

"You're stalling, Marcus. I don't know why, but I'll give you a quarter of an hour."

I need more time. And I need Talus.

CHAPTER FORTY-FOUR

Talus

King's Throne, Cyrenaica, May 7

TALUS GAZED UP at the cliff face below the King's Throne but saw only darkness. It was forty feet to the top. A moment ago, a shower of small rocks had rattled down, and he heard voices, but now all was silent.

He resumed his sitting position on the ledge. He had spotted it from the ridge during lightning flashes. Marcus had reluctantly agreed to his plan to climb up the cliff at dawn and attack Kleon from the rear.

Once below the view of Kleon on the upper level, Talus had picked his way along the cliff face, making good progress until he reached a gap where part of the ledge had fallen, blocking his path. He retreated, awaiting first light.

Talus fought sleep until light unexpectedly opened his drooping eyelids. He sprang up, searching the ridge, wondering why Marcus would light a fire. Unable to find a light source there, he peered up the cliff. He spotted her then.

Dangling overhead was Electra, suspended by a rope from a tree. Her legs kicked the empty air.

Mars, what is going on up there?

Talus moved along the ledge trying to get a better angle.

"Electra!" It was Marcus.

"Marcus." The word, barely audible, came from above. It sounded like a woman.

"Is that you, Marcus?" Hearing the accursed Kleon, Talus suddenly understood and listened to the heated exchange going on above.

Talus pressed his back against the cold stone, and as he often did before a desperate battle, he waited. His time would come.

CHAPTER FORTY-FIVE

Marcus
King's Throne, Cyrenaica, May 7

MARCUS GATHERED HIS archers. His face was calm, but within, he agonized over his plan of action. He couldn't go along with Kleon's proposition—he didn't trust Kleon. If he and his men rode down the ridge, Kleon could escape with both Electra and the scrolls. And Marcus would be back to where he had been for over a month—chasing Kleon across the world. He had considered many variations of his plan. Before he could say anything, one man spoke out.

"Where exactly is Talus? Those men down there need him to lead them." At Marcus's withering stare, the bowman gazed at his feet.

"Do you need Talus to draw your bow for you? Or aim it? Or release your arrow?" His voice was firm.

The man who had spoken glanced up but said nothing. He shook his head.

"Any of you?" Marcus examined the faces of the others.

"No, sir," came the answer.

"Listen, you're all good men and excellent bowmen. I'll lead the men across the neck. Here's the plan. Lukos, I want you to take a blunt arrow and aim for the bag of scrolls. You must knock it back as Kleon's man swings it away from the fire. Timing is critical."

"I can do it, Marcus."

Marcus addressed the next archer. "Demos, I need you to hit Kleon's hand and knock that blade away from the rope. Can you do that?"

Marcus followed Demos's gaze across to the outcropping where Kleon stood, dagger against the rope that held Electra from death. Light from the flames danced on the shiny blade.

"Commander, I can make that shot in my sleep."

Marcus knew the man could back up his words. "Just in case, stay awake for this one." No one laughed.

"What about me, sir? Shoot and kill Kleon?"

"I want you to put an arrow in the chest of the man swinging the scrolls."

"Aye, sir. Consider him dead."

"Marcus, do I take Kleon?" Lukos asked.

"He's yours. I want you to kill Kleon with your second arrow. By Jupiter's balls, you can use four arrows if you want." He wanted to kill Kleon personally but fought against the guilt of that primitive desire. This was war, justified war, he told himself. Justice for Papa if nothing else.

Marcus turned back to Lukos. "His wound will distract Kleon from seeing your second arrow. I'll have my bow as well and will back up anyone in case of a miss. When all your targets are down, support our attack across the neck. Any questions?"

"Talus is going to miss all the fun," said Demos, chuckling.

"I'm sure he's already had two lifetimes of fun," Marcus replied.

This time the three archers found his remark humorous, but Marcus knew Talus's heart. He'd rather be a farmer on his own plot of land in a peaceful, remote corner of the Roman world.

"To your positions, men. Signal when you're ready."

The archers spread out to positions advantageous for their targets.

Marcus rubbed his face. Fatigue clouded his thoughts. He took a gulp from his waterskin and then poured some over his head, letting the liquid trickle down his face before drying himself on his tunic's sleeve.

He hoped his body was up to tonight's challenge. More critically—was he hardened enough to fight and kill? He had been near delirium when he killed Decimus.

When Marcus inspected the line of archers, they each gave the signal.

They're ready. Am I? Gods, help me.

He turned to his remaining men. "Gemellus," he called over to his man in charge of the swordsmen, now lined up to charge Kleon's position.

Gemellus hustled over. "Sir?"

Marcus explained what the archers were doing. "I'm not sure how many men Kleon has. No more than ten, I suspect. After the archers fire, I'll signal you to charge across the land bridge and onto the promontory. Be careful of the edge. Speed of attack and surprise are critical." Marcus clasped the man's shoulder. "Are your men ready?"

"Commander, we've been ready. I await your command." He pounded his chest in salute and ran back to his position.

Marcus scrutinized the two men across the open space. The man swinging the scrolls over the flames was still at it. As for Kleon, he held the dagger steady against the rope.

He was confident that Kleon could not see his men's movements. The glare of the flames ensured that.

It was time.

He raised his sword to waist level, wishing Talus was by his side. He brought the flat of the sword down on a rock, sending a sharp metallic crack into the night. In the blink of an eye, three arrows launched over him, the sound of their flight merging into one shrill song of death.

Marcus watched Kleon's blade. When he saw the dagger fall and heard Kleon's cry, exhilaration surged through his body.

In front of him, Demos jumped up and skipped forward, waving his bow in the air. "Got the bastard," he yelled in triumph.

"Demos!" yelled Lukos, sidestepping as he nocked another arrow for his second shot. "Get down. You're blocking my shot."

Lukos had to take Kleon down.

"Lukos! Kill him!" Panic filled Marcus's voice.

As Lukos's second arrow flew across Marcus's vision, he swung his head back toward Kleon. To Marcus's wide-eyed horror, Kleon dove to the ground, and the arrow sailed over him.

"All archers on Kleon!" Marcus screamed, reaching for his bow. Fumbling to nock an arrow, he watched helplessly as his enemy, the murderer of his father, rolled away from the light and into the shadows.

Electra screamed.

Her terrifying cry shook Marcus, and he tossed aside the now useless bow. Drawing his sword, he charged along the ridge. "On me," he cried, slicing pass Gemellus's swordsmen and onto the narrow neck of land.

"Kleon! Kleon!" Above his screams, Marcus barely heard the men behind him take up the charge, their hoarse cry of attack ringing along the ridge.

Ahead of Marcus, a line of seven or eight men emerged from the shadows running to meet his sword. Three arrows whistled over him, and two of Kleon's men fell. His sword crashed against his nearest opponent's sending a shock through Marcus's arm. A moment later, Gemellus and his men smashed into the enemy's line.

Marcus and all around him fought like wild animals. Blood splattered his face as he pounded relentlessly against his opponent's weapon. He focused all his pent-up anger, frustration, and hatred on the hammered steel that was now an extension of his body. Using a move Talus taught him, Marcus killed his first man with a thrust of his gladius into the man's throat. When he withdrew the blade, the man dropped like a stone.

Looking up just in time, he avoided a sword jabbed at his head. The man's thrust propelled him past Marcus, who slashed his weapon across the back of the man's thigh, severing the hamstring. The man crumpled to the ground. Marcus saw an opening in the enemy line and charged through it toward the tree where Electra dangled.

She was still screaming, but he had no breath to answer. He sprinted for her with all his strength.

Almost there, my love.

Horror replaced hope as Kleon emerged from the shadows. Marcus's heart leaped in his chest.

"No!" he cried.

Kleon had recovered his dagger. His bloody hand pressed it to the rope holding Electra. He glared at Marcus and with a flick of his wrist, sliced the line.

Everything now moved extraordinarily slow. At the edge of his vision, Marcus saw Electra start to fall. Ahead, Kleon dove back into the shadows. An arrow whistled by Marcus and struck the ground where Kleon had been. The rasp of the rope slicing around the tree trunk filled Marcus's ears. For an instant, the rope caught on something, but then a sharp crack rang out as the force of Electra's fall snapped the dead branch that had held her.

Marcus came to a sliding halt on the wet ground as the rope unwound from the trunk. Before him, the line whipped up a spray as it raced through the grass. He dived for the slick rope, but it danced through his fingers as he fumbled to get a grip. The rope end slithered toward him. At the last instant, Marcus managed to press the line between his chest and the ground, allowing him time to grab a firm hold.

Electra's weight took up the rope's slack, dragging Marcus toward the cliff edge. He tried to dig his sandals into the soft ground, but the effort barely slowed his slide. The darkness at the edge loomed before him. Desperate, he reached out with his free hand for anything to stop Electra's fall.

Snagging a prickly dry bush, he yelled in pain as the force of Electra's fall tore through his arms and shoulders. It stretched his body between the rope and the bush, but he had stopped Electra's fall.

How long can I hold her?

Marcus tried to see if Kleon was still around, but he saw nothing of the man. He heard the fight going on behind him. Were his men winning?

"Marcus?"

His name came from below the cliff edge. It was Electra. "Electra? I'm holding you." His voice faltered from his exertions. "It... it will just... be a minute, and we'll... pull you up." His heaving lungs forced his words out. The rope slipped slightly through his grip. "Is there anything you... can grab onto?"

The rope shuddered for a long moment. "There's nothing, Marcus. Only rock and air." Electra's voice was soft but strong.

She hasn't given up trying.

His shoulders screamed, and he felt the strain in his face. Clenching his teeth, he held on using the strength built up as a rower in the *Neptune*. He blocked everything out, concentrating on his tenuous grip on rope and bush.

"Marcus?"

"Not now," Marcus croaked.

"Marcus, down here," came the same voice, louder and more urgent this time.

It wasn't Electra. "Talus? Is that you?"

"Drop her, Marcus. I'll—"

"Marcus, I see Talus," cried Electra. "I don't want you to fall. Let me go."

"Drop her?" Marcus rasped. Then there was a snapping sound.

The branch he was clinging to started to yield. Marcus slipped a hand's width toward the edge. He tried to get a better hold. Instead, his hand slid closer to the end of the branch.

Abruptly, he heard a sharp whistle. It was the command whistle that Talus used to initiate an exercise or maneuver during their arms training.

Marcus didn't know if it was because of the instincts drilled into him by his training or the realization that his grip on the rope was slipping away. Perhaps the bush broke. Whatever the cause, he released the rope.

A short high-pitched scream from Electra shattered the night. Marcus scrambled on all fours to the lip of the precipice and called down. "Electra? Talus? Do you have her?" He peered into the black void below.

Silence.

A groan broke the quiet. A sound like a slap rang out.

"Got her, Marcus," came Talus's reply.

"Thank the gods," Marcus exclaimed in relief. "Is she all right?"

"She's alive. No blood, but groggy from the fall."

"Stay there. As soon as there's light, we'll come down to help move her."

Marcus, his strength depleted, lay back on the wet ground. There's was one final thing he had to do tonight.

I must kill Kleon.

Kleon
King's Throne, Cyrenaica, May 7

Kleon ran as soon as his blade cut the rope, sending Electra plunging down. The deed was done; it was time to escape. But how? The cliff was too steep and the night too dark to climb down.

He proceeded along the side of the promontory facing Cyrene and shielded from the ridge by a thick band of underbrush and low trees. As the cliff curved around toward the land bridge, Kleon took to the bushes hoping to avoid detection before making a dash across to the ridge.

There was a rustle ahead of him, and Kleon froze. He was weaponless. As a dark bulk moved toward him, Kleon's arms flew up to cover his head.

"Kleon? Is that you, sir?" came a voice.

Kleon lowered his arms and found one of his men a foot away. "Who else, you fool." Maybe he wasn't going to die tonight. "Where are the others?"

"Dead, I think," the soldier replied. "I'm the only one left."

"Do you have a weapon for me?"

"I've only a dagger besides my bow and—let's see—two arrows." The man handed the dagger to Kleon.

"Let's get away from here," Kleon said.

Making use of the dark and the vegetation, they crept to the edge of the clearing before the narrow connecting strip of land. From the light of the dying bonfires, Kleon spotted two of Marcus's men standing guard—one swordsman and one archer.

"Can you take them out?"

"I have a clear shot on the swordsman, but he's blocking my view of the archer," said the soldier, removing an arrow from his quiver.

"Take the shot," ordered Kleon, crouching down and clutching his dagger.

The man nocked his arrow, drew back and released. The arrow whistled through the night and struck the swordsman in the head. While his soldier reached for his last arrow, Kleon stood up and readied himself for the run to freedom.

But the enemy archer already had an arrow on his bow string. He swung the bow up, aimed and released.

Kleon heard the thud of the arrow's impact on his archer's body.

The man collapsed to the ground. Across the way, the enemy archer was slow in readying another arrow.

Now's my chance.

Kleon dashed out of the underbrush, his long legs churning, covering a third of the distance before the enemy archer could react. A low howl erupted from Kleon's throat as the archer fumbled to ready an arrow on the bowstring. The loaded bow whipped up as Kleon closed the gap. The thud of collision, the twang of the bow, and the crunch of the dagger into the archer's chest all simultaneously filled Kleon's ears. The two men crashed to the ground.

Kleon gasped for air, lifting his head to stare into the dead eyes of the archer. A sharp pain in his right side forced him to sit up. Feeling his side, he found his tunic sliced and a light nick in the skin. He had dodged death.

He scrambled to regain his footing and peered ahead to the land bridge seeing only darkness. The way was clear for his escape. Kleon stumbled forward, increased his pace to a jog, and crossed to the ridge. He heard the snorting of horses.

I'm alive, Marcus. I will yet triumph.

CHAPTER FORTY-SIX

Electra

King's Throne, Cyrenaica, May 7

ELECTRA WOKE WITH a gasp. She rubbed the back of her head and the images of last night came to her like falling shards of glass. She felt a rope around her waist and realized Talus had roped them together.

"It's nice to see you back with us, Princess," said Talus.

"I'm not sure how you did it, Talus, but I owe you a great debt for saving me. And it's Electra, not Princess."

"Ah, yes, Electra. Let's head up. It may still be dark on the ridge but here there's enough light."

Electra could see a ribbon of pink along the horizon.

"Don't look down," Talus warned.

She took a deep breath. "I won't," she replied, but she caught one terrifying glance as they edged along the cliff face.

When they reached the path climbing up from the ledge to the ridge top, she stopped. "I can't. Too tired. I'll slip," she said, angry at her exhausted body.

Without a word, Talus picked her up and carried her the rest of the way.

In the dim light of the ridge, she saw Marcus dash over. He helped her stand, and as they embraced, a wave of relief coursed through her. His arms protected her; his body warmed her. She could hear his heart beating as she rested against his chest.

"Come over here, dear, and we'll get some food and water for you," Marcus said.

She followed him through the camp to water and took a long swig of the liquid, immersing herself in its restorative powers as it cleared her mind's lethargic fog.

Dropping the waterskin, she turned to Marcus, pressing herself against him. "I don't know what to say. I'm so glad to be with you and away from that monster. Thank you."

Marcus frowned. "I failed to hold you. If not for Talus…"

Electra balked at his protest. "You did save me, Marcus. You stopped my fall. You gave Talus time to catch me. I heard the men talking about your wild charge. That's bravery. And you killed Kleon." She stared at the ground. "Where's his body?"

Marcus bit his lip and looked away. "I'm sorry, dearest," replied Marcus, his voice barely audible. "Kleon escaped. I've sent men hunting for him. But," his voice brightened, "we saved the scrolls from—"

Electra stepped back and raised her hand. Her anger rose to such an intensity that she wanted to slap Marcus. This man she loved—so good, so brave, so smart, but so insensitive right now. Did he not see the equivalency he was making between her and the damn scrolls? What kind of deal did he make? She searched her memories of last night. She had faded in and out, and nothing came back to her.

"Marcus, were the scrolls that important? I thought we…" She couldn't finish. What could she say? Cared for each other? Loved each other? Feelings for Marcus had been growing in her—until this moment. Now, she was confused.

"No, no, Electra." Marcus reached out to her. "It's not what you think. My focus was on you. Kleon held the advantage, and I didn't trust him with any deal. There was no guarantee that he would let you live, so I double-crossed him. I wanted to save you. Anything else, the scrolls, was a far, far secondary consideration."

His words sounded sincere. Electra took a deep breath, letting go of her worst anger. "Oh, Marcus. I understand. I'm grateful—I truly am—for what you've done, but... but after being in someone's total control, I will never let anyone control me again—not Kleon, not Cleopatra, not even you."

"Electra, I don't want to control you. I—" He stepped over to her and took her in his arms.

"I know, dear." She lay her head against his shoulder. "Just take me home."

Despite his words, an unsettling feeling filled her heart. And raging next to it was her hunger for revenge on her tormentor—Kleon.

CHAPTER FORTY-SEVEN

Marcus

Apollonia, Cyrenaica, May 10

MARCUS LEANED AGAINST the *Neptune's* rail and gazed up at the lighthouse, perched on a spit of land near the Harbor of Apollonia, port for Cyrene, Pentapolis's largest city. Open seas lay ahead.

Talus walked up. "How did the *Neptune* come to be in Apollonia?"

"You always told me to think strategically," said Marcus. "When I left *Neptune* to chase Kleon, I ordered Socus to Apollonia to await my arrival. I was confident where the desert chase would end."

Being aboard the *Neptune* again raised painful memories. He shook off his feelings of shame.

Marcus thought back to King's Throne. Kleon's escape angered him. He had sent riders to scour the countryside, but with an hour head start, Kleon had eluded them. The rough terrain held many places where he could have taken refuge.

"How are you feeling about yourself now?" Marcus saw apprehension on Talus's face.

"Except for the joy of rescuing Electra, I'm feeling a bit numb."

"You saved those Archimedes scrolls. Has to feel good."

"Yes, it does. Those documents are vital to my scholar's life. Still, Kleon got away."

"He's out there somewhere. We haven't seen the last of him. Patience." Talus clapped him on the back.

Marcus stared at the water sliding by the hull. He should be happy, but Electra's rebuff and subsequent refusal to talk weighed on his spirit. Should he have concentrated solely on her rescue? That's what his heart told him. Logic said his plan had been sound, with a high chance of success—if Demos had not blocked Lukos's kill shot.

To what should he have listened? Heart? Mind? And what was Electra feeling? Anger? Betrayal? Sorrow? Disappointment? Regret? Possibly all. Hippolytus always said he needed to work on his empathy.

"I miss Papa and Hippolytus," Marcus mused aloud.

"I'm not a father or a philosopher, but I'll help you any way I can."

"Thanks, Talus."

Without the counsel of Hippolytus and Papa, it had all fallen on his shoulders. Hippolytus had said to trust no one. He had trusted Kleon, and disaster followed. He had also trusted Electra. He still did. Their partnership in decoding the scrolls, her compassion after he escaped slavery and their continuing delay in exploring their feelings for each other were all based on trust. Even her positioning of their relationship to be incorporeal was to protect them both. Cleopatra could arbitrarily force Electra into a politically expedient marriage. If that happened, Cleopatra must not find Electra to be impure. Marcus had no control over Cleopatra's actions.

He watched as the land slid below the horizon. "Octavian is supporting Kleon now. With Roman resources, he could build ships with steam-driven catapults. That would give Octavian an advantage against Antony and Cleopatra."

Talus grunted. "I'm not a navy man, but an enemy with superior artillery? Doesn't sound good."

"If Octavian wins the civil war, what kind of civilization will we get? Millions more conquered people would be enslaved." His stomach tightened at his words. "Power, and power alone, would rule the world, and neither heart nor mind would find space there."

"Not a pretty place, Marcus." Talus saluted. "Need to check on the men and the horses." The big man walked aft.

The land was a mere sliver now; the seabirds no longer circled overhead.

Octavian's rule didn't appeal to Marcus at all. If he did nothing, could Antony and Cleopatra still win? Unlikely. Egypt would fall, and the knowledge from four collaborating geniuses would be revealed.

Somehow, he must keep Archimedes' technology from the wrong hands—the only solution was to offer to help Antony and Cleopatra defeat Octavian. Such a victory would give him some negotiating power with those two. He would get them to support his goal to end slavery—maybe not immediately, but in time. He shook his head.

Two years into manhood and he was to plea before two of the most powerful people in the world.

There were alternatives to slavery. Machines, perhaps? Machines—to do man's work. The title of one of the new scrolls gave him hope. Written in large script in olden Greek, it read, "The machine will lessen your burden."

Captain Socus's hail interrupted Marcus's thoughts.

The captain removed his straw hat. "Pardon, sir. Have you decided where we're heading?

"Yes, Captain. Athens."

"Athens, sir?" Socus shrugged. "Athens it is."

Athens and Cleopatra. That should make Electra exuberant. Or maybe not. This empathy thing is hard to understand.

CHAPTER FORTY-EIGHT

Electra

The Mediterranean Sea, near Athens, May 15

ELECTRA SENSED HER cabin walls closing in. Needing fresh air, she proceeded to the main deck, finding the ocean breeze refreshing. She glanced around for Marcus, wanting to avoid premature contact and needing time to collect her thoughts.

If only she could talk to Cleopatra. The queen knew men and would understand Electra's feelings. She felt disconnected from her queen and from the man who had captured her heart. Electra realized the enormous value of the scrolls, but did Marcus likewise value her? Did he recognize her part in breaking the riddle of Archimedes' work? What would *she* have done that night on the mountain? Ignore the scrolls entirely?

Her anger in Cyrene had been immature. The deprivations of the past month and the near-death experience had temporarily unhinged her mind, causing her to act with raw emotion.

After making her way to the port rail, she looked back to the stern of the ship. There was Marcus, standing at the starboard rail on the upper deck, staring down at the water.

As she watched him, he never moved. Was he thinking of her or the scrolls?

Marcus suddenly straightened up, and their eyes locked before she could avert her gaze. He had an unusual expression on his face and appeared penitent as if caught in a grievous act.

With gazes locked, he called out, "Electra."

He was coming down the steps toward her. She could make a run to her cabin, but she told herself that now was the time. If ever they were to have a future together, they somehow had to get past this unfortunate crisis in their relationship.

"Electra, may we speak?" Marcus asked when he reached her.

Electra tried to stay calm by closing her eyes but upon opening them found Marcus studying her. She fidgeted with a lock of her black hair. She needed to start this, now.

"Well, certainly. Out here?" The open space gave her some relief from her feeling of being trapped.

Marcus scanned around. "I'd rather not. I'd prefer my cabin where we can talk freely."

Did that mean a loud argument? She hoped not, wishing he would be forthcoming with an expression of his feelings that night on the mountain.

"As you wish. We can't continue to avoid talking about what happened. If we do, it will destroy us."

Since that horrible night, there had been an emptiness inside her. During her captivity, her helplessness had unsettled her, and she fought now to rebalance herself. Resiliency had been her strength all her life. She needed it now.

They had to clear up the situation, and the sooner, the better. As it was, the idea of a conversation with him had her either depressed or furious with irrational anger. "Please, lead the way," she said.

Marcus's cabin was much larger than hers. When they first came on board, he had offered to switch cabins with her, but she had refused.

He showed her in, leaving the cabin door open. "It will be cooler with the door open. Have a seat."

"Good," she replied, sitting in a chair before a large desk. "Marcus—"

"If it's all right, Electra," he interrupted, "I must say some things first. Things I should have said long before now."

Electra nodded. "Fine, proceed."

"First, my words back in the mountains were insensitive and foolish. I want to start over," Marcus inhaled sharply, "and restate my feelings." Marcus came and knelt beside her. "I cannot imagine what my life would be like if Talus had not caught you."

"I reiterate, you also played a huge part in my rescue." That was true, but her emotions still churned. His plans to save the scrolls seemed incongruent with the feelings he now expressed. "Marcus, let's put this behind us." She clenched her shaking hands.

"Electra, I'm in pain whenever I think about what happened to you. I made a horrible mistake. I allowed my hubris to overcome my heart. In that long month spent chasing Kleon, all I thought about was having you back and in my arms again. When the new scrolls showed up, my mind spun in insane directions. My heart never changed, but my focus should have been entirely on you."

He was admitting his mistake, but his words did not satisfy her heart. She started to get up but sat back down when Marcus grabbed her arm.

"I admit my mistake, Electra. You're the most important part of my life. Without you, my life would be aimless. Gods, I'd probably end up being a bureaucratic librarian like poor Philotus."

Electra laughed. "Yes, I can see that."

"Hippolytus once told me: 'Marcus, sometimes you must stumble on your first step before you know where you should be going.' Back there, I stumbled. Not my first, but my biggest."

"So, where are you going now?" The walls were starting to close in again for her.

Please hurry.

Marcus sat back down. "There's something I've held from you.

It's kept me from expressing my feelings for you, for thinking I was not worthy of you."

"That's nonsense."

"Let me explain," Marcus continued. "On the *Neptune*, I was subjected to a lot of abuse."

"It must have been awful. The beatings, the physical strain, the horrible food."

"Those I could live with. There was something else, a horrible thing. Something no man should suffer."

"What could be so——" She realized what he was trying to say. "Oh, no, Marcus."

For a moment, Marcus covered his eyes. "The pirate captain, he... you know... did unspeakable things... violated me." His eyes were wet from the memory.

"Oh, goddess, have mercy." Electra rose from her chair and knelt by his side.

"I pushed you away and hid my feelings. I didn't want to get hurt or to hurt you."

She held his hands. "Expressing your pain will never hurt me, Marcus. Can you tell me what those feelings are?"

"I feel damaged and unworthy."

"I can understand that, but...." She paused searching for the right words. "It's nonsense. Your actions, your words show me the opposite." She squeezed his hands.

"I can't see my future without you in it."

His hands were warm on her skin. "Why is that, Marcus?" She found herself staring into his blue eyes. A warmth spread through her; she felt something—a wholeness. As she glanced away, uncertain of this new feeling, the earlier emptiness began to seep back in.

"Why? Because I love you, Electra. I always have. From that night at Cleopatra's dinner until this very moment. Even before you stole my clothes." He smiled at her.

At last, his revelation expressed the words Electra wanted to hear. She was relieved, overjoyed. The emptiness was gone.

"Marcus, I too was stirred that day. I realized…" she searched for the right words, "I felt somehow that you and I shared a destiny."

Marcus looked at her. He wiped his eyes and moved his lips, but no words came out.

Their weeks-long separation made her realize she could no longer deny or suppress her feelings. She loved Marcus. That feeling overruled Cleopatra's rules for their relationship.

She laughed—a full, uninhibited laugh. He laughed too—a laugh she had never heard before. She jumped at Marcus, sending them both tumbling to the ground. She lavished kisses on his face.

He tried to keep up but after a moment broke away long enough to say, "The bed would be softer."

"Well, it seems you know where you're going now." She lowered her eyes, then slowly raised them.

Marcus picked her up, kicked the door shut, and carried her to the bed. She lay back. He pulled his tunic over his head, and her eyes widened as she took in the taut, hardened muscle of his chest.

"Marcus, I love you. I want you."

He sat down next to her and began removing her clothes. "And I love you, darling," he replied, fumbling with her undergarments.

She sat up. "Here let me." She completed disrobing and lay back down. "Well, I'm naked. How about you?"

She watched as he quickly shed his loincloth.

Because Cleopatra had made her watch the naked men and women copulating at several of her and Antony's wild parties, Electra had seen much but had not participated. Now she was finally ready to share her love and her body but only with Marcus.

"Yes, that's better," she said quietly. Passion fired her body as she reached for his rising member, but he intercepted her hand, brought it to his lips, and kissed the back of it.

"First, I want to kiss you, taste your sweetness. I want to kiss you slowly, deeply." He laid on the bed facing her.

Electra turned to him and slid her tongue over her lips, leaving them slightly parted. She reached out and touched his face. Joy filled her.

Marcus brought his body down on hers, and fiery heat rose in her body.

Hours later, in the dark of the cabin, Marcus turned to her. "Does this mean I'm forgiven?"

She propped herself up and whispered into his ear. "You're forgiven, more or less—" She squealed when he tickled her ribcage. "And I'm off the marriage market. Tainted, you know." Her smile turned into a frown. "Oh, gods. I hope Cleopatra doesn't banish me."

CHAPTER FORTY-NINE

Marcus
Athens, June 1

MARCUS WATCHED FROM the bow as the *Neptune* glided into Piraeus, its harbor bristling with the masts of warships. After anchoring, Marcus and Electra rode back with the harbor pilot to the wharf, where Marcus secured a wagon for the five-mile trip to Athens. Once in the city, Marcus found rooms near the Acropolis.

From his third-floor room, Marcus could see the governor's impressive house. He had read that Pompey once used the house for his headquarters in the civil war against Caesar. Now, Caesar's right-hand man occupied it with Cleopatra.

Electra dispatched a message to Cleopatra, informing the queen of their arrival and recent events and requesting an audience with her and Antony. Cleopatra had acknowledged Electra's letter, and now all they could do was wait.

Marcus bought a copy of Pausanias's travel book, *Descriptions of Greece,* and toured Electra around the city and countryside viewing the Acropolis and the numerous monuments, temples, and theaters throughout the area.

Despite the activity, Marcus often found himself staring out the window of their rooms. He practiced the speech he'd be giving to two of the mightiest rulers in the world, but sitting idle day after day was driving him insane. He began pacing around the sitting room.

"I can't take this waiting," he said to Electra. "I'm going insane."

Electra didn't look up from the letter she was writing. "Marcus, you must have patience."

Marcus glared at her back. "Patience is a bad idea while Kleon remains free. They might see me as a young idealist and send us on our way. Can't they see I'm offering them victory against Octavian?"

She turned around in her chair. Her face was hard. "Don't you think this waiting wears on me as well? Only a month ago, that evil bastard sent me falling to my death. Believe me, I want my revenge. But you can't rush Cleopatra."

Marcus hurried over and knelt by Electra's side. He took her face in his hands. "Forgive me, dearest. I know you suffered terribly under Kleon. You've been so strong, and I've been too wrapped up in my own affairs since we arrived. I don't know how you've kept your sanity." He kissed her forehead.

"I've never told you this, but my attitude against slavery is based on more than an intellectual decision. It was my life until I was nine."

Marcus was taken aback. "What? I don't understand. How can this be? You're Cleopatra's cousin."

"Yes, it's complicated; so, pay attention. I'm not a legitimate Ptolemy. My grandmother, Melissa, was the youngest sister of the King of Samos. While visiting Rome, she had an affair with Ptolemy Alexander the Second, who was living under the protection of the dictator Sulla. Alexander and Melissa had an illegitimate child, my mother, Demetria. When his uncle, Ptolemy Soter II died, Alexander returned to Egypt and brought along my grandmother and mother. Alexander married his uncle's widow and ruled for a few weeks as King. The ambitious Alexander then killed his very popular wife. Shortly thereafter, an angry mob killed him. After Alexander's death, Cleopatra's father, Ptolemy Auletes, assumed the throne. My grandmother died soon after and my mother ended up as a maid, a slave, for Auletes' daughter, Berenice—"

"Berenice? Wait, wasn't she Cleopatra's sister who Antony killed in Ephesus on Cleopatra's orders?"

"Yes, Berenice ruled Egypt for a few years after Ptolemy Auletes, father of Berenice and Cleopatra, fled a revolt in Alexandria and took refuge in Rome. My mother was one of the mistresses of Archelaus, Berenice's husband. I was born posthumously after Antony killed Berenice and Archelaus, my father."

"That's awful, Darling," said Marcus.

Electra slowly walked to the window before continuing. "My mother was a slave in Antony's household for a while and was treated well. When I was three, we and several other Antony slaves ended up as part of Cleopatra's palace staff, though still slaves. My mother became one of Cleopatra's favorites."

Marcus took Electra in his arms. "I'm so sorry, my love. Why hadn't you told me?"

"I've tried to forget those days and have until recently. I'm not proud of my heritage. But I've survived."

"You must hate Antony," said Marcus, shaking his head.

Electra sighed. "I suppose I could, but I never knew my father. My mother never spoke of him. I heard he was not a nice person. It was Cleopatra who ordered their deaths. A Ptolemy's worst enemy is likely to be another Ptolemy."

"You're a wonderful, resilient woman, and you should be proud of that," said Marcus, squeezing her tight.

Electra leaned back. "Thank you. My mother died when I was nine. When Cleopatra learned of my mother's death, she had her steward investigate my background. When she discovered I was her grandniece, she took me in. My grandmother's father and Cleopatra's father were cousins, so Cleopatra considers me her cousin."

"Gods, to have survived all that. I respect you even more."

"It wasn't that bad a life. I wasn't ever beaten or abused. Still,

I know something of what it's like to be a slave. Now, back to our situation here. I can tell you, Marcus, Cleopatra isn't going to send us away. I've told her about my kidnapping, Kleon's involvement, and your rescue of me. It probably won't be necessary, but if Cleopatra doubts my commitment to your cause, I can remind her of my early years. In my letter, I emphasized your crazy, brave charge against Kleon's men to save me. She'll see us if only to thank you."

"I wish she'd hurry up."

At that moment, Marcus heard a knock on the door. "Maybe this is it."

When Marcus opened the door, a messenger handed him a scroll. Marcus broke the seal and unrolled the message at Electra's desk. "It's for you from Cleopatra."

She quickly scanned the note. "This is it. Listen."

My Dear Electra,

How surprised I was to receive your letter. I am horrified that attackers took you from the sacred temple and dragged you out to sea and desert. You must have suffered terrible deprivations. I am thankful for your safe return and am in debt to young Marcus Bassus.

War planning continues. Some of the Legates and advisers are telling Antony to invade Italy before the enemy has built up his naval forces. Others say to move north and take a position to defend the Via Egnatia. Some good news is that Antony has divorced Octavia. He is free.

We finally have some time to see you and to thank Marcus for saving you from that dreadful man, Kleon. Antony is intrigued to hear about the proposition Marcus has for us.

Come to the Governor's house at the sixth hour. We await the details of Marcus Bassus's proposal.

Cleopatra

"It's about time," cried Marcus. He glanced out a window to check the sun. "I'll need to change clothes and review my notes."

"Be quick. It's getting late."

"Not to worry." Marcus narrowed his eyes. "Just don't wear your silks today. Not around that seducer, Antony."

Electra shook her head. "That's foolish, Marcus. But to help you relax, I'll wear something else."

Two hours later, he found Electra dressed in a radiant stola, a Roman matron's dress. He had changed into a fine robe he had purchased earlier. He had considered a toga but decided to straddle the line between Roman and Egyptian.

They hurried through the streets of Athens to the governor's house, soon finding themselves in a large room off the main entrance. The far end of the room opened out to the house gardens, where Antony had posted two legionnaires armed with a spear and belted gladius. Servants led Marcus and Electra to chairs lined in a row and facing a raised dais with two ornate wooden thrones.

Soon, Cleopatra entered the room and rushed straight for Electra, who stood. Marcus followed her example. The queen embraced Electra and then kissed her on the forehead.

"You poor girl." Cleopatra sounded deeply concerned. "What an ordeal you must have gone through. You will come back for dinner and tell me the details. None of this would have happened if you had a husband."

"Well, I'm working on that," replied Electra, her eyes shifting sideways to Marcus.

"What? Marcus?" The queen appeared taken aback. "We do need to talk."

Antony stomped into the room followed by a string of military tribunes, two centurions, and various sycophants and followers. A slave girl carrying a silver pitcher trailed after them. It had been six years, back when Marcus was still a naive fourteen-year-old since he had last seen Antony. Time and the war had not treated him well. He had gained weight, and his face was puffy with dark rings under his eyes.

"Electra, it's good to see you," Antony said. "Dreadful experience you had." As he hugged her, Marcus thought of the man's murder of Electra's father.

Electra bowed and stepped back.

"Ah, Marcus, my boy. Well, maybe not a boy, more of a man now. Unlike that boy in Rome who plays at being a Roman consul. Soon, I shall crush him, and we'll have peace again."

Marcus tried to ascertain the veracity of Antony's statement. Octavian was a shrewd and cunning opponent, and he also had Agrippa, Rome's best general.

With a signal, Antony sent his followers into the garden. He stopped the slave for a cup of wine and waved her out as well.

"Time is critical," Antony said. "Since deciding to move my headquarters to Patras and the fleet to the Ambracian, chaos has erupted. Let's get started."

"Yes, my love. Come take a seat up here by me." Cleopatra took her seat after settling Antony into his. Marcus and Electra returned to their places.

"Now, Electra, from your letter, I understand Marcus has a proposal. Correct?

Electra bowed. "Yes, my Queen."

"Don't expect any handouts, boy." Antony wagged his finger. "War is not cheap."

"Ha. I'm supplying the money," Cleopatra injected. She patted Antony's hand.

Antony rubbed his temples. "Go on, Bassus. Keep it simple. What's on your mind?"

Marcus rose, eying the wine pitcher. He could use a drink. Instead, he took a step toward the dais. "Thank you, Proconsul, and thank you, Queen Cleopatra, for allowing me this audience."

"Yes, yes, go on." Antony took another swig of wine.

"I offer you the power to defeat your opponent, Octavian, without losing a man—"

Marcus halted when Antony's wine caught awkwardly in his throat, nearly choking the Roman general.

"Get out, boy! Are you crazy? A magician, are you? You must have been sunstruck in that desert." Antony rose to leave.

"Please sit down, dearest. I'm sure Marcus spoke poetically. Right, Marcus?"

"As it happens—"

This time Electra interrupted. "Please, hear Marcus out. You will not regret it, I promise."

"Go on," grumbled Antony, waving his hand.

Marcus started again. "I will try to be brief. I have built a device, a weapon that allows me to shoot projectiles—bolts and stones—at great distances and with great accuracy."

"I already have ballistae and scorpions," said Antony. "What else do you have?"

"Proconsul, can your weapons shoot a thousand feet and cave in six inches of timber? Mine can."

"Impossible," scoffed Antony.

"Not only is it possible, but that's not all it can do. These catapults can rapidly fire multiple bolts. To demonstrate, I'll clap my hands every time my catapult fires a bolt." Marcus held his hands apart and then clapped them together. Antony looked at Cleopatra. Marcus waited for ten heartbeats before clapping his hands again. "By winter, I'll have a working model for a field demonstration."

Antony blew out a blast of air past his lips. "Cleopatra, surely you are not buying this horse shit?"

She stared back at Antony. "If Electra believes in him, then I do as well. You do believe in him, Electra?"

Electra stood up straight and fixed her eyes on Antony. "Yes," she answered, "with all my heart. And mind."

"Gods." Antony pinched the bridge of his nose. "Fine. I'll indulge your fantasy for now. How will you defeat Octavian?"

Marcus relaxed and took a deep breath. "I'll build a large ship with twenty or more catapults. With the ability to strike at a distance, with a rapid firing rate, and with deadly accuracy, I can destroy any naval force Octavian can throw at me. After that, your ships can be sent anywhere with impunity."

"Right," said Antony. "And what will this ship cost me?"

Marcus felt the sweat trickling down his underarms. "Two things. First, I'll need 500 talents of gold—"

"What?" bellowed Antony. "I don't have that kind of money. I'm sorry, Marcus." There was sarcasm in his voice.

Cleopatra leaned forward. "I'll provide Marcus with the gold, my love. What else, Marcus?"

Antony frowned at Cleopatra.

Marcus looked at Electra. She smiled and nodded her encouragement.

"After we defeat Octavian," said Marcus, observing the effect of his words on Antony, "I plan to construct machines the likes of which the world has never seen. I'll use the machines in transportation, mining, pumping, milling, and construction. They'll be more effective and cheaper than slaves."

"Slaves are cheap," replied Antony. "The whole Roman economy is built on slavery. Why should anyone risk that set up to try these mysterious machines?"

"With your help, Proconsul, and I know this could take decades, perhaps generations, I intend to use the machines to… end slavery."

This time Antony flung his empty wine cup across the room. His face turned a deep shade of red. He sputtered, trying to get the words out. "Were you not listening to me? Ending slavery will topple Rome's power."

Cleopatra went over to him and embraced him, cooing gentle words to calm him.

After Antony composed himself, he turned to Marcus. "You've got balls, sir. I'll give you that. End slavery? That's an impossible dream, a dangerous dream. Or a nightmare. But if—and that's a big if—you can defeat Octavian as you say, then yes, you have my oath that I, reluctantly, will help you with your crazy scheme to replace slavery. I assume you've figured out how to substitute machines for men as well." He scratched his beard. "Now, I have legates clamoring for my attention." Antony clapped his hands, and his retinue reappeared and followed him out of the room.

Cleopatra was about to make her exit when she turned to Marcus. "Forgive Antony. The stress of the war…" Her voice trailed off before she continued. "I have two hulls under construction in Paraetonium which are yours for your ship, and I'll give you 200 talents instead of 500. Agreed?"

"Agreed," Marcus said, though it meant he would need to add more from his funds. He watched Cleopatra leave and then turned to Electra, picked her up by the waist and twirled her around. "We did it!" He set her down.

"You did it, Marcus. Just tell me. How are you going to free all the slaves?"

"The Archimedes scrolls will have the answers," Marcus replied, confidently.

I hope.

Marcus
The Mediterranean Sea, near Athens, June 4

Marcus spotted Electra on the helmsman deck. She wasn't usually up at dawn. She waved, and he made his way over.

"Well," said Marcus, giving her a gentle kiss. "You're up early."

She hugged him, then turned back to the sea. "I couldn't sleep. I wanted to see one of those sunrises you're always talking about."

"Beautiful isn't it?" Marcus leaned on the rail.

"Magnificent."

"Why couldn't you sleep?"

"I keep thinking about the arrangement with the queen and Antony."

"As do I, and I worry whether we can trust Antony. No telling what he might pull."

"Don't worry. Cleopatra can control Antony."

Marcus rubbed a hand across his face. "Hades, I worry as much about Cleopatra."

"Well, don't. Tell me this—can you build that ship before the war gets critical?" She pushed a stray lock off her face.

"The partially completed hulls will cut four to six months off the construction time. Still, Quintus doesn't have a completely tested boiler, though he should in a few months."

"And you must get a working catapult, right? You haven't even started that. Have you considered all the missiles you'll need to attack and destroy an entire fleet?"

"Yes, and I've calculated the numbers we need to carry. I'm working with Talus on a space-efficient method to store the missiles."

"And the catapult?" asked Electra, wrinkling her brow.

"With the designs we took from Kleon's base, we'll have a working model in six months."

"Six months." Electra shook her head. "From the reports Cleopatra showed me, not much will happen this campaign season except securing supply lines and building up harbor defenses. That means your monster ship must be ready by this time next year. Are you sure, Marcus?" She pressed her palms together.

"Ships like this have been built before by you Ptolemies. I've reviewed those ship designs kept in the Library. We'll be able to shortcut some of the mistakes they made before."

"I'm worried about time." She frowned. "I dread the consequences if we don't deliver."

"I'm confident." Marcus moved close to Electra and looked

into her eyes. "And when we get to Alexandria, I'll show you all the designs, plans, and schedules."

"I believe in you, Marcus, I do. It's just—"

"I know, I know." Marcus paced along the short rail. "If we fail to deliver the ship, then no matter who the victor is, we won't be around for the victor's triumphant march."

"But if this is too risky, if the price of failure is so high…?" Electra reached out and stopped Marcus.

"You know why. The slaves. If Cleopatra and Antony provide even minimal help, we can start the process of ending slavery, at least in the Roman world. This endeavor isn't for today's slaves but for their unborn children, grandchildren and great-grandchildren who will perhaps have a life of freedom. And I'll be using the knowledge of the ancient Greeks—a dream of mine since I was ten."

"Ending the practice of slavery is a noble cause, a cause worth living or dying for." She watched the waves for a moment before turning back to Marcus. "Do you know how you're going to handle Kleon if he shows up?"

Marcus cleared his throat before answering. "Handling Kleon is another part I haven't figured out yet."

A pained expression spread across Electra's face, and she turned back to the sea. Marcus heard her faint whisper.

"Goddess, help us."

CHAPTER FIFTY

Marcus
Alexandria, July 2

SOON AFTER DARK, Marcus and Talus entered the large meeting room attached to the Bassus warehouse. Papa had often used the space to entertain Ptolemy bureaucrats and rich Nile Valley land-owners. His father had adorned the room with expensive frescoes, ebony furniture and sculpture, but Marcus had sold off both. Over the frescoes, assistants had placed long strips of papyrus upon which Marcus and his naval architect, Quintus Fabius Buteo, had drawn the designs for various components of the warship.

As Marcus inspected the plans, he vowed to keep his promise to Cleopatra and Antony. He would build this new ship and destroy Octavian's fleet.

The room's occupants sat at an oversized worktable. Besides Quintus and his three assistant engineers, there were a logistics chief and a handful of Cleopatra's senior shipwrights. Marcus had stopped construction on Cleopatra's two hulls upon his return from Athens. His ship's final plans weren't complete yet, and rebuilds would be costly.

The naval architect greeted Marcus and Talus. "Everyone's here now."

Talus scanned the sketches. "This results from spending weeks working over a bunch of drawings?"

Quintus folded his hands together. "It's only a design now," he pointed to the walls, "but when finished, it will be the most powerful ship on the sea."

Marcus clapped Talus's shoulder. "Care to join the shipbuilding?"

Talus grimaced. "No, sorry. I'm better at destroying ships. Quintus, I can't wait to shoot your special catapults."

Marcus chuckled. He'd told Talus not to use the word "steam" around the shipwrights. The less they knew, the better. "You'll get your chance at that, don't worry."

Quintus addressed the men, many of whom were studying the drawings. "Let's get started."

Soon, everyone's eyes were on Quintus, but he deferred to Marcus.

Marcus rose to speak. He needed to emphasize secrecy, to put the fear of the gods in the men. "Everyone here has sworn a blood oath to keep secret the plans and work related to the ship's construction. You have made this oath to the goddess Isis, incarnate in Cleopatra." He examined their faces. It was time to stress the importance of the mission. "Break this oath, and a curse will fall upon you and your progeny, barring them from the Afterlife. If anyone wishes no part of this, leave now."

Marcus waited for several moments. Everyone remained seated.

"So, we're committed to the work." Marcus eyed the eager men seated at the table. Something wasn't right. There were one too many faces. Marcus tugged his ear, signaling Talus to prepare for trouble. The big man returned a slight nod.

Marcus whispered to Quintus. "Do you know every man here?" He turned to the group, addressing them in a normal tone. "Where to begin?"

Quintus touched Marcus's arm. "The man at the end on the left," he whispered, "I don't recognize him."

Marcus examined the man before pointing a finger at him. He noticed Talus moving around the table. "Who are you? Name yourself."

In a sudden movement, the man jumped up from his chair. With the way to the door blocked by Talus, he turned and charged toward a low, boarded-up window. He hurled himself at it, smashing through with a violent cracking of wood.

"Talus, he's a spy!" Marcus yelled, but Talus was already in pursuit, climbing through the broken window.

"Well, I'm sure Talus will get his man," Marcus said as the room settled, "so let's not let a few broken boards stop us." He focused on the shipwrights. "To begin, let's review the overall design."

He rolled out a scroll on the table. "As you can see in this drawing, we plan to build a twin-hulled ship."

At these words, chatter erupted from the men around the table, filling the room with excitement, awe and skepticism.

"We'll use the two half-built hulls Queen Cleopatra has in the Paraitonion naval sheds. Each hull will be two hundred and forty feet long with a thirty-foot beam and will carry twelve hundred rowers in two watches. Three masts for each hull—the main set aft of amidships, and two smaller masts, one aft of the main and the other forward. We'll have the normal two helmsmen per hull."

Marcus tapped the drawing. "We'll connect the two hulls with three arched bridges, spanning a horizontal gap of twenty-five feet."

One shipwright stood. "Bassus, will the bridges alone give enough stability to hold the hulls together?"

"Good question. No, they won't, but Cleopatra has promised timber beams of fifty feet or more from her cypress groves in Lebanon. Four two-foot by two-foot beams will lie under each bridge, and we'll attach them to heavy frames in each hull."

Another man stood. "That won't be enough, sir."

Quintus looked over to the man. "We've studied the design of the massive, double-hulled ship built by Ptolemy Philopator two hundred years ago. Our ship will be half as long and won't have the huge platform that spanned both hulls and the gap between them. We won't have four thousand marines stomping around that platform either. We have it figured out, so while it may not be a fast ship—eight miles per hour tops—it will dispense overwhelming damage from our new catapults."

Marcus pointed to the walls. "You're free to examine the drawings. Note the extra ribbing frames we will add to the existing hull. Questions?"

From every direction, a cacophony of voices assailed Marcus.

He wouldn't be meeting Electra later.

*

In the fifth hour of night, Marcus and Quintus left the building and found Talus waiting. He stood relaxed, cleaning his sword.

"You people can talk," Talus observed. "Still talking when those shipwrights left."

Fatigue hit Marcus, but he wanted Talus's report. "We had many details to discuss. How did your evening's work turn out?"

"Bah." Talus spat. "Spies are cowards. They can keep a secret even if you threaten to slit their throat, but tell them you'll cut off their privates, feed it to them, and then cut their throat—they get very talkative."

"It's an unpleasant business we're in," Marcus mused. "Did he talk?"

"Chased him across town to the Western Harbor. The stinking gutter-rat thought he gave me the slip. He talked when properly persuaded. I dumped his body in the water."

"So, who hired this spy?" asked Quintus.

"Who do you think?" asked Talus, shaking his head. "Our old friend, Kleon."

"Are you sure, Talus? That's what he said?" Marcus shouldn't be surprised. Given the defections in Antony's camp, he expected Kleon knew his plans. These spies gave the man an advantage. "We need to check everyone involved in the ship construction to make sure no more Kleon spies bother us."

"Yes, sir. Kleon will get nothing from tonight's spy. If you don't mind, Marcus, my exercise has made me thirsty."

"Have a good night, Talus." The night soon swallowed his hulking form. "Walk with me, Quintus." Marcus smelled the salt in the air as they left the docks.

"I've arranged a secure location to store our plans, so they're safe for now," said Quintus.

Marcus nodded. "When do your engineers build the boiler?"

"Tomorrow we're moving the desert workshops further west to avoid curious visitors and will begin construction after that's completed. Do you expect more steel?"

"I've sent buyers to every potential source, including Parthia. I regret we don't have time for India."

"Marcus, you can't have enough idle rowers in Bassus Trading for our needs."

"The Bassus rowers are free men working for wages now," said Marcus. "To encourage them to join us, I'll offer double wages— thanks to Cleopatra's gold. That will add several hundred, and Talus is going to Rhodes and Crete to recruit rowers and sailors. I want to have the men ready by late spring next year."

"This is a long project. The boiler and steam piping installations alone will take three months. Add another month for installing the catapults. And another for sea trials."

Marcus stopped at the street leading to Quintus's quarters. "Quintus, now we know what we'll be doing for the next year. Go, get a good night's sleep. We start tomorrow."

Building a massive ship and keeping Kleon's spies away were big challenges, but there was one last problem.

Will Electra and I survive this year-long commitment?

CHAPTER FIFTY-ONE

Marcus
Alexandria, December 12

As the *Neptune* slid past the Pharos, Marcus gazed up at the lighthouse's ever-burning flames. Alexandria's harbors were quiet. After Octavian's declaration of war on Egypt in October, most navy squadrons and many of Egypt's troops were in Greece.

Winter storms had delayed his return trip from the naval yard at Paraitonion. On the voyage, his mind never stopped reviewing necessary work to finish the massive warship. Quintus had fitted his new boiler design with what he called a "release valve." Tests of the first crude steam catapult had sent a ten-pound stone ball through a two-inch thick plank at five hundred feet. He expected even better results as the design matured.

During the past month in Paraitonion, Marcus had worked on construction problems with the naval architects, fighting to keep the ship construction on schedule. Marcus had named it *Vulcan*, after the Roman god of fire, proper for a ship with a belly of fire and steel. The next phase was to connect the support beams and bridges to each hull.

At the docks, Marcus waved when he spotted Electra and Talus. Electra was stunning in a blue silk dress. Gods, how he had missed her. Their arrangement was that Marcus would spend equal time in

Alexandria as in Paraitonion, staying busy with ship construction and Bassus Trading activities.

Marcus gave Electra a long embrace and kiss. He clasped forearms with Talus.

"Good to see you, sir," said Talus.

"I need to talk to you Talus. Coming, Electra?" When Marcus looked into her eyes, he exchanged a silent conversation of love, want, and mutual respect with her.

Electra grabbed his arm. "I'll not let you escape. I go where you go."

Marcus laughed. "I want your company, dear."

"Hey, you two, stick to business," said Talus, grinning.

Marcus led them to the *Vulcan* design review building where the walls again displayed the colorful frescoes.

"Before you start, sir," said Talus, "I've wanted to ask you something for a while."

"Sure." Marcus glanced over at Electra. She raised her eyebrows.

"You're a Roman citizen now," said Talus. "Whoever wins this war, you go on with Bassus Trading, pulling in the gold. Octavian would not want to disrupt Bassus Trading and its important grain trade. So why fight at all?"

"Octavian would never let me keep Bassus Trading. I've never filled you in on my motives, Talus," replied Marcus. "Electra and Quintus know them. My motivation is moral. Octavian has the ambition to conquer the world, to finish what his Uncle, Julius Caesar, couldn't do. Octavian's actions will cause death and enslavement of millions. He has the military power to outdo even Alexander."

Talus's face brightened. "There's glory in that." He cast his eyes at the ground. "I jest, sir. I don't want that to happen."

Marcus chuckled. "This military power is for Octavian's glory and that of the Roman elite, and I want to stop it. Our fight with Kleon, however, is also a personal matter for me and for Electra."

Electra looked at Talus. "I don't want Marcus in a war. But if he can stop Kleon…" Tears welled in her eyes.

"It'll be fine, dear." Marcus put his arm around her shoulders, knowing how raw her memories of captivity still were. "My foremost motivation is to keep the powers in the Archimedes scrolls out of the hands of evil men like Octavian and Kleon. I'm not sure if Hippolytus and his Oracles should have them either. Maybe we should destroy them. I don't know."

"Well, sir, that's something to think about, though I worry my simple mind might explode." Talus patted his head. "What did you want to ask me?"

"Will you accept military operations command for the *Vulcan*, including marines, archers and artillerymen?"

Talus showed an ear-to-ear grin. "Thought you'd never ask. I accept. I'll be in my legion days again, with better weapons. Wish I could tell my old man. When do I take command?"

"Good question," said Marcus. "I suspect late this spring."

Electra covered her ears at Talus's curses.

"Sorry." Talus scratched his head. "I worry that we can't recruit the best troops. They're all in Greece."

31 B.C.

CHAPTER FIFTY-TWO

Electra
Alexandria, May 1

ELECTRA STEPPED OUT of the litter and onto the road in front of Marcus's house. She was glad to be out from behind the stifling curtains which shielded the interior from any Octavian spies lurking in the city. Only days ago, as Caesarion returned from the Gymnasium, a mob, angry over the increased taxes levied to pay for Antony's war, had chased the boy through the streets.

At Marcus's urging, Electra had increased her security to ten men, including two mounted troopers. Once a week, she allowed herself to leave the palace complex while Marcus visited her twice a week. With the workload she had in the palace, she found the restriction bearable.

On her weekly outings, she went to visit Marcus when he was in Alexandria. These days he was as likely to be in Paraetonium, supervising his ship's construction. She savored their conversations, not of war or building ships, but of everyday events. When there was time, they often read out loud. She loved Greek poems and hearing Marcus's voice reciting them. In turn, she read history to Marcus, fighting to stay focused on the scholarly material.

At the street, Bassus bodyguards escorted her through the gate and into the house. There Titus met her and led her to a sofa by the fountain in the atrium. Soon after, a servant girl came up to her.

"Something to drink, Princess Electra? Water or fruit juice? Something a little stronger?"

"No, I'll have water and a slice of lemon." Though it wasn't a command, Cleopatra had asked everyone to call Electra princess. Electra didn't want the title or any part of the throne. Her mother had been an illegitimate child of a cousin of Cleopatra's father—not the proper provenance for royalty.

"At once." The girl hurried out of the room.

Electra was soon sipping the refreshing drink beside the fountain—its melodious sounds soothing her. As soon as Marcus entered the atrium, she ran to his embrace and gave him a long, passionate kiss. She wished it could last until the dreadful war was over and Cleopatra was back home.

As she slid her lips away, she pressed her cheek against Marcus's chest, feeling his heart's strong rhythm. She longed to make love, but she had received a letter from Cleopatra and wanted him to know the contents.

"I've received a letter from Cleopatra." She waited for his attention. "Can I read it to you?"

"Yes, please do."

Electra retook her seat, making room for Marcus to settle in beside her. "It's short."

Dearest Cousin,

Antony and I hope you are well. Caesarion writes that you are keeping to his language lessons. I know he must pester you for more practice of his archery or swordplay. He so wants to join this war, but I will have none of that.

We are well enough, though our army suffers from disease and lack of provisions. Antony moved his main camp to the northern promontory. I remain at the Actium naval headquarters on the southern side of the Gulf of Ambracia. Octavian and Agrippa have taken Methone in the Peloponnese and cut our lines to Alexandria.

The courier comes, so I must close. Take care of my Caesarion, the future of Egypt.

Cleopatra

Electra clutched the letter in her hands. "The conditions must be awful. From this letter, it sounds like she needs a woman's comfort. She needs me, Marcus. I wish I could be there."

"That's illogical, dear." Marcus placed her hands in his. "Cleopatra asks you to care for her son, not to go commiserate with her. Besides, she has other women in her court."

Electra felt a darkness closing in on her. The fountain was no longer soothing; instead, it marked the slow passage of time. Marcus's words sounded right in her mind, but her heart found them blocking her need to act.

"Besides," Marcus continued, "it would be dangerous to reach her as Agrippa blocks all the sailing lanes, and Octavian's legions watch the overland routes through Greece."

"You're right." Electra said standing. "But I need to do something."

Marcus took her in his arms. "Write her a sympathetic letter. Tell her Caesarion is healthy and progressing in his studies and that you will be there for him if something happens to the queen."

"Yes, that will ease her mind." In his embrace, the warmth of his body seeped into hers, giving a comfort and a tranquility she hadn't had since her mother's death years ago. She traced a finger down his cheek and along his jaw. "I love you, Marcus."

"And I love you, Electra." He gave her a soft kiss on the lips.

She murmured two words. "Love me." She needed his warmth, his strength inside her.

Marcus smiled. "I'm doing that right now with my eyes, but I can involve more of me."

Electra moaned as familiar arms lifted her. With great care, Marcus carried her away from the fountain and time froze, if only for their love.

CHAPTER FIFTY-THREE

Electra
Alexandria, June 5

"So," said Electra, as she and Marcus watched the activity in the Great Harbor from a window in her palace room, "you're leaving for Sicily in two weeks?"

"Yes, darling, that's been my plan," answered Marcus.

"And do you expect me to stay in Alexandria while you sail off to war?"

Say it's not true.

Marcus wiped a hand across his face. "We've talked about this. I appreciate all the support you've given me this past year. Your love has sustained me through some difficult days. But a sea battle is a dangerous place for a—"

"For what? A woman?" She glared at Marcus before throwing her arms out. "You expected me to sit around while the love of my life enters the jaws of death? Better change your expectations, foolish man." She felt her face flush with ire.

For a moment, Marcus seemed at a loss for words. "What if I fail? I don't want Octavian or Kleon to get near you. And what about Caesarion?"

"You won't fail, Marcus. You have the most advanced ship and weapons ever built. As for Caesarion, Cleopatra has confined him to the palace with his war council and his military trainers."

"You're smart, resilient, and tough. A shared fate then?" Marcus offered his outstretched arms.

Electra slipped into his arms. "Shared fate is what we are all about, Marcus. Shared minds, shared bodies, and shared danger. When I agreed to help with the scrolls, a bond formed between us." Her voice trembled. "We were not sharing a simple academic endeavor, but one of shared danger, shared adventure, and shared achievement—Goddess Isis, little did I know."

"It was more than either of us bargained for." Marcus walked to the window with a harbor view.

Electra followed his gaze to the Pharos, still spreading its luminosity across the sea. "How many men get the chance to positively affect the path of history? It's noble. I want to share it beside you."

Marcus wrapped his arms around her waist. "It's risky, but all my fears flee in the face of your courage. How can I doubt this path I, *we*, have chosen?" He looked down into her eyes. "Anything could happen, but our combined strengths will give us better chances. Yes, I do want you there, my love."

She pressed against his body. "I'm glad you've seen the wisdom of being together. It will inspire the men to see you bring me along."

"I hadn't thought of that. But I make one request. I want you on the *Neptune*, not the *Vulcan*." When she started to object, he pressed a finger over her lips. "I'll give Captain Socus strict orders that you're in command. The *Neptune* won't engage in the fighting but will be there in case events don't go as planned. Regardless of what happens, we're going to face it together... to the end."

"It's a compromise, but I can live with it." Electra was satisfied. This was the best she could have hoped for.

"Good. I didn't want to tie you to your bed on sailing day."

"You're dreadful, Marcus Bassus." She lowered her eyes. "But

I understand beds are good for forming… shared bonds." She ran her hands down his hard chest.

Marcus laughed. "Is that so?"

"Race you," she said and took off running. She would enjoy today. War, looming on the horizon, might soon sever their bonds forever—at least in this world.

CHAPTER FIFTY-FOUR

Marcus
Alexandria, August 2

NEAR SUNSET, MARCUS and Electra climbed to the upper observation level of the Pharos. Bathed in the setting sun's light, they stood at the waist-high wall and watched the sea.

"Where will the ship come from?" asked Electra.

Marcus pointed out to sea. "The *Vulcan* will come from the west. It left Paraitonion three weeks ago for sea trials. Absent major problems, Quintus and Captain Pollio will bring the ship to Alexandria at sunset and set anchor near Pirates Harbor just north of the Pharos."

"And we'll leave tomorrow, my love?"

"Yes. Are you packed? Including good, heavy sandals?"

"Yes. Those shoes are ugly. Even Medusa wouldn't wear them." Electra wriggled her fingers through her hair mimicking the snakes that formed Medusa's hair.

Marcus couldn't control himself and burst out laughing. Electra joined in.

"Hey, what's that?" asked Electra, shading her eyes.

Marcus followed her gaze. Even at five miles distant, the ship was awe inspiring. It plowed through the sea under four huge, billowing sails. The twin hulls and triple connecting bridges gave it a bizarre appearance, like some deformed sea monster.

"It's the *Vulcan*!" Marcus did an excited little dance.

"It's a behemoth, Marcus."

"It's beautiful," Marcus said in a low, reverent tone.

"My handsome man has a beautiful ship," Electra said, hugging him.

"Tonight, Talus and I will transfer to the *Vulcan*. In the morning, Honorius will take you to the *Neptune*, which will sail out to meet up with the *Vulcan*. Tomorrow, the race to reach Actium begins. If we win, we'll destroy Octavian and his fleet."

"Race? What happens if we lose that race?"

As the light faded, Marcus took one last look out to sea. "In that case, Antony and Cleopatra will try to break their fleets out. Likely, they'll be destroyed."

Electra's face paled. "You must succeed, Marcus. You must." Her eyes teared. "If Octavian wins, he takes Egypt. If Kleon defeats you," she paused, choked with emotion, "I'll kill myself."

She embraced Marcus.

Her trembling told Marcus the scars from her captivity ran deep. Defeating Kleon's ship and Octavian's fleet would not be easy, but necessary if he were to reach his goals. A life with Electra was his priority, but he had to stop Kleon first. "Don't fret, my love. All will be well."

That magnificent ship will lead us to victory.

Marcus

Alexandria, August 2

Marcus wiped the perspiration from his brow and took one last look at Alexandria as the pilot guided the small harbor craft past the reefs at the mouth of the Western Harbor. As Marcus stared up at the lighthouse fire, it abruptly flared up, brighter than ever.

Was that an omen?

They glided past the western Moon Gate. At the tip of Pharos Island, the lights of the Temple of Poseidon slid by.

Behind him, Talus mumbled a prayer to the traditional Roman war god and goddess—Mars and Bellona. Marcus added his own silent prayer to Poseidon, Greek god of the seas.

His thoughts turned again to the dilemma he faced. If he interceded in this war using the technology of the scrolls, he risked releasing a devastating weapon upon man. If he stayed away, he risked Kleon doing the same, except it would fall into the wrong hands—Octavian's.

Maybe Hippolytus was right. Maybe mankind needed wiser men to guide them down the path to technology forged from nature by man's imagination.

He shuddered with apprehension. It was too late to stop what was already in motion. He just needed to win.

I wish I had never opened those cursed scrolls.

CHAPTER FIFTY-FIVE

Kleon
Sicily, August 3

KLEON TOSSED A coin at the feet of the inebriated woman, a whore from the tavern below. The golden head of Octavian stared at him from the mud. "Go back, woman," Kleon ordered, wiping the light rain from his face. "I'm going to the top of the hill."

Yesterday's downpours had left the hillside soggy and slippery. Using bushes for handholds, he reached the crest, where he had a panoramic view of the shipyard on Sicily's south coast. The huge trireme dominated the scene. Scores of men scurried around preparing for tomorrow's sea trials.

Kleon had three enemies—Antony, Cleopatra, and Marcus Bassus—so he had named his great ship *Cerberus*, after the three-headed dog with lion's claws and a serpent's tail who guarded the Underworld. The ship, with its name carved in huge letters on the stern, may be a product of Octavian's gold, but his steam catapults would carry the day.

Marcus better not be hiding like a coward in Alexandria.

The spy reports from Egypt indicated someone was building an unusual warship in Paraitonion. Cleopatra or Marcus? It didn't matter. As long as he witnessed Kleon's victory, Marcus could be rowing a river punt.

Kleon unslung his wine skin and raised it to the sky. "To victory and the death of Marcus Bassus," he cried. He squirted the wine into his mouth but immediately spat it out. It was bitter, undrinkable. He ignored the fleeting shadow of an omen and tossed the skin. Soon, he'd have sweet victory.

He left the hill, leaving his victory wine to trickle out into the mud.

CHAPTER FIFTY-SIX

Marcus

The Mediterranean Sea off Sicily, August 27

"READY ARROWS," MARCUS commanded the bowmen on the *Vulcan's* stern connecting bridge. "Pollio, bring us to a stop."

Marcus gave the order, and a flurry of flaming arrows streaked skyward, signaling the *Neptune* to close.

An hour later, Marcus briefly embraced Electra before joining Talus, the two captains, and the chief engineer, Meidias, on the ship's upper deck.

Marcus addressed the men. "We've been off Sicily for a week with no sign of Kleon. We're out of time. Captains, set sail for Greece and the Gulf of Ambracia. Two-hour rower shifts. Our goal: break Octavian's blockade." He turned to Meidias. "Extinguish all boiler fires except for forward catapults. Save your fuel."

"Yes, sir," replied Meidias. "Sir, does Antony know of our plans? A breakout attempt before we arrive could mean…"

"I know," replied Marcus. "That would mean defeat. His last dispatch told of disease, low morale, and food shortages. He's desperate. I sent dispatches from Alexandria telling him to await our arrival on the first of September and to attempt no breakout until after the full moon on the fourth. If he makes an attack before our arrival, Octavian will destroy his fleet."

Marcus addressed the group again. "Keep a sharp lookout. Any warships we spot will be Octavian's. We must avoid engagement at all costs. If we don't arrive on time, our year's work will be for naught."

I can't let Electra down. And damn the gods if I'll let Kleon win.

Marcus
The Ionian Sea off Zakyntos Island, September 1

"You're right, Captain," Marcus said, dropping a few feet to the deck from the main mast.

Marcus rubbed his palms, red and scraped from the rough wood. The masthead view was exhilarating, although scary. Up there, he could see for miles.

"That's the island of Zakyntos." He slapped the mast. "We're too far south." Marcus was sweating but not from climbing. He was angry that the wind had pushed them far off course.

"Curse Jupiter's eyes!" cried Talus. "If that's Zakyntos, we'll not make Actium today."

"Captain, head to the northwest, top speed," Marcus ordered.

Marcus and Talus hustled up to the small, aft-most deck of the portside hull above the helmsmen where they had a battle command center of signalmen and runners.

Talus eyed the four helmsmen heaving against their tillers to turn the huge ship. "We won't make it, Marcus. Wind's against us. And more storms are likely today."

"Gods, have I failed?"

What would Hippolytus tell me?

"Nay. If Antony does as you asked, we can be a day late."

"He's hotheaded. I hope he'll be patient."

Four hours later, both shifts had worked the oars. The *Vulcan*, clear of Zakyntos, turned north, steering to stay away from the lee shore of the islands of Kefalonia and Lefkas. The plan was to lower sails at sunset and continue by oar power for a few hours during the night. Tomorrow morning, they would be near enough to Actium to start the attack.

"Sail!" came the masthead's shrill call.

Captain Pollio looked aloft. "Where?"

"Coming off the port beam."

Marcus, high up on the command deck, peered in the indicated direction. A smudge of white showed on the horizon. Was it Kleon? Or Octavian warship? He paced the narrow deck.

Half an hour later, Talus climbed up to Marcus's position. "Do you see the thin trail of smoke coming from that ship?" the big man asked.

"I was beginning to wonder if that was smoke. It's likely Kleon. Son of a bitch!" Marcus gritted his teeth.

Talus snarled. "Our friend is back."

At the rail, Marcus called down to Captain Pollio. "Captain, set course to intercept."

"Aye, sir, but that north wind will slow us."

"Understood, Pollio." Marcus turned to Talus. "We're going to get that bastard, by the gods."

"I'll get the boilers stoked in case we catch him before nightfall," said Talus, scrambling down the stairs.

*

With the last of the light fading, the *Vulcan* turned northeast in the enemy ship's wake. Marcus looked up to the eastern sky, where a three-quarters moon was rising behind thin clouds. The sky was clearing after intermittent rain much of the day.

He turned to his flagman. "Give Talus the signal to open fire with the forward catapults."

On the forward bridge, Talus's man acknowledged the signal. A few moments later, there was a sudden jarring crack and a howling as the catapult's ten-pound stone streaked toward Kleon's ship. Three more balls quickly followed. A cloud of white steam engulfed the bow before the wind scattered it. A cheer arose from the crew and the fighting men, which soon turned to groans as the stones splashed well short of their mark.

Then, a puff of white engulfed the stern of the enemy ship.

"Incoming!" came the cry from the bow. Marcus ducked behind the low rail. A moment passed before he heard several distant splashes. Kleon's shots also fell short.

Ahead, Kleon's ship was fading into the night. The ships were close enough now that sounds would guide Marcus. In the morning's first light, Kleon would be out there, waiting.

Their hatred would at last find resolution, and men would die; a way of life would fall, and a new one rise from the ashes. Would good or evil triumph? Would he and Electra find happiness and love from a life together? Only the gods knew.

He thought once again of the world he wished to build. A world powered by machines, freeing man from his chains. A defeat tomorrow would end that dream and put the Roman boot on the neck of the world.

I won't sleep tonight.

CHAPTER FIFTY-SEVEN

Talus
The Ionian Sea near Lefkas Island, Greece, September 2

TALUS HATED SURPRISES. Before sunrise, boilers fired and checked, he inspected the missiles arrayed in their storage bins below decks. Time for catapult testing.

He had trained one hundred artillerymen for *Vulcan's* catapults. The man helping him test, Fabius, was the brightest. He had even adjusted Quintus's rangefinder, improving accuracy. Talus stopped at the port bow tower. "Last tower. Two more catapults."

"Eighteen down and two to go," quipped Fabius.

Each of *Vulcan's* twin hulls had five catapult towers: three amidships, one at the bow, and one in the stern. Two deadly steam catapults topped each tower.

Fabius fired several five-pound stones from the first catapult.

Talus whistled. "Fine shots."

"Number nineteen's a sweet one."

At the last catapult, Talus loaded a full rack of sixteen bolts into the circular repeater cylinder. Pulling the loading level would drop a bolt into the firing chamber. A firing lever released the steam, shooting the missile out. Ten heartbeats later, the steam recharged, and he could launch again. Quintus's remarkable repeater, for bolts or stones, was beyond Talus's comprehension. The mechanism was their real secret weapon.

He jerked the lever, loading a missile, and then slowly pulled the firing lever. A wet, hot cloud burst from the catapult. A quick moment later, the projectile splashed down a quarter of a mile away.

"Take that, Kleon, you murdering bastard."

I'll never fail Marcus again because of you. The Vulcan's *ready. I'm ready.*

Electra
The Ionian Sea near Lefkas Island, September 2

Electra was on *Neptune's* deck at dawn. Yesterday's storm had moved on. A lamp glowed near the main mast, casting flickering shadows as the crew tended their business. Near the upper deck stairs, Electra spotted Neema. Maybe she had updated news. Electra hastened over to her.

"Good morning, Miss." Neema bowed slightly.

"Neema, I'm desperate—any idea what will happen today? Did Captain Socus say if Marcus would attack Octavian?"

"We'll know soon. He's headed over."

Electra saw the captain scampering across the deck. "Captain Socus?"

Socus stopped. "Yes? Many things to do right now."

Electra didn't like the man's curt manner. "What news? What will happen today?"

"Happen?" The man shook his head. "Bassus will start the most significant battle since Carthage fell. The world will never be the same."

"What will the *Neptune* do?"

"We've exchanged signals. Bassus is about to attack Kleon. The *Neptune* will move beyond engagement range. Five miles.

We'll still see the battle and their signals and be close enough to offer assistance."

Electra exchanged a glance with Neema. "What kind of assistance? We have no catapults and only a few mercenaries."

"Being toothless may allow us to live if the battle goes poorly," replied Socus. "Worst case—we can pick up *Vulcan* survivors. Cabins, both of you." He pointed below.

Electra felt cold, and her chest tightened. She saw the maelstrom of activity around her. The crew raised sails, and the ship was turning away from Marcus.

"Marcus," she whispered.

Neema took her arm. "Don't worry, Electra. Marcus has a powerful ship. And Talus. Come, let's get below."

Walking in a daze, Electra looked back to where she had last seen the *Vulcan*.

Marcus, if you get yourself killed, I'll never forgive you.

CHAPTER FIFTY-EIGHT

Marcus

The Ionian Sea off Lefkas Island, September 2

MARCUS STRAINED INTO the twilight beyond *Vulcan's* bow, searching for Kleon. The sun was lighting the tops of the mountains of Kefalonia and western Greece when Marcus heard the lookout's call.

"Sail! Off port bow heading northwest."

"What's this?" cried Talus, spitting on the deck. "It's moving away from Actium?"

Marcus frowned. "Are we sure it's him?"

Marcus ran to the port side with Talus. There was enough light to see the large black shape of Kleon's ship two miles away.

Captain Pollio joined Marcus. "He's trying to draw us away from the Octavian fleet. We should stay the course for Actium."

Talus scoffed. "What? Would you have Kleon come up our backside? He'll smash us before we can disengage from the fleet."

"Talus is right," said Marcus, his voice taut. "We must neutralize Kleon before we attack Octavian."

"How long do we chase him?" asked Pollio.

"A half day at most," Marcus replied. "Tomorrow, or the next day, Antony will attack. We'll catch Kleon. Don't fail me, Pollio."

Pollio nodded. "The winds are light and west by southwest. It will take a while, but my sailors and rowers will give their best."

The *Vulcan* had six hundred rowers in three banks on the two outer sides. Another six hundred were in reserve and for relief. Marcus recruited most from Bassus Trading while the rest he found in various ports.

Marcus checked his weapons—sword on hip and dagger in boot—before turning to Talus. "In two hours, get all six boiler fires back up."

"Aye, sir. Time those twenty-five lazy firemen earned their keep. Can't wait to see what Kleon's up to. My gut says he's not running."

*

Three hours later, under a blue and cloudless sky, Marcus sensed the wind pick up from the west. He observed the ruffling stern sail.

"Trim that sail, Theosus," commanded Pollio. Sailors attacked the lines. Pollio operated the ship with twenty officers and one hundred and twenty sailors and craftsmen.

"Marcus," called Talus. "Kleon's making a move." He pointed out over the bow at the ship a mile away. "He's turning to port, trying to cut across our bow and rake us with all his catapults."

"Captain," came the call from the masthead. "Ship ahead carries the name *Cerberus*."

"Acknowledged," came the return call from Pollio. "Eagle eyes up there."

Talus scoffed. "*Cerberus*, the three-headed dog. Kleon's keeping this in the family, the son of a bitch."

Marcus glared at Kleon's ship. "If we turn away, we'll head dead into the wind. We have to do it. Captain, turn to port. Head southwest."

"That will be a big turn for this double-hulled ship," said Talus. "Kleon will have the advantage."

As Marcus watched, the *Cerberus* continued to move closer.

When the gap closed to half a mile, a cloud of white burst from the port side of Kleon's ship. "Everyone down," Marcus yelled.

"Get down, fool," Talus cried to the helmsmen. "I'm headed for the bow catapults, Marcus," he called as he hurried down the steps. He dashed across the deck.

Marcus lost sight of Talus. The *Vulcan* was beginning the swing through the wind when he heard the splashes of Kleon's catapult stones.

"Short," said Pollio.

"But he's still got more range than we do," observed Marcus. "We must close in if we are to hit Kleon's ship."

"Looks like we have another volley coming in. Heads up, everyone," Pollio shouted.

This time catapult stones rained down on the forward sections. Marcus heard several screams, including that of an archer on the forward connecting bridge who lost his balance and toppled overboard. Marcus clenched his fists. He could do nothing for the man.

On the bow, Marcus saw a blast of steam as Talus launched a return volley. In the time it took Kleon to fire a single volley, Talus loosed four stones from each catapult. Marcus slapped the rail when he saw all the shots fall fifty paces short.

A few sailors grabbed loose lines as the sails flapped against the masts. They were head up into the wind. Marcus growled in frustration as the *Cerberus* continued its turn, and gaining the wind over its starboard quarter, Kleon's ship shot ahead. As the *Cerberus* reached a point off the *Vulcan's* bow, white steam clouds again engulfed the enemy ship.

"Incoming! Get down!" Marcus cried.

This time Kleon fired long, sharp bolts. Marcus flinched as one hit and stuck in the stairs below him. Several penetrated the sails, leaving small tears in their wake. He looked forward in time to see a burst of steam from Talus's bow catapults. A heartbeat later, Marcus got the results he was hoping to see.

Hit!

Cries of triumph erupted from Talus' crew and from the fighting men across both hulls. Several of the catapult's stones crashed against the enemy ship's hull.

Marcus pumped his fist. "Kleon, your three-headed dog now has one less head." He stood and detected a sudden change in the wind. It was more from the north, and it was stronger. "Captain, this is our chance. Get the sails trimmed to the new wind and give me attack speed from the rowers. Pull in behind *Cerberus*. At close range, we'll devastate them."

The captain barked orders. Marcus could hear the cries of the drum masters below decks. A moment later, wind and muscle power propelled the *Vulcan* forward. The deep boom of the drum synchronized with his heart.

Marcus raced down the deck, alerting his catapult crews in the towers to prepare to fire at will on the enemy ship. "Aim for the steering oars and the helmsmen."

He reached the forward mast and called to Talus in the tower. "Talus, we'll be crossing behind Kleon's stern. Watch for my signal."

"Excellent, Marcus. We'll shoot him in the ass."

Marcus sprinted back to the command deck. His mouth was dry, but his palms were sweaty. He relayed to Pollio the plan to disable *Cerberus's* steering.

Pollio called over his signalman before replying. "That could cripple Kleon. Knock him from the fight."

"That won't be enough, Pollio. It's critical we destroy that ship so no one can ever use it again."

Marcus peered over the port side as the *Vulcan* lined up the enemy's stern. Marcus looked over at the signalman.

Almost. Hold. Hold.

"Fire!"

As soon as the signalman waved his flags, a long series of whooshing sounds erupted. Talus fired a full rack of stones, a dozen missiles. A huge cloud of wet steam enveloped the *Vulcan* like an angry volcano. A moment later, the cloud rolled over and off the ship's stern. Marcus looked skyward to watch the flight of stones arch their way toward Kleon's ship. It seemed forever before they slammed the enemy's stern.

At this range, Marcus could hear the cracking of wood and the thud of stones. *Cerberus's* stern exploded, sending wood and men flying into the air. Debris littered the water. Men wailed.

Focused as he was on the damage, he jumped when the next round of catapult firings erupted. More missiles impacted the enemy than before though a few shots splashed in the sea.

"Look, Marcus," cried an excited Pollio. "We've shot *Cerberus's* steering oars away. They can't maneuver now, so the helmsmen have deserted the stern deck."

"We've breached a good bit of the stern planks," Marcus added. "Make another pass across his tail. Maybe we can sink the bastard."

What a waste of lives.

"And set the rowers back to cruising speed. We've knocked out several catapults, too."

"It will take time to reverse course. I'll get the crew going." Pollio moved to the rail at the front of the command deck and called out his orders.

Talus came pounding up the stairs. "We kicked Kleon's ass with that last volley." He gave several beast-like howls. "Something I picked up in Gaul," he said with a sheepish grin.

"It's not over yet, Talus," Marcus reminded him. "We will make another pass and hope—"

"Incoming!"

Marcus, Talus and the helmsmen reacted at once, moving into a crouch. A crunching sound behind Marcus made him turn. A stone had crushed the signalman's face. He lay against the stern rail. On the deck, a bloody stone rolled with the ship's motion. Cries of pain from the bow and from the starboard hull were signs of more injuries. Pollio called up two men to take the dead signalman below decks.

"Jupiter's balls!" yelled Talus. "We've got to be careful. He's still got catapults that can hit us."

Marcus turned to Pollio. "Captain, make sure you get men to carry the injured down to the doctor and his medics."

Another cry from the mast sent everyone to the deck. This time, Marcus noticed the shots landed well short of the *Vulcan*.

The *Vulcan* took a half-hour to make the turn and run across the stern of the *Cerberus*, which had continued straight along its southward course, unable to turn. This time Marcus had his catapults in two groups. The first group fired stones, followed by bolts from the second group. He sent Talus around to check each catapult's accuracy.

With the high firing rate, each catapult could launch five or six shots, making this new round's devastation as great as the earlier firing. Kleon's ship speed slowed as many of his rowers—exposed through the damaged stern—took hits. Oars became tangled, further slowing the enemy ship's progress.

Damage from the enemy's return fire horrified Marcus. Half the oars on the starboard side were useless. A few stones penetrated the starboard hull.

The chief fireman sent up a message that all boilers were undamaged and working, but one of the hull breaches had exposed the main boiler. That worried Marcus, and he had Pollio send down carpenters to repair the hull as best they could. He knew the damage an exploding boiler could do.

Marcus called Talus up to the command deck. "Talus, are your marines up to repelling boarders?"

"Sir, I only have fifty men, and repelling boarders wasn't planned for."

"I know. That was my decision. That's why we must finish this."

Use the Greek fire at your three best catapults." Talus seemed to pale at the words.

"Are you sure, Marcus? That stuff is a two-edged sword." Talus grimaced. "I advise against it."

Marcus took in a deep breath.

When he had bought the "Greek" fire from an Arabian merchant through the Bassus trading post in Petra, he hoped he would never need to use it. Creating the substance required mixing palm oil, pitch, quicklime, sulfur and charcoal and pouring it into terra cotta jars sealed with lead. Volatile and explosive when exposed to a flame, oil-soaked linen wicks triggered a fiery blast when the jar shattered.

Greek fire was flammable beyond any other substance, which was why storage was under water in the bilge using special metal-lined crates. Instead of inert stones, they would now fire hazardous pots of Greek fire.

A chance explosion could happen during the catapult launch, but the current situation overrode that risk.

"We can't afford any more damage, or we'll be useless to Antony. I don't want to risk a boiler explosion, either. Talus, this has to be the death blow to Kleon." Marcus was desperate.

"Yes, sir. I'll need time to get the Greek fire from the bilge."

"Understood. Hold fire until my signal." Marcus watched the man dash away.

One thing about Talus: he was loyal.

It was midday when the *Vulcan* neared the *Cerberus*. Talus had three conventional catapults ready on the port side deck, armed with the Greek fire.

"Five hundred feet, Marcus," advised Pollio.

"Keep us close," Marcus ordered. Already the enemy ship had fired its catapults, though its slow reloading meant that his ship would only suffer through two or three volleys at most.

But as Marcus observed the enemy ship, something unexpected happened. The oars on *Cerberus's* starboard side increased their speed, while those on the port side held their oars stationary, blades against the water, angled back. The enemy ship turned hard to port toward the *Vulcan* and in minutes had completed a half-circle. Kleon now had the *Cerberus* set up to fire its full starboard set of working catapults.

"Four hundred feet and closing," advised Pollio.

"Fire!" cried Marcus. The *Vulcan* erupted in another cloud of steam. A heartbeat later, two puffs of white steam came from the other ship.

"Incoming!" cried Captain Pollio.

As soon as the enemy fired, Marcus realized that the projectiles were not stones or bolts. They were grapnels.

"Abort! Hard to starboard, Captain," Marcus yelled. "Don't let them grapple us."

At the sound of metal clanging, Marcus knew it was too late. Down on the deck, the grapnels shot back to the rail as the double-hulled ship's headway pulled in the slack. Sailors and marines rushed toward the iron-spiked weapons, ready to cut them loose, but a cloud of arrows descended upon the men, killing or wounding at least seven or eight.

The *Vulcan* lurched to a stop. Marcus grabbed a rail to keep his footing. The grapnel lines and the rising north wind worked against them.

"Archers, return fire," yelled Marcus. "Talus, fire your catapults. Have the remaining catapults reload with bolts. Take out those archers." Another two grapnels slammed onto the deck. More men rushed to cut the grapple lines, but again enemy archers killed many and drove the others below deck. The screams of the dying and wounded filled Marcus with dread. He dived to the deck as another wave of arrows whistled overhead.

Over a hundred archers were firing at the *Vulcan*. Marcus's inexperience had made him blunder and turn a long-range duel of steam catapults into a conventional battle.

"Everyone below," ordered Marcus. "You helmsmen, too."

Instead of following them below, Marcus sped across the stern-most connecting bridge. At the starboard hull, he found the missile fire much lighter. With only two of four tillers operating, he ordered the helmsmen there to stay at their posts and grabbed a few of the sailors to add additional muscle power. He told them to keep low.

Why did Talus wait?

In answer, there was a sudden explosion of noise and a new level of screaming. Marcus peered back through the drifting steam clouds to the *Cerberus*. The Greek fire had smashed onto the upper deck of Kleon's ship. Burning men were running around frantic as their shipmates tried to douse the flames. Marcus knew water couldn't extinguish Greek fire. In desperation, blazing men jumped into the sea. They would drown or burn to death.

The enemy crew continued to pull the *Vulcan* toward the *Cerberus*. Marcus could see why. Winches connected to two of the grapnel lines provided tremendous pulling power while a hundred marines and sailors heaved on the others. Marcus raced back across the bridge to the central catapult tower. He paused, his heart pounding in his chest.

What was taking the catapult teams so long to switch to bolts?

Marcus climbed to the top. There he found only one catapult working. Enemy arrows had decimated the men. The rest—including the wounded—were working to switch to bolts. Marcus peered at the action on the main deck below. Talus was carrying a huge mercenary shield moving toward the nearest grapnel line. Arrows hurtled by, one after another.

The man must be crazy.

From around his shield, his gladius hacked at the rope. Most naval grapnel lines had copper wire running through it. Even with Talus's strength, it took four or five hacks before he severed the line.

More archers were targeting Talus now. "Talus, you crazy fool, get out of there!" Marcus yelled. Somehow, his words must have penetrated Talus' thick skull, because the giant retreated to the forward tower.

The two ships were less than fifty feet apart now. Marcus grasped his isolation, separated from Pollio, Talus, the helm and his marines. An hour ago, an easy victory had seemed at hand. Where had he gone wrong? At least Kleon's ship was on fire. He breathed easy knowing Electra was far away and safe.

Then his spirits rose when one of the starboard hull catapults began a steady fire of deadly bolts against Kleon's marines. The catapult in his tower joined in, too. Talus's head popped up in the forward tower. He seemed unhurt.

Marcus's eyes swept back to Kleon's ship, and his heart dropped. The enemy marines were erecting a corvus, a boarding ramp, and using it as a shield against Marcus's catapults. With many of his marines down, an overwhelming number of enemy fighters was about to storm aboard the *Vulcan*.

CHAPTER FIFTY-NINE

Marcus

The Ionian Sea off Lefkas Island, September 2

THE TWO HEAVY vessels slammed together, sending a shock through both hulls and hurling men to the decks.

As Marcus looked on from the center tower, Kleon's men continued to secure a boarding ramp between the ships. With ropes and pulleys moving the ramp, the enemy men swung it over the gap between the ships.

A burst of light drew Marcus's attention. The *Cerberus's* stern mast and sail were aflame as was much of the starboard side of Kleon's massive ship. Marcus could still hear the screams from the enemy fighters as both burning and panicked men jumped overboard. Kleon's marines would fight a desperate battle with nowhere to retreat.

Marcus peered over the tower wall back toward the starboard hull towers. The catapults there, unable to aim low enough, struggled to target Kleon's men. Marcus searched in vain for Talus on the forward tower.

He turned to one of the catapult loaders. "Take a message to Captain Pollio below. Tell him to organize the rowers to fight any fires. Get everything that can hold water. Wet clothing and pieces of sailcloth and be ready to fight fires. Go!"

Marcus peeked over the tower wall at the *Cerberus,* then ducked when several arrows shot overhead. In the quick glimpse, he spied over a dozen of his marines on deck, hiding behind the three catapult towers. Talus was with them.

A huge resounding crash came from below, and Marcus risked another quick look. The heavy boarding ramp now spanned the short gap between the ships, and Kleon's marines were charging across it and onto the *Vulcan.* Many carried long tridents.

"Get the bastards, boys!" cried Talus. The marines charged from behind the towers. The lines crashed together, the tridents giving Kleon's fighters an advantage. Several of *Vulcan's* men fell victim to the long weapons.

As Marcus watched, Talus stepped in and showed the men how to disarm a trident fighter. He blocked the trident's thrust with his gladius, using the sword to force the three-pronged weapon downward. Then he stomped on the shaft, wrenching it from his opponent's hands. Weaponless, the panicked man fell back.

Above all the noise—steel clanging against steel, arrows slamming into shields, the crackling of burning timber, the intermittent howls of agony—Marcus yelled to the catapult crew. "Grab a weapon. Get down there."

The engagement line stretched from bow to stern. Kleon's superior numbers pressed the *Vulcan* fighters back against the towers. Fear gripped Marcus. His mind seemed unable to focus before he spotted Kleon behind his men, a vile sneer on his face.

It reminded Marcus of Kleon's boastful and demeaning smile when he bested Marcus in their childhood days. Kleon, four years older, had been the master. He won all the games, finished first in the foot races, pinned Marcus, countless times, in their wrestling matches. Kleon always gloated. Marcus cleared his mind to focus on one goal—wiping that grin off Kleon's face.

Acrid smoke from the blazing wood and sails of the *Cerberus* filled Marcus's nostrils. There was also another stench in the air—burning human flesh.

Marcus drew his gladius and checked the blade. His chest burned. He needed rational options, but only one thing could quell the raging fire inside him. Kleon had to die.

Marcus climbed up on the tower wall, chose a target below, and jumped.

The enemy marine, whose shoulder Marcus landed on, went hard to the deck with a cry of surprise and pain. Marcus also fell to the deck with his knees and elbows taking his weight. He scrambled to his feet. The fighter was up on one knee when Marcus thrust his sword point into his chest. The man collapsed, writhing.

Marcus was now behind the line of enemy fighters and cut off from his men. Desperate, he scanned up and down the line of combat searching for Kleon.

There he is.

At the sight of his rival near the boarding ramp, Marcus tensed and took in a ragged breath. On the top of a mountain in Cyrenaica, Kleon had been thin and weak, unkempt and dressed in tattered clothes. Tonight, across the *Vulcan's* deck, he looked robust and confident, dressed in a clean white tunic. And he wore a triumphant look was on his face.

Not for long.

Marcus took a deep breath. In a guttural voice, he roared a single word. "Kleon."

Kleon glanced around before finding Marcus. The smile dropped. He pulled out the blade on his hip, a long cavalry sword, and strode toward Marcus, who did the same. Marcus stopped ten feet from his vile enemy.

Kleon glared at Marcus, sneering. "Seems you don't give up, do you, Marcus? You always come back, no matter how many times I best you."

"Crete, King's Throne. I'd call those defeats for you, you scum."

"Oh, Marcus. Names. They don't hurt me. Is that Egyptian bitch of yours aboard? I expect to ravish her tonight."

Marcus tensed, balancing on the balls of his feet. He tried not to react to Kleon's words, but a mixture of bloodlust and hatred rose inside him.

"Enough, Kleon. Let the steel speak for us."

Marcus bellowed and sprang forward, swinging his gladius in a wide arc—left, right, left.

Kleon avoided the reckless blows, parrying the last one. Their swords crossed, and Kleon pushed Marcus's weapon back toward him. "A gladius, Marcus? How Roman of you."

Kleon shoved Marcus, sending him reeling backward, and then advanced, thrusting and swinging with his longer weapon.

Marcus was ready. He waited for the right maneuver, the right angle, the right weight shift before countering Kleon's blow, knocking the long sword from his opponent's grasp.

The weapon clattered across the deck, and Kleon moved to retrieve it, but Marcus blocked his way.

As Kleon retreated, his boot hit something on the deck.

A trident. Snatching it up, Kleon pointed it at Marcus and roared in triumph. "I win again!"

He thrust the great, three-pronged weapon at Marcus, who sidestepped and retreated. Sweat ran down his forehead. His grip on the gladius seemed slippery.

He's playing with me now.

Kleon took several swipes at Marcus with the weapon and laughed. The wicked smile had returned.

Marcus danced back, biding his time until he could use Talus's maneuver. He turned to check his retreat, but it was too late to prevent disaster. He tripped over the fallen marine he had killed earlier, fell backward and landed flat on his back, his head bouncing hard off the deck. The gladius broke free of his grip and slid along the deck.

Shaky from the hard landing, Marcus rolled on his side, pushing himself with his boots as he thrust his arm out toward his sword.

Kleon rushed up and jabbed the trident at Marcus' arm.

Marcus howled in pain as a trident point caught his upper forearm. Pinned to the deck, he groaned in agony.

Kleon snatched up the loose gladius and jumped atop Marcus. He pressed the sword point against Marcus's throat.

"Well, Marcus. Should I kill you with your Roman sword?" Kleon said in a casual voice.

Think. Think. Think.

"I never wanted this, Marcus. But you're so infuriating. This is all your fault. You leave me no other choice." Kleon glared at the weapon in his hand. "I can't use this cursed Roman sword." He tossed it to the deck. His hands flashed out and gripped Marcus's throat. "Time to die now, Marcus."

Kleon squeezed his throat. Gasping for air, Marcus tried to punch at his executioner with his free hand, but he could only reach as high as Kleon's shoulder.

Kleon squeezed harder.

Think.

Marcus brought his left leg toward his hand. His lungs were burning.

Air.

He fumbled for his heavy boot.

His hand found it.

Dagger.

He thrust upward once between the ribs and again before Kleon fell away.

Marcus gasped, sucking in a precious lungful of air. Then the pain in his right arm screamed at him, and he struggled to roll onto his side. Like an animal caught in a jagged trap, he labored to work the trident out of the deck and his forearm. He shrieked as the trident tore through and out of his flesh. Dropping the weapon, he rolled upright as blood began to ooze from his wound. He saw Kleon, dragging himself along the deck, leaving a trail of dark blood behind him.

Marcus hissed when he touched his bloody forearm. He had to stop the bleeding. Spying a loose rope, he cut a short piece with the dagger and then, using fingers and teeth, tied it around his upper arm. Marcus winced at the new pain, but at least the blood flow slowed to a seep. He pulled a bandana off a dead sailor and tightly wrapped the wound.

Picking up his gladius, Marcus staggered back on his feet. Sounds of steel against steel and man against man filled the deck as the fighting raged around him. His men fought like mad dogs, holding the line. A wisp of black smoke whirled by him, leaving the pungent smell of death and destruction.

He was alone, behind the enemy's line with a single sword against a hundred. By Jupiter's providence, none of Kleon's men had noticed him.

Behind him, a cracking sound, sharp as the snap of a whip, pierced the din, forcing him to turn. The *Cerberus's* stern mast, weakened by the fires, had fractured at the base. Though still tethered to its lines, the mast leaned toward him.

Marcus turned to move from the mast's path, but two of Kleon's men were now edging toward him. He tightened his hold on the gladius and thought of Electra.

Please forgive me, Darling.

Marcus crouched as his enemies advanced. The fires crackled behind him.

CHAPTER SIXTY

Talus

The Ionian Sea off Lefkas Island, September 2

TALUS WINCED AS he eliminated the man in front of him with an upward thrust to the man's groin. It was a horrible way to die.

He stepped back from the line, and the man behind him stepped forward. Talus evaluated the struggle for control of the *Vulcan*. That's when he marked a single man standing motionless near the rail behind Kleon's men. The enemy took notice, too.

Shit! That's Marcus. How in Hades?

With no time to think, Talus turned his mercenary shield horizontal. Time for a bull charge. "You men, follow me!"

Talus bellowed a war cry from the dark woods of Gaul and charged. He crashed through several enemy marines, creating a big hole in their line. The *Vulcan's* marines quickly took advantage of the gap and began flanking the *Cerberus* fighters' line.

He continued his rush toward Marcus, who was defending against two swordsmen. Talus stabbed one in the back while Marcus sliced open the belly of his distracted opponent.

He glared at Marcus. "Shit! What are you doing over here, sir? Are you *trying* to get killed? Oh, never mind." He looked down at the dying form of Kleon. "Guess it was worth it."

Marcus's chest heaved as he nodded.

At that moment, Pollio burst out of the forward gangway, swinging a naval sword. Charging behind him were many of the *Vulcan's* rowers, also armed. Talus roared a battle cry as dozens of armed rowers attacked the enemy. The *Vulcan's* archers joined in, taking down more targets.

Talus spotted two of the marines that had followed him through the gap in the line. "Mossimo! Leotis! Cut those grappling lines."

Back to work.

He charged the backs of the enemy.

CHAPTER SIXTY-ONE

Kleon
The Ionian Sea off Lefkas Island, September 2

KLEON KNEW DEATH was close. His strength diminished, each breath brought frothy red bubbles from his mouth and nose. He tried to yell out but only a hoarse whisper and blood came out.

He was unable to crawl any further. The pain was too great. He rolled over onto his back, easing his suffering somewhat.

Why doesn't Marcus finish me?

He slapped the deck repeatedly with his hand.

I'm over here. Come on. Kill me.

Marcus appeared in his vision, standing over him. A moment later, he sat down and picked up Kleon's head and shoulders, cradling him in his lap like a child.

"Kleon... I'm sorry," Marcus said.

"Stay... with me." Kleon's words came out slowly between gasps for breath. "As children... secretly admired you. Couldn't be you... so hated you." Kleon spit blood. "... wanted scroll's power."

Marcus bent down to hear his whispers. "That was wrong, Kleon. If only—"

Kleon cut Marcus off with a coughing fit. With an effort, he continued. "You were... friend. I loved... you. Don't... want to die."

Marcus shook his head and surveyed the surrounding scene. "You caused all this for power and riches." Marcus wiped his eyes. "I can't forgive you. You killed Papa. You took Electra."

"Regret that... but wanted Electra. You... win war... and her—" A sudden pain shot through Kleon's heart. He waved Marcus closer.

"Tell... you a secret." Kleon took a deep breath, wincing with agony. Marcus put his ear next to Kleon's mouth.

Marcus jerked back. "No, that's not true, Kleon. Tell me it's not true!" Marcus cried, shaking him.

Kleon stared past him. He saw a bright light behind Marcus, growing...

CHAPTER SIXTY-TWO

Marcus
The Ionian Sea off Lefkas Island, September 2

MARCUS CHECKED KLEON'S breathing. Gone. He stood and stared down at Kleon, not knowing if his emotions were from victory, remorse or closure. Black smoke burned his eyes.

He heard shouted warnings and glanced over at the *Cerberus*. Its main mast was falling right at him. Marcus dashed aside as it slammed onto the *Vulcan's* deck, showering burning wreckage. Some shot overboard, but most landed on the decks of the *Vulcan*. The mast's blazing sail engulfed the center tower. Fires leapt up like lions on a gazelle.

Battle sounds died and weapons clanged to the deck as Kleon's exhausted men, leaderless and isolated by the fires, yielded their weapons. They, like his own men, were covered in blood, sweat and ashes. Many collapsed.

Nearby, the two marines hacked the last grappling line joining the two ships.

Pollio ran over to him. "Sir? Are you injured?" Blood stained the captain's blade.

"Never mind me. Get what rowers you can to fight these fires. Pull away from the *Cerberus*."

"Yes sir. I'll get them working." Pollio hurried below deck.

Over on Kleon's leaderless ship, total chaos ensued. Panic-stricken rowers were emerging from every hatch and passageway, crowding onto the deck like cattle. Many jumped the thirty feet to the water. On the far side, sailors and fighters were lowering the ship's only shore boat. Men fought their way toward it.

An immense explosion from below the *Cerberus's* decks erupted, sending Marcus to the deck. Searing hot clouds of steam burst from every crack, seam and opening in the ship's skin. The screech of metal pierced through the howling of scalded men. The enemy ship's boiler had become an angry, vengeful machine, rounding on its masters.

Marcus shook his head. Hippolytus had said mankind wasn't ready for the forces contained in the Archimedes scrolls. Was he right?

A loud cracking brought Marcus's attention back to the drowning ship. The deck was splitting across the vessel's beam. The boiler, low in the warship, had smashed the ship's spine, the heavy timbers of the keel. *Cerberus* was sinking at an extraordinary rate.

"Pollio," Marcus yelled. "Get us away, quickly!" Marcus feared the massive ship would pull *Vulcan* down with it.

"We're underway," Pollio yelled.

The drumbeats began from below as he raced to the command deck. With the fires spreading on both hulls, Marcus called in his last reserve.

"Pollio, signal the *Neptune* to come to our position."

Warm wetness rose on his arm as fresh blood dripped from his wound. The rope on his upper arm had fallen off somewhere. He felt dizzy and weak. His vision dimmed as the deck rose toward him.

CHAPTER SIXTY-THREE

Electra

The Ionian Sea off Lefkas Island, September 2

ELECTRA WAS BELOW when she heard the explosion and bolted topside to find Captain Socus.

"Please tell me, Captain, that horrible sound wasn't the *Vulcan*." She tried to stay calm, but her voice faltered. Her breathing became strained, and she closed her eyes to steady herself.

Socus turned to her after scanning the battle scene. "The explosion wasn't from the *Vulcan*. It was the *Cerberus* and—"

"Marcus is fine?" interrupted Electra.

"Hard to tell. There's significant fire on both ships, which may still be grappled together."

"Isn't there something we can do, Captain?" said Electra, folding her shaking arms across her chest

"Marcus gave me orders to stay off until needed." He returned to watching the battle. "Jupiter's balls!"

Electra gasped and peered out to sea. "Oh, goddess. There's only one ship!"

"The *Cerberus* is gone."

"Goddess, how do we know if Marcus is all right?" She pulled on Socus's arm. "We should help him. I beg you." Electra hugged her stomach where a cold knot had formed.

"Princess, go below to your cabin, or I will have someone take you there."

"Captain," called the helmsman, "A signal."

Electra stared out at the distant battle.

Marcus, you better not be dead.

CHAPTER SIXTY-FOUR

Marcus

The Ionian Sea off Lefkas Island, September 2

MARCUS AWOKE, GROGGY and disoriented, to find himself rocking, lying on something soft. He blinked and saw a deep blue sky above him.

This can't be the underworld.

When he pulled himself upright, his head spun, and his vision blurred. He wanted to vomit.

"Ah, back with us. Just lay back down."

It was Talus. Marcus lay in the stern of a small rowboat with Talus working the oars, the muscles in his arms bulging. Over the hulking giant, Marcus saw a ship.

"It's the *Neptune*. Why—"

"Because they have a surgeon to stitch you up. Lie down," Talus ordered.

"Where's *Vulcan*?" Marcus twisted around to search the sea. When his arm bumped the side of the boat, he winced.

"Remember that little scratch? You were bleeding out at Pollio's feet. I saved your ass… again. Bound you up, got you into this boat. Almost there."

"Thank you, again." Marcus turned and observed the *Vulcan*, three hundred feet behind them. Fires continued to burn on her decks.

"Oh, Mother, no!" Talus's voice held a panic Marcus never expected to hear from the man. He was as pale as moonlight, his jaws clenched.

"We have to go back." Talus worked a single oar to turn the boat.

"Why?" Marcus asked.

"The Greek fire pots. They're still in the forward tower."

"Shit! Talus, turn—"

At that instant, a concussive shock crushed the air from Marcus's lungs. Then a wall of sound, loud and deep, assaulted him, and his heart shook in his chest.

Chunks of wood and metal splashed in the water all around them. Pieces landed in the boat.

The explosion dazed Marcus, setting his ears ringing like a thousand hammers striking a thousand anvils. Shredded pieces of sailcloth and clothing floated from the sky. Something hard and wet struck Marcus in the shoulder. On the boards by his feet lay a human hand.

Marcus recoiled in horror.

That's when he saw the *Vulcan*. The explosion had split the ship by separating the connecting arched bridges from the port hull. As the heavy bridges sank into the water, their weight pulled the starboard hull onto its side. On the port hull, the Greek fire had blown out the forward half, its midships section sinking amidst rapid popping and cracking sounds, forcing the tiller oars out of the water. Marcus watched men jump into the sea. He knew they'd die from either the forty-foot drop to the sea or the Greek fire burning on the water's surface.

Another explosion, less intense, rocked the starboard hull and blew out its right side, now facing the sky. Marcus watched as the explosion propelled shattered pieces of the boilers and chunks of the ship's side high into the air. Water gushed through the gaping hole.

Marcus swung back to Talus but found the big man bent down, hands covering his face. Marcus's ears throbbed, but he heard Talus sobbing.

He looked back to the *Vulcan* and watched in horror as the quick death of the huge warship played out. Cries of trapped and drowning men dissipated after a few minutes into an eerie silence that hovered over the twin pools of whitecaps momentarily marking the ship's grave. Then all trace melted into the vast sea.

A thousand *Vulcan* sailors, rowers and marines found a watery demise. Add to that death count an equal number on the *Cerberus*.

"I'm to blame," whispered Marcus. Anxiety squeezed his throat.

"No, I'm to blame," said Talus. "I'm an arrogant wretch." He looked to the *Neptune*, grabbed the oars and began rowing again with powerful, steady strokes.

As they approached the *Neptune's* bow, Marcus thought it odd that no one on deck came to meet them. The oars rested in the water, motionless, and both main sails were furled. The ship was drifting.

"Hello on the *Neptune*. Throw us a rope." There was no response. Where was Socus? Where was Electra?

"Let's go around to the stern," offered Talus.

The head of one of the mercenary marines popped above the rail.

"Hold on," he called. "I'll get a rope."

"Wait in the boat," Marcus whispered to Talus before tying the rope around his waist. The crewmen above hauled him to the deck where he found four mercenaries facing him. "Where is everyone? Where is Captain Socus?"

One mercenary pointed to the stern. Marcus turned and saw Socus coming up a ladder that led to the cabins.

"Captain, what's going on?" Marcus called.

Socus looked at the passageway where another mercenary ascended and pointed his sword at the captain's neck.

Startled, Marcus took a few steps forward, but one of the other mercenaries stopped him with a sword. Marcus backed off from the blade. When he looked forward, Electra had ascended to the deck. Her face was twisted in distress.

"Electra," he called. "Are you all right?"

"Marcus, you're hurt. Dearest, just do as they say."

"Do as who says?"

Electra glanced at the ladder where Marcus saw a hooded figure ascending to the deck. He had a dagger. He snatched Electra—who let out a sharp cry—and put his blade to her throat.

Marcus surged forward again, but this time two of the mercenaries blocked his way. One struck him on his wounded arm causing Marcus to hiss in pain. "Who are you? Let her go. What is going on?"

"Can't you guess?" The man pulled his hood down, uncovering his face.

Marcus froze for an instant. *No, it can't be.*

"Hippolytus! What are you doing? Release Electra. Now!" Marcus tried to comprehend the inconceivable scene. Hippolytus was his friend, not his enemy.

"I can't do that, Marcus. Come closer, so we can talk." Hippolytus beckoned him forward.

Marcus studied Hippolytus as he walked toward the stern. Absent six years, his former tutor had aged beyond his years. What did he want? Was he still one of the Oracles? Marcus, confused and still reeling from the horrible deaths he had witnessed, addressed his mentor. "You don't look good, Hippolytus."

"And you're not that skinny library rat anymore. More muscle on your bones now. But to answer your question, I've been running from the Oracles."

What did Hippolytus want? Why was he threatening Electra?

"Why? I thought the Oracles held you in high esteem. Oracle Master and all."

"True. But each Oracle vows to prevent the release of Prime Knowledge into the world. Their attitude changes if you fail that vow. Why did you do it, Marcus? Why didn't you wait until I returned?"

"I thought you were dead, killed by the Romans. You abandoned me. You never contacted me to say you were still alive. After all our years together, now you betray me?"

"Did you not betray my trust with Kleon, Marcus? That disappointed me. And incensed the Oracles against me. I've spent the last two years living in a cave in Spain. That ages a man."

"I'm sorry about Kleon. It was a lack of judgment on my part. I took the scroll back when I saw his ambition." He resisted the feeling, but Marcus still experienced shame.

"Once the unlearned taste power, it is all they crave. You were both playing with the gods' fire. And it burned you." Hippolytus pointed out to sea, the fresh grave of many men. "You weren't able to control it, either of you. The Oracles will study the scrolls in relation to the totality of man's knowledge." His old mentor pointed out to sea. "Now you see the danger to man when unproven technology is unleashed. Didn't I teach you anything, Marcus?"

"You taught me truth and honor, the beauty of mathematics, the wonder of the great cosmos around us. I trusted you. We trusted each other back in Ephesus. You once told me not to trust anyone. I detected a discontinuity in that, a circle of illogic. Can you trust the words of someone after they tell you not to trust at all?"

"Excellent reasoning, Marcus. See these men around us? Do I trust them? No, but I trust their desire for gold. Greed you can trust, Marcus. But you can't trust Octavian or Antony. They're Romans. They believe in conquest, in their destiny, ordained by the gods. Bah. Romans… plunging onward, eyes forever closed."

Sensing Electra's increased agitation and worried she might try to break away at any moment, Marcus cautioned her, "Electra, stay calm." He focused cold eyes on Hippolytus. "Why do you hold her, Teacher? She's harmless."

"You've become a cunning and resourceful man, Marcus, as I expected. Can I assume there's not another ship lurking out there?" Electra arched her neck away from Hippolytus's blade. "No, Electra, dear, you will stay right where you are. I trust you and Marcus will do nothing foolish."

Hippolytus sheathed his dagger.

That gesture relieved a little of Marcus's concern for Electra, but an old conflict arose. Should he use the scrolls for the good or sequester them once again, as Hippolytus wanted?

"Don't these scrolls offer hope for man?" asked Marcus. "They could lead us to a more civilized world. Think of the steam-powered machines that could benefit—"

"They could also lead to our destruction or rule by evil, corrupt men." Hippolytus' face flushed. "I'm sorry, Marcus. As much as you may distrust the Oracle, they aren't evil or corrupt."

"So, you say. Following the path of the Oracles, mankind may never know great knowledge. The Oracles, in their infinite wisdom, will keep it all to themselves."

"That's where you're wrong, Marcus. Every advanced technology has a malevolent and benevolent side. The Oracles, whose wise men—and women—have studied the past, know how to curate knowledge, to set controls on it."

"That's where your blind spot is, Teacher. I grant you, technology has a good side and a bad side, but there's also the unknowable side. It's the consequences of technology and knowledge that no one can prepare for or predict, until it happens."

"That's a good theory, son—"

Marcus bristled at the word. "I'm no one's son now."

"Your father's death saddens me. He was a good man. He was a victim of the evil you destroyed today."

"Yes, he was a good man and a good father whom I never appreciated."

Marcus's voice cracked, and he turned away. The memory of his father's death brought back his unatoned, unending guilt. Marcus paced the deck for a moment before turning back to Hippolytus. "You understand while men enslave men, civilization will not advance. Steam power could be a solution. It could power machines and undermine the economics of slavery. Isn't it worth trying to save the millions of slaves and the untold millions of potential slaves not yet born?"

"Perhaps you're right, Marcus. The Oracles will figure that out, using means which are methodical, sane, and wise. Trust me on that."

"I wish I could, Hippolytus. But I'm all out of spare trust."

"Marcus, please. Whatever he wants, give it to him," begged Electra. "We'll get on with our life."

Hippolytus pulled Electra tighter and unsheathed his blade, holding it close to her throat again.

Marcus glared at Hippolytus. "Hippolytus, there's no need to threaten Electra. Tell me what you want."

"You know what I want. The Archimedes scrolls. Electra's already given me the original two we stole from the temple. I want the ones you—or was it Kleon—dug up in the desert. You give me those scrolls—which I haven't been able to find on this ship—and I'll give you Electra."

"Fair enough, but like I said, I have no trust in you, Hippolytus…"

Marcus edged to the rail and looked down at the water. Talus had worked his way below him and now pointed around the stern. Marcus gave a slight shake of his head. *Even Talus can't take on ten mercenaries.* "Even if you release Electra, you can still kill us and take the scrolls."

"I understand that you can't trust me, Marcus. You know that

I will sacrifice everything," Hippolytus said, looking directly at Marcus, "even my own son."

Marcus worked his jaws, trying to maintain control over his anger. "Then we are at an impasse, Teacher."

"You always were smart. Here's my proposal. Since I'm sure the scrolls are hidden on the ship in some clever place, we will sail over to the Roman port on Lefkas, where my friends and I, and Electra, will disembark. You will toss one scroll down so I can verify their authenticity. If all is well, you will toss down the rest, and I will release Electra. I will go my way, and you yours."

"And with all the customs officials and legionnaires walking around Lefkas, you can't slit our throats."

"Yes, that's how I see it," replied Hippolytus. "Oh, you better bring your man up now. It's a long row to Lefkas."

"Good plan. What if…?" Marcus paused, glancing over at Electra. He loved her. She was everything he wanted in life. They completed each other. She was worth every scroll in the Library of Alexandria. He needed no further negotiations.

"Marcus—" Electra choked off her words and winced as Hippolytus pressed the blade against her throat.

"I don't like the way you're treating her!" Marcus yelled. "Your conflict is with me, not her. Put that knife away, now!" He stormed toward Hippolytus, but a mercenary stepped up and backhanded him.

"Come, come, Marcus. Don't make me resort to violence."

Marcus wiped his bloody lip. "Fine. I'll do as you say. Now, let Electra go."

Marcus glared at Hippolytus, who laughed. "That will not happen, Marcus. Patience, dear boy."

"Hang on, Electra. This will be over soon, darling." Electra nodded. "Hippolytus, can you have the surgeon sent up? I have this scratch on—"

"By the gods. Look!" Captain Socus' cried. He pointed to starboard.

Marcus darted to the other side.

A few miles out to sea, ship after ship of Egyptian warships, an entire fleet, streamed southward. In the center of the formation was the royal flagship of Queen Cleopatra. It could mean only one thing. Antony had lost; Octavian ruled the Roman world. Marcus dropped to his knees. He pressed his forehead against the rail and closed his eyes. It was the final blow to his hopes. He sat back on his heels. The effort to decode the scrolls, to build the *Vulcan*, it came to nothing.

"No!" The wailing voice was Electra's.

Marcus spun around to the woman he loved. Tears ran down her cheeks. Even Hippolytus seemed sympathetic. He released his grip on her.

*

Marcus watched as the *Neptune* docked at Lefkas. Hippolytus, Electra, and the mercenaries disembarked.

Marcus, suffering less since the surgeon stitched his arm, brought the bag of scrolls up on deck. After Hippolytus verified the scroll's authenticity, Marcus tossed the rest to the dock. Hippolytus released Electra, who hurried to Marcus's waiting arms. His old mentor flung the scrolls over his shoulder and walked away along the dock.

Marcus hoped to never see Hippolytus again.

"Prepare us to leave, Captain," Marcus told Socus.

"Yes, sir." Socus barked orders to his sailors.

After settling Electra in their cabin, Marcus returned to the upper deck and found Captain Socus looking out to sea. Marcus imagined he was wondering whether he would see his wife and children again.

Socus looked up. "Ready to cast off, sir. What course?"

Marcus spied a distant group of men running along the mole toward the *Neptune*. It was Hippolytus and his men.

"Take us south to Gaza, Captain. And hurry."

Confident of their escape, Marcus went below to Electra. The course of their shared future was now uncertain. Their voyage would involve much discussion, an abundance of compassion, and healing of mind and body.

Marcus balled his hand into a fist.

I'm not ready to give up my dream just yet. I have one more act left to play.

CHAPTER SIXTY-FIVE

Marcus

The Ionian Sea off Lefkas Island, September 2

MARCUS, HIS LEFT arm in a sling, stood with Electra on *Neptune's* upper deck and watched the solemn rite nearing its end on the lower level.

He glanced to the side where Talus stood, his body rigid, his face twisted into wretched mourning. Many of the dead were ex-legionnaires Talus had recruited. His eyes were dry, but Marcus could see the inner struggle. Earlier, after leaving Lefkas, the man had begged Marcus to flog him for his failure to secure the Greek fire.

"It will help me forgive myself," Talus had pleaded. I cannot live with the guilt."

Marcus would not consent to Talus's foolish request. "I will not flog a man who's saved my life many times over. You can atone by helping us rid the world of such men as Kleon and Octavian."

"Sir, I'll need guidance because I don't understand what I should do."

"I'll let you know our plans after Electra and I talk."

Below, Captain Socus intoned the final words of his short and inadequate eulogy. "And we ask the gods and goddesses— great Zeus, Poseidon, and Isis—to guide the fallen—the sailors and marines of the *Vulcan*—through the dark Underworld to a rewarding place in the Afterlife."

After his words, a trio of archers launched flaming arrows into the evening sky that arced over the sea, landing with a hiss.

Marcus stared at the sea as the crew dispersed in eerie silence, back to duties, back to living. The dead went to the Underworld, while their hopes and dreams and secrets fell to ashes.

I wish Kleon had taken his secrets with him.

When Electra came up to him, he bent and kissed her cheek. "I can't believe all those men are dead," Marcus said. "Gods, I pray I never lead men into battle ever again."

"I won't let you. War's horrible. It's not for you, Marcus."

"I'm glad my father wasn't here to witness all this." Marcus took a deep breath. "I need to tell you some things."

"Oh, Marcus, can it not wait?"

"No, because it concerns our future."

Electra squeezed her eyes shut for a moment. "Fine, I yield you the rostrum of insanity to which this day has led us."

Marcus studied her face. It seemed a mixture of anticipation and dread. "I'm sorry, but I acted on a few things before we left. There were so many things going on."

Electra shook her head. "I don't like it, but I understand. I too had a thousand tasks to complete. Leaving Caesarion wasn't easy."

"Yes, that's a duty you took to heart. I focused on defeating Kleon and on our future. I considered the consequences if we won and if we lost. However, I never envisioned Hippolytus in my plans."

Electra took his hand. "That must have been a shock. I tried reasoning with him while we waited for your return, but all he could talk about were the Archimedes scrolls. He's obsessed with them. How could he put those scrolls above his relationship with you?"

"Yes, I can't believe his treachery. Anyway, here's what I did.

First, Bassus Trading is no more. If we had defeated Octavian, I couldn't trust Antony to stick to our bargain. If we lost, Octavian wouldn't let us live. Alexandria is no longer safe. The world has changed. Rome's Republic, though a flawed democracy, is now dead, with no chance of resurrection. The Roman juggernaut has replaced it. Rome will suffer as a dictatorship, now and forever, until, like all civilizations, it too falls into ruin. Unless—"

"I know. Unless we had the full knowledge of the Archimedes scrolls, which we don't. You're not thinking of going after Hippolytus, are you?" Electra walked over to the port rail. "We don't know where he went. And Octavian is still out there."

Marcus joined her. "No, I've countered Hippolytus."

"What?"

"Let me finish telling you what I've done. Before we left, Honorius started negotiations to sell everything. He'll convert the proceeds and the gold and silver bullion in my bank into precious gems. We'll meet him in Gaza."

"So, that's where we're going." Electra frowned. "What about the house in Alexandria?"

"Also sold. I gave Titus and the other household servants a large bonus. They'll be fine. Neema will travel with us. She's a good cook. As for Honorius, I have given him the *Neptune* for his many years of service to Papa and me."

Electra touched Marcus on the shoulder. "Where shall we go, Marcus? What shall we do? Dear, there's nowhere safe wherever Rome rules."

"You're right. Octavian's victory has poisoned the Roman world for us. We should go east."

"Parthia?" asked Electra, her face downcast. "I'd rather jump into the sea."

Marcus chuckled. "Not Parthia. I'm talking of India."

"Cleopatra told me good things about India."

"I'm not sure how I fit in there. Perhaps set up a Greek

school. Many Greek colonists live in India. The money gives us many options."

"I could teach the children of the rajah's court new languages like Greek and Latin." Electra's face brightened.

Marcus took Electra's hand. "With your love of children, you would enjoy that. Perhaps one day, you can teach our children."

Electra gasped. "Marcus!" She swatted his chest. "Don't tease me."

"Who said I was teasing?" Marcus grinned.

"Is this your way of negotiating a marriage contract? You use innuendo?"

"Let's hold that discussion for later, in private, darling."

"I'll hold you to that. Now, there's still one thing looming over us," she said, winking at Marcus.

"Ah, yes, the voyage to India." Marcus leaned against the rail. It was getting dark.

"Not that. I was talking about the hulk on the deck." She nodded her head.

Marcus turned. "Talus?"

"I swear to Jupiter, I wasn't listening in," pleaded Talus from across the deck. "Just... thinking."

"Talus will journey with us to India and perhaps return to Italy."

"Somebody has to save your ass," muttered Talus.

"I heard that. Perhaps next time, I'll save your ass."

"Right," said Talus, laughing.

"What are your plans once you're back in Italy?" asked Electra. "Not the arena again?"

Talus laughed. "By Jupiter, no. Never again. I'll go back to my hometown in the Po River Valley. With the money—undeserved—that Marcus has given me, I'll buy a farming estate, settle down, get a wife. Run for city magistrate. Be respectable... stop... killing."

Marcus couldn't make out Talus's face, but the tone of his last words showed anguish and self-disgust. "You may like the new lands, Talus."

"Aye, maybe. Well, goodnight." Talus wiped his hands across his face. "Will this cursed day never end?" He disappeared below deck.

"Poor man. He blames himself for what happened to the *Vulcan*. Anyway, dear, I've taken care of everyone," said Marcus.

"Except us."

Marcus put his free arm around Electra. "If you will marry me, we'll make a life in India."

"Oh, Marcus, with no reservations, I'll marry you." She cocked her head to one side. "I want a full life, including children, but I will not sit home and make babies all the time."

"No, my love. I shall let you be my guide on that subject."

"Thank you. But, Marcus, am I too old?"

"I won't dignify that question. I love you for who you are, not for anything else. But there is one other thing—"

Electra wrapped her arms around his neck. They kissed and the day's tension wilted away from Marcus, their passion replacing it. Electra broke away. "You were about to tell me about that bag of Archimedes scrolls in your chest, right?"

"You knew about that?"

"I know everything, dearest." A big smile appeared on her face but faded. "Those scrolls scare me, Marcus. They're like a Pandora's box."

"They scare me, too. It's dangerous, but I can't resist this need to study them. And they're the originals. The scrolls I gave Hippolytus are fakes. The one he examined was filled with symbols I copied from the first two scrolls when I was trying to decode them. The others are all blank. Instead of checking them, he trusted me to fulfill my promise. He was right about one thing... trust no one."

"Marcus, how could you? Now the Oracles will be after us."

"I couldn't give them what they wanted. No telling what the

Oracles' plans are for them. The scrolls can help make our world a more civilized place."

"Marcus, you are an enigma. Skeptical of powerful men but willing to bargain with them. You seek knowledge, yet you're suspicious of those who hoard it."

"You've made your point," Marcus admitted. "So, what should we do with the scrolls? Someone should study them."

"Or we can throw them into the sea. No one will know. The Oracles will leave us alone if we do that."

"But, Electra. We could be the instrument that takes humanity to a new level of civilization. Don't you want that adventure?"

Electra laughed. "Oh, Marcus. If you're at my side, I'll go on any adventure you want. Now let's go pretend we're married."

Marcus laughed. He loved this woman.

ABOUT THE AUTHOR

Tom Roberts is the author of an historical novel and a short story collection. At the Florida Writers Association's 2019 Royal Palm Literary Awards, his historical novel, *Lost Scrolls of Archimedes,* was awarded Gold for best unpublished historical novel. A software engineer in a previous life, Mr. Roberts began writing in 2017. He is avid reader of ancient history and technology and a member of the Florida Writers Association, the Atlanta Writers Club, and the West Florida Literary Federation. His favorite authors are Bernard Cornwell, Patrick O'Brian, Steven Saylor, and Arthur C. Clarke. An Air Force veteran, he loves dogs and enjoys hiking, classical music, video games, and college sports. He lives with his wife in Pensacola, Florida.

To find out more about Tom Roberts and his writings, visit
www.tomrobertsauthor.com

Acknowledgments

I am indebted to a host of people who helped bring this novel to fruition including editors, fellow writers from my critique groups and writing conventions, beta readers, friends, and family. Foremost, I wish to thank my wife extraordinaire, Charlotte Cheney, and my children, Melissa Klawinski and Andrew Roberts. Without their support, I likely would have given up. And thanks, Dudley.

I want to thank my editors, Terra Weiss of The Plot Doc, Don Weise of The Writers Ally, and Maria D'Marco of TigerX Global. They were critical in honing my complicated plot into something readable. My English proofreader, Griffin Smith, was amazing at catching all the small errors that tried to hide in the prose. Though their part was smaller, I am also indebted to these literary professionals for helping me along the way: Elizabeth Buege, Richard Bradburn, Heather Cashman, Stephanie Eding, Kaitlyn Johnson, Meg LaTorre, Chuck Sambuchino, Kathy Ver Eech, and the editors at Scribendi.

Beta readers I wish to thank are Patricia Black-Gould, Doug Clark, Elle Fort, and Aimee Walker. Many thanks go to my critique group members who had to suffer through the early drafts of Lost Scrolls of Archimedes. They include Tabitha Barrow, Charlie Davis, Judy Fawley, Elizabeth Holmes, Anne Howard, Linda Miragliotta, Patrick Sims, Diane Skelton, Ron Tew, and John Waite. I probably missed somebody but please accept my thanks.

Kudos to Melinda Saunders for the Ephesus map.

Any historical inaccuracies in the text or maps are strictly my fault.

Made in the USA
Monee, IL
06 September 2020